Ninety-Nine Promises

BOOK 3 OF THE NINETY-NINE SERIES

ELISHEBA HAXBY

JESSE RIVAS

ABOVE THE
SUN

Contents

For those of you who are walking through the fire and are choosing to hold on to faith, this book is dedicated to you.

CHAPTER 1

December 23, 5:20 p.m.

TAMARA

"When is your check out date?" The rail-thin man behind the counter asked.

Great question. My head throbbed behind my temples. I pulled out the debit card to Joe's and my joint account—the one we'd been adding to for months—the one meant for our wedding and honeymoon. A lump formed in the middle of my throat as I pushed the card toward the man. "I'm not sure."

He gave me a tentative smile and picked up the card. "The system needs a date. You can always change it if need be."

I looked down at the fake hardwood floors and swallowed hard. "How about a week?" Hopefully that would be long enough. Maybe my parents would invite me to stay with them for a while. Yeah, right. If they reacted anything like Dakota, they'd slam the door in my face and send me packing.

"Okay, perfect. We have you checking out the thirtieth then." He slid the card back to me, along with two room keycards. "You'll be in Room 206 for the week." He gave directions to the room and told me where the guest laundry was. "If you have any questions, just dial nine."

I gathered my things and drug them across the parking lot. Outside was frigid and damp with an arctic breeze rolling off the

1

water from the harbor. Aberdeen Washington was on the southern tip of the Olympic Peninsula and had the constant smell of salt water in the air. It made me ache for the ocean. Somehow, I'd have to find a ride to Ocean Shores while I was here. Perhaps then I could find Charlie and finally thank him for his kindness years ago. *Two birds. One stone.*

Thoughts of me standing in front of the water, watching the waves roll on the shore and seagulls mining the beach for food comforted my heart. I *definitely* needed the ocean now. I walked up the stairs to the second floor, pulling my duffel bag behind me. My room was the sixth door down. The inside was basic and clean, but it had a musty old carpet smell, not too different from my apartment in Vancouver. I plopped down onto the bed and sighed. What now? My stomach growled, but I ignored it.

Lying back, my mind spun around the next possible move. When I had mapped it earlier, my parents' house was a mere four-minute walk from this hotel. Besides the affordability, this was the number one reason I had decided to stay here. But now that I was this close, my courage waned. What was I going to do anyway? Knock on the door with Gabriel's ashes, only to tell them their son was dead, and that Dakota had been his victim for years without them noticing. Bile stung my throat, and I closed my eyes. Taking in a large breath, I waited for the sick anxious feeling to pass. After a few minutes calming myself, I rolled off the bed and headed to the door, leaving the jar of ashes. The bad news could wait for now.

Before I could talk myself out of it, I marched toward my parents' house, determination in my steps. I hadn't walked away from everything that mattered in Vancouver to chicken out now. The sun dipped behind the horizon as I walked, and the sky glowed with an intense orange hue. Slowing, I took in the beauty. For a brief moment, peace washed over me, strengthening me to move forward. A few minutes later, I stood in front of the address Dakota had left me. The place was small and plain but taken care of. An older home with light brown siding, the windows trimmed with white. Definitely an upgrade from the trailer park.

On the street in front of the house was parked a burgundy log truck semi, its rear tires folded up over the front ones. I took a closer look. In the dim lighting, it was hard to read, so I pulled out my cell phone and switched on the flashlight. The logo on the side of the truck said Jensen's Trucking. Nice. After all those years of dreaming about it, my dad finally owned a business. I turned back to the house. It was fairly dark, but a light beamed from a window in the middle of the building.

A flurry of wind rushed through my hair, and I wrapped my jacket tighter around me. I glanced up and down the street. The neighborhood was quiet, everyone settled in for the winter night. I noticed then that the driveway was empty. I slowly crossed the manicured grass, feet unsteady as I crept to the lit window. My heart raced as I peered through the glass. My father sat in an old leather recliner, a beer in hand. He looked exactly how I thought he would, thick salt and pepper hair and a tad more weight around his midsection. Other than that, he looked the same as he always had. A ruggedly handsome face with a sturdy jawline set like the world had been hard on him. He focused on a boxing match on the fifty-inch flat screen television across the room from him. The new appliance didn't match the rest of the room. The floors were chipped hardwood with an ancient oriental rug in the center covering its flaws. The furniture was mismatched—an array of Goodwill specials, no doubt. The television, though, appeared almost brand new. Priorities. On the screen, the two men pounded each other. Head shot. Head shot. Abdomen. Dad winced a few times and made the occasional air jab along with the contenders.

Behind the television, the walls were lined with photographs of children I didn't recognize. At the end of the line of photos was a portrait of a family. Was that my brother Nathan? His arms were around a beautiful brunette with two small children in front of them. Emotions prickled in my throat. Nathan was married?

From the picture, he looked quite happy. And I was an aunt? What else had I missed? Why did they only have pictures of them on the wall? Where was Josiah? Had he disappeared too?

Sounds of an engine coming around the corner startled me from my spying, and I ducked behind the house. The car stopped in the driveway and a door slammed.

"Paul!" the woman hollered. "I need help with these groceries."

My heart jumped at the sound of her voice. *Mom.* I hadn't heard that wonderful sound for six long years. My body screamed to run to her, but I stayed perfectly still. Frozen. A few moments later, I shook myself out of it and crept back to the window. Mom came through the door, two brown paper bags loaded with groceries in her arms.

"You gonna help me? The car's full."

"Not now. The fight's on." Dad took a swig of his half-finished beer.

Sadness and then frustration flickered in her tired eyes. *Oh Mom.* Longing made my stomach twist as I took in her appearance. The years hadn't treated her well. Her dark hair, once vibrant and thick, was now dull and stringy. She was thinner than I remembered, which made her face a bit sunken, but if I looked long enough, I could still see the beauty in her vacant features.

She sighed and set the bags on the table before heading back outside. My heart ached for her. In that one interaction, I saw the loneliness she had endured over the years at the selfishness of my father. Why couldn't he just pause the stupid fight and help her for five minutes? The door opened and closed four more times before the car was unloaded. Why so much food? Did other people live with them? Or was it Christmas dinner? That was probably it. Would Nathan and Josiah be in town for the holidays?

I ducked away from the window. This was the time to let them know I was here, but somehow, I couldn't. I was frozen. Literally and figuratively.

"Theresa!" Dad yelled as if she was far away. "Grab me another beer."

"Grab it yourself. I'm putting the groceries away."

My heart pounded against my chest, and for a split second I was a helpless little girl hiding under my bed, praying for the fighting to stop. I peeked into the window again and saw my father rising to his feet, face red. He stomped into the kitchen and took hold of my mom's arm, squeezing it hard. She winced, pain mangling her features.

"I don't work all week for this. When I say get me a beer, that means get me a beer. Got it?" he yelled in her face.

After all these years, nothing had changed. My entire childhood played before my eyes. The fighting. The abuse. The overwhelming sense of being alone. It all shattered inside of me at once. Why was I here? Why would God tell me to come? Why would God bring me back to the brokenness and pain? Before I could think of another agonizing question, I ran with all my might back to the hotel room.

I burst through the door, chest burning, gasping for air. My body ached for Joe. I wished desperately he was with me now, to have his strong arms around me, holding me together. Why would God lead me to face this alone? It seemed cruel. I paced the hotel room, wishing for answers, hoping for comfort, but nothing came. A thousand memories crashed over my mind at once, good mingling with the bad. My mom, when she was home with us, had been a great cook. On special occasions, the house would be riddled with pastries and cookies she'd made from scratch. When my dad was in a good mood, the house would be filled with his baritone voice, singing and being silly with us kids. Those moments were rare, though, and usually ended with someone being beat or my parents arguing. Sounds of my dad's angry voice berating my mother pounded in my ears. *How dumb are you, Theresa? It's like your paralyzed from the neck up.* Why hadn't she left him years ago? Why hadn't she protected us from him?

Maybe Joe had been right this whole time. Finding my family

was a mistake. It wasn't like I could change the past, and I sure as hell couldn't change a thing here. I wasn't strong enough for this. I picked up my phone and scrolled to Joe's name. The injured look on his face right before I had left him sitting on his couch came before me. I'd hurt him deeply, and I wasn't sure there was a way to fix the damage between us. God had brought us back together before. I hoped beyond reason he would do it again.

Dejected, I sat down on the bed, with nothing to distract me from the sorrow and loss. Nobody here to hold me as the emotional turbulence came. My whole being longed for Joe. Guilt came with a massive torrent of grief as his last words played through my mind.

So that's it, you're leaving me two days before Christmas to clean up this mess by myself?

I didn't deserve his comfort. He needed mine, and I had left him for *this*. I scrolled to his name once more, finger hovering over the send button. Maybe it wasn't too late. Maybe I could plead insanity. Maybe if I begged hard enough, he'd forgive me and come rescue me from this hell. Tears rolled down my face, and I tossed the phone aside. As much as it hurt, I'd left this morning because I felt God leading me here. If I gave up now without giving him a chance to show me why, it would haunt me for the rest of my life. Besides, I couldn't go back to Vancouver yet, not without at least talking to my parents and telling them the truth.

Dread crashed over my soul. Facing my parents with the jar of Gabriel's ashes, telling them the secret Dakota had held all these years, suddenly felt like an impossible task.

God, I need your help, I'm sinking here. I buried my head in my hands, grief drowning me in its undertow.

Several times over the last few days, I'd heard God clearly, but now his voice felt a thousand miles away, and all I could think of was the way my dad clutched my mother's arms as he yelled at her. The act was mild in comparison to what he was capable of. Why had it set me off like it had? Angry tears fell down my face. That one act showed that nothing had changed.

They may have been in a nicer house and owned their business, but underneath the rage was still alive and as active as it ever had been. I wiped my face and tried to shove down the memories that battered my insides like the boxers on my dad's big screen TV.

Snatching the remote, I flicked on the television to distract me from the unbearable torment in my chest. I flipped through the channels quickly, but nothing caught my interest. I needed to talk to someone. I needed to sort out this mess inside of my heart. I grabbed the phone again, scrolling through the names. Claire? No. Trudy? Definitely not. Joe? I stared at his name for a long time, praying that he'd call me. That he'd send me some sort of sign that we would be okay, but nothing came, and the agony in my heart increased. Finally, I swiped the contacts away and opened the safari app and googled Midways in Ocean Shores, hoping Charlie still worked there. I tapped on the phone number, and it dialed.

Three rings and someone answered. "Midways, this is Charlie."

For a moment, my voice was lost in shock. What would I even say after all this time?

"Hello. Anyone there?"

"Charlie?" It was all I could spit out.

"Yes? Can I help you?"

"Um... It's Tamara. I was just—"

"Tamara Jensen?" His voice changed from polite to surprised. "My goodness, how have you been? I can't believe it. I was seriously just thinking about you."

"Really?"

"Yes, really. You were on my heart when I woke up this morning. I said a prayer for you."

I smiled through the tears that had spilled over. The praying bartender. God had his soldiers in the most unlikely places. Back in Ocean Shores before I even had a thought of God, Charlie had been there, pointing the way toward him like a lighthouse in the midst of a storm. "Thank you for that. I could use all the prayers I can get right now."

"What's wrong?"

I pinched the bridge of my nose and sighed. "It's a really long story."

In the background, someone yelled out a drink order. "Hold on a sec." There was a muffled response from Charlie, and then he was back. "Sorry about that. What's going on with you?"

"This probably isn't the best time. You sound busy. What are you doing the next few days?"

He hesitated before answering. "I was actually heading out of town for Christmas. My family has a cabin rented up the McKenzie River in Oregon. It's the most central location for everyone."

Christmas. Of course, he wouldn't be available. I glanced around the dingy hotel room. This was what my Christmas would probably look like. "Okay, yeah. That makes sense. I was calling because I'm in Aberdeen. I'm not sure how long I'll be here. I thought it would be great to see you while I'm close."

"I would love that. I'll only be gone a few days. Why don't you give me your number, and I'll call you as soon as I get back into town?"

"Perfect." I said, but disappointment and loneliness weighed down my insides. I rattled off my number with the promise of connecting before leaving town and hung up.

I stood, went to my duffel and pulled out Gabriel's ashes. No matter what my childhood had been like, my parents deserved to know the truth. Then and only then could the healing actually begin. More tears came. Could there ever be true healing for us? Was God big enough to put the shattered parts of my family back together? Did I even want that? In every dark corner of my past, there had been brokenness and heartache. Anger welled up inside of me. All of the abuse and neglect had led to this. My sister molested and turned junkie. My brother—her abuser—dead. I hated him for what he did to Dakota, but my Lord, is this what he deserved? To die at the hands of a psychopath, burned to oblivion on a heap of ash? Stomach wrenching, sobs clawed up my throat. "God, why? It hurts too much. I can't do this alone!" I cried through a gasp. "I hate what Gabriel did. I hate what my parents did." I set the ashes aside and pounded the bed with my fist. "I'm angry, God! I'm so angry. Why did you let this happen to me? Why didn't you stop it?" For hours, I cried, the bitter sorrow crashing over me in turbulent waves, ebbing and flowing with the inner storm. As the tears subsided, a strange calm rested over my soul, and I heard the faintest whisper.

I'm angry too.

Was that God? He was also angry? That didn't make sense. I flipped over and more tears rolled down my cheeks. As I closed my eyes, a picture came into my mind, playing before my vision like a movie projector. I was five or six years old, waiting for my dad to come home. He'd been on the road an extra week, and last time I'd spoken to him, he'd promised he'd bring me home a surprise. After school that day, I'd put on my prettiest dress and had my mom braid my hair. Back then, I was Daddy's little girl, and he could do no wrong. Sure, he got angry sometimes, but it was never toward me, and in my underdeveloped mind, my siblings or Mom were at fault.

That day, when Dad came home in his semi, I ran to meet him. He had climbed from the truck, a huge smile on his handsome face. Then he'd lifted my tiny frame and twirled me around. "So good to see you, Cupcake. I missed you."

"Missed you too, Daddy." He set me on the ground, turned to his truck, and brought out a large stuffed blue dog with floppy ears and a curly tail. I squished the dog against me, joy lighting my mood. "Thank you, Daddy. I love it." He'd tousled my hair and regarded me with a fond expression. "Now you'll have something to snuggle with when I'm on the road."

Tears spilled over at the memory. There was more to my dad than the anger and abuse. Under the pain lived a man who loved his children. A man who loved me. Could we somehow return to the simple love we'd shared when I was a child? Could there be healing for him? For us? In the middle of the questions, another phrase played through my head. *I will restore to you the years that the swarming locust has eaten.*

Chills covered my body. Another promise ...? I crossed the room and fetched my journal from my purse. I flipped it open to the page of promises I had written.

Beauty for Ashes
Dad will walk me down the aisle to Joe.

I stared at the second line, a flurry of emotions overwhelming me. With the anger I held toward my dad, I wasn't sure if I wanted him in my life, let alone to be in my wedding. There would have to be a lot of changes inside of me and even more changes inside of him... *Lord, help me with this.*

Underneath the short list, I wrote down the words *The years of my life will be restored.*

I closed my journal and my eyes again and whispered a prayer asking God to help me believe these promises would be fulfilled. There was a chance I was completely losing my mind, but these new words breathed fresh life into my being. There was still a ton of hurt under the surface, but perhaps tomorrow, after a good night's sleep, I'd have the courage to face my parents.

CHAPTER 2

December 24, 10:15 a.m.

TAMARA

Pulse thudding, I slowly made my way up the sidewalk leading to my parents' home with only my wallet and keycard in my pocket. For hours this morning, I'd worn tracks in the old carpet in my cheap motel room, praying, no—begging—God to give me strength for whatever lay ahead. Too quickly, I reached the front of the house. The muscles in my legs clenched as my shaky hands reached for the doorbell. I turned around and waited, a part of me hoping they were gone.

"Theresa!" Dad's voice bellowed from the other side of the house. "Get the door."

"I can't. My hands are covered with meat."

A few choice words spewed from my father's mouth. Something about not wanting surprise visitors on Christmas Eve. I edged away, berating myself for setting off my dad. Maybe I should come back after Christmas.

The door creaked open behind me, and I spun around. Mom stood in the doorway, wiping her wet hands on her jeans. "Can I help—" Her mouth snapped shut as recognition dawned and the color in her face drained.

I swallowed the emotion stuck in my throat, making it impossible for me to speak.

Her eyes shone with tears. "Tamara." She gasped. "Is that you?"

"It's me, Mom." I took a tentative step forward.

"Oh, thank God!" She came close and threw her arms around me, hugging me tight, pressing her wet face against mine. "I can't believe it. I can't believe it. You're actually here."

I embraced her tiny frame, realizing how much I'd missed her over the years and how much I'd suppressed the longing for my mother. "I'm sorry, Mom. I'm so sorry. I shouldn't have stayed gone for so long."

"Theresa!" my dad's voice bellowed again. "Who is it? You're letting out the heat."

Mom withdrew and searched my face. A thousand words passed between us in a single moment. Was I ready to face my dad? I blotted the tears with my sleeve and whispered a quick prayer. Ready or not, his footsteps were heading toward us.

"Are you deaf? I don't work my butt off to heat the great—" He stopped as he took in my appearance. Surprise and anger flashed in his countenance. He clenched his jaw, then stalked into the house.

Good to see you too, Dad.

Mom motioned me to follow. I hesitantly trailed after her. Dad grabbed a PBR tallboy from the fridge and paced the living room, taking large chugs of his beer. Mom took a bottle of wine from the cupboard and offered me a glass. I shook my head. It was only ten past eleven, for goodness sake. Besides, last time I drank with family, it had *not* gone well. I glanced over at Dad. He stared at me now, a curious yet bitter expression on his face. Anger flared in my core. What's wrong with him? If it were my child coming home after these years, I would be thankful they were alive. I'd shower them with affection and let go of the past, even if it cost me my pride.

Apparently, the burden landed on me to make the first move. "Hi, Dad."

His upper lip twitched, but he said nothing.

"I'm really sorry for leaving like I did."

"You're sorry?" He shook his head and took another long chug.

"Yes, I'm sorry for running away and staying gone as long as I have."

His face scrunched like he'd tasted something bitter. "That's it?"

"What do you mean?" I asked, confusion making my head ache.

He threw his free hand in the air. "Do you have any idea what it's like to be a parent? You disappeared for years, Tamara, and you waltz in and say sorry and expect what? How did you even find us?"

A hundred different responses came to my mind. Yes. I did know what it meant to be a parent. That's what had caused me to search for them in the first place. But I couldn't tell him that. He'd probably assume the worst. He always assumed the worst. I looked at the floor to hide how much his words cut me. Mom placed her hand on my shoulder, giving me the strength to speak. "Dakota gave me your address."

"Dakota?" He spat out her name like a curse word.

"I found her first. With her record, she was easier to find. She was supposed to come here with me."

"No." Dad shook his head, and a vein pulsed on his temple. "No way. Dakota's not allowed here. She knows that."

"Why?"

"Because she's worthless. Last time she stopped by, three hundred dollars went missing from my wallet. To support her drug habit, no doubt." Dad crumpled the can in his hand, returned to the fridge and clutched another beer.

She'd stolen from me too, but I'd never completely shut her out. This might be harder than I expected. "Dakota needs help, Dad, not the silent treatment. She needs to know that she's loved, no matter what."

A deep flush climbed my father's neck as he turned to me.

"Oh, that's how it is? You're all grown up, thinking you can give your old man some parenting advice? Give me a break, little girl. You don't know a thing." He paused long enough to open his beer and slowly walked toward me. "What happened to you to make you think you can come to my house and disrespect me?"

Fear crept down my spine. Last time he accused me with this tone, he beat me senseless. I took a step backward. Mom's hand curled around mine, seemingly scared to let me go—perhaps afraid I might disappear again.

He stopped a foot from me and spoke with an unnatural calm. "When you were born, I thought you were special, that you were going to make something of yourself, but you have done nothing but poison this family. Because of you, Dakota got addicted to drugs—"

"That's enough, Paul." Mom cut him off.

"Be quiet, Theresa. Nobody asked you."

Rage exploded inside of me, and the words came before I could stop myself, "Those weren't my drugs, Dad. I only said they were to keep you from killing Dakota. I'd been protecting her from you. But even if they were my drugs, instead of beating me, why did you not ask me why I was taking them? I'm not the one who poisoned this family. You are!"

He jabbed his pointer finger at me, poking me in the chest. "Don't you dare talk to me like this in my house! I gave you kids everything, and this is how you repay me? You spit in my face! Why did you come here anyway? To insult me? Get the hell out, and don't come back."

"No, Paul, please!"

His expression soured, and he stomped into the living room.

"I'm sorry, Mom. I'll be at the Travelodge for the next few days if you want to talk," I said and hurried through the door before the emotions overwhelmed me.

CHAPTER 3

December 24, 11:27 a.m.

JOE

The dull gray light from the window poured in from under the curtain. What time was it? Who actually cared? I rolled over in bed and groaned. Everything hurt. My head. My body. My soul ... I heaved the blanket over my head and inhaled deeply. Big mistake. I gagged on the odor of whiskey mingled with stale sweat. A shower would have been a spectacular idea, but at the moment, nothing mattered except making the torment stop. I threw the blanket off me, sat, and glanced around the messy room.

Knick-knacks from my dresser lay strewn across the floor along with six empty beer cans. The lamp was tipped over next to a half-empty bottle of booze. Beside that was a picture of me and Tamara, ripped to shreds. Like my heart ...

My head throbbed, and shame ripped through me. I had told Tamara I would follow her to hell. Well, I did, and then she abandoned me there, soul burning in heat and ash. My phone buzzed from across the room, but I ignored it and reached for the bottle of whiskey instead. There wasn't anyone in the world I wanted to speak to right now. Not even her. I stared at the light brown liquid, contemplating drinking away last night's hangover and yesterday's heartbreak. The serenity prayer flitted across my brain like an old habit, impossible to kick. *God help me accept the things I cannot change.* I winced at the thought.

Things I couldn't change.

Number one—Tamara walking out on me.

My parched throat ached, along with the rest of my body.

She left me. She's truly gone.

Number two—The diner was gone.

Burnt to the ground at the hands of a psychopath. On the bright side, he was dead, so there's that. But his death didn't change anything. Life as I knew it had been destroyed. Decimated beyond oblivion. And she was gone. She abandoned me like it was nothing to her. Like *I* was nothing to her. Tears stung my eyes, and I closed them tight.

This wasn't real.

This couldn't be real.

Any moment I'd awaken from this cruel nightmare. Tamara would walk through the door, and this terrible dream would be over. I scanned the messy room, seeing the chaos I had created. Another round of shame served with a heaping side of guilt. I twisted the cap off the bottle. The sweet smoky scent filled my nostrils, and I took in a long inhale. Forget Tamara. Forget the diner. Screw it all.

The phone rattled again, and I hesitated before setting the booze aside and stumbling across the room to fetch it. Ten missed calls and seventeen text messages. Six from Betty. Three from Trudy. Two from Frank. The rest were from Claire. Not a single one from Tamara.

My head ached again as I clicked on Claire's latest text.

Hey Joe, I'm sorry to hear about the diner. I hope you and Tamara are okay. I'm praying for you.

You and Tamara? I resisted the urge to throw the phone across the room. I took in a deep breath and counted to three, pressing the phone against my throbbing forehead. Another text came through. Hesitantly, I brought the phone from my temple and peeked at it.

I hate to ask, but we're getting paid this Friday, right? I'm going to need the money while I search for a new job.

The words crashed against my chest like a wrecking ball.

Number three—the money was gone. Who knew if the cops recovered it, and if they did, how long it would take for them to process it? I barked out a humorless laugh. I could pay them out of Tamara's and my wedding fund. It wasn't like we were going to be needing it. Yeah ... that would only cover a few employees and leave me deader than dead broke.

I trudged to my bed and plucked the bottle off the dresser, the serenity prayer skipping through my head once more. "Enough!" I didn't want to think of God or any higher power that would allow this. That would rip away everything I ever cared for like he had with my mom.

The doorbell chimed, a ringing noise that cut through my skull like a splitting maul. Who would be here? Tamara? No. It would definitely not be her. And if it were, I'd slam the door in her face. The doorbell rang three more times in quick succession, then I heard the front door open. What in the— Maybe it was Tamara. She was the only one who had a key to the place.

"Joe?" a male voice called. Caleb. Of course. He knew where I hid my spare key. "Joe? You here, buddy?"

Silence. Then footsteps climbing the stairs. Panic struck, and I regarded the bottle of whiskey in my hands. Damn. There'd be no hiding what I'd done. "Give me a—"

The door twisted and Caleb walked into the room. He scanned the trashed room, gaze landing on me. "What's going on, man?" He tried to keep his voice light, but clearly this whole scene spooked him.

I raised the bottle in the air, grimacing. "Let's just say it's been a rough twenty-four hours."

"Yeah, the diner made the news. I've been trying to call you." He crept toward me like someone approaching a skittish animal.

A sardonic chuckle sputtered from me. "That's barely half of it. The money's gone, the employees need to get paid, and did I mention Tamara left me?"

His mouth dropped open. "She left you? Like left you, left you?"

"Is there any other kind of leaving?" The words sounded bitter as they left my mouth.

"Whoa."

Another sick laugh that sounded more like a cry. "Right?"

He eyed the whiskey in my hand. "Hey, bud, why don't you let me have that?" He cautiously worked the bottle from my grasp and disappeared into the bathroom. The liquid made a glug glug sound as it emptied into the drain. "Do you have any garbage bags in here?"

I ignored his question and thought of Tamara instead, feeling my insides implode. She hadn't dumped me like Susan had, but she ditched me, leaving me with the aftermath of her sister's cyclone. I'd never be able to forgive her for that. My guts twisted. This was the second time in the last year that I'd fallen off the wagon. Both times were because of Tamara. Loving her wasn't good for me. No one else, not even Susan, had ever gotten to me the way she had. I needed to stop loving her. Quit her cold turkey. Dig a moat around my heart that would keep her out forever. Otherwise, in the end, there'd be nothing left of me.

"Found them." Caleb waltzed out of the bathroom, a white plastic bag in hand and started picking up cans and garbage.

"Come on, man. You don't gotta clean my room."

He ignored me and continued cleaning the mess. "Is there any more alcohol in the house?"

I shook my head.

He raised a suspicious eyebrow.

I held three fingers in the air. "Scouts honor, bro."

"Scouts honor? We haven't been scouts since the fourth grade."

I raised my hands in mock defeat. "It still counts. Check the whole house if you must."

"Why don't you shower while I look around?" He lifted a piece of garbage with the tips of his fingers and crinkled his nose.

"Come on. I don't need a babysitter or a maid."

"I beg to differ." He eyed me from head to toe. "Now go get in the shower before I hose you down. We're heading to a meeting."

I glared at him. "A meeting?" Why couldn't he just leave me to my demise?

"Yeah, Phillips, a meeting. I know your life just took a terrible turn for the worse, but I'm not going to sit by and allow you to self-destruct. Now get in the shower."

I rose and hurried to the bathroom. I'd go to the stupid meeting to get him to leave me alone.

"Where's your duffel? I'll pack you an overnight bag."

"What?" I stuck my head out from around the bathroom door.

"Never mind. Found it." Caleb said with a grin. "Mom insists you stay with us tonight."

I shook my head. "No way."

"For Christmas, dude. You know she won't let me in the house without you."

Yeah, right. I slammed the door behind me. His mom probably didn't even know I was coming. This was Caleb's way of hovering. Controlling the situation. I undressed and stepped into the shower, mind circling on ways I could dodge Caleb and Christmas with his folks. Not a single part of me wanted to celebrate the birth of God and the blessed hope he offered. Nope. I wasn't in the mood at all.

CHAPTER 4

December 24, 12:20 p.m.

TAMARA

After leaving my parents' house, I walked to the pier to sort through my emotions, but after nearly an hour it hadn't helped. Teeth chattering, I started back to the hotel. I'd expected things to be strained with my dad, but I thought he'd at least have some sort of positive reaction to seeing me. Then again, he'd believed this whole time that I'd been the one who had brought drugs into his house. That I'd been the reason Dakota had started using. *You have done nothing but poison this family.* His words pounded in my head, spinning and catching like a scratched record. Fighting tears, I jogged up the stairs to my room and cranked the heat to full blast before running a hot bath.

My phone vibrated on the nightstand. I thought I'd brought it with me, but I must have forgotten it. I hadn't even missed it. Probably because I knew I wouldn't be hearing from anyone I cared for. Specifically, Joe. Thinking his name caused that familiar longing to bud in my chest. I missed every part of him. His tenderness, his caring, his love. If he were here, he'd pull me close, warm me with his embrace and assure me that I'd be okay.

The phone buzzed again, and I ambled toward it. I lifted the cell and scrolled through the notifications. Eleven text messages and several missed calls from people from the diner, checking in to see if Joe and I were doing okay after the fire. A voicemail from Claire had come through seven minutes ago. I clicked on the message and brought the phone to my ear.

"Hey, girl. I'm worried about you and Joe. I've been texting both of you this whole morning and getting no response. The news said there were no injuries in the fire, but not hearing from either of you is scaring me. Please let me know what's going on."

Guilt made my stomach clench. I wanted to let her know I was safe, but I wasn't ready to tell her the rest of the story. Why hadn't Joe gotten ahold of her? He had always been the responsible one. Why hadn't he called a meeting? Maybe he was doing worse than I expected. Maybe he'd been crushed under the weight of my family drama and his destroyed dreams. All I had to do was press one button and I'd have the answer to my worse-case scenarios. The need to hear his voice crashed over me like a tidal wave.

Holding my breath, I scrolled to his name and hit send. The phone rang four times before going to his voicemail. My heart broke a little more as I hit end without leaving a message. Was he ignoring me? I hit send again and waited for it to go to voicemail. I should have at least left a message.

"Hello." He answered after the third ring this time, his voice hollow.

"Hey." A long deafening silence pervaded as I gathered my thoughts. "I'm calling to see how you are."

Another extended silence. Long enough that if I didn't know better, I would have thought he had hung up. "Joe?"

"What do you want me to say, Tamara?" A hardness in his tone I'd never heard him use before came through. Not toward me anyway.

My eyes stung as tears flooded them. "I'm sorry, Joe."

A sarcastic chuckle. "What? Things aren't going well with your folks? Didn't see that one coming."

His words felt like sandpaper on my shredded soul. That was all right. He was hurt. I deserved that. But I didn't know what to say. "Claire tried to get ahold of me. She sounded worried. Have you contacted anyone, or do you want me to do it?"

He sighed deeply. "I don't even know what to say to them. They want their last paycheck, but you know as well as I do the money's gone."

I rubbed my temple, my head suddenly aching. "I can call them, Joe. This is my fault."

More silence. This gap between us felt far too wide to mend.

"Sure," Joe said, his voice distant.

"I'll work on it this afternoon. Take care." I wanted to say the normal I love you, but the words lodged in my throat. Despite the strain between us, my feelings for him would never change. He owned me until the end of forever.

"Yeah." With that, the phone went silent, and my heart shattered. Not even a goodbye. No tenderness in his words whatsoever.

I threw the phone aside, walked into the bathroom, and shut off the running water before it overflowed. I stared at the water, my conversation with Joe stuck on repeat, doubts flooding over me. I wanted to believe that God could restore us. That God could restore me, but after the blows I withstood over the last few days, I couldn't see how.

And Joe ... he'd never spoken to me like that. Even after the mistake I'd made with Kyle, Joe had never given up on us. I had run from him, and he'd chased after me. But this time, it was different. The distance and coldness in his voice told me that he may be done fighting for us, and I couldn't blame him.

Gnawing my lip, I fought back an avalanche of sorrow as my plethora of mistakes bombarded me. I'd bullied him into taking me to Washington. I'd abandoned him to face Trudy alone. And then I left him to deal with the mess I created. After the many times he'd been there for me, I'd failed him again and again. *God, be with Joe. Please help him through this.* I went to the bedroom and grabbed my phone. I didn't know how to help him, but I would start by doing what he asked. I found Claire's number and hit send, searching for the words to say.

She answered on the first ring. "Oh, my goodness, Tamara. Where are you? How's Joe? I've been worried sick!"

Shame burnt the lining of my guts. I should have contacted her sooner. "Hey, Claire," I said, my voice weak. "I'm so sorry for not getting ahold of you earlier."

"Oh dear, you sound awful."

"It's been a hard few days, but that's no excuse. I should have called earlier."

It took a few moments to gather my thoughts. Might as well tell her the whole story; she deserved a confession. I told her how because of my mistakes the money was gone, then launched into my story of Dakota coming to my apartment with Gabriel's ashes and the onslaught of insanity that followed. "When I woke yesterday, Dakota had stolen my car, which triggered a huge fight with me and Joe. In the end, I took off to Aberdeen without Joe to tell my parents about Gabriel. It seemed like the right thing to do."

"Wow. This is insane. I thought my life was crazy."

"Yeah, well, it hasn't gotten any better since I arrived. When I went to my parents' house, my dad freaked out on me, called me poison and kicked me out." My voice grew hoarse as I spoke. "And to top it off, Joe is barely speaking to me."

"That's awful, Tamara. How can I help?"

I swiped a stray tear that had escaped. "Thanks for the offer, but I need to take care of this. It's my mess. I need to clean it."

"Don't do that. It sounds like you have a ton to deal with regarding your family. Let me help you."

I bit the side of my cheek, overwhelmed by her kindness. Recounting this story to the rest of the employees would be exhausting. "Thanks, Claire. I really could use the help right now. Would you mind calling the other employees for me?"

"Absolutely."

Relief momentarily washed through me as I felt the weight of the task lift.

"What do you want me to tell them?"

I stared at the green and gold flecks in the carpet, clutching the phone, mind spinning. What would Joe say? As I thought of his strong leadership, words formed. "Please don't give them the personal parts of the story I shared but let them know that the diner was a complete loss. The money's gone, which means until the insurance settlement comes through, there is no money to pay anyone, but everyone should be eligible for unemployment. Also, if anyone needs a letter of recommendation or reference, Joe or I will gladly oblige." I probably shouldn't have spoken for Joe, but a part of me knew he would say the same thing.

"All right. I'll let them know. People won't be happy that they're not getting paid, but it's not like it's your fault."

Her words stung. In reality, it was my fault. Maybe my dad had been right. I was poison. Joe had finally seen it too.

A light rap on the door drew me from my self-loathing.

"Hey, Claire, I gotta go. Thank you for everything."

"You're welcome. Please stay in touch."

"I will." After hitting the end icon, I tucked my phone in my pocket and crept to the door, unsure. Was it housekeeping? It seemed too late in the day for that. Plus, I was pretty sure they would have announced themselves. I peered through the peephole. Mom stood on the other side of the door, eyes red-rimmed and puffy. Pulse thundering, I unlatched the lock and swung it open. Was she coming here against my father's orders? How much would that cost her later?

We gazed at each other for a few awkward seconds. "Can I come in?" she asked.

I nodded and stepped aside.

She walked inside and turned toward me. As a child, I'd been told I looked like my mother, but standing here now, I couldn't see it. Except for the slight build and oval face. The rest of her appeared tired and aged like she'd lived a million years in the last six.

"I'm very sorry for the way your dad treated you."

Was he sorry? I highly doubted it.

A low cry came through her trembling lips. "Please don't leave again. I prayed for you to come home every day for the last six years."

I stood in front of her speechless, clueless on how to respond.

"To have you, Dakota, and Gabriel home for Christmas would be a dream come true."

I glanced at my duffel where Gabriel's ashes were safely stowed. I prayed for the strength to tell her the truth, then averted my gaze, unable to speak. No wonder Dakota had kept it to herself over the years. Some things were too awful to say out loud. "Mom, I want that too. I'm the one who has been trying to track our family for months now. But it's like they're in hiding."

"What do you mean?" Her eyebrows pinched together, deepening the crease in between them

"No one even has any social media. I had to find Dakota through her arrest record, and she told me you guys had moved here. But I have no idea where Nathan and Josiah are."

A tiny smile appeared on her lips. "Well, Nathan's here in town. He's doing great. He has two kids, Ivy and Colton, and he works with your dad with the trucking company."

Sadness trickled through my insides, making my stomach heavy. Why had I stayed away for so long? I had missed so much.

"And Josiah's in North Dakota working in the oilfields. He and his wife had a baby girl named Mia this last year."

North Dakota? I guess that didn't surprise me much. The summer after Josiah's eighteenth birthday, he headed to Alaska to work on a fishing boat. Of my siblings, Dakota was the only one I'd been close to when we were kids.

"But we only moved a few years ago. You could have returned to Quilcene before then," Mom said.

A few years ago? More like close to five. But honestly, as much as I'd wanted to reunite, I was only recently serious about it. "I'm sorry, Mom."

"It's okay, sweetheart. You're here now, and that's what matters."

"But, Mom. How can we move forward if Dad won't even talk to me?"

She placed her hand softly on my arm. "Just give him some time. You took him by surprise."

An unexpected ball of anger erupted in my stomach. "Time? It's been six years. How much more time does he need?"

"Come on, sweetie. You know how your dad gets."

"Yes, I do. I have the scars to prove it."

She flinched as if my words were weapons, assaulting her battered heart.

I took in her quiet demeanor and more anger rose. "Why did you let him abuse us, Mom? Why didn't you ever stop him?"

"Oh honey, I know he got rough sometimes, but it was only when he was disciplining you kids."

Disciplining us? Had she forgotten the verbal abuse toward her? "You think that justifies it? Mom, he abused us, and you didn't even try to stop him."

"You think I didn't want to? Your father is three times the size of me."

I threw my hands in the air. "You could have left him, got the cops involved, or filed a restraining order."

"You're right. I'm a terrible mother, but did I deserve this? To have three of my children completely abandon me?"

I reigned in my emotions. Lashing out at her wouldn't help. "I don't understand why you didn't leave him."

"I love him." She fiddled with her wedding ring, a small simple bronze band she'd worn for years. "I wanted us to be together as a family. I wanted you kids to have a better life than me. Obviously, I failed."

Taking in her injured expression, my anger drained away. She was hurting too, like the rest of our family. Closing the distance between us, I rested my hand on her shoulder. "You did the best that you could, Mom. That's all that any of us can do."

She gaped at me through the tears. "I'm sorry, Tamara. Please forgive me."

Tears poured down my face too. She put her arms around me, and I buried my head into her like I did when I was a child.

She caressed my head. "You have always been my strong baby girl," she said between sobs. "You're so beautiful and smart. I'm sorry I wasn't there for you the way you needed."

I burrowed my face deeper into her, allowing her words to heal a small place within me. My dad seeped into my thoughts, and I wondered if this, right here, could ever happen with us. A part of me recoiled at the thought, but from a deeper place, I prayed beyond hope that somehow God could work that big of a miracle for us.

CHAPTER 5

December 24, 7:35 p.m.

JOE

Turns out, it was harder to find an AA meeting on Christmas Eve in Vancouver than Caleb had bargained for. We had already missed the morning AA gatherings, and there wasn't another until late evening at St Luke's Lutheran church. After cleaning my house, Caleb took me to Denny's for a late lunch and dragged me around for the rest of the day doing last-minute Christmas shopping. By the time we made it to the meeting, my head pounded, and my throat ached for another drink. The place was packed as we held hands to say the Serenity Prayer. I mouthed the words without any conviction, wary of asking God for serenity. There were a few announcements, then they passed around the collection bucket.

The focus of the meeting today was Step One—admitting we were powerless over alcohol and that our lives had become unmanageable. A dark chuckle escaped me, and I hoped no one noticed it. Caleb nudged me with his knee and shot me a look that said, *what's so funny?* Truth be told, there was nothing funny about it. Because my life had become far from manageable before I'd taken my first drink this time, and now it seemed the only thing that could touch the wretched ache was a half a fifth of whiskey.

A woman in her mid-twenties with dreadlocks and a tattoo on the left side of her neck stood. "Hello, my name is Angel, and I'm an alcoholic."

The crowd chanted their reply.

"This is day three, and I have to say that it's hell. The doctors prescribed me Librium for the withdrawals, but I'm trying not to take it. I don't want to get addicted to another substance, ya know?" She paused, wringing her shaky hands together. "As this step says, my life has become unmanageable. My kids were taken from me last week." Her voice broke, and she sobbed, a guttural thing that sucked the air out of the room.

Damn. Why did life have to be so hard?

She composed herself after a few seconds. "They say some of us have to hit rock bottom before we reach for the help we need. This is definitely my bottom."

Rock bottom ... I could one hundred percent relate to that. I'd thought I hit my bottom more than once, but I kept locating new depths. The ironic thing was, it wasn't even because of my drinking. It was Tamara. She had been the addiction destroying my life. She had somehow rewired my brain the same way heroin does to its users. She was the drug I would do anything to get. The ache that caused me to sacrifice myself.

A tear slid down my cheek, and I wiped it away. I had to quit her before she destroyed me. Grief overwhelmed my soul. The entire day I'd been so angry with her. It had kept the sorrow at bay, but now the only thing I felt was the miserable ache for her, the part of me that wanted her so bad it nearly killed me.

For the rest of the meeting, Tamara completely engulfed my thoughts as I mourned the things I loved about her. Her smile, her laugh, her free spirit, and spontaneity. The way she felt when I held her close. There was so much good in her, but could that outweigh the damage that had been inflicted this last month? She left me to take care of the destruction her demons unleashed, and that didn't feel like love to me. In fact, it seemed like I didn't matter to her at all. The meeting dismissed, and I hurried through the door before anyone I knew could find me.

Caleb followed me, and we walked in silence to his car. He unlocked his Chevy Malibu with his key fob. We both climbed in. "That was kind of a bummer, wasn't it?"

I nodded. "Yeah, man. Not the best way to spend Christmas Eve."

Caleb started the car and backed out of the parking space. "Did it help?"

"Maybe a little," I said to make him feel better. There wasn't anything that could help at this point.

He took a left on Mill Plain, heading toward his parent's house. "I'm sorry you're going through this, but we both know drinking isn't going to help."

I did know that, but it didn't stop the helpless need to numb the pain.

"You're strong, Phillips. This is tough, but you've made it through worse."

Caleb was right. Losing my mom had definitely been worse than this, but why did I have to go through any of it in the first place? Why couldn't I have a happy life surrounded by family and love? Was that too much to ask for?

Caleb exhaled. "You know I'm terrible at this stuff. I don't know what to say to help you right now."

Dealing with me in this state was way out of his wheelhouse. As much as I loved the guy, he didn't know the first thing about true suffering. He was better at the lighter side of life, like shooting hoops, joking and flirting with women.

We pulled into Caleb's driveway. His house looked like Christmas had vomited on it. Red and white lights were strung perpendicular across the roof, and icicle lights hung from the gutters. In the front yard, to the left, an inflatable Santa stood erect in his sleigh with eight reindeer attached. The right side contained a life-size nativity scene, complete with Baby Jesus in his manger surrounded by the wise men and his parents. I rolled my eyes as I exited the car and retrieved my bag.

Caleb opened the door and flipped on the light. "My folks are at the candle lighting service, and who knows where Megan is."

Nodding, I entered and climbed the stairs. Caleb lived in a split-level house with the kitchen, living room and master suite upstairs. Downstairs consisted of a fun area, with a pool table, wine cellar, and Caleb and Megan's rooms. Surely, they would put me as far from the wine as possible. I stepped into the living room and set my bag on the floor. The television and couch were moved to the side to make room for the large Christmas tree, adorned with lights, ornaments, and tinsel.

"I'm going to grab us some water," Caleb said. This part of the house was one big open floorplan. The kitchen and dining room extended into the living room.

I sunk into the beige sofa, feeling exhausted, wishing I could curl up and sleep for days. At the end of the couch sat a neatly folded blanket and sheet that Judy must have set out for me.

Caleb returned and set the glass on the end table. He sat next to me and placed his hand on my shoulder. "Hey, man, I know we joke around a lot, but there's nothing I wouldn't do for you."

I inhaled deeply. "I know, man. I appreciate it."

"I hope you don't mind me saying, but I think you should get ahold of your sponsor."

Inwardly, I cringed. Nick-the-drill-Sergeant-Stone. I'd rather put a bullet in my head, or, less dramatically, drink myself to death. He was what I had needed in the early days of my sobriety, but once I had my feet underneath me, he'd become a bit much. When it came to the program, he clung to it rigidly and acted over-the-top by the book in his approach.

The last few years, I'd started avoiding him. I thought maybe I'd outgrown him. I hadn't even contacted him after my slip back in April. Instead, I had dived into my rediscovered faith and relationship with Tamara and acted like it never happened. I would attend meetings here and there, but I hadn't felt the need for them. Nick would have told me that was my first mistake. *You have to work the program in order for it to work. Never forget what the Big Book says: alcohol is cunning, baffling, and powerful. It will bite you in the ass when you expect it the least.*

"Sure, sure," I said, but I probably wouldn't call him.

"Think about it. I'll let you rest." He stood and entered his parents' room. A few seconds later, he returned and chucked a pillow at me with a smile. "You're gonna be fine, Phillips. You always land on your feet."

I tried to return the smile, but it felt more like a grimace. "Thanks, bro."

"Take care." Caleb headed downstairs.

I settled onto the couch and adjusted the pillow, a familiar sadness returning. I'd slept on this couch for months after my mom died, and somehow, I was here again during the second biggest loss of my existence. It's crazy how life had a way of bringing you full circle. Tears threatened to come as I watched the lights on the tree twinkle against the green. This was supposed to be the most wonderful time of the year, but since losing my mom, it had been the hardest. She had taught me that the true meaning of Christmas was love and family, but since she died, I didn't have a family. I'd tried to with Susan, but that had failed. I thought this year with Tamara would be different. I had been ready to vow myself to her for the rest of our lives, but now she was gone. Abandoning me like my mom. My mom hadn't chosen to leave me, but she had left me here—an orphan on this cold and brutal planet. I rolled away from the Christmas tree. Here I was once again, the night before Christmas, completely alone.

$\mathcal{D}$ecember 24, 11:30 p.m.

DAKOTA

Where was I? My eyes fluttered, but I couldn't keep them open. My stomach swirled, and my body hummed in the most delicious way. Perhaps I was dead. I'd somehow escaped this nightmare called life. No, if I were dead, wouldn't my soul be burning in the deepest dungeons of hell? For half of a second, my eyes opened and landed on the big sign that read *Mt. Shasta Brewing Company.* It went dark again.

Memories crashed down on me, ruining the most pleasant high I'd had in weeks. Ryan finding me at Tim's house, beating me senseless, choking me until I passed out. Me escaping and then fleeing to Tamara's place. And the worst part—recounting the story of how Gabriel had lost his life. The way Tamara cried as I told her the awful story. Ryan may be dead, but what he took from us could never be made right. Tamara thought our family could heal, but we were like Humpty-freaking-Dumpty. All the king's horses would be at a loss.

My eyes flickered again, and I began to piece together the last twenty-four hours. After the fire, as I lay on Joe's couch, taking an inventory of the damage, guilt grew inside me. Tamara had wanted me to take my story to the cops and go with her to face our parents. I'd tried to tell her that wouldn't work, but she had insisted.

The last time I'd seen them, three years ago, my dad had busted me for stealing money from him. For a solid fifteen minutes, he'd yelled at me, telling me what a worthless person I was. I'd given him the finger and told him I had inherited it from him. Then he'd gotten in my face, jabbed his finger against my chest and told me to never come back.

That had been over money.

How much worse would it be when he heard the news of Gabriel's death? Dad wouldn't see the situation like Tamara had. He'd blame me for the whole thing the way he had when the trailer burned.

On top of that, I knew Romeo blamed me for his diner burning. Everywhere I went, things turned to ash. The longer I lay there, dwelling on my family and the overwhelming losses, the knot in my guts intensified. In the end, I had to escape, and the quickest way happened to be Tamara's car.

For hours I'd driven south, wanting to put as much distance as possible between my sister and myself. But as I drove, the destructive thoughts had grown louder, and I knew only one way to quiet them. Then I had driven into the city of Weed, a little town south of the California border.

Ironically, scouring drugs in Weed had been a struggle. My mangled face had made it difficult, but eventually, it worked to my advantage, and I sweet talked a guy into dipping into his personal stash of OxyContin. Twenty-five milligrams of time-release with a few shots of Fireball had worked wonders for a few hours at least.

A new round of guilt, shame, and self-loathing devoured my soul like vultures attacking a decaying animal. What kind of person steals from her sister after she'd shown them nothing but kindness? A worthless piece of white trash junkie was who. I was no good. I should head to the police station and turn myself in for stealing Tamara's car. Truthfully, she had probably already reported me. In a matter of days, I'd be thrown into a tiny cold cell and left to rot. A shiver worked its way through me, and the bruise above my right eye throbbed. I turned the car on and blasted the heat, surprised I hadn't frozen to death last night. Sleeping in a car in the middle of winter near the mountains of Northern California was brutal.

I retrieved the rest of the pills I scored last night and eyed the bar. Time for round two. Another onslaught of guilt overtook me. I'd promised Tamara I'd go somewhere and get some help, but I didn't truly think there'd ever be help for someone like me.

When had I started caring anyway?

Life was easier when I didn't.

The only hope for me was in these tiny white pills. Perhaps I should take them all at once and end it now. I could find a liquor store and swallow them with some Mad Dog. As James Dean said, *Live fast, die young, and leave a good-looking corpse.* Ha, good-looking? Yeah, right. Maybe a week ago before Ryan mangled my face.

But the thought was tempting.

Swallow these pills and fade into oblivion where I could never hurt anyone again. I opened the car door and stumbled toward the bar, suicidal thoughts beckoning me like the Pied Piper. There was only one way to stop the war within and around me. This would be the perfect way for me to leave. Almost poetic.

I swung the bar door open. I didn't need a full bottle to execute this plan. A few doubles and a handful of pills should do. I pushed through the door into the dim room. *Hurricane* by Luke Combs played from the speakers mounted on the wall. A few people sat at the bar, and a couple of guys were off to the left side of the room playing darts. The bartender, an older man with a gray handlebar mustache, polished a glass behind the counter. I ordered a double of top-shelf vodka. If I was going out, it might as well be in style.

The man retrieved the bottle of Grey Goose and free-poured it into a tall shot glass. "That'll be twenty-two fifty, darlin'." He scooted it toward me with a wink.

Darlin'? Puke. I grimaced and set twenty-five dollars on the bar. "Keep the change," I said and gulped the shot. "And I'll take another. Let's go with Stoley's this time."

He raised a bushy gray eyebrow and turned around, grabbing a bottle. He poured again and took my money. After he handed me the shot, I headed to the ladies' room. I stepped into a stall, locked the door and dug the bag of pills from my pocket.

Fear trickled into my core. Seven oxys should do the trick. I set the vodka on the toilet and dumped the pills into my hand. In a matter of minutes, the torment, shame, and loss would be gone for good.

Thoughts of Tim invaded the dark moment. *I love you, Dakota. I always have.* The last words he spoke to me sent gut wrenching sorrow through me. Why would he love me? I was a monster. Garbage.

You didn't deserve what Gabriel did to you. Or what your dad did.

Whether I deserved it or not, it *had* happened, and I *had* become this. Someone so lost and broken they could never find their true humanity. This is who I am, Tim. I deserve to die.

I put the first pill in my mouth and swallowed it with a sip of vodka.

You deserved to be protected. If you were, I know you would have made better choices.

"How do you know that, Tim?" I yelled and punched the door. Pain radiated through my hand, but I didn't care. That would be gone soon enough.

Someone pounded on the bathroom door. "Are you okay in there?" It sounded like the bartender.

Buzz off, perv. "I'm fine!" I looked at the pills in my hand, stomach turning with guilt and nausea.

I love you, Dakota.

Why wouldn't his voice leave me alone? Why couldn't he let me die? He'd gone to great lengths to protect me from Ryan, but he could do nothing to save me from myself. I'd been self-destructing for years, and nobody could save me from it. I swallowed another pill and let the next one swim around in my mouth. If I crushed it with my teeth the medication would release all at once.

Take care of yourself, Dakota.

Tears spilled down my face, and I spit the pill into the toilet before grabbing my phone. I scrolled to Tim's number and stared at it as sobs climbed my throat. Calling him would be selfish. Ending my life would be the most loving thing I'd ever done for anyone. I'd never been anything but selfish though. I pressed the green icon and put the phone to my ear.

"Dakota?" Tim answered.

Another sob rose in my throat.

"Dakota," he said again, voice pitch rising with concern. "Where are you? What's going on?"

I stared at the pills in my hand. "I'm in Weed," I rasped through the tears.

"California?"

The room started to spin, and I sat on the toilet. Had I already taken too much? "Yes. I'm not..." I paused, eyes fluttering. I only took two pills, right? "I'm not feeling so well." I slurred.

"Where are you, Dakota?"

"I, I ..." I tried to focus on my phone, but it seemed like there were three of them. After a few moments of confusion, I sent him my location, hoping I'd still be conscious when he arrived.

CHAPTER 7

December 25, 6:20 a.m.

TAMARA

A loud knock startled me from a deep sleep. Disoriented, I looked around the darkened room. My gaze landed on the glowing red letters of the digital clock. Twenty past six? Who would be pounding on my door at this time in the morning?

Another round of knocking. I threw my blankets off and stumbled to the door. I peeked through the peephole, and my mood lightened at the sight of my brother wearing a Santa Claus hat. He was taller and more muscular, but it was certainly Nathan. He held an adorable blond boy with cherub-like cheeks. I swung the door open.

"Merry Christmas, sis." Short dark curls stuck out from under his hat, and a crooked grin lit his brown, deep-set eyes. "Welcome home."

The little boy rang a small bell. "Mawwy Clismass."

Was I dreaming? "Nathan?"

"Who else? The ghost of Christmas past?" He laughed.

I chuckled, and a light warmth filled me. Nathan was always the joker of our family.

"I'm here to invite you to Christmas breakfast."

He hadn't seen me for six years, and he wanted me to come to have Christmas breakfast with his family?

The boy continued to ring the bell and hummed Santa Clause is Coming to Town.

"How did you know I was here?"

"Mom, how else?"

I yawned and rubbed my eyes. "And who's this little guy?"

"This is Colton, but this morning he's Santa's little helper."

I smiled, resisting the urge to tousle Colton's hair. "He's adorable."

Colton's teeth chattered. "Daddy, I cold."

"Sorry, bud." Nathan turned to me. "You gonna come to spend Christmas with us or not?"

"Umm." There were so many things to catch up on, and Christmas morning didn't seem like the right time. Then again, there wasn't any bad blood between Nathan and me, besides the fact that when we were kids, he'd been the biggest nark in the known universe. "Sure. Give me a minute."

"Great, we'll be in the car where it's warm." He pointed to the silver minivan across the parking lot. I watched for a minute as Nathan interacted with his son as he walked to his car. From our tiny conversation, I got a pleasant vibe from him, like the stuff that marred me and Dakota so badly had barely touched him, but who could tell in such a short conversation?

After the other reunions with my family members, I would have expected bitterness or rejection from Nathan, not for him to invite me to his house for Christmas. But honestly, Nathan always had been the one bringing humor and lightness to our family, even in the hard times. Why hadn't I searched harder for him instead of Dakota? He could have been more of a support, rather than dragging me through a bunch of insanity like Dakota had. And he and Joe may have become friends.

Chest aching, I closed the door, grabbed the first outfit I could find, and ran to the bathroom. After brushing my teeth and other duties, I threw on my clothes and gathered my hair into a loose ponytail. Was I crazy to accept his invitation this soon? No, this would be a good thing. It would be nice to meet his wife and become acquainted with my nephew and niece.

On my way through the door, I snatched my jacket and threw it on as I ran to his van. The door slid open automatically as I approached. I climbed in and put on my seatbelt.

Nathan looked at me from the rearview mirror, eyebrows wagging. "Cool feature, huh? I call this baby the Enterprise. It's not a minivan. It's a freaking spaceship."

I chuckled. "Beam me up, Scotty." The interior, though sleek, was littered with kids' toys, McDonald's cheeseburger wrappers, and a few forgotten French fries.

"Warp one, engage," he said, and he backed out of the parking space and pulled out of the motel lot. Nathan's playfulness felt like a breath of fresh air to my savagely beaten heart. His humor had obviously served him well over the years. Why couldn't I have been more like him?

"It's good to see you, Nathan. Thank you for inviting me to Christmas with your family. I'm excited to meet them."

"Absolutely. Mom called me pretty late last night, otherwise, I would have come sooner. It's been way too long, sis. And Amanda is dying to meet you."

I nodded, my throat feeling thick. I couldn't believe I had missed this much being gone for so long.

Beside me, Colton rang his bell again. "Daddy, I hunny."

"We're almost home, bud, and Mommy's making us a big breakfast."

The little cherub's face brightened. "Wif pantates and swawballeys."

"Yeah, bud. And whip cream too."

I smiled at their conversation. Nathan seemed like a good dad with a genuinely sweet connection with his little boy. In some ways, I'd been afraid to become a parent, believing that somehow, I'd repeat the mistakes of my mom and dad, but this little glimpse of sanity gave me hope. Maybe someday Joe and I—I killed the thought immediately. I couldn't go there.

We turned on the next street and after passing a few houses, we pulled into Nathan's driveway. The house was painted a soft yellow with white trim and a fenced-in yard. The grass was a tad overgrown but not too bad. A few stray toys speckled the lawn. Nathan rounded the vehicle, took Colton from his car seat, and we made our way toward the house.

The smell of bacon mingled with coffee and cinnamon hit my nose as soon as we entered. The house was as warm and inviting as it appeared on the outside. The walls were a rich caramel color framed with crown molding and hardwood floors. Christmas carols played, and someone with a lovely voice, across the house sang along.

I followed Nathan down the hall, stepping around stray toys.

"Sorry for the mess," Nathan said as we entered a large living room.

"No worries. You have a beautiful home," I said, a bit confused. Sure, there were a few toys here and there and a tad bit of clutter, but other than that, it was almost too perfect. The furniture set was leather and immaculate. In the corner off to the left set a six-foot grand fir tree decorated elegantly with white lights, silver bells, and big blue bulbs. Underneath, the Christmas presents were piled high.

We rounded the corner into the kitchen, and there stood the brunette from the pictures, stirring ingredients into a pot, body moving with the music. Plates full of bacon, pancakes, waffles, cinnamon rolls and a bowl of strawberries covered an island near the stove. On the opposite side of the room was a large dark wood table with matching chairs, set with five place settings.

Nathan put Colton on the floor, and the boy ran to his mom, throwing his arms around her legs. She spun around, a startled expression on her face. "Oh my, I didn't hear you come in!"

Nathan chuckled and kissed her cheek. "Sorry, babe. This is Tamara, the long-lost sister I told you about."

She turned to me, and a big smile brightened her soft features. Though she was pretty with symmetrical features, and perfectly white, straight teeth—the kind that probably cost her parents a small fortune in orthodontic work—she had this wholesome girl next door vibe. She greeted me, arms wide, and drew me into a hug. "Nice to meet you. Welcome to our home."

I returned the hug, not quite sure how to respond. It felt backward that she was welcoming me to *her* family. "Nice to meet you too."

"I hope you're hungry. Breakfast is almost ready, and there is plenty."

I felt a bit queasy, probably from the lack of sleep, excitement, and the fast food I'd been eating. "It smells delicious."

"Is Ivy awake yet?" Nathan asked.

"Still dead to the world. I hoped the music would rouse her. I swear that girl could sleep through anything."

"Mommy, up." Colten reached in her direction, closing and opening his hands.

She lifted him and set him on her hip. "This one though, he woke me at five."

"Open pwesents, Mama."

Nathan laughed, a deep baritone from his gut. "The kid knows what he wants. I'll go awaken sleeping beauty," he said and walked out of the kitchen and down the hall.

"We do presents after breakfast, sweetie."

Memories of Christmas in my home as a child flitted through my mind. Our parents never waited until after breakfast. Once we kids woke up, it had been a free for all until the presents were unwrapped, then we'd have homemade donuts topped with buttercream frosting. I smiled at the memory. It seemed like lately, more good memories were resurfacing instead of seeing my whole childhood painted in darkness. "Do you need help with anything?"

Amanda glanced around the room. "I think everything is good to go."

Nathan entered the kitchen again, carrying a sweet girl with soft features, sleepily nuzzled into his neck. She appeared to be a year, maybe a year and a half, older than her brother. Her fine, dark hair hung in disarrayed ringlets to her shoulders.

"Good morning, sleepyhead," Amanda said and tousled her hair. The girl scrunched her face into a scowl and burrowed deeper into her dad.

Nathan chuckled and whispered in her ear. "Come on, sweetie, wake up and meet your Aunt Tammy."

I cringed at the nickname my brothers used to call me. I never liked it and when they realized that, they did it all the more.

Her head snapped to attention. "I have an aunt?"

She had two aunts. Had she not met Dakota? Sad.

"You're adorable. How old are you?"

"I'm Ivy. I'm four." She raised her hand, flashing four tiny fingers somewhat awkwardly.

"Nice to meet you, Ivy," I said, heart swelling with fondness. "You can call me Aunt Tamara."

She gave a big smile. "Okay."

"All right, you little rascal, it's time for breakfast and then presents." Nathan placed her in a booster seat at the table, and Amanda set Colton next to her.

"Presents!" Both of them chimed at the same time.

I thought my heart may explode from cuteness overload.

"Want some coffee, sis?" Nathan stepped toward the counter on the opposite side of the room.

"Yes, please."

He took two mugs from the cupboard, filled them both, and opened the cabinet underneath. A variety of liquors lined the bottom shelf. He pulled out a bottle of Bailey's Irish Cream and a fifth of Irish Whiskey. An odd shiver crept over the length of my spine. Maybe Nathan's picture-perfect life wasn't so perfect after all. Not that drinking was necessarily wrong but drinking at seven in the morning on Christmas day seemed a bit off.

"Do you want me to make yours Irish?" He looked at me with a gleam in his eye.

I shook my head and flashed a fake smile. "Just cream and sugar for me."

"Suit yourself. I make a heck of a good Irish Coffee though."

"Maybe later." Probably not though. Not drinking with family, no matter how normal they seemed, felt like a good rule of thumb at this point.

We sat at the table and enjoyed the most delicious meal I'd had in a while. The spread made me think of Joe, but I tried not to let the sadness of missing him steal from the moment.

Over breakfast, Nathan told me that he'd met Amanda when they moved to Aberdeen while finishing his senior year in high school. It sounded like a bit of a whirlwind romance, and a month after they graduated, they discovered they were pregnant. Before breaking the news to either of their parents, they ran off and eloped. The first few years were hard financially for them until Nathan started driving truck with Dad, and Amanda learned to do the books for the company. Overall, they seemed happy. They rented the house they lived in, but someday soon they hoped to be able to purchase a home. They didn't ask why I'd shown up after being gone for so long. Instead, they kept it light, telling stories and making silly jokes with the kids.

After breakfast, Nathan put on a Santa Claus beard and jacket and handed the presents to Colton to disperse to Ivy, Amanda and himself. Then they took turns opening presents, taking delight in each one as they tore off the paper. Once the gifts were unwrapped, Nathan took off his Santa Claus outfit, left the room and returned minutes later with a final gift, a tiny rectangular box wrapped with shiny red paper.

The children were preoccupied with their stash of toys and Christmas candy. Nathan handed the gift to Amanda and whispered in her ear. A light flush tinged her cheeks, and she paused before ripping off the paper. She opened the velvet black box and gasped. She stared at the elegant necklace for a long moment, then focused on Nathan. "It's beautiful. I love it."

He kissed her, and I glanced at the floor. I twisted my

engagement ring and thought of Joe. Should I be wearing this ring? We hadn't said we were calling off the engagement, and as long as there was breath in my lungs, I'd pray that God would show me how to make things right with us. I brushed off the thoughts, stood and began collecting the wrapping paper strewn across the floor.

"You don't have to do that," Amanda said, rising to her feet. "You're our guest."

"I don't mind helping." I grabbed another piece of crumpled paper. "It's the least I could do after that epic breakfast you made."

"I'm glad you enjoyed it, but seriously, you can relax," she said with a pleasant smile.

Nathan started helping as well. "The extra help is good. Amanda gets nervous when she knows the folks are coming."

My head snapped to attention. "I hadn't realized they were coming."

"Of course, they are. It's Christmas. They should be here within the next half hour. You okay with that?"

I nodded and hoped the apprehension wasn't showing on my face. "Um, yeah. Things didn't go well with Dad and me yesterday. I'm not sure he'd want to see me again." Especially not on Christmas.

Nathan waved me off. "It'll be fine. I told Mom I planned to invite you today. I'm sure he'll expect you to be here, and I'm sure he'll be happy to see you."

I gave him a wary glance. "Yeah, right. You know how Dad is."

He flinched, brows knitting together. "What's that supposed to mean?"

"How do you not know what that means?" I said sharply.

"Oh, come on, sis." He raised a hand in the air and turned toward the kitchen. "Not you too."

My cheeks flushed, but I followed him, confused.

Nathan took a Budweiser from the fridge and cracked it open.

Already two Irish Coffees and now a beer? Did he drink like this often?

He took a big chug of beer and turned to me. "I don't understand you and Dakota's problem with Dad. Sure, he disciplined us when we needed it, but he never abused us."

My jaw dropped open. Was he delusional? I'd seen Dad break a board over his butt more than once while swearing and calling him names. And that was mild compared to what he did to Gabriel. Did he not remember?

"You don't know what it's like to be a parent. We were a rowdy bunch. We needed discipline."

I did know what it was like to have a child. It meant doing the best for them no matter how much it killed you on the inside.

"I don't know what happened between you and Dad yesterday, but he's been nothing but helpful to me and my family. He helped me get a CDL and gave me a job running a log truck for his company. And one of these days when the timing's right, I'll be a full partner." He paused and took another long swig. "He's been a great dad to me, so don't be coming to my house bad mouthing him in front of my kids, all right?"

My eyes pricked with tears, and my mind spun with confusion. "Okay, yeah, I'm sorry." He walked into the living room, and I stared after him, trying to pull myself together. It didn't make sense. Were we raised in two different households? I walked to the sink and turned on the hot water to fill it for the breakfast dishes, working to shake off the strange interaction. I put the stopper in the drain and poured dish soap into the sink.

"We have a dishwasher." Amanda's voice startled me.

"I know, but I'm used to doing things old-school." And the menial task felt like a good distraction.

She gave a sad smile, crossed the room and took a towel out of the drawer. "I'll dry."

I put a stack of plates into the sink and scrubbed the first one before rinsing and handing it to her.

She dried the plate and set it in the cupboard. "Don't mind Nathan. He gets a bit defensive of your dad."

I rinsed another plate and tried to think of the right response. A part of me wanted to tell the truth from my perspective. I wanted her to know what being raised in my home had actually been like. That her and Nathan's life didn't make sense to me with all the love and happiness tossed around, like Nathan hadn't experienced the same childhood I had. But what would be the point of that? Maybe Nathan had constructed this idea of our childhood so he didn't have to face the pain from our past. Maybe that was how he was able to build this beautiful life and be happy. "It's fine. I didn't mean to upset him."

Sounds of Nathan's booming laughter floated in from the living room. "Climb on the horsey, Ivy, and hold on tight."

Amanda giggled. "Sounds like he's already over it."

I hoped so, because before our little spat I'd thoroughly enjoyed being here with their family. Watching Colton and Ivy play with their dad filled a place in me I hadn't realized had been desperately empty. I dumped the silverware into the sink and scrubbed a fork with the washcloth. Amanda and I slipped into a routine, and within ten minutes, the dishes were clean and put in their proper places. I wiped the counters while she cleaned the table.

"Thanks for the help." She rinsed the dishrag with hot water and wrung it into the sink. "All clean, in time for me to make a mess again."

"Do you need any help? Joe does most of the cooking, but I could do something simple."

"Who's Joe?" She grabbed a bag of potatoes from the cupboard.

I quieted for a moment, unsure of how to respond. "My fiancé," I said quietly. "I can peel those if you like."

Her almond-shaped eyes grew wide. "You're getting married? When?"

My stomach fluttered. Why had I mentioned Joe? I took the

bag of potatoes from her and brought them to the sink. "We're thinking March, but it's a bit in the air right now."

"March? That's soon!"

I swallowed the onslaught of emotions gathering in my throat. "Like I said, nothing is concrete."

"Well, if you need any help, let me know. I used to dream of having a proper wedding, but the way things happened..." She was quiet for a few beats. "Not that I regret the way things went, but I love weddings, and I do have a passion for decorating."

I gave her a half-smile. The woman did have an eye for beauty. Her home, though somewhat messy from the children, had a classy touch with a homey feel. "Thank you. I'll definitely take that offer once we have a solid date."

She squealed. "It's so exciting to have a sister."

Her words hit me in a strange way. I had a new sister, but where was my old one? I hoped that she was safe and doing what she'd promised and got the help she so desperately needed.

"Are you okay?" She snatched a potato peeler from a drawer and handed it to me.

I shook my head. "Just thinking of Dakota."

"Yeah? Nathan doesn't talk about her much." She took the cutting board off the hook and leaned against the counter.

I rinsed a potato and peeled it before setting it on the cutting board, my mind jumping from Dakota to Josiah. Did he ever visit? I would have to get his phone number from Nathan. Was Josiah like Nathan, living in complete denial when it came to our childhood? Or had moving to North Dakota been his own way of running from the past?

The sound of a motor interrupted my thoughts. I peered through the window. Mom and Dad walked toward the house. Mom held a dish of some sort, and Dad had a large bag of what I assumed were gifts. The front door opened.

"Gwandpa!" Colton squealed, and there were footsteps running in the opposite direction.

"Hey, little buddy." Dad's voice sounded almost cheerful.

"Up, Gwanpa, up!"

A loud belly laugh filled the air. It sounded a lot like Nathan, but I thought it may have come from Dad.

"Vrrrrmmm. Vrrrmmm."

I set down a half-peeled potato, dried my hands on the front of my jeans and popped my head around the corner. Dad had Colton raised above his head, playing airplane with him. Colton's face beamed with delight. Dad smiled, genuinely enjoying this interaction. His face seemed years younger and softer than I ever remember seeing him.

Mom stood by Ivy as she showed her the new doll Santa had brought her for Christmas. She looked good. She wore a red shirtwaist dress that revealed her slender physique. She'd blow-dried her hair, which gave it more of the body it used to have.

I ducked into the kitchen and continued my peeling duties before either of them spotted me. Inwardly, I prayed that things would go smoothly with my dad, but I wasn't counting on it.

CHAPTER 8

December 25, 9:45 a.m.

JOE

I woke to the sound of clanging pots. Startled, I sat up.

"Sorry," Judy whispered, guilt lining her features. "That was an accident."

I rubbed the sleep from my eyes. "No worries." The smell of coffee, blueberry muffins, and fried potatoes mingled in the air.

"Would you like some coffee?" She wore a red and white Christmas apron over a velvet green dress. She'd teased her short hair to give it body and her make-up was bright with holiday colors.

"Coffee would be great." I stood, folded the blanket and laid it on the end of the couch. It was beyond awkward crashing in on their family's Christmas.

She poured me a cup and added an ample amount of sugar cookie creamer before handing it to me. I took a sip. "Thank you." Too sweet for me, but I was used to the way Judy prepared my coffee.

Caleb's dad, Ted, appeared in the doorway of the master bedroom dressed in slacks, a white oxford shirt, and a green tweed sweater vest. "Merry Christmas, Joe."

"Happy holidays." I glanced at the jeans and hoodie that I'd slept in last night, feeling underdressed. I wondered what Caleb had packed me. He surely knew that his parents liked to dress to the nines on Christmas morning.

"How's breakfast coming, hun?" Ted kissed Judy's cheek.

"It'll be ready soon." She blushed a little and pushed him playfully away.

I averted my gaze, yearning for Tamara.

Why did this scene make me miss her so badly? My phone buzzed, but I ignored it. Probably more work stuff. I wasn't ready for that. Hopefully, Tamara had contacted the employees like she said she would. The tiniest amount of guilt worked its way through me for how cold I'd been on the phone with her yesterday. She had sounded genuinely sad—I stopped the thought. I couldn't allow myself to go there. Not now. Maybe not ever. "Do I have time for a shower?"

She waved a hand. "Afterward. Food's almost ready."

I gave a half-smile and took another sip of coffee, trying to keep my focus on anything but Tamara and the diner. Both were off-limits today.

A few minutes later, Caleb emerged in his Oregon Duck pajamas. At least he'd dressed casual. "Smells great, Ma," he said and poured himself some coffee.

"Make yourself useful and set the table," Ted said and handed him a stack of plates.

"Merry Christmas to you too, Dad." He took the plates and set them around the table.

"I can help," I offered, stepping into the kitchen.

"You take it easy, dear. The food will be ready in a few minutes," Judy said with a smile, a hand on her hip.

"Okay." I lifted my hands in surrender, there was no arguing with Judy.

Ted dug the silverware from the drawer and followed Caleb as he set the glasses on the table. Megan climbed the stairs wearing a red fitted dress with silver bells for earrings, her strawberry blond hair pulled into a high ponytail and her lips glossy.

"Hey, Joe," she said with a smile, pink tinting her neck. "I didn't realize you were joining us this morning."

"Hey, Sprout," I replied. Caleb's kid sister had a bit of a crush on me. Well, she wasn't much of a kid anymore. She was nineteen and adorable in her own way, but to me, she'd forever be Caleb's baby sister.

She shot me a glare, but her lips curved at the edges, then she took a seat at the table loaded with food. Judy and Ted sat, and I squeezed in next to Caleb.

"The meal is amazing, hun. You really outdid yourself this year." Ted rested his hand on Judy's affectionately.

"Thanks. Why don't you bless the food, and we'll dig in?"

We held hands and bowed our heads. While Ted prayed, I zoned out, thinking of my mom instead. This was exactly the kind of extravagant brunch she would have prepared if she were here.

A knot formed in my throat, and I swallowed hard. I had to find a way to leave. Spending the day with Caleb's happy family would be pure torture for my shattered heart. I would have much preferred to be holed up in my bedroom eating pizza while binge-watching *Dexter* or something psychotic like that. One of those shows that makes one think that their life isn't so bad. My life may be falling apart, but at least I wasn't the freak addicted to murdering the bad guys.

Instead, I was stuck in a holiday with the Mayberry's and a perfectly cooked meal of country potatoes, bacon, pancakes, eggs, muffins, and fruit. Overall, it was an exquisite feast, enough to feed an entire basketball team. I reached for a pancake and contemplated my exit strategy. I wouldn't be sticking around for the awkward round of opening presents.

"How's Hailey doing?" Ted asked.

Caleb shook his head, making a cutting motion with his hand to his neck.

I took a large swig of coffee. "Who's Hailey?"

"Just a new girl I'm seeing." He shrugged and snatched another piece of bacon.

Judy chuckled. "Just a girl? He's spent practically every waking moment with her for the last few weeks."

"Yeah, and when he's not with her, he's talking about her," Megan piped in with a goofy grin.

"More like gushing," his dad said, a playful teasing in his voice.

"You guys knock it off." Caleb shoved a bite of pancake in his mouth, red spreading across his face.

He was blushing over a girl? Strange. I thought Caleb was terminally single. Guess things can turn around without a warning. Why hadn't he mentioned it to me? Probably to save my feelings.

The rest of the meal was filled with conversation about dreams, plans for the New Year, and ribbing each other. It was hard being in the middle of a cheerful family yet being the odd one out. I thought of the dream I'd had after my and Tamara's night together, the one of us on the beach, happily playing with our children. Sorrow swam in my guts. That was what I wanted for us: a simple life, full of joy and connection.

"You okay, Joe?" Judy asked.

"Yeah. I'm fine. I'm honestly not that hungry. I think I need some air." I stood and hoped it didn't seem rude. I couldn't stay another moment in this beautiful home, surrounded by beautiful people reminding me of what I didn't have. I hurried down the stairs and stepped through the front door into the brisk morning air.

"Hey, hold on!" Caleb followed after me. "Where are you going, man?"

I turned to him. "I appreciate you helping yesterday, but this." I made a sweeping gesture with my hands toward his house. "It's like salt in a blistering wound. I need to go home."

He sighed and ran a hand through his blond hair. "All right, man, I'll take you."

"No, you should get in there and enjoy the day with your family. I can walk home. Exercise will do me well."

His eyebrows pinched together. "Don't you want your stuff?"

"I'll get it later."

He nodded as his shoulders drooped. "Okay, but do me a favor?"

"Sure, anything." I hated putting Caleb through this.

He was silent for a minute. "I really think you need to call your sponsor."

Not this again. "I'd rather not. You know how Nick can be."

"I know, but I'm worried about you. When's the last time you talked to him?"

"It's been a while, but don't worry. I'll be fine." I berated myself for lying, but Caleb needed to be with his family instead of worrying for me.

"You're not fine, Joe." He lifted his pointer finger toward me. "You've fallen twice in the last year. You need to call your sponsor and tell him what's going on."

"Fine. I will."

"You promise."

I lifted three fingers with a cheesy grin. "Scouts honor, bro."

He chuckled and punched me in the arm. "I'll check in with you tomorrow."

On my walk home, I passed by houses decorated for Christmas. Through the windows, I could see families spending time together, laughing and smiling as if their lives were perfect. Why couldn't that be Tamara and me? Why couldn't we be healthier with functional families? My hand fumbled around in my pocket, gripping my phone. A huge part of me wanted to call her. To hear her voice, to let her love comfort this deep ache inside me, but that would change nothing. I couldn't go back to how things were. Too much damage had been done. I'd tried so hard to be strong for her, but it wasn't good enough. *I* wasn't good enough.

Taking a deep breath, I pushed forward, shaking off the onslaught of thoughts. I tried to pray, but it only made me miss her more. Across the road, I spotted the convenience store I used to frequent. The bright red light in the window told me it was open. The muscles in my abdomen tensed, and my throat felt dry.

God grant me the serenity—I squashed the thought and headed across the street, mind racing, circling around the people I'd be letting down once again. Caleb, Levi, my mom, Tamara ... My soul fractured a bit more at her name and the broken dreams it represented. The pressure became too much, I couldn't do this anymore. I couldn't think or feel for another second today. I needed to numb the pain away. I pushed through the glass door into the store and walked straight to the alcohol.

CHAPTER 9

December 25, 10:30 a.m.

DAKOTA

I rolled over in a soft bed and found my face drowning in a down pillow. Where in the actual hell was I, and how did I get here? The aroma of freshly brewed coffee mingled with sautéed onions and garlic wafted in the air. My mind spun around images of me in Tamara's car and stumbling into the bar in Weed. Sirens went off in my brain. Was I in a stranger's house? Perhaps the guy I had scored the oxys from?

Wait, no.

I had taken those pills and called Tim. *Tim.* A twinge of shame and embarrassment shot through my guts. Had he once again played the role of my guardian angel?

Damn it.

I wasn't some stupid damsel in distress. And he wasn't my friggin' knight in sparkling-fairy-tale-bull-crap armor. He was a goody-two-shoes cop, and I was a used-up drug addict. Water and oil, baby. The two didn't go together. Not even a little bit.

I scanned the room. It was earth-toned, the color of mud, with plants scattered around in random places. Above the bed hung an elegant dream catcher, adorned with various types of feathers and beads. Definitely not Tim's house.

The grog in my brain made it hard to sit, but I managed it.

Coffee. I needed coffee. Stat. Like mainline it into my veins, please. I placed my feet on a Native American rug that covered half the oak floor. The floor creaked as I took a few steps toward the door. I turned the knob and wandered into the hallway. I could hear a few muffled words.

"I care about her a lot. I hope I can help her." Tim's voice became clearer as I approached.

"I don't know, if people don't want to change, there is no help for them." A woman's voice now, a bit low and gravely, like she had smoked for the last twenty years.

I rounded the corner into the kitchen. Tim sat at a stylish oak table drinking coffee across from a slender woman with olive skin and dark salt and pepper hair. They both turned toward me as I entered.

Tim slid his chair from the table and stood. "Dakota, nice to see you awake. This is my Aunt Sage."

"Hello, Dakota," she said with a big smile, and laugh lines appeared around her mouth. "Happy Holidays. So nice of you to be able to join us."

I forced a smile, and my left cheek ached. Thanks to Ryan, my face looked and felt like it had been beaten with the notorious ugly stick.

"Thanks," was the only thing I could think to say. I hadn't celebrated Christmas since I was a kid. Why pretend now? As I approached the table, confusion crumpled my features. "Where am I, and how did I get here?"

Tim and Sage exchanged a glance, before he spoke. "We picked you up from the bar last night."

I squinted, racking my brain. The last thing I remember was taking those pills in the bathroom. The rest was blank. Had I blacked out?

"You were pretty drunk when we found you. We're in WhiskeyTown ... California. I'm staying here with Sage for the holidays since I was already in the area for work." Tim stood and pulled out a chair for me.

"WhiskeyTown?" I chuckled and winced at the pain that shot through my skull. First Weed and now WhiskyTown? Californians sure did like their substances.

I took a seat next to him, and an awkward silence drifted over us. I should probably thank him for rescuing me once again, but I'd rather not acknowledge it.

"You hungry?" Sage asked.

I shrugged a shoulder. "A little." Truth be told, I was starved. I couldn't remember my last meal.

Tim rose to his feet, walked to the fridge and pulled out a plate. "We didn't know how long you were going to sleep so we already had breakfast, but we saved a plate for you." He unwrapped the cellophane, popped it in the microwave and pressed a few buttons.

"Uh, thanks." Heat climbed my neck. Now he was serving me food? On top of that, I was at his aunt's house on Christmas morning after his big confession of love on the telephone. I wasn't sure what to do now that those feelings were exposed. It wasn't like we were a couple or anything.

The microwave dinged. Tim pulled out the food, brought it to the table and slid it in front of me. A strong sting of attraction hit me as I looked up at him.

"Bon appetit." His full lips curved into a fond smile.

I quickly glanced at the plate, berating myself for these unwanted feelings. He probably found me disgusting with my ruined face, courtesy of Ryan. "This breakfast is a lot. Thanks again." The plate brimmed with two eggs Benedict with hollandaise, avocado slices, and homestyle potatoes.

Sage gave a nonchalant wave and leaned forward in her chair to grab her coffee. "It's nothing, sweetie. I love to cook and don't have much opportunity to entertain nowadays."

"Coffee?" Tim asked.

"Oh, yes."

He went to the cupboard, retrieved a mug, and filled it to the brim. As he handed it to me, his hand brushed against mine, and another wave of heat went through me. Ignoring it, I took a sip. The flavors mingled in my mouth, exploding with hints of hazelnut. It had to be, no contest, the best coffee I'd ever tasted.

I glanced around the room, noticing marble countertops, backsplash that lined the wall behind the sinks and stainless-steel appliances. This place was seriously posh. My world didn't make sense anymore. Two days ago, I had stolen my sister's car after barely escaping death at the hands of Ryan, and today, I was living it up in what felt like an episode of *The Lifestyles of the Rich and Famous*. Any moment, an old guy in a coupe would drive up and ask me if I had any Grey Poupon.

"Go ahead and eat, you must be starving after the night Tim said you had." I nodded and grasped my fork. How much of my business did Tim tell her? How much did Tim even know? He must have heard that Ryan was dead by now. Hell, the Jefferson County Police Department was probably throwing a big party to celebrate justice finally being served to Ryan Cooke.

I nodded and dug into the eggs Benedict. As suspected, even reheated, they were delicious.

Tim rested a hand on my arm and leaned in a bit. "How are you doing, Dakota?"

He was always so warm. It made my skin tingle and my stomach too. I withdrew from his touch. No matter how great Tim was, whatever he was making me feel could never work. I finished chewing a bite of potato and threw him a snarky smile. "Oh, you know, livin' the dream."

Sage laughed and made eye contact with Tim. "I like this one."

What did that mean? Did she think we were together, and did she approve? A police officer and a drug addict? Hilarious. I shoved another bite in my mouth and ignored the questions taunting my brain.

"Me too," he said under his breath.

Heat flooded my cheeks, but I disregarded it and them as I continued to eat. The topics drifted toward safer subjects for the next few minutes as I finished my food. Sage didn't mention my wrecked face or the fact that I wasn't spending the day with my own family, which meant Tim had shared my business. When I finished the meal, Tim took my plate while his aunt refilled our coffees.

"Let's relax a bit in the living room and let our meal settle," Sage said.

A part of me wished that I could sneak off with Tim and tell him the details of what had happened since seeing him in Quilcene. Or maybe I wanted to be alone with Tim and do everything but talk. My stomach quavered at the thought, and I inwardly cringed. I grabbed my coffee and followed them into a large living room. A small live Christmas tree sat in the corner, but luckily, there were no other holiday decorations. Off to the left were a few Himalayan salt lamps and a layered water fountain in the corner. Sage settled into a recliner next to an open fireplace. Through the window, a few evergreen trees swayed in the wind behind a garden in the front yard.

I sat in the loveseat perfectly angled to face both Sage, the fireplace, and the big open window.

Tim sat next to me, and I found myself wishing there was somewhere else to sit.

"So how do you guys know each other?" Sage asked, curiosity in her tone.

There it was. The judgment I'd been expecting the whole time.

Tim spoke, filling my pause. "We grew up together, and we were neighbors for a season. We used to play together and build our own forts in the woods. They were never anything special, but we liked them."

I nodded. I had to admit, those times with Tim were the highlight of my childhood. For some reason, adventuring with him through the woods made me feel safe.

A timer went off on Sage's phone and she shut it off. "It's time for chores. This farm doesn't run itself."

I glanced at Tim. "We're on a farm?"

He smiled. "A small one. A few horses, chickens, and two cows."

Sage rose and headed to the door. "It's the only way you can be sure of the food you eat. Grow it yourself. That's what my papa taught me."

Her papa? This lady was a bit different.

"Do you want any help?" Tim offered.

"Naw, I like doing it myself. It gives me time to meditate and reflect."

Meditate? Great. Just what I needed. Another spiritual freak shoving their beliefs down my throat.

She left, and the door shut behind her.

I turned to Tim, and there were a few awkward moments between us as he studied my face, his appearance sad as he took in every inch of what Ryan had done to me. I glanced at the mug in my hand, unable to handle his stare.

"I got you a gift." He broke the silence.

My head jerked toward him. "For Christmas?"

He nodded with a slight smile.

"You shouldn't have done that."

He took hold of my hand, opened it and put a wrapped square box in it. "It's nothing."

I swallowed hard and stood, confused by the feelings this small gift could stir in me. I wanted to open it, but I couldn't do it in front of him. Not when he was affecting me like this. "Give me a minute, would you?"

"Sure."

Gift clutched in my hand, I hurried toward the bedroom I had slept in last night, trying to cram my feelings in the black hole where they belong. It was like my heart had been under a deep freeze for years, and Tim had begun to unthaw it.

Once in the room, I closed the door and latched the lock. I wasn't ready for my heart to melt. Too many things were stuffed in there, under the surface, that I wasn't ready to face. But I wasn't sure how to stick it back in the freezer. Between Tim and Tamara, something unexplainable had happened inside of me, and I didn't know if I could ever return to being who I was before. The terrifying thing was that I also didn't know how to move forward.

CHAPTER 10

December 25, 12:03 p.m.

TAMARA

A few minutes after Mom arrived, she entered the kitchen, and for the next hour or so the three of us prepared for lunch, though I was stuffed from the breakfast feast. Amanda and I slipped into an easy banter, Mom interjecting now and then about the grandchildren and how cute they were as they played with their Christmas toys.

Playful screams and giggles echoed from the living room where Dad and Nathan were with the kids. As I had expected, Dad didn't even bother to come to say hi to me. Even though I'd known it would be like that, it stung. I thought maybe the Christmas spirit might soften him a little, an empty hope that added to the sadness squeezing at my chest.

Several times over the last hour, I nonchalantly peeked around the corner to watch Dad bounce Colton on one knee while tickling Ivy with his free hand. As I watched, a longing formed in me, remembering the times he'd been like that with me as a child before the brokenness between us. I may have been a grown woman, but watching him with my niece and nephew, I felt like a little girl craving her father's attention.

Amanda gave me a curious glance as I took my place at the

counter cutting tomatoes for the salad. "You can go be with them if you'd like. We can finish up here."

"That's okay. They seem pretty absorbed."

"Those babies love their grandpa. It's so cute it warms my heart." She smiled wistfully and crossed the room to check on the ham baking in the oven.

My eyes stung as I cut through a tomato, and I wished it were an onion to disguise the tears. How could he be so good with the grandchildren but terrible with his adult kids?

Ivy waltzed into the kitchen, her face split into a huge grin. "Gramma, come play with us."

"I can't, honey." Her hands were in a bowl covered with the dough she kneaded. "I'm helping your mama make dinner."

Her lower lip protruded, making an adorable pouty face. "How 'bout you, Aunt Tammy?"

"Ahh, sweetheart, I'm helping too." I could have easily set my job aside and gone to play with her. That's what I wanted to do, and if it weren't for my dad, I would have.

Her face fell, and my heart did with it.

"Dinner should be ready soon," Amanda said. "Why don't you go find your pretty Christmas dress and Mommy will come help you change."

She still wore the purple princess Jasmine pajamas she had on when she woke. "Okay." Head down, she marched toward her room like she was mad.

"I can go help her get ready if you would like," I said. I'd have to walk past Dad, but he probably wouldn't even notice.

Dad came around the corner, holding Colton. His countenance seemed to darken when he saw me. "When's lunch going to be ready? I'm starved."

"Somewhere around a half hour," Amanda said.

I ducked around Dad and hurried down the hallway before he had a chance to say anything to me. The way he looked at me was painful enough. Closing my eyes for a brief moment, I said a prayer for strength. I made it here by the grace of God, and by that same grace, he would carry me through this day—hopefully without another explosion between me and Dad. I stopped at the room with the Frozen movie poster on the door and knocked three times.

"Who is it?" Ivy's voice rang through the door.

"It's Auntie Tamara." I hoped saying it enough would change the way she said my name.

"Aunt Tammy?" She opened the door, wearing a frilly dress with a red princess cut top that poofed into a black skirt at the waist. "I can't button the top." She turned around.

Kneeling next to her, I threaded the button through the hole. "You look pretty."

She smiled briefly, her cheeks tinted a light rose color, then she ran to her bed. Her room was decorated with Disney Princesses. Her twin bed had a pink comforter with Sleeping Beauty, Cinderella, and Snow White standing together in front of a castle. Her dresser had different characters from Frozen scattered over it.

"Would you like me to brush your hair?"

She scrunched her face. "Only Mommy can brush my hair, 'cause Daddy hurts my head when he does it."

"I promise to be super careful. I used to do my sister Dakota's hair when we were younger and my hair too, so I have lots of experience."

She stuck her pointer finger in her mouth. "You have a sister?"

"Yup. She's your auntie too." I grabbed the hairbrush off her dresser along with a hair tie.

She smiled as I sat on her bed, placed her onto my lap, and softly ran the brush through her hair.

"Can I meet her? I like having an aunt."

"I don't know, sweetheart. I hope so." My heart melted and broke at the same time. So far, being an aunt was wonderful, but I wasn't sure when or if she'd meet Dakota. I ran the brush through her hair several times until it smoothed and gently pulled it into a ponytail.

She jumped off my lap, ran to the mirror and inspected herself in it. "Now I look like you."

"Like me?"

"'Cause the ponytail."

"I think you look more like a princess."

"Really?" She beamed while swaying back and forth.

"You better believe it." I tapped the end of her nose.

She threw her arms around my leg. "You're the best auntie ever."

I lifted her and gave her a firm squeeze. She was quickly becoming my favorite child on the planet. Was this what having a little girl would be like? A twinge of sadness made the moment feel heavy. Would Hope grow up to be as amazing as Ivy? I bit the side of my cheek and pushed back the onslaught of images this question brought. "Do you want to go show your mom your pretty outfit?"

She nodded with vigor, and I set her on the floor with a sad smile. I wished so badly Joe was here to see this part of my family, to see there wasn't all bad here. It would also be nice for him to hold my hand and walk me down the hall to give me the strength to face my dad once more. Instead, I held Ivy's hand and silently prayed again as we walked toward the kitchen.

Dad and Nathan were in the living room discussing the trucking business when we passed by. Both held half-empty bottles of beer in their hands. Once in the kitchen, Mom and Amanda oohed and awed over how adorable Ivy was in her Christmas dress.

"You're going to be a great mom someday." Amanda eyed my engagement ring and winked.

I averted my gaze. Someday ... It felt strange how kind she was to me with barely knowing me. Part of me wanted Christmas with the festivities it entailed to disappear so I could lay myself bare in front of them. I wanted to tell them of Hope's adoption and why I'd finally tried to find them, but it wasn't the time, and strangely, no one had asked what I had been doing over these years.

The next fifteen minutes were spent putting the finishing touches on dinner, cleaning, and setting the table. It was quite the spread. Ham, mashed potatoes, green bean casserole, stuffing, rolls and three different pies for dessert.

We gathered around the table, and to my surprise, Dad insisted on saying grace before eating. It was a quick prayer of thanksgiving for his family and food, but his words touched a tender place in my heart. Had God begun to work in him too? Nathan dished Colton's food and cut it into small bites for him while the rest of us passed the platters around.

Amanda poured herself a glass of merlot and offered me some. I politely declined and dug into the mashed potatoes. Nathan stood and made him and Dad a couple of rum and cokes. Goodness, I hoped they didn't get drunk. This day could go south pretty quickly with the amount that they were drinking. So far, the alcohol hadn't affected Nathan much. He seemed his normal jovial self. And Dad seemed normal too as he intently devoured the ham and potatoes in a ravenous manner.

"I have an idea," Nathan said as he slid the cocktail in front of Dad.

Dad stopped chewing mid-bite. "What's that?"

Nathan sat in his chair again. "Next year, we should do a family trip for the holidays. Maybe rent a log cabin in Montana so Josiah wouldn't have to travel so far."

"That sounds like a wonderful idea," Mom interjected. "I'd love to see Josiah and baby Mia."

Dad chewed his food, brows furrowing. "Sounds expensive."

"If we pitched in, it wouldn't be too bad," Amanda interjected.

"Yeah, Dad," Nathan said. "We could pitch in as a family. You in, Tamara?"

"Sure. I mean it's a whole year from now, but I don't see why not."

"Great. Maybe by then, Dakota will get her crap together," Nathan said.

"Don't count on it, son." Dad snorted. "There's something wrong with the women in our family. It'll probably take her six years too."

Amanda and I exchanged a glance. A pool of anger swelled in my abdomen. *Stay in control, Tamara. Don't let this turn into a scene like yesterday.*

"This ham is pretty good, Amanda," Dad said after a moment.

"Thanks," she said and helped Colton with a bite of food.

"I mean, I prefer turkey on Christmas, but this isn't half bad."

She gave a weak smile and eyed her plate.

"I think your idea has merit, son. It would be good to see Josiah. It's been way too long. And we both know he'd be able to pitch in. He's doing good for himself in the oilfields." He paused for a minute, cleaning his teeth with his tongue. "If nothing else, my boys have done real good for themselves."

Acid churned in my guts at the subtext in Dad's words. His boys had done great, and his daughters were losers. Nothing like he hoped we would be.

"Tamara's done great for herself too." Amanda's voice had a tinge of defensiveness in it. "Have you not noticed that engagement ring on her left hand?"

Dad choked on his drink.

I slid my hands in my lap to hide the ring. What was Amanda thinking? She didn't have to defend me like that, and I sure the heck didn't want her to draw attention to my strained relationship. Too many things I wasn't ready to discuss in present company.

"You're engaged, honey?" Mom asked, a bit of hurt in her tone. "Why didn't you tell me?"

"Why are you hiding the ring?" Dad asked.

My head jerked toward him, and I looked him straight in the eye, startled by my own reaction. Those were the first words Dad had spoken directly to me the whole day.

I averted my gaze and inhaled deeply before bringing my hands above the table. "Sorry, Mom. It just hadn't come up yet. And I'm not hiding it. It's been on my hand the whole time, and the only person who's asked me about it was Amanda."

"Well, who is he?" Mom asked, her voice curious.

My throat tightened as I gathered my thoughts. How could I keep this conversation in safe territory? "His name is Joe." I swallowed the jagged shards clawing at my throat. "He's wonderful." I hoped they couldn't see the sadness I was trying to mask.

"Wonderful?" Dad repeated the word with accusation. "What does he do for a living?"

I took in another long breath. If there was going to be an explosion today, it wouldn't be from me. "He and I have been managing a small diner in Vancouver for the last eight months, and he recently purchased it."

"Businessman, huh?" Dad cut a piece of his ham.

"Yeah." I gave a weak smile though I was dying on the inside. Half the truth felt like a lie, but I couldn't tell the rest of the story.

"Well, good for you, kid. Maybe you'll make something of yourself after all," Dad said.

I nodded as tears stung my eyes. The backhanded comment had been the nicest thing he'd said to me since I'd arrived. Earning his respect seemed like the only path into his good graces, but how would he react when he learned the rest of the story?

"When's the big day, sis? Were you planning on inviting us?" Nathan threw me a cheesy grin.

"Absolutely. That was one of the reasons I came."

"Excellent." He leaned back and took a large swig of his drink. "This is perfect then. Tamara will definitely be able to pitch in on the trip with her having a well to do fiancé."

Well to do? Yeah right. I wasn't even sure I had a fiancé anymore after making this trip.

"Now we just need Gabriel," Nathan said.

Darkness descended over the room at the mention of Gabe's name. I glanced around the table at their unassuming faces. They had no idea the bomb that I carried with me, ready to blow them to shreds as I pulled the pin. I had to tell them, but I didn't know if I was strong enough.

CHAPTER 11

December 25, 12:30 p.m.

DAKOTA

For hours, I paced the room, occasionally glancing at the small package on the bed, summoning the courage to open it. I was such an idiot. Why would a simple gift cause this intense fear to rise in me? It was an inanimate object. Why had Tim bought me a gift in the first place? When did he even have time? My phone dinged, and I ignored it. Tim had already texted me several times to check if I was all right, probably terrified to knock on the door.

You know what, screw it. I snatched the gift off the bed, ripped open the package and lifted the lid off the box. A tiny pendant hung from a sterling silver bracelet.

The pendant said, "Allies forever."

I bit my bottom lip to resist the tears that threatened to come as memories played through my thoughts. Tim and I were kids, eight or nine years old. I'd been in the woods at our secret hideout escaping another one of my dad's moments of rage over something one of my brothers did. Tim showed up moments later.

He pricked his finger and had me do the same and vowed that moment to be allies forever. With that pact, we promised we would be there for each other no matter what, and we'd forever keep each other's secrets. It was a stupid thing kids did. Over the years, I'd forgotten our pact. Turns out he hadn't. He had kept his side of the vow without wavering.

A tear slid down my cheek, and I wiped it away, embarrassed by my own emotion. I'd been crying an awful lot lately. Good thing I hadn't opened this in front of Tim. I could never let him know how much it affected me. How much *he* affected me.

I sat in my bed as the tears overtook me. It was useless to resist. I didn't want to return to the cold barren wasteland of drugs and partying. I was done numbing myself from the hurt and pain. A moment of clarity illuminated my mind. If I was to ever get clean, this was the time. I had promised Tamara that I'd get the help I needed, not that my word had ever meant anything. But a fresh determination welled in me, a force of life that quickened me to believe that I could change.

I could get sober. Tamara wanted to be the change in our family. She believed we were able to be made whole even after the abuse and losses. Thoughts of her taking the beating for me those many years ago invaded my mind. Even then, she'd shown me the meaning of true love before anyone had taught her. Hopefully, one day, I'd be strong enough to let her know how much that impacted me. I owed her so much.

A tap on the door, brought me from my thoughts. I straightened and readied myself to face Tim. "Come in."

He opened the door and regarded me, concern shading his dark eyes. "I didn't mean to upset you. It's just Christmas and ... I don't know." He leaned against the doorframe and shoved his hands in his pockets.

I nodded and suppressed a fresh wave of emotion threatening to come. So annoying. Shedding tears in front of Tim would *not* happen. I'd never even cried in front of him when we were kids, and I wouldn't start now. "When did you even have time to get me this?"

"I bought it when I first got to California. I thought you may have been at my house for Christmas."

I exhaled a cynical laugh. "Well, that idea went poof in

smoke." I took the bracelet from the box and slid it on my wrist. "It's cool. I like it."

Tim crossed the room and sat on the bed next to me. A nervous feeling opened in my stomach at his nearness. He searched my face again. That same expression he wore earlier overtook him, and he lifted his hand to lightly touch the bruise above my eye. The feeling in my center increased, sending shockwaves through the rest of my body.

"I hate what he did to you," he whispered and brushed the bruise on my cheek.

I stiffened at his touch and stood. "Well, he's dead now, so he can never do it again."

From the corner of my eye, I could see the hurt flash in Tim's countenance.

"Listen, Tim, I'm grateful for what you've done for me and I know you care for me, but this"—I gestured between us, with my pointer finger and thumb. "It's not going to happen."

He nodded, lips forming a thin line. "What are you afraid of, Dakota?"

"I'm not *afraid*. I'm just saving you the trouble. In case you haven't noticed, I'm a complete mess. You're a cop, and though Ryan's dead, I still have secrets." Not to mention that I came here in a stolen car. "Do you have any idea how many illegal things I've been involved in? You could risk your job just associating with me."

Tim stood and took hold of my wrist, causing an unfamiliar heat to pulse through me. "I'm not worried about my job, Dakota. I'm concerned for you. I'm not asking for anything from you, but I do want to be your friend again. I'm sorry if you felt I was coming on to you. It wasn't my intention."

My gaze caught his. "Friends?"

"Allies." He smiled sadly. "Forever."

Emotion caught in my throat. "I could use an ally right now."

"You got one."

I stayed silent for a minute, considering his words. "I want to get sober, Tim. Like really sober. No drugs. No vodka. Honest to goodness sober."

"That's great, Dakota. How can I help?"

I shook my head. "I'm not sure."

He took a few moments to respond as if he was scared to make a sudden move or say the wrong thing. "Sage would be a good person to talk to, she's a recovering addict. You wouldn't be able to tell by looking at her now, but she has fifteen years under her belt and has built a pretty great life for herself."

Sage didn't seem like the kind of person I could see myself opening up to. "Not to change the subject, but how did I get to this house?"

"You don't remember? I came and got you."

"Where's my car?" Or should I say Tamara's car?

"It's in Weed. Sage came with me, but I didn't know which car was yours."

"We have to go get it." I could *not* lose Tamara's car.

"Like, right now?" Tim's forehead creased with confusion.

"Yes. Please."

"Okay ... Whose car is it?"

"It's Tamara's. She loaned it to me." The lie slipped from my mouth way too easily. "We need to get it before it gets impounded."

"She loaned you her car?"

"Yes, Tim." I grabbed my coat and put it on. "Can we go?"

"Okay, yeah." He turned around.

I followed him down the hallway, wondering if he believed me.

CHAPTER 12

December 25, 5:20 p.m.

JOE

I grasped my mom's picture in my right hand, a bottle of beer in the other as tears spilled off my cheeks. Why did the people I love get taken from me? Why couldn't I control this demon that was constantly waiting in ambush, ready to pounce as soon as I had a weak moment? Why did life have to be so damn harsh? I tried so hard to be a good person, to truly care about the people in my life, and this is where things ended up—my dream burned to the ground—abandoned by the one person I loved the most.

I took the last swig from the bottle and stood, stumbling across the dim living room into the kitchen. I threw the empty bottle into the recycling bin with a sardonic smirk and set my mom's picture on the counter. Shame stung my insides as her hazel gaze stared at me. She would be so disappointed in me right now.

"I'm sorry, Mom, but it hurts so bad." In my mind's eye, I transported back to that terrible moment when my whole world split apart. I'd only been seventeen years old, sitting in that cold sterile room, holding my mom's icy hand in mine as I begged God to heal her. An eerie sensation had crept into the room, and the beeping of the heart monitor stopped. An alarm had gone off, and

I'd screamed for help as doctors and nurses poured in, yelling orders and starting chest compressions.

"Get him out of here!" the doctor had commanded.

A nurse pushed me toward the door, but I'd resisted. "No, Mom, No!" I'd cried. "Please don't leave me."

It took three of them to force me out of the room. I had felt powerless as I wrestled against them and wailed for them to save her. An hour later, the doctor found me in the waiting room, his expression weary, but I already knew she was gone.

Sorrow cut through me as I lingered on the memory, and I ran my fingers over the picture on the counter. She had been more than a mother to me. She'd played the parts of both parents so many times, but truly, she had been my best friend and greatest advocate in my life. She'd always believed in me despite my bad choices that teenagers tended to make. Even now, the loss of her shook me to the core. I reached for a bottle of port and lifted a wine opener, focusing on my mom's picture.

"All I wanted was to be a man you could be proud of. Why does it have to be so hard?" I pressed the corkscrew into the top and twisted it in. Tamara and my broken dreams flitted through my thoughts. "No, that's not true. All I'd wanted was a family to share the love that you placed in me."

There's still hope, son.

Chills racked my body, cutting through the buzz. Were those words from my mom or God? It sounded like both. I lifted the bottle in my hands. Hoping hurt too much sometimes, but medicating wasn't helping either. It only made it hurt more.

"I don't want to do this!" I yelled as I slammed the bottle in the sink. Red liquid sprayed over the counter as the bottle burst. It looked like blood. "I can't keep doing this!"

For a long moment, I gazed at the shattered red glass in the sink. What was I doing? This wasn't me. I was stronger than this. I'd already defeated this demon years ago.

I cleaned the mess and found my phone. Nick would probably kill me for calling him half-drunk on Christmas night, but I didn't have another choice. I needed help and accountability, and Nick was the best person to whip me into shape. I scrolled through my contacts and found his name.

The last time I'd talked to him was at the meeting where he'd presented me with my three-year sobriety chip. Since then, I'd seen him in passing at meetings only. I sighed, gathering courage. Calling him meant admitting I was a failure.

I pressed send before I could think of a reason not to. I'd promised Caleb I would do this, but I knew I needed it.

He answered after the fourth ring.

"Hey, Nick, it's me, Joe."

"Phillips?"

"Yeah, man," I said.

He let out a low whistle. "Boy howdy. It's been a while, and you're calling on Christmas, so this can't be good."

Quite the pessimist. Some things never changed. "I could be wanting to wish you a Merry Christmas."

"Come on now, Philips. We both know you're in trouble, so why don't you cut to the chase."

"It's been rough," I admitted, shame searing my core. "I've fallen off the wagon a few times this year, and I realized I'm going to need help."

"Now we're getting somewhere." His gruff voice had a ring of delight in it.

I inhaled deeply and continued my confession. "The time earlier this year was only a few drinks, but this time—"

"Did I not teach you anything? There's no such thing as just a few drinks, you know that."

Head pounding, I rolled my eyes, waiting for the textbook words I knew he would say.

"One is too many, and a thousand is never enough."

"I know, you're absolutely right." I did know better, but it hadn't stopped me. "That's why I'm asking for help."

He heaved out a long exhale. "All right, I'll help you, but we do it my way."

I cringed, my head throbbing harder. "Agreed."

"That means you get your butt to three meetings a day no matter what is going on. I'm busy tomorrow, but I can meet you on the twenty-seventh when we start going through the steps again. You're starting at ground zero, and it's time to rebuild."

Ground zero ... that was exactly what my life felt like, and I didn't know if I had what it took to start over.

CHAPTER 13

December 26, 6:28 p.m.

TAMARA

I stood in the middle of the motel room, staring at the jar of ashes. It was time. This was why I'd come here. I thought of the vision I'd had after Dakota had told me of Gabriel's passing. Jesus had taken the ashes from me and sprinkled them over the plot where the trailer had burned. Then a beautiful garden sprouted forth beneath our feet.

Could it be that these ashes I held were the key to our family's healing? Once the secrets were revealed and the tears were shed, could God use this tragedy to bring us together? I whispered a prayer for strength and set the jar at the bottom of my bag. No wonder Dakota had kept this secret for so long. Some things were easier to deal with locked deep within, where they could hurt only me.

I put one strap over my shoulder, grabbed my phone, and left my motel room, ambling toward my parents' house. I wasn't sure of Dad's work schedule, but I had waited until evening in hopes they'd both be home. Mom had told me she worked at Duffy's, a local seafood restaurant, and most days she was off by six. It was six-thirty now. Surely that would be enough time to do her end of shift duties and drive home.

I reached for my phone and scrolled to the number Mom had

given me at Christmas lunch. It went to voicemail after the fourth ring. That probably meant she was still at work. I slowed my walk and circled the block to give her more time, inhaling the smell of saltwater mingled with seafood cooking at the surrounding restaurants. It made me think of Joe and the date he'd taken me on a little over a month ago. I thought by now he would have called me at least to give me an update on the diner situation, but I hadn't heard a word. I missed him terribly. Especially yesterday when hanging with my niece and nephew. He would have loved them as much as I had.

How would things have been different if I had found the rest of my family before Dakota? Would Joe be here with me now, enjoying the good part of my family? Of course, he would have hated the way my dad treated me, but he would have hit it off with Nathan for sure, and my mom too. I peered at my phone again and scrolled to Joe's name. Would he be less angry with me by now? Was there a way to make him understand why I had to come here? If I begged him hard enough, would he forgive me? My phone shrilled, and my heart jumped. An unknown number appeared on the screen.

"Hello."

"Hey, Tamara." Charlie's voice came through the line. "I wanted to check in with you about getting together. You still in Aberdeen?"

"Yup. I'm here," I said, tightening my jacket as the cold wind blew around me.

"Awesome. I'll be passing through there tomorrow evening around seven. Would a late dinner work for you?"

"That would be great. I'm looking forward to seeing you and catching up." Spending the evening with someone that I had no bad history with sounded wonderful.

"Me too. You said you were at the Travelodge, right?"

"Yes. Room 206."

"Great. See you tomorrow night."

I hit end and checked the time. 6:40 p.m. Surely by the time I reached their house, Mom would be there.

I trekked forward, feet heavy with the secret about to be shared. Three minutes later, I stood in front of the house, pondering whether I should go in or not. Dad's truck was parked on the road near the sidewalk, but Mom's old Honda was nowhere in sight. Dropping the heavy news on my dad alone didn't seem like a wise idea, but I could try to keep it casual before Mom got home. I tapped on the door.

A few moments later, Dad opened the door, his brow furrowed. "Tamara?"

My pulse sped, and I shifted my weight from foot to foot. "Can we talk?"

"Why not?" He motioned for me to come in, walked toward the kitchen cabinet and reached for a bottle of scotch. He grabbed two glasses and poured some in both before handing me one. I took it without arguing. A little something to help steel my nerves.

He shot his and poured another. "What's on your mind, kid?"

I smiled at the endearment and took a sip of the scotch and coughed a little. "Where's Mom?"

"Working." He took the bottle with him into the living room.

I followed. "I thought she was off at six."

"She's pulling a double. Covering for one of those worthless college kids." He sat in his recliner and placed the bottle on the coffee table.

Taking a long steadying breath, I settled onto the couch. Was this conversation meant for the two of us alone? I took another sip of my drink and set it on the end table. I glanced over at my dad, who unlaced his work boots like he had when I was a kid after a long day's work.

Tears welled in my eyes. I wished there was some way to bridge the gap the last six years had made between us. I wished I could somehow fix things. Though Dad had erected a wall to keep me out, a part of me knew it was because I had hurt him. Before I'd taken the fall for Dakota and left home, Dad had an affection for me that seemed deeper than with the rest of the kids.

There were only a few times throughout my childhood that he'd actually abused me. Most of his anger had fallen on the boys, but in some ways it was worse to see my siblings being beat than being hit myself. Each time I had witnessed it, a part of me would break. It was a terrible feeling to watch someone I loved be abused and being completely powerless to stop it.

From a young age, I had learned to stay quiet and do what I was told, which gave me a certain amount of favor in his sight. The night I lied to him about bringing drugs into his house had completely changed his image of me.

"So how have you been all these years?" My words felt stupid as they left my mouth. How was I supposed to reconnect with him after the lies and years of distance? How could I let him know that I loved him despite the heartache we caused each other? There had to be a way to break through his defenses and start over.

He shrugged. "Life is good. Business is good. I guess I can't complain." He took another swallow and filled both his and my half-full cup with more. He lifted his glass to me as if to prompt me. I clutched my drink and clinked it against his. We both sipped together in awkward silence. I shouldn't have been breaking my new rule of not drinking with family, but the exchange was comforting. At least he wasn't yelling at me or telling me to leave.

Dad quietly relaxed in his chair. I bit the side of my cheek as sadness overwhelmed me. Wasn't he the least bit interested in my life or where I'd been for the last six years? Apparently, once again, I would be leading this conversation.

"You know what I don't understand? I come here after six years and no one even asks why," I said, my pulse increasing.

He pursed his lips. "I figured you finally came to your senses."

"Right. I guess that's part of it, but aren't you the least bit curious to know why I stayed away so long?"

The lines on his forehead deepened, and his eyebrows lifted slightly. "Now that you mention it. Sure."

I shot the rest of my scotch and grimaced as it burned my throat. "I was running from Ryan Cooke. I would have come home years ago if it weren't for him. Once I thought he was in jail, it had been so long, and honestly, I didn't want to face your disappointment. I knew what you must have thought of me, and I didn't have the strength to face you."

My gaze met his. His eyes seemed softer than they had a few moments ago. "Earlier this year, things changed." I paused and eyed the empty glass, feeling a bit woozy. Did I want to go here? To tell this man who had hurt me so deeply, the gritty details of my life? It felt like the only way. The only possible road to healing. The full and ugly truth. "I was a victim of date rape and got pregnant as a result."

"You have a child?" His voice pitched heightened.

I shook my head. "She was adopted."

I peeked at him. A sad tenderness softened his face as if he saw me as his little girl again. A faint hope flitted through me. "Along the way, I found Jesus and met Joe. We got engaged when I was pregnant. He would have been a father to my baby if I'd chosen to keep her. Giving her up made me see how much I'd been hurting you guys. I knew then I needed to find you and Mom."

Were those tears welling in his eyes? "It did hurt, Tamara. More than you know."

"I'm sorry, Dad. I really am." For the first time in a long time, I felt a spark of connection between us. A part of me knew I had broken his heart long ago, but in this moment, it was apparent how deeply I'd hurt him.

He nodded. "Thank you for apologizing, kid. It means a lot."

Were we finally taking a step forward? "You are welcome, Dad. We both hurt each other, and I'm ready and willing to forgive if you are."

He glared at me. "What exactly do you think you need to forgive me for?"

His words slammed against my chest, awakening a torrent of anger. "For the abuse. I left that night because you beat me senseless."

"Oh, come on, now. You know as well as I do, I never beat you or any of my children. I disciplined you when it was necessary, but that's it."

"Seriously?" I blinked rapidly in confusion. How could he be in complete denial? "You beat the crap out of me while cursing and berating my character. That is not discipline. That's abuse."

"Listen, little girl. You don't get to come to my house and spew your lies. Was that whole rape story a lie too? A ploy to manipulate your old man? What a bunch of bull."

I threw my hands in the air, exasperated. "Dad, I just want you to acknowledge that you hurt us."

His face creased in disgust. "Are you kidding me? I gave you kids the best life I could. You're so ungrateful. I'd hoped you changed, but you're exactly the same. Why don't you disappear for another six years and come home when you can find some respect?"

"Is that what you want, Dad? Why can't you admit you abused us?"

"I never abused you!" Dad stood and threw his glass against the wall, shattering it to pieces. "Get the hell out of my house!" he yelled, following with a string of curse words.

I bolted to the door and ran to the motel room, weighed down by the ashes in my backpack. I was sure I'd made things worse than ever. One day soon I hoped I'd be strong enough to have a healing conversation with him, but with his denial and accusations, restoring our family felt more impossible than ever.

CHAPTER 14

December 27, 6:30 a.m.

JOE

I walked through the Highway Ninety-Nine Diner parking lot, taking in the remnants of my restaurant, the remnants of my dream, the remnants of my life. Charcoal debris littered the property, and ashes swirled in the wind. Why had I come here? Perhaps to torture myself, to remind myself why I couldn't call Tamara, to remind myself why I couldn't let her back in no matter how much I missed her.

I shivered and lifted my latte to my mouth and took a drink, wishing I could have added a shot of whiskey to numb the sorrow building within me. I climbed into my Jeep and started the engine, ready to leave this desolate place. Coming here was a mistake. I knew I needed to deal with it, but I wasn't quite ready. The wound was too fresh.

My first AA meeting of the day would start soon, and I needed to make a few phone calls before I arrived there. Today's schedule was going to be full, with three meetings plus lunch with Nick and the other stuff I'd put off for days. Yesterday I'd taken a regroup day. I made it to only two meetings, of which I was sure Nick would jump my case for, and the rest of the day I binged on Psych, letting humor and mystery numb my brain instead of alcohol. My head was cloudy from the depression, but my mood had shifted enough to give me the strength to press forward.

I took a final look at the heap of ashes, put the car in gear, and left the diner parking lot. How would I actually recover from this? How long would I be out of work? I had sunk most of my savings into purchasing the diner to secure Tamara's and my future. Now that future appeared as dismal as the Great Depression.

God grant me the serenity to accept the things I cannot change.

I needed to focus on the tasks in front of me. One foot in front of the next. I peeked at the list I'd made for myself earlier this morning. The first item on the agenda was to get ahold of the employees and let them know they'd not be getting paid anytime soon, not until the insurance settlement came through. Tamara said she'd do it, but I didn't trust her to keep her word. I pinched the bridge of my nose, fending off the tension the thought brought me.

After that, I needed to call the insurance company and start the claim. Then I'd get ahold of the clean-up crew to have them start on the debris removal. I'd talked to them yesterday, but they said they needed a claim number before they started to make sure they'd get paid.

I turned on Burnside and took a long sip before grabbing my phone. I called Trudy first. She obviously wasn't an employee, but she'd been leaving me messages for days, and had sounded worried sick. Also, she, of everyone, would be the hardest to face. After four rings, it went to voicemail and relief worked through me. Perhaps she was in physical therapy. I left a message, letting her know that I was all right and to call me as soon as she could. I clicked end and scrolled through the list. Claire would be next because except for Tamara, of the people at work, I was closest to her, and she had called the most over the last few days.

"Joe?" Claire's voice came through my Bluetooth.

"Hey, Claire. I'm sorry it's taken so long to get in contact with you."

"It's okay. You sound awful."

I felt awful. "I need to let you know that I won't be able to pay you or anybody until the insurance settlement comes through and knowing insurance companies it could take a while."

"I know, Joe," she said, sounding confused. "Tamara told me a few days ago, and I've already let the other employees know what's going on. Didn't Tamara tell you?"

My stomach clenched, a mixture of guilt and sorrow. "I haven't spoken to her."

She said nothing for a few beats, and the feeling in my gut intensified. "I see."

Those two words felt heavy as if she knew information I wasn't ready to hear. "It's complicated right now."

"I know. It's just … I know how much you two love each other, and you're both going through so much."

I worried my lip as longing budded and with it the familiar ache that her absence brought. A huge part of me still wanted her, but … things could never be the way they had been. The relationship we'd built over the last year had been unsafe and unsustainable. I needed more than she could give.

"It's hard to be the bigger person, but Tamara needs you, Joe. Things with her family haven't gone well. The day she arrived, her dad seriously freaked out on her and basically called her poison."

Thoughts of Tamara's face twisted in anguish as her father spoke those harsh words tore me in two, and guilt dug deeper into my soul. Should I be there with her? No, I couldn't keep doing that to myself. I couldn't keep sacrificing myself for her. That's what had led me to drink in the first place.

"What do you want me to say, Claire? I'm not her savior. This is the path she's chosen, and I'm not going to chase her into crazy land anymore."

"That's harsh, Joe."

Anger replaced the guilt in a half second. "Do you know why you haven't been able to reach me for the last few days? It's because I've been on a bender, drinking myself into oblivion. I love Tamara, but sometimes love isn't enough. She's not good for me. I have to do what's right for me for a change."

"I'm sorry. I didn't mean anything by it."

I took in a deep breath to reign in my frustration. Last time I'd seen Claire I'd asked her about her sobriety, but she should have been asking about mine. "It's fine. I know you care, and I appreciate that. I gotta go though. I have a lot of ground to cover today."

"Take care of yourself. And don't concern yourself with the employees, I've already talked to them. They understand. Some of them were relieved. People didn't feel safe after Trudy was shot."

People were relieved? After all the work I'd put in to save the place and people didn't even want to work there? My heart plummeted into my guts. I pressed on the gas pedal as I hit the red icon. My throat ached with that familiar thirst. The next AA meeting couldn't come fast enough.

CHAPTER 15

December 27, 5:45 p.m.

DAKOTA

Tonight's dinner was crazy good, like last night's had been and every other meal I'd had since I'd been there. Ribeye steak topped with caramelized vegetables sautéed in Dijon butter. On top of normal mashed potatoes, Sage had prepared creamed spinach and sweet potato gnocchi. And I had thought staying at Tim's house had been bad for the waistline. This was a whole other level.

Tim smiled at me as I sat at the table, but Sage regarded me with a strange expression. She seemed quiet this evening as she prepared the meal, like something was eating at her. Over the last day and a half, I'd done my best not to be alone with her and kept the conversation between us light. I wasn't ready to reveal my deep dark secrets to this complete stranger. Tim had said she was a recovering addict, but that had been eons ago, and her life seemed pretty perfect on her little slice of heaven she'd been obliged to share with me. That had to be it. She didn't know me from Eve, and though I'd been doing my best not to be in the way, she must have been sick of having me around. Or maybe she thought I was bad news for her beloved nephew.

I shoved another bit of potatoes in my mouth, but this time, they didn't taste quite as good. Tonight would be my last night here. It had been nice having a place to rest for a few days, but it was time to move on and take care of things on my own.

"So, Dakota, what's your plan?" Sage asked, cutting into her ribeye.

"My plan for what exactly?" Had the lady been reading my thoughts?

"Tim only has until New Years before he has to return to work. Are you heading north with him?"

I took a bite of steak, chewing it slowly, giving myself time to answer. The way the flavors mingled in my mouth was divine.

"You know you're welcome to stay with me for a while," Tim said around a bite, shielding his mouth with his hand. "The problem you were having in Quilcene has been taken care of."

I shook my head and swallowed. "I can't do that. It wouldn't work." Ryan may have been dead, but the people I'd associated with in that town were druggies. I didn't stand a chance of staying clean if I went home with him.

Tim nodded, with understanding in his gaze.

"I'll figure it out."

Sage set her fork on the table and leaned forward. "That's the thing, Dakota. You can't just figure things out. I know we don't know each other, and you might tell me to piss off. But when Tim brought you to my house, completely inebriated, face injured like it had been mauled by a mountain lion, you became my business."

Tim and I exchanged a glance. His expression held an apology.

"You gotta have a plan, Dakota. Tim told me you were trying to get sober. Is that true?"

"I am getting sober," I said firmly. I was done with drugs and the party scene. If I didn't stop now, I'd find myself in a worse situation and most likely die within the year.

"If that's true, you need a plan. You need a job. You need stability. You can't keep sleeping in your car and expect to stay sober."

I slammed my fork down. "What do you want from me, lady? I'm two days in!"

"It's okay, Dakota." Tim placed his hand on top of mine. "She's trying to help."

I withdrew my hand and crossed my arms in front of me. "Yeah, well, I'm not loving her energy."

"I'm sorry, Dakota." Sage's voice softened. "You have a very long road ahead of you, and I want you to succeed. The only way that is going to happen is with stability and accountability."

"Why do you care? You don't even know me."

Sage lifted her knife toward Tim. "This guy right here. He's my favorite nephew, and he obviously cares for you."

A half-smile crept up one side of Tim's face, and my abdomen tightened. It always came back to him. "I don't need your help, okay. I'm planning on leaving tomorrow. I can tell I've outstayed my welcome."

"What? No. Please don't leave," Tim said.

"It's not your house, Tim," I said. "You don't get to decide."

"Again, Dakota, I think you're misunderstanding me." Sage gave a curt smile. "I'm only saying what I am because I want to help. You can stay here until Tim leaves, but after that, I think it would be good for you to stay at a sobriety house in Redding. They can help you get on your feet while you get a job and start working a program."

"A program? Like rehab?"

"Not exactly." She took a sip of her sparkling water. "Those never worked well for me. I mean, they dried me out and gave my body time to heal so I could go for the next round, but nothing like Narcotics Anonymous has done for me."

Narcotics? That was a surprise. When Tim had told me she was a recovering addict, I figured it was alcohol or another legal substance. Maybe it was prescription drugs? "What's your poison?"

She leveled her gaze on me. "Oh, I've done it all, honey. I dropped my first hit of acid when I was thirteen years old."

That was hard to imagine. Then again, thirteen had been around the time I'd done my first line in the girl's locker room with an older girl named Marcy who used to work for Ryan.

"That was only the beginning though. I dabbled a bit in crystal meth, cocaine, pills of all kinds, but my favorite was heroin." She paused for a moment, and it seemed as though she was somewhere else, thinking of a whole other life.

This lady was seriously hardcore. I had never tried heroin and I *never* used needles. It seemed dirty to me. I may have been a druggie, but I had my standards. I mostly stayed with meth because it was cheaper than coke or pills. "What made you stop?"

Her gaze met mine, and I could see the remnants of the other life behind her eyes. "I watched the love of my life die of an overdose." She blinked rapidly to fend off the tears. "I don't know what was more painful, the grief or the withdrawals. Both almost killed me."

Damn. That was almost as tragic as my story. Maybe even worse. What would I say to that kind of sorrow? Grief mixed with withdrawals. I'd heard coming off heroin was gruesome. Another reason I'd never touched the stuff. "Sounds awful."

"It was a living hell." She observed her barely touched dinner and sighed. "But that was a lifetime ago now."

Silence crept over the table as we went back to eating. My thoughts turned to the sobriety house Sage had mentioned. I couldn't imagine it. I had barely any work history and no high school diploma. What kind of job could I get anyway, fast food or maid work? I grimaced at the idea of serving greasy food to overweight people and cleaning hotel rooms after they'd been partied in.

I guess we all had to start somewhere, and if I seriously wanted to change my ways, I needed to listen to people who'd been through this before me. Sage seemed to know plenty on how to get on the right track, but it sounded like the whole experience was going to be one big crap sandwich.

CHAPTER 16

December 27, 6:00 p.m.

TAMARA

I laid on the bed, journal splayed in front of me, mind on the fight with Dad last night. How could his version of the story be so different from mine? How could Dad interact so well with the kids on Christmas and terrible with me? The family I'd witnessed on Christmas was incongruent with my reality. I wanted to confront them all over the situation, but what if Mom agreed with Nathan and Dad? That would leave me appearing delusional. Dakota would back me up if she were here, but I didn't know if I'd ever see her again. The truth of the situation wrenched my insides, stealing my breath. I picked up the journal and read the list of promises once more to garner strength.

Beauty for ashes
Dad will walk me down the aisle to Joe.
The years of my life will be restored.

The lines blurred through tears as I stared at the page. Nothing felt more impossible than those three measly lines. I wasn't even sure if I'd want my dad at my wedding. Not if he wasn't willing to admit his wrongs and seek the help he needed. Besides that, Joe still wasn't talking to me.

Earlier today, I had called him four times. Each time it went to voicemail. Each time I didn't know what to say to his machine. He never called me though, and as the day wore on, I became more certain that he wouldn't. Not today. Possibly not ever. It had been three days since we talked, and the silence felt like a punctuation mark—a period at the end of our sentence. We were over. I'd somehow destroyed the best thing that had ever happened to me. The bridge between us had burnt the moment I decided to come to Aberdeen without him.

A light knock on the door. I closed the journal, rolled out of bed, and glanced in the mirror before heading to the door. Not that it mattered. It was only Charlie. I'd made minimal effort by showering and applying mascara to brighten my eyes, but nothing more. I wore skinny jeans and one of Joe's sweatshirts I'd swiped from him months ago.

I opened the door and Charlie stood there, wearing dark jeans and a polo shirt. His auburn hair was short and spiky, and his sideburns came to ear level, accentuating his sturdy jawline. He'd grown a goatee since the last time I'd seen him, which seemed to suit him. Definitely more attractive than I remembered. He smiled, revealing his pearly-white teeth, and his arms came around me, crushing me into a bear hug. "So good to see you. It's been way too long."

I hugged him and breathed in, allowing his embrace to bring comfort, but mostly it made me miss Joe. "Way too long." I echoed. "Your generosity pretty much saved my life."

"It was nothing," he said with a smile as he stepped back

"Nothing? A thousand dollars is definitely something."

His lips curled at the edges as he shrugged. "I mean. It wasn't much for me. A single guy with no responsibilities. Besides, I'm glad it meant that much to you."

"It really did. I'm sorry it took me so long to say thank you. I wanted to call a thousand times, but nothing I thought to say seemed to do what you did justice, and then the months turned to years—"

He waved me off. "Seriously, Tamara. Don't worry about it. I had a feeling that it was bigger than me."

Smiling, I nodded. In retrospect, that was one of the moments in a trail of many I could see God reaching out to me.

"You ready for dinner?" He gestured toward the door. "Cause I'm starved."

"Yeah, sure." I grabbed my purse and followed him outside. Most of the day I hadn't eaten, except for a bag of almonds and an apple earlier that afternoon. I'd awoken queasy and stayed like that most of the day. The greasy diner food I had the night before hadn't agreed with me. I'd made a mental note not to eat there again. The night air hit my face, and I shivered as I walked behind Charlie. The sky was clear though, and a crescent moon shone brightly.

Charlie stepped up to the midnight blue Altima and opened the passenger door for me. I slid into the leather seat. I would have reached over and unlocked his door, but he'd already clicked it open with his key fob.

"Nice car," I said as he settled into the seat next to me.

"Thanks."

I slid my hand over the sleek dash. "You bought this on a bartender's salary?"

Pursing his lips, he raised an eyebrow. "Bought it for cash, baby. And correction, I'm a bar owner now." He started the car.

"You bought Midways?"

"Sure did."

"Congratulations!"

He laughed as he put the car into reverse. "The thing is a pain in my butt. The money has been good, though."

"Well, from what I remember, you practically lived at the place."

"Still do." He made a right turn out of the parking lot.

"And Shelby? Is she still in Ocean Shores?"

Charlie threw me a skeptical side glance and turned his

blinker on. "Shelby's, you know, Shelby. I think she's an Ocean Shores lifer."

"She hasn't settled down?"

"Not even a little."

Sad. I'd hoped maybe she got her life together after I'd left.

Charlie pulled into the parking lot of a nice restaurant. I regarded my outfit, self-conscious. I'd dressed for a burger joint, not for an upscale place.

"This place has great gnocchi," he said, pushing his door open.

I exited the vehicle, unsure if I'd ever had gnocchi. "Sounds great," I lied as I matched his steps to the restaurant.

"It also has the best Sunday brunch. If you stick around, you should try it." He made an okay symbol with his hand. "It's top-notch."

I nodded and smiled, though his words made me feel strange. I was unsure how long I'd be here, and though the motel was cheap, I'd been spending money I didn't have. And once Joe noticed I'd used our wedding fund, it would dig the knife in deeper.

The restaurant was bright and modern with high ceilings and crisp hardwood floors. It was a bit more casual than I thought from the first appearance, which put me at ease. The place was busy, nearly three quarters to capacity. A waitress with dark hair approached us. She had full red lips and her hair was pinned into a twisted bun with stray hairs spiking out. "Just the two of you this evening?"

"Yes," Charlie said.

She grabbed two menus and a water pitcher. "Right this way."

After seating us, she ran through the specials and gave the details of their famous wine list.

Charlie scanned the list for a minute. "Oh, they have a Lemberger. That sounds good. It's only by the bottle though. Would you help me drink it if I ordered it? I'm buying dinner, by the way."

"What? Charlie, no. If anything, I should be paying for you."

He set the menu aside and looked at me. "Nonsense. Tonight's my treat. Now, you in on that Lemberger?"

I didn't know what Lemberger was, but Charlie obviously knew how to order wine. "I could have a glass."

"Excellent."

When the waitress returned, Charlie ordered the wine and appetizers while I continued to scan the menu. As I glanced over the prices, I was thankful he had offered to pay. I couldn't afford to eat here, or anywhere else, for that matter.

"What have you been doing since I last saw you? What brings you back to these parts?" Charlie asked.

Goodness. I didn't even know how to answer those questions. "I never told you much of my story, did I?"

He shook his head. "You were always ..." He put his finger on his chin and glanced toward the ceiling. "I don't know. Mysterious."

I laughed. That was a nice way to put it.

His eyebrows furrowed. "But I got a good vibe from you. Like you cared for the people around you."

"Thanks, Charlie. What do you say we talk about you for a while? It's been a hard few weeks, and I'd rather not rehash it at the moment."

He tilted his head to the side. "Are you sure? People tell me I'm a great listener."

I leaned in, smiling. "I know you are. I'm sure you have to listen to people's crazy stories every day at your job."

"Girl, you don't even know. If I were a writer, I'd have a whole volume of material."

I giggled. "Maybe I shouldn't tell you anything then. It may wind up in some smutty novel."

"First of all, I'm not a writer. Second, if I were, I would never cast you in smut."

I laughed again, the weight of the last few days dropping off my shoulders. The waitress interrupted us with the bottle of

Lemberger and hot bread with butter. She poured a little for Charlie to taste and he seemed pleased. After a nod from Charlie, she filled both our glasses. "You ready to order?"

"I think so." He glanced at me and I smiled.

"Would you judge me if I ordered the burger?" The other items on the menu made me nauseous.

He chuckled and raised his glass of wine. "Nope. A burger sounds mighty fine to me. We'll both take the classic burger. I'd like the works on mine."

"Me too."

The waitress smiled and gathered our menus before leaving.

I took a sip of wine. It had a rich deep flavor that made it go down easy. "Come on, Charlie, I want to know what's been happening with you. Besides buying Midways, is there anything new in your life? Are you seeing anyone?"

Charlie took a sip of his wine, eyes dancing with humor. "I'm pretty sure I'll die single."

Sad. That seemed like such a waste. "Seriously? There hasn't been anyone since I left town?"

"I've dated here and there, but no one that stuck. No one that I could see me spending the rest of my life with."

I smiled sadly, swirling the wine in the glass.

"Looks like things have been better for you."

My eyebrows pinched together. "What do you mean?"

He pointed at my engagement ring, and my face instantly heated.

"Somebody must love you an awful lot. That's a nice ring."

I set my glass on the table and hid my hands in my lap, sorrow clawing at my throat. Joe had loved me more than I would ever deserve.

Charlie cocked his head to the side. "What's wrong?"

Tears threatened to come, but I swallowed them back. "I'm wearing the ring, but I'm not sure where we stand right now. We had a big fight right before I headed this way." I grew quiet for a moment, thinking over the things that had gone wrong. "We never fight, Charlie."

Charlie reached across the table, placing a hand over mine. "I'm sure you guys will be okay. Just give it time."

I looked at him through glossy eyes. "I hope you're right." With the fighting and the silence, I wasn't sure.

The waitress came with our food, only interrupting us for a quick moment.

"So how long have you two known each other?" Charlie asked and popped a fry in his mouth.

I swallowed a bite of the burger. It was delicious. The patty had a savory garlic and flame broiled taste. "We met the day I left Ocean Shores. My car broke down in Vancouver, Washington, and he came to my rescue. I ended up settling in there and getting a job with him at the diner he worked at. Over the next year, we became best friends, but it bloomed into more."

"I love that. See, that right there is exactly what I want." He wiped his hand on his napkin and took a sip of his wine. "It seems like the women I've dated want this over-the-top romance, but how can it be that genuine if you don't know each other first?"

I set my burger on the plate and wiped my lips with a napkin. "Right? I've had it both ways now. Danny was this intense romantic who wrote me songs and a bunch of that other stuff, but what I have with Joe is way deeper than any of that. I hope that you find that kind of love, Charlie. You deserve it." I paused, thinking of Joe and everything he meant to me.

Charlie refilled his wine glass and added a smidge to mine. "I'll drink to that."

My phone rattled in my purse, and my heart beat hard. Could it be Joe? I reached into the side pouch and clutched it. Nathan's number lit the screen. "I need to answer this," I said to Charlie before hitting the green icon.

"What in the hell, Tamara?" Nathan's angry words came through the line.

Confusion spun through my brain. "I don't understand. What's going on?"

"Oh, don't play innocent with me. You know exactly what's going on!" His voice grew louder.

"I promise you, I don't."

"Did you come here to make trouble? You have no right!"

I took a gulp of wine to settle my nerves. "I'm sorry, but I don't understand."

"Don't act stupid. I'm talking about you starting crap with Dad. He said you came over to the house last night spewing lies and accusations."

My stomach churned, collapsing in on itself. "That's not true."

"Whatever. We don't need your lies here, Tamara. Our lives were perfectly fine without you in them."

My pulse raced. I didn't understand. I didn't want to hurt my relationship with Nathan. I loved being with him and his family on Christmas. "I'm sorry, Nathan. This is a misunderstanding."

"It doesn't seem like that to me. You're not welcome in my house until you make things right with Dad." With that, the line went dead.

For a moment, I stayed completely still, mind reeling, not having a clue what to say.

"You all right?" Charlie asked, concern in his voice.

I stood and set my napkin on the table. "I need a few minutes." I ran to the bathroom, my guts twisting and turning like I might hurl. This didn't make sense. Dad had turned Nathan against me? I splashed water on my face and stared at myself in the mirror. What was I doing here? Why had I come? That old familiar part of me wanted to run—to leave this place without a second thought, like I'd been doing for the last six years.

Be strong and courageous for I am with you.

When I'd first heard those words, I never imagined I'd be facing this. It felt like all the doors of my life were slamming shut.

First with Dad last night, Joe ignoring my phone calls and Nathan kicking me out of his life unless I made nice with Dad.

Did he expect me to act like I'd fabricated the abuse in my head? Did he want me to act like nothing had happened? I couldn't live in those sorts of lies. I couldn't construct that sort of make-believe world like he had. Was it wrong that I wanted some sort of acknowledgment of the wrong Dad had done to me? I blotted my tears and adjusted my hair before heading to the table.

The lines of Charlie's face held apprehension when I returned. "I don't want to pry, but is there anything I can do?"

Taking a deep breath, I decided to tell Charlie the story of the circumstances leading to this moment. I started with my family history, then of me running away and staying away this long. I ended with sharing about Gabriel and how Dakota saddled me with the responsibility of telling my family he was gone. By the time I finished talking, the bottle of wine was empty and a stack of crumpled up napkins that I'd use to wipe away the tears sat next to my plate.

"I'm really sorry, Tamara. This is a lot for you to walk through alone. No wonder you've been on my heart lately."

I nodded, fighting back another onslaught of emotion. Charlie had been such a good friend to me over the years, even when I wasn't present in his life. "Thank you, Charlie. I really appreciate you."

"You're welcome." He lifted his glass and drank the last of his wine. "So what do you think the next step is?"

"I don't really know. It doesn't feel right to head back to Vancouver yet, but it seems like every door here has shut in my face."

Charlie's expression turned thoughtful.

"What?"

"I don't know... I had a thought."

"Yeah?"

"Why don't you come stay with me for a bit while you sort through things?"

I flushed, unsure. Charlie and I had only ever been friends, but at one point, he did have feelings for me. What would Joe think of me staying with him? "In your apartment? That place is tiny."

Charlie grinned. "My old place was tiny, but I've upgraded since you left. The house I have now is much bigger, with a guest bedroom and all. And it's right on the beach. Just think about it."

"I don't know. I really need to find a job and start making money again." Dipping into Joe's and my wedding fund killed me every time I had to do it. We were only able to save a little over a couple thousand, which already wasn't enough for a nice wedding. I'd have to find a way to repay what I took if there was any hope for Joe and me to still be married.

"You could work at Midways. I could use the extra help through New Year's."

Tempting offer. Leaving this town for a few weeks sounded like a good idea at this point. I could cancel the daily hotel charges and maybe even start repaying the fund. Also, staying that close to the ocean sounded even better. I imagined standing on the beach, waves crashing against the shore, feeling the ocean spray against my face. It didn't matter that it was the middle of winter, I'd take my shoes off just to squish the sand between my toes.

"Why don't you pray about it," Charlie said, his grin growing wider.

I laughed. How many times had he told me that years ago, when I'd been wrestling through my demons? Inwardly, I said a quick prayer. A feeling of peace settled over me along with a few inviting thoughts. Getting out of Aberdeen and being with a good friend seemed to be what I needed for now. I didn't know if it was God leading me or not, but it did feel right. "Okay, I'm in," I said and hoped I'd chosen the right path.

CHAPTER 17

December 28, 12:30 p.m.

DAKOTA

Most of last night I tossed and turned, thinking of Sage's story and her offer to help. What would life possibly be like for me, clean and sober? Living at a sobriety house, getting a crappy job, learning to live a structured life. Would I be strong enough to make those changes?

Around three in the morning, I decided to make a run for it. I packed my belongings and tiptoed to the car. When I went to start it, the engine made a strange whirring sound but didn't turn over.

I tried again. Same noise.

Was the battery dead? I cussed and glanced at the darkened driveway, contemplating hitchhiking out of here. But then where would I be? Homeless without a car to shield me from the elements. I pounded the steering wheel and cursed again before going inside.

I crept down the hall to the guest bathroom and found a bottle of sleeping pills behind the mirror. I shook three into my hand and swallowed the pills before heading to bed, hoping they were the fast-acting kind.

For the next forty-five minutes, thoughts swirled around my head, like an army of pissed off bees, each one stinging and leaving a nasty welt. Eventually, I drifted off, only for those thoughts to turn into nightmares. My dad looming over me the night he found the drugs under my pillow, Tamara's cries as she took the beating for me. Waking the next morning finding her gone, knowing it was my fault.

I woke hours later, around noon, with a splitting headache, relieved to escape the nightmare. I stumbled into the bathroom to find the Tylenol. My skin itched for something stronger, but I ignored it and gulped down the medicine.

Staring at my reflection for a few beats, I took in the lightened bruise around my eye. It had faded from purple to an ugly light green. Within a few days, I'd be able to hide it with a bit of concealer. The gash above my nose would take longer to heal, but my top lip was almost to its normal size.

I blew a stray hair from my face. Could I actually do this sobriety thing? Thoughts of Tamara invaded my mind and the way she had so easily forgiven me, the way she hadn't judged me for my plethora of mistakes. After everything, she seemed to think I was still worth the beating she took for me. If nothing else, I had to try for her. I needed to fight to become who she thought I could be.

After going to the bathroom and washing my hands, I ran them through my hair a few times and headed to the kitchen. In the hallway, I heard my name in conversation and paused.

"This might be a tad much," Tim said. "Dakota's somewhat like a wild stallion. You gotta make slow movements to earn her trust, otherwise, she'll bolt."

"Listen, Tim, you have to understand, she has a hard road ahead of her, and she needs as much help as she can get," Sage said.

"I hear you, but you pushed too hard at dinner last night. We won't be able to help her if she disappears."

I braced myself and stepped forward. What was Sage trying to do now? Why didn't I hitchhike out of here last night?

"Good morning," Tim said as he spotted me, face wary. Both of them sat at the oak table, drinking coffee. Sage had a laptop, a big blue book, and a notepad in front of her.

"Morning." My tone sounded flat. I went to the cupboard and grabbed a mug. "Doing homework this morning, Sage?" I poured myself some coffee and watched the steam as it rose from the cup. It smelled amazing. Hopefully, this would help the headache more than the Tylenol.

Sage sighed. "It kind of feels like that."

As I turned around, Tim was glaring at his aunt. I took a seat across the table from Tim. "Just so you know, I heard you guys talking about me before I came in."

"What?" Tim asked, averting his gaze.

I rolled my eyes and took in a dramatic breath. "I don't know, something about me being a wild stallion and Sage being a bit too much." I shot him a smirk, scooped the hair away from my face and took a sip of the world's best coffee.

Tim's olive toned skin turned red. "Dakota—"

I raised my hand to quiet him. "It's cool. The truth is the truth, right? I am a wild stallion, and Sage is definitely too much." I took another sip. "Not that I love being talked about."

Sage laughed out loud. "You're something else, girl."

I shrugged my shoulders. "Just keeping it real."

"It's good. I like it," Sage said. "You have fire left in you. That will help you through the next few months."

Fire? She was nuts. I was as burnt out as they get. "That may be a stretch. I just don't like BS."

"Neither do I, so I'll get to the point," Sage said.

"Sage." Tim shot her another look. "Why don't you let her finish her coffee first."

"Because I have stuff to do. Besides, it's already afternoon and some of this information is time-sensitive."

"Fine." He raised his hands in frustration.

What had Sage done that had Tim so on edge?

"Remember our conversation last night? About you staying at a sobriety house in Redding?"

"How could I forget?" I'd lain awake half the night in turmoil over it.

She chuckled at my sarcasm. "Well, I have a few connections around town, so I called to see if I could get you in."

Wow. And she thought *I* was something else. She needed to take a good look in the mirror.

"The houses are pretty full right now, but I put your name on the waiting list."

"So that means when Tim leaves, I'm homeless?"

"Not exactly. There was one place that had a room available."

I frowned. "I thought you said—"

"It's not a sobriety house. It's a safe house for abused women."

"Excuse me? Last I checked I was an addict, not some battered woman."

"You look pretty battered to me."

I gaped at her, incredulous. "You can't be serious."

"Actually, I am. I'm good friends with Cathy, the director of the house, and since I vouched for you, she's willing to let you in."

She vouched for me? Unbelievable. Tim was right. I wanted to bolt through the door and stay gone forever. "Did you know she was doing this?"

He nodded and observed his coffee, avoiding my gaze.

Stupid question. Of course, he knew. I needed a cigarette. Big time.

"Dakota, I'm trying to help you. I have made an appointment at two for you to meet with the house manager."

Another big eye roll. "Well, you've thought of everything, haven't you?"

Sage tilted her head and arched an eyebrow. "I guess you could always sleep in your car and hope for the best."

"Maybe I will. At least that way I wouldn't owe anybody."

"There's not always an angle, Dakota. Sometimes people do

care." She lifted a big blue book to me that said Narcotics Anonymous on the front.

I stared at it, mouth agape. This lady wouldn't stop.

Her gaze bore into me. "If you truly want to get sober, this is the best place to start. It's full of stories of people who've been through the same thing you have."

I snorted. I highly doubted that.

"Just take the damn book."

"Fine," I said through gritted teeth and stood before retreating out the front door and lighting a cigarette. I paced the front porch, acid churning in my guts, feeling the weight of the book in my hands.

Who did Sage think she was? Housing me at a battered women's shelter? That's not me. Sure, I'd witnessed plenty of abuse in my life, but I was never abused until Ryan. My focus landed on Tamara's car. What choice did I have? For the moment, I was stuck at the hands of that flipping ex-addict control freak.

Tim stepped onto the porch, his countenance shaded with concern. "Hey, I'm sorry. Sage means well."

"Seriously? She planned my whole sobriety program according to her terms. And then she wants me to go to some women's shelter. I'm not a battered woman, Tim. I'm an addict." I sucked in a quarter of the cigarette in one forceful drag.

Tim raised his hands in the air. "I get it. I tried to tone her down a bit, but she wouldn't listen to me."

I took another pull off my smoke and kept the rest of my bitter thoughts to myself.

"Hey." Tim put a hand on my shoulder.

I tensed as my gaze landed on his hand, irritated with the fluttering sensation in my guts.

"Sage is definitely a lot to deal with, but she'd be a great advocate in these first few months of sobriety. Why don't we at least go check out the place? If you don't feel comfortable, you don't have to stay there."

I flicked my cigarette to the ground. "Fine, yeah. Okay." I

didn't want to but getting out for a while would be nice. Once in town, maybe I could find my escape route.

"I'll go grab my keys." Tim went into the house and closed the door behind him.

I considered lighting another smoke, but I probably didn't have time.

A minute later, Tim exited the house and tossed me a granola bar on the way to his Bronco. The vehicle was clean and smelled of some fruity air freshener. He started the car and BareNakedLadies', *One Week*, blared from the speakers.

I laughed. "Is this the radio?"

He gave me a sideways smirk. "Playlist."

"No way." In my mind's eye, I was transported to age ten, when Tim had brought this CD to my house. We had spent the entire week memorizing the words to that song. In secret, Tim had gone the extra mile and choreographed the most ridiculous dance to it. He had arrived at my house that day wearing thick shades with his hair spiked on top and a long-sleeve, buttoned shirt two sizes too small for his chubby boyish body. He dragged me to his house where he performed his dance. I laughed so hard that day I almost peed my pants.

Tim chuckled. "It's still my favorite song."

"You're such a dork." I reached for his phone. "What else is on the playlist?"

Tim held the phone away from my grasp. "You'll see soon enough."

"Oh, come on, Timmy." I gave him a mock pout like I did when we were kids. "I wanna see."

He shot me a glare, but his lips twitched. "Fine, but no messing with it. I've finally perfected this thing." He released the phone and drove down the driveway.

I scrolled through the playlist and smirked. The whole thing was an ode to our childhood. His fervent love for old 90s music had made me fall in love with it too. Over the years, he had introduced me to Weezer, Hanson, Alanis Morissette, and to top it off, Weird Al Yankovic. I laughed again. Amish Paradise was another song that Tim had made a dance too. A strange feeling weighed down the laughter that bubbled from me.

"When did you make this?"

He shrugged, gaze on the road. "Over the last few weeks."

"Oh." I stared through the window at the lake and the trees that surrounded it, taking in his confession, unsure of how to feel.

"You being around made me remember the old days."

I set the phone aside, an overwhelming ache crushing my heart. I wished I could press rewind and stay in the past before the worst of the bad stuff had happened. When Tim's jokes and laughter made my whole world seem brighter. "You were pretty funny as a kid."

"Hey. I'm still funny."

I raised a skeptical eyebrow. "Ehhh ... I don't know. When we were kids, I thought you were going to be a comedian when you got older. Never in ten billion years would I have thought you'd become some brooding, intense cop."

"Whatever. You don't really know me, Dakota. You have this idea of who I am, but because I'm a cop you see me in this one certain way."

"You've seemed a bit intense since I've been around." I tore the wrapping off the granola bar and took a bite.

"Maybe because I was worried for you. Because I care. But truthfully, my life is pretty chill. I play softball in the summer in a league. I love to spend time at the lake on hot days." He chuckled again. "Not that there's many of those in Quilcene."

"Right?" I said around a bite. Ironic by Alanis Morissette played from his list.

"I love nature and good music," Tim said, tilting his head with a silly smile.

"I don't know if I'd consider this good music." I jabbed his side.

He chuckled. "Okay ... Are you like a music snob now? What do you consider good music?"

I pondered this as I finished the last of the granola bar. I thought about throwing the wrapper out the window to mess with Tim, but instead, I crumpled it and wedged it under my lap. I'd take care of it once we stopped, which would probably be soon since we were rolling into the outskirts of Redding.

"The Verve Pipe by The Freshman."

Tim pursed his lips. "Great song. I've never quite known what it means, but that melody, it hooks you."

"I know. I never really understood it either, but when it comes on, I'm hypnotized. Let's play it. Do you have it on your phone?"

"Uhhhh," he said with a crooked grin. "Does a bear crap in the woods?"

"I think that's a yes." I laughed, reached for his phone and scrolled through his music until I found it. I hit play, and the haunting melody flowed from the speakers. For the next few minutes, we listened to the song as Tim drove through Redding. Before the tune ended, he parked in front of a light green home with a large front yard and a white picket fence. The house had a large wrap-around wood deck. "What is this?"

"It's the address that Sage gave me."

I did a double-take. This was the women's shelter? The place was gorgeous yet homey. Definitely *not* what I had expected. We exited the vehicle and ambled to the front door. Tim and I exchanged an inquisitive glance and then he knocked on the door.

A woman opened the door with a smile. "Hello, you must be Dakota." She reached for my hand and gave it a firm squeeze. "I'm Naomi."

"Hi," Tim introduced himself as Sage's nephew.

"Nice to meet you. Please, come in."

The place wasn't bad. In fact, it was quite nice, but like everything else involving Sage's version of my sobriety, I couldn't imagine it. I watched Tim as we walked through the house, interacting with Naomi. A part of me wished I could go stay with him for a while. As I envisioned living with Tim, my mind took me down roads that scared the crap out of me. Living with Tim wasn't safe for my heart but staying here in this place that Sage was trying to carve out for me felt suffocating. Would I ever really belong in this world? Would I be able to actually stay sober? Truth be told, I didn't know.

CHAPTER 18

December 28, 4:00 p.m.

TAMARA

Standing at the edge of the water, I breathed in and watched the waves crash against the shore, feeling the ocean spray soft against my skin. The clouds had gathered overhead, threatening to release its storm. It amazed me the deep emotion standing in front of this vast body of water stirred in me. I missed Joe as I thought of the day he took me to Cannon Beach and held me close to him as we watched the storm gathering over the ocean. That day, I believed there was nothing in the world that could separate us. Now it seemed like the chasm between us was impossible to cross.

The thing that killed me the most was it seemed like I had sacrificed us for nothing. I'd come here believing that God had led me to reunite with my family and to tell them the truth, only to be rejected by my dad once again. It didn't make sense. Somehow, I must have heard wrong. God wouldn't have led me to hurt Joe like that. I thought of the sadness in his eyes the morning I left him and almost doubled over. Tears fell down my cheeks, and I prayed with everything I had that God would heal Joe and if it be his will, that he'd mend the broken pieces of our relationship. If we ever did reunite, I'd hold onto him for everything that he was worth.

Drops of rain fell from the sky, and a huge wave crashed

against the shoreline, bringing my attention to the water. My life was in the hands of the creator of this epic display of raw power and creativity. Surely, somehow, someway, even though I couldn't see how, he had to be able to help me fix things.

I inhaled deeply and walked the shoreline toward Charlie's house, rain drenching me. Charlie expected me at Midways in half an hour, but now I was going to have to stop for a change of clothes first.

A few minutes later, I was in the house, digging through the contents of my duffel bag. I found a clean pair of jeggings, and a teal top, and shoved them into a plastic bag to keep them dry on my walk to work.

Moments like these caused the irritation of not having a car to surge through me. Why did Dakota feel the need to steal mine? Where the heck was she anyway? Was she all right? Was she getting the help she promised she would? Silencing my thoughts, I said another prayer for her, releasing forgiveness for the hundredth time for her abandoning me to face our family alone. Although, with the way Dad had spoken of Dakota, her being here would have only made it worse. I gripped the bag and headed through the door.

When I arrived at Midways ten minutes later, I dripped with water. The place was dead for the moment and exactly the way I remembered it. A large open room with the bar on the right side, two pool tables toward the back, and a place to play darts. The room had plenty of tables and chairs for people to relax with a beer or cocktail and eat fried food. And off to the left was a small stage that held a whole different lifetime of memories.

Danny making his way onto the stage and singing the song he wrote about a woman on the run. Internally, I flinched. Before Joe, Danny had been the only man I'd ever loved. But the way Joe loved me had more than made up for the pain I'd been through with Danny. Joe had made me believe again.

"You all right?"

I turned to Charlie's voice and nodded. "Yeah, um, this place holds a lot of memories."

"Are you sure you're ready for this today? We could start training tomorrow if you need more time."

Shaking my head, I waved him off. "I'm fine. I've had way too much downtime. I need to stay busy. Besides, if I'm going to be any help to you on New Year's I need to get whipped into shape."

Charlie smiled with a nod. "All right. Let's do this."

"I'm going to go change first." I beelined it to the bathroom and changed my clothes, the whole time batting off feelings of deja vu. I checked myself in the mirror and ran my hand through my wet hair before walking to the bar and placing my stuff underneath the counter.

"That was quick." Charlie polished a glass and put it on the shelf. "Tonight should be fairly slow. I think, for now, I'll have you wait tables since you're most familiar with that. You just gotta stay on top of the orders, and me or one of the other bartenders will make the drinks."

"Sounds simple enough."

"It will be tonight, but it can get crazy in here."

"Oh, I remember." Shelby and I had spent most of our twentieth year together here at Midways. Charlie had never called us on our fake I.D.s

Charlie gave me a knowing smile and began instructing me on how to use the till. The ordering system was computerized, which made things a bit more complicated, but I'd have a handle on it soon enough. While it was slow, I took the time to memorize the bar menu. It was somewhat simple, hamburgers, chicken strips, fish and chips, a few different types of sandwiches and appetizers.

Around seven, things got busy and stayed steady until nine where it died down again. Charlie was encouraging as we worked through the rush, giving me an occasional fist bump when I got things right. At 9:17, Charlie was showing me how to pour a beer from the tap without making it foam when the bar door swung open, and a blond-bombshell stepped through the front door.

Shelby.

She dressed per usual in a skintight mini-skirt, flaunting her size six curves. Her hair was perfect, not a lock out of place, and her make-up was piled on thick, accentuating the contours of her face. My insides ached at the sight. I knew working here there was a strong possibility that I'd run into her, but I wasn't expecting it to affect me like it had before. I thought I'd forgiven her months ago but seeing her caused the memories of that last day in Ocean Shores to surface, stinging my core with the harsh betrayal of it. She'd been my best friend and she'd committed the worst of the worst of crimes in girl code.

"Tamara?" She crossed the room, heels clicking against the wood floor. "What are you doing here?"

I averted my gaze to the beer glass in my hand. Not thinking, I brought the cup to my lips, took in a large chug and peered at Charlie. I hoped he wouldn't fire me for drinking on the job the first day.

Charlie gave me a reassuring smile and spoke for me. "Tamara's in town for a visit, and while she's here, she's giving me a hand."

"Oh." Her voice sounded unsure.

I kept my gaze on the floor and thought of the time I'd run into her in Portland while at the bar with Kyle.

"It's good to see you, Tamara. Whether you believe me or not, I'm sorry for what I did."

My head jerked toward her. Sadness and sincerity lined her features. I still had the urge to slap her, though it wasn't as strong as last time. "It's fine," I said curtly. I'd forgiven her, but I wasn't ready to let her into my life again.

"Charlie, can I get a double Jose Cuervo?" Her lower lip quivered as she spoke, and she withdrew a debit card from her wallet. "And keep the tab open. I'm going to be here for a while."

I felt nauseous and a little dizzy. Why would she want to stick around? There were other places in town to drink. I didn't know if I could handle watching her drinking the whole night while hanging all over the guys that came through.

Charlie grabbed the bottle of tequila and poured a double into a glass with lime before sliding it to Shelby. She drank it in a quick gulp, then set the glass on the counter and sucked on the lime, wincing. "Thanks, Charlie, I'll have a Long Island."

"Why do you do this?" I asked, my stomach clenching. "You could be so much more than a slutty barfly."

Her mouth dropped open, and Charlie's eyes grew wide.

"Wow. Thanks, Tamara, for your great insight into my life. It's not like you know me anymore."

"I know plenty, Shelby. I know that you're beautiful and smart. You could have any guy you want, but you chose to go after the one guy that *I* was in love with." Where was this coming from? I thought I'd let this go eons ago but loads of anger and boldness were exploding to the surface from nowhere.

Charlie set Shelby's drink in front of her, and she played with the straw. "Come on, Tamara. You of all people know how damaged I am. I'm sorry for what happened with Danny, but what did you expect from either of us? He was as screwed up as I am."

"I expected you not to sleep with my boyfriend, Shelby!" I seethed. "I expected you to act like my best friend!"

Charlie's hand gently touched mine. "Hey, why don't you get some air?"

I glanced around the bar. Upwards of twenty people who were there, focused on us. I nodded, put the glass that had been clenched in my hand on the bar and started toward the door.

"I don't think it's a good idea for you to be here tonight," Charlie said to Shelby.

"Are you serious? You're eighty-sixing me? She's the one who's lost her mind."

"Only for tonight, Shelby. She needs some space."

Leaving their voices behind me, I pushed through the back

door, my heart raw. It seemed like wherever I turned lately there was more heartache.

CHAPTER 19

December 30, 6:55 p.m.

JOE

The last few days were a flurry of AA meetings, dealing with insurance paperwork and the menial tasks that entailed. The hardest moment—though every second seemed to have an awful aching quality to it—was talking with Trudy about the gritty details of the diner, Tamara, and falling off the wagon. She'd been kind and full of compassion, but she asked me a ton of questions concerning Tamara, and like Claire, she thought I should call her. Truthfully, I almost had at least one hundred times over the last few days, but I never could bring myself to pull the trigger. The pain surrounding her and what had happened still felt fresh, not to mention that I'd have to confess my drinking again. I couldn't face that yet, so I pressed on, going through the motions.

The second hardest thing had been meeting with my sponsor. He'd been so hardcore when it came to working the program. When I told him my woes, he told me to buck up and be a man. When he said that, I wanted to yell and cry at the same time. I wanted to tell him everything I'd done for the last few years to be the best man I could, despite the challenge's life had thrown at me. Instead, I nodded, determined to deal with whatever he dished out.

Tonight though, I decided to skip my third AA meeting and head to Hope Chapel instead. Right before Tamara and I left, the church had announced it was launching a new men's group named *Wholehearted Man*. This was the night that they met, and I felt a pull in my spirit to go. It took me almost nine years after my mother died to find God again and to learn to trust him. This time, I wouldn't allow myself to stay in the dark, running from his love.

All of the steps of AA spoke of opening yourself to a higher power and having a spiritual awakening. I had rediscovered my higher power a little over eight months ago, and I couldn't keep shutting him out. It hurt too much not to let him in. I parked my car in front of the large building and went into the church.

Two men stood at the entryway with welcoming smiles on their faces. They shook my hand and pointed me to the sanctuary. As I stepped in, clusters of men, young and old, were talking with each other. A few men sat off by themselves, playing on their cell phones. Across the room, Levi and David chatted with a muscular guy with a tattoo sleeve. I made my way in their direction, bracing myself for their unwanted sympathy. I stood back, waiting for them to finish their conversation, regarding the homeless ministry that the tattooed guy led.

Levi spotted me first. "Joe?" He reached for a handshake and pulled me into a hug. "Great to see you."

I returned the hug, my eyes feeling grainy like sandpaper. I stepped away and gave a half-smile.

David patted my shoulder. "Glad you could join us this evening. We're ready to get started."

"You can sit with us." Levi gestured toward the tattooed guy. "Randy, this is Joe."

Randy offered a firm handshake. "Nice to meet you."

"Likewise."

David stepped onto the podium, and I followed Levi and Randy to a seat in the third row. David told some jokes and rattled off a few announcements and then invited Joshua, the associate pastor, to take the microphone before exiting the stage and taking a seat next to us.

"Welcome, everyone, to the Wholehearted Man. We want you to know that this is more than a support group." Joshua gestured to the back of the room. "When you walk through those doors, you're family. We believe that the key to freedom, whether you struggle with pornography, alcohol, drugs, or any other addiction, is daring to live wholeheartedly. This involves connection. Connection with God and connection with each other. This is a safe place where we'll cover you and walk together on the journey to live wholehearted."

Wholehearted ... That sounded excruciating. My heart felt so fractured, I didn't know if it could be made whole.

After his introduction, he asked a few guys to share testimonies. One man spoke on his addiction to porn and how after many years of struggling, he understood it had nothing to do with lust, rather that he felt lonely and craved intimacy. He mentioned that for the last few months, instead of acting on the impulse when he felt the pull, he had been calling friends to talk through his issues. So far, it had been working.

Another guy said that he and his wife had gone through years of struggle with communication which consequently had hurt their sex life. This week though, he said they finally had a deep conversation and worked through their feelings which had led to the best sex they ever had. The room stood and applauded after each one spoke, genuinely celebrating their victories.

Joshua took the microphone and spoke again. "Thank you, Landon and Alex, for sharing. I cannot congratulate you enough for being powerful men who choose to engage with your needs rather than self-medicating. Most, if not all of us have had challenging upbringings, be it abuse, fear, neglect, or any number of pains we did'nt have the tools to deal with. And to top it off, the world wants to tell us that true men don't have emotions, that we need to have our lives together, and we can never show vulnerability. Well, I'm sorry, but that's crap, and it's killing us. Ignoring our emotions and trying to uphold the image that we have everything together has only led us to live isolated, depressed, addicted lives, and turning to sin to numb our pain."

He scanned his notes on the podium. "But addiction is not a sin problem. It's a legitimate unmet need that we try to meet in an illegitimate way. God is not mad at us for trying to protect ourselves when we were younger, but now he wants to give us the courage to express our needs so he can help us meet them legitimately. He wants us to let him into every area of our hearts so we can live wholeheartedly, bear the weight, and feel his love." He looked around the room, making eye contact with the crowd. "I implore each one of you to re-engage. It's time to reclaim the places of our hearts by courageously confronting our pain and surrendering the pull to disengage and self-medicate."

Shame cut through me, bringing a feeling of heaviness. Medicating was the only thing I had been capable of lately. If it wasn't alcohol, it was Netflix or staying busy so I wouldn't have to feel.

"The shame researcher and author, Brene Brown, says, 'There are many tenets of wholeheartedness, but at its core is vulnerability and worthiness; facing uncertainty, exposure, and emotional risks, and knowing that I am enough.' Men, you are enough. We are men who will be present. We are men who dare to enter the arena with our whole self, holding nothing back. We are men called to stand side by side, waging war for each other and the ones we love. We can no longer be weak men running from our emotions. We are men who fight to live wholehearted for God, ourselves, and for our families."

His words were powerful, but did I have that kind of fight left in me? Heck, I wasn't even sure what I'd be fighting for. Tamara was gone. The diner was gone. What else mattered?

When he'd finished talking, we broke off into small groups.

Levi invited me to join his, and I gladly accepted. Two other guys joined us. Logan was a short guy in his early-twenties and Rod was in his mid-forties. He was tall with a bald head and goatee.

"We usually each get five minutes to share and then we pray for one another," Levi said to me. "Since you're new here, if you want to share, you could go first or last."

"I'll definitely take last." I cracked my knuckles, unsure if I wanted to speak at all.

Logan chuckled. "I get that. The first few times I came, I didn't even talk."

"Now we can't get him to be quiet," Rod said with a grin.

"I'll go first," Levi said, then wrung his hands and exhaled. "I'm not going to lie. It's been a long week. Hope's been extra fussy. I think she might be cutting her first tooth."

Joining Levi's crew may have been a bad idea. Hearing his struggles with Hope would lead to only one thing in my mind. Tamara. But truth be told, I constantly thought of her, whether I wanted to or not. I hated myself for it.

"Sarah and I've barely slept the whole week. Then yesterday, I got a flat on the freeway on the way home from work in the middle of that rainstorm. When I arrived at the house, my wife greeted me with a fussy baby and asked me why I was late. I pretty much lost it. I acted rude to her and completely ignored her feelings. The fact is, she'd been worried, and I should have at least messaged her to let her know what had happened. It took a ton of willpower to let go of my own needs, change into a dry shirt, and apologize."

Logan nodded and spoke. "I completely understand. I mean, I hate to sound like a jerk, but I don't know how you do it, Levi. I don't have the same sort of patience you do. I want to, and I do try, but when I'm working all day and come home to a messy house and Addison curled up in bed asleep, it infuriates me. The other day when I got home, the baby was in her crib screaming for her mother, and Tyler, our four-year-old, was in the kitchen, scooping peanut butter from the jar with his bare hands." He relaxed into his chair and sighed. "I know she's struggling with postpartum, but she refuses to get help."

As much as I hated it, his words made me think of Tamara again. Her struggle with depression after her pregnancy had been brutal. Longing sprouted in my chest and tears stung my eyes.

"On top of that, she won't let me near her. We haven't had sex for months, which has caused me to start slipping into pornography again." He became quiet for a while, seeming to search for his next words. "I know it's not her fault, but a part of me blames her for it."

I felt bad for the guy, but I had no words for him.

Levi leaned forward in his chair. "Thank you for being honest. What is the emotion you are feeling right before you turn to porn?"

He pondered the question for a few seconds. "I don't know. Fear? Maybe a little bit of hopelessness, like worried that we will never have sex again," he paused. "And a bit of selfishness."

"Have you talked to Addison about this?" Levi asked.

He snorted. "No. You know the last time I confessed my struggle, she went nuts."

"I don't mean sharing the details, but I encourage you to tell her you are afraid, and to reassure her that no matter what, you will always choose her. When is the last time you took her on a date and helped her feel attractive?"

"I'm not sure. It's hard with the kids and work."

"I know it's hard, but it's important."

Rod agreed. "If there is anything Melanie and I can do, please let us know. We'll gladly take your kids for the night so you and Addison can get some quality time together."

"Thank you, guys. Enough about me, though. How was your week?" he said as he looked at Rod.

"It's been a mixed bag. Melanie recently released her first novel, *One Woman Falling*, and it's going well. I'm so proud of her. But because of her success, it's created some problems for me and my business. For the past ten years, she's been my bookkeeper, but with the book tour and writing the next book in the series, she's too busy to work for us. We've had to hire someone to fill the position, and it's been a complete nightmare. Because of a mistake the new girl made with the books, some of the employee's paychecks bounced on Friday. We got things taken care of for now, but I had to fire her."

"Sounds stressful," Levi said.

"It has been. Melanie's been doing her best to clean up the situation while working on her book stuff, but I don't like it. I want her to be able to follow her dreams without my added stress."

"That's really hard. Is there any way we can help?" Logan asked.

Rod scratched his head. "Practically, if you know a good bookkeeper, send them my way. But other than that, I'd appreciate your prayers."

"Absolutely. We have you covered on that front," Levi said.

A long beat of silence fell over us, and I realized it was my turn.

I cleared my throat and considered what to say. My life was a train wreck compared to theirs. "I honestly don't know where to begin. My life is a mess."

"It's all right, Joe," Levi encouraged. "Whatever you feel comfortable sharing."

"Okay." I wiped my sweaty palms on my jeans, praying for courage. "I'm a recovering alcoholic. I had three years sober, but eight months ago, I stumbled but stood quickly. That night I committed my life to Christ again." I glanced at Levi.

He smiled softly and nodded, probably thinking of the same memory I was.

"Over the last month, my life's become a warzone. My fiancé and I started having big problems. It's a long story, but last week, the diner I'd recently purchased burned to the ground and then Tamara left me to put the pieces together by myself."

Levi's mouth fell open in shock. "She left you? You broke up?"

I took in a deep breath.

"I'm not sure. She's in Washington with her family, and I'm here dealing with the mess. Anyway, after she left, I went on a two-day drinking binge, but I knew the alcohol wasn't making anything better." I swallowed the massive lump building in my throat. "I called my AA sponsor this week and have gone to three meetings a day. I'm sober, but on the inside, I feel like a dead man walking."

"That's tough, Joe." Levi said. "It sounds like it's been awful."

"It's been hell." My guts wrenched as I spoke, and I wished for some sort of release. "I don't understand why the AA meetings and working through the steps seem to almost make it worse. It's like despite the hard work I've done, I'm here again at the bottom. It makes me feel like an utter failure." I paused to reign in the sadness rushing over me.

"It could be that you need a new avenue of healing," Rod said. "The Bible says you're a new creation in Christ. Perhaps he has a different path for you to travel this time."

"I don't know. I guess that's possible." I tried to accept what he said, but I needed more than a scripture verse. "It seems hard no matter which way I go." I adjusted my position and raked my hands through my hair to distract myself from the building pressure in my torso. "I tried so hard to be a good man, to love Tamara well, but our lives completely unraveled."

"Look at me, Joe," Levi said.

I met his piercing gaze. "You are a good man, Joe. You've stood by Tamara through the trying times, and you've loved her so well."

A massive lump formed in the back of my throat. I'd loved her with everything in me, but in the end it didn't matter.

"It might feel like hell," Logan said. "And in some ways, it probably is, but you *will* get through this."

"Can we pray for you?" Rod asked.

I nodded and bit the side of my cheek. The guys leaned over and prayed for me to receive hope in the situation and to honor the feelings that were surfacing. They asked Jesus to enter my brokenness and heal my heart. Choosing to feel my pain sounded good in theory, and I hoped it would be, but it could very well crush me.

CHAPTER 20

December 31, 10:00 a.m.

DAKOTA

From Sage's front deck, the big red barn and horse corral were in plain sight. I stood on the patio, sipping coffee as Sage rode the thoroughbred in circles around the corral and Tim worked under the hood of Tamara's car. A part of me wished I could stay here for a bit. The shelter had been way nicer than I had expected, but with that many women and kids under the same roof, it seemed like it could be a lot. I preferred the quietness and simplicity of this place. Being in nature, hidden from the drama, was soothing. And a part of me liked Sage's peacefulness, even with her domineering control issues.

Every morning since I'd been here, Sage had the same routine. After breakfast, she'd head to the barn, feed the horses, clean their stalls, saddle one of them and ride for at least an hour. This was the first day I'd watched her though. The fluid motion of the horse along with the ease of Sage's movements stirred a yearning in me. Would I ever be that free? Would I ever be that happy? With all the drugs and secrets, I highly doubted it.

Sage had been through worse than I had, and there she was with the wind in her hair, riding that graceful animal, moving along free from the heaviness I held. The moment almost felt sacred. Holy. I breathed in deep and stared at a crack on the porch. It had been seven days since my last drink of alcohol and my last pill, and some moments my muscles crawled with the ache of wanting one more hit, so badly I wished I could rip my skin clean off. I lit a cigarette and focused on Sage. No, I'd never be that free. Not in a million years.

The hood slammed shut, and I startled, turning my focus to Tim. He wiped greasy hands on the front of his jeans. "I think I fixed the problem." He glanced at me and smiled, then stepped to the driver's side of the car.

A sting of attraction zipped through me. His hair was a bit disarrayed, and scruff lined his jawline, which gave him more of an edgy look. He slid into the car and turned over the ignition. It roared to life. What a huge relief. With Tim leaving tomorrow, it would be nice not to have to rely on people for rides. Guilt nagged at my guts. Where did that leave Tamara?

Tim shut off the car, got out, and came toward me, a gleam in his eyes. Why did he have to be so attractive? Why couldn't he be that chubby little boy I used to hang with? Why did his closeness make my insides hum?

"So, I was thinking."

"Oh no. Don't do that." I threw him a playful wink.

He grinned. "Since it's my last night in town and it being New Year's Eve." He hesitated for a few beats. "Well, I wanted to know if you'd want to go out." He pulled two tickets from his pocket. "I did some checking around and found that Bob Segar is playing at the Civic Center tonight."

"Shut up!" I snagged the tickets and examined them. I didn't know Segar was still touring.

"You in?"

I looked at him. His lips were curved into a sexy crooked smirk that made my core tighten. "Hell yeah, I'm in."

"Excellent. It's a date."

A swell of butterflies rolled through my stomach. For a brief moment, my gaze landed on his mouth and flashes of our kiss ran through me. What was this man doing to me? Over the years, I'd steered clear of the opposite sex. I never had a boyfriend and only a few sexual encounters that I'd rather forget. My history made it hard to want to be touched like that.

With Tim lately, I'd felt an underlying current between us whenever he'd walk into the room and sometimes at night when I couldn't sleep, I'd imagine sneaking into his room to curl in next to him on his bed. My gaze hit the ground as I berated myself for feeling this way. *A date.* Tomorrow, Tim would be gone, and I would go back to normal. Not that I even knew what normal was anymore.

CHAPTER 21

December 31, 5:30 p.m.

JOE

"I have good news." Trudy sat across from me in her rehab room, countenance bright. "In three days, I'll be able to go home."

"That's awesome!" It was nice to hear good news for a change. "Let me know if you need help getting home."

"I'll be all right. Roger will take care of me. After this whole ordeal, he's asked me to move in with him." Fondness lit her face, causing her to appear ten years younger.

"That's a big step."

"I know, and I'm not sure if I will. He's been so great through this whole fiasco." Her cheeks turned a light pink shade. "I think he might actually love me."

I smiled, though inwardly, sadness overtook me. Love ... it was a complicated thing.

"Anyway. How are you doing? How is the insurance stuff going?"

I exhaled a deep, long sigh. "Awful. Itemizing the whole restaurant is a way bigger task than I realized. It would be a lot easier if Tamara were here to help."

"Have you spoken with her yet?"

I shook my head and peered out the window to avoid eye contact. For the last few days, Tamara had been the only thing I

130

thought of, and truly, I wanted to talk to her, but I wasn't ready to come clean about my drinking. There was this constant ache in my chest that could only be soothed by her voice. But more powerful than the ache was the wall I'd erected the day she left me, the day she chose her dysfunctional family over me.

"I know you're hurt, Joe, and you have every right to be, but sometimes, our own pride can add to our suffering." She adjusted her position, "When I got word that the person who shot me had been caught, at first I hoped he would get sentenced for a long time. But then I saw his punishment, no matter how just, would never satisfy me. I had to let go of my hurt and forgive him."

"Yeah ..." Perhaps she was right, but the person who'd hurt me was the one who was supposed to love me, not a stranger.

"You have any plans for New Year's?" she asked, obviously changing the subject.

A low chuckle came out. "I'm thinking a Kill Bill marathon is in order."

Trudy crinkled her nose. "Or you could do a road trip. I hear Aberdeen is a nice place."

Irritation surged through me. "Trudy! Would you please drop the Tamara thing?"

"Fine." She adjusted the blanket on her lap. "I'm sorry."

"I gotta go. There's a bit more I wanted to get taken care of before the businesses close for New Year's." My errands were already done, but I wasn't in the mood to deflect conversations centered around Tamara. I walked over and wrapped Trudy in a hug. "Take care of yourself."

"You too, Joe."

I left the room and ambled down the hall, retrieving my cell phone from my pocket along the way. I found Tamara's name and stared at it for a few seconds, my heart nudging me. She had quit calling me five days ago, and I wondered if she had given up on me. On us. I pushed through the hospital doors and sucked in a large, frigid breath. Dark clouds loomed in the distance, and wind swayed the evergreens back and forth. A storm was brewing.

I ran to my jeep, climbed in, and gave my phone one last look, lingering on Tamara's name, allowing the full force of missing her to overwhelm me. I shouldn't have ignored her phone calls. She probably thought I hated her, but I could never do that. I still loved her as much as I ever did. I still longed for her with everything in me. I still hoped that after the dust settled, we'd find a way to work through our issues. *God, I know it's time to forgive, but I don't know how.*

I started my car and drove out of the parking lot. Driving through the Portland traffic, I continued to wonder why Tamara had stopped calling. Perhaps the tide had turned with her family, and she'd been so busy reconciling with them that I hadn't been a thought in her mind. My phone rang, and I jumped, hoping it was her. Caleb's name appeared and disappointment struck my core. I answered the phone.

Caleb's cheery voice came over the speakers. "Hey, hey."

"Caleb, how's it going, man?" I tried to match his tone but could hear the falseness in my own voice.

"Just checking in with you, bro. How are you doing?"

"I'm sober." I changed lanes in hopes to go faster. I should have visited Trudy earlier in the day to avoid this traffic.

"That's a step in the right direction."

"True." Ahead of me, a guy slammed on his brakes.

"You have plans for New Year's?" Caleb asked, a hint of concern in his voice.

I squashed the regret that tried to come. I couldn't erase my drinking mistake, but I sure wished Caleb had never seen me like that. "No, man, I'll probably head to bed early."

"Going to bed early on New Year's Eve? Are you sure? I'm heading to a party tonight with some girl, but I can ditch and hang with you."

Some girl? Was he referring to the girl his family had been teasing him about on Christmas? "It's cool. I'm good. You go have fun."

"All right, bro. Let's do brunch tomorrow and catch up."

"Sounds like a plan." My phone vibrated, sending an alert that a text message came through. I checked the road in front of me and peeked at the phone. Tamara's name illuminated the screen. "Hey, man, I gotta go." I hit the red icon and pulled to the side of the road, pulse quickening.

Dear Joe, I don't know what's going on with us right now. I know you probably hate me for leaving like I did, and I guess I can't blame you. I'm concerned for you, and I'm sad that you've chosen not to return my phone calls, but I understand why you haven't. I want you to know how much I love you. That will NEVER change. You have been the absolute best part of my life. With all my heart, ~T

A tsunami of emotions crashed over me, and tears welled in my eyes. I typed a response and then deleted it, the words a shadow of what I wanted to say. I needed to call her. I needed to hear her voice. I needed her to know I didn't hate her. There were so many things to work through between us, but this felt like it could be a start.

I merged onto the freeway, praying for the cars to part so I could get home faster. This conversation needed to happen without distraction.

A little less than an hour later, I was home. I walked down the hall, stepped into the kitchen, and filled a tall glass of water from the fridge. I took a large chug, set it in the sink and brought out my cell phone, energy pulsing through my veins. Why was I so nervous? Taking in a long breath, I found Tamara's name. Another shot of adrenaline hit as I hit send.

One ring.

Two rings.

Three rings.

Voicemail.

Why hadn't she answered her phone? She messaged me less

than an hour ago. I hung up and hit the green button again. It rang and rang and rang. I pressed end and dialed her again.

One, two, thr— "Hello. Tamara's phone." A guy's voice came through the line. Confusion mixed with anger swirled in my guts.

"Where is Tamara?" More importantly, who are you and why are you answering her phone?

"She's ah ... in the shower. Can I give her a message?"

"Who the hell is this?"

"It's Charlie."

My head pounded as anger surged through me. The Charlie she told me about from Ocean Shores? Was this the reason she hadn't called me? Because she'd been with him? *You have been the absolute best part of my life.* The words from her text message played through my mind, but this time they had a different ring to them. They suddenly sounded more like a goodbye. Jagged shards clawed at my throat, making it hard to speak. "Forget it." I hit end and flung the phone across the room.

CHAPTER 22
December 31, 6:35 p.m.
TAMARA

After blow-drying my hair and applying make-up, I stepped out of the bathroom ready for work. As I entered the living room, Charlie's face was etched with worry.

"What happened?"

"Joe called while you were in the shower."

I jumped for my phone, feeling excitement, relief and then ... fear. I paused mid-step looking at Charlie. "What's the problem?"

"I answered it."

My eyebrows pinched together as confusion settled over my features. "What? Why?"

"I don't know. It kept ringing. I thought maybe it could be an emergency."

I pinched the bridge of my nose to suppress the tension headache, building in my skull. "What exactly did he say?"

"I don't know. He asked for you. I told him you were in the shower. He asked who I was. I told him. He sounded pissed and he hung up. I'm so, so sorry, Tamara."

"It will be okay," I said, more to myself than him as I pressed on Joe's name in my phone. This wasn't a big deal. I just needed to get ahold of Joe to explain. He had finally called, which had to mean he was ready to talk. If I could explain what was really going

135

on, he'd realize that Charlie had only ever been a good friend and there was nothing going on between us.

The phone rang once and went to voicemail. My heart sunk. Was he purposefully ignoring me? I pressed send again and prayed that he'd answer. A half a ring and voicemail. A sick desperate feeling gathered in my core. If I had my car, I would have gotten in and driven a hundred miles an hour the whole way to Joe's house and pounded on his door until he answered and made him listen to me. But I was stuck here. An onslaught of dizziness swirled around me, and I sat on Charlie's couch as the room spun.

"I'm so sorry, Tamara."

I drew my knees to my trunk and wrapped my arms around them. "It's okay, Charlie. You didn't do anything wrong. You've been such a good friend over the years. I don't think Joe understands that right now."

Charlie sat next to me on the couch and slid a hand around my shoulder. "He'll cool down, and you can explain it to him then."

I pushed my head against my knees, wishing he was right, but my gut said otherwise. Too much damage had been done between the fire and me leaving. I had sent him that text message earlier, but he could have been calling to end things for good. Tears fell like waterfalls off my cheeks and onto my jeans.

Charlie massaged my shoulder. "I know you were planning to work tonight, but you don't have to."

I wiped away the tears. "I can do it. I just need to redo my make-up," I said with a sad smile, eyes still brimming.

"The bar will be fine. I hired an experienced bartender this week and scheduled three other cocktail waitresses. You take care of yourself."

"I don't want to be here by myself. Staying busy could help."

"How 'bout you come and hang at the bar. You could probably use a drink right now, and if we get too busy, we will put you to work." He stood and reached his hand toward mine. I took hold of it, and he dragged me to my feet. A dark cloud crowded around my soul. Having a drink did sound good. Hopefully it would help shake the nausea that'd been hounding me since leaving Vancouver. In moments like this, though, it intensified. I followed him to his car, the wind and rain swirling around us.

A few minutes later, we pulled into Midways. We had to park around the bar because the lot was full. Charlie had booked a cover band that claimed they could play every hit written since 1977. The band consisted of three men and a woman and reminded me a bit of an 80s hair band. They were playing Bon Jovi's Bad Medicine when we walked in. I made my way through the crowd, following Charlie to the bar. The different scents in the crowd hit my guts in odd ways, making it turn.

"Are you sure you don't need my help?" I yelled over the music to Charlie.

"We'll be fine. Can I get you a beer?"

Ignoring the nausea, I nodded. "Sure. I'll take a Bud Light."

"You got it." He walked around the bar, took a cold glass from the fridge and filled it.

"Thanks." I handed him a five, but he refused it.

"Your money is no good here, friend," he said, an apology in his eyes.

A blond girl standing near the bar glared at me. She must have been waiting for a while. Oh well, that was the perks of being friends with the bartender.

I pushed my way through the people and headed outside for some fresh air. The wind howled, and tiny drops of rain misted my face. No matter. Getting a little wet was worth the quiet. Sipping the beer, I dug my phone out of my pocket and stared at the picture of me and Joe on the screen. I hit his name one more time. It went straight to voicemail. A large knot formed in my throat, and I swallowed hard.

"Hey," my voice sounded weak. "Joe, please call me. I need to talk to you. I love you so much. Please, please call me." I prayed to God that he'd hear the sincerity in my voice. A gust of wind blew hard around me. I shivered and headed into the bar.

The band was singing *Time After Time* by Cyndi Lauper when I walked in. If my whole world wasn't imploding, I may have enjoyed this group. They were skilled musicians, and the woman's voice had a deep husky quality that brought the songs to life. But at this moment, it made me sadder as I walked through the bar searching for a seat.

Suddenly, I felt exhausted. At the end of the bar, I spotted an open stool and hurried to it before anyone else could snag it. I settled in and took another sip of beer, stomach trembling. A hollow, aching feeling gathered in my chest, making it hard to breathe. The room spun a bit as I regarded my barely touched beer. Why was I so dizzy? I massaged my temples as the music droned on.

Coming here was a mistake. I should have stayed at Charlie's house. That way, I could release this sorrow stuck in my body that was causing my heart to feel like it was on the verge of fracturing. I lifted my beer and took a large swig. Why hadn't I ordered a stronger drink? One that would dull the edges of my heart as it shattered to smithereens.

"You seem sad, girlfriend." Shelby's slurred voice came from beside me.

Understatement of the year. I was too sad to be mad at her in that moment. I wished I could take back the drama of the last month of my life and go to that one perfect day before our love had burnt to ash. The day Joe had surprised me with the trip to Cannon Beach, taking us to the places we'd been on our first date and proposing to me for the second time. I had been so safe and loved that day. Now I was lost. Alone. Broken.

"Earth to Tam." Shelby waved her hand in front of my face. "You, okay?"

"Not really." I circled the rim of my glass with my finger.

"You're not going to have me eighty-sixed again tonight, are you?" She slurred, wedging in between me and the guy sitting next to me. "'Cause this band is amazing, and that drummer is super-hot."

"I hadn't noticed."

She put her hand on my shoulder. "You never notice anyone."

"More like you notice everyone."

"Tomato, *Tomoto*."

I regarded her hand. So, this was it. I had officially come full circle. I had no family, no boyfriend, and my only friend besides Charlie was a barfly. The good news was, there was only one direction I could go from here.

"I know you hate me," Shelby said, coming in close. "But I can't handle you over here looking so sad."

I sighed and took another drink of my beer. "I don't hate you, Shelby."

"Really?" She beamed.

"I don't particularly like you." I smirked with a shrug.

She laughed hard and smacked the bar. "Well, now we're getting somewhere."

I chuckled, remembering for the briefest moment why I had loved this girl. She always knew how to lighten the mood.

"Are you going to tell me why you're so sad?"

"Rather not." I gnawed my bottom lip, fighting tears.

"That's cool, but I know a great cure for sadness."

"Oh yeah?" Knowing Shelby, it was some sort of booze.

"Blue kamikazes, baby." She raised her hands in the air, eyes growing wide with excitement. "They're the best to make your problems disappear." She slung her arm around me. "Believe me, I know from experience."

"I think I'm good." Doing shots with Shelby would only make things worse.

"Oh, come on, chica, for old times' sake."

Behind us, the band played *Mister Jones* by Counting Crows.

I turned to her and raised an eyebrow. Those old times were almost as painful as the current times. "I don't know."

"Please." She stuck out her bottom lip in a mock pout.

I threw my hands in the air. "All right, fine. One shot."

Shelby flagged down Zack, the bartender assigned to this side of the bar tonight and ordered our kamikazes with a flirtatious gleam in her eye. At the other end of the bar, Charlie busily prepared cocktails and poured beers. Zack grabbed a metal shaker, muddled some lime in the bottom, filling it with ice before mixing in vodka and blue curaçao. He gave it a good shake and poured the contents into two shot glasses.

"Twelve dollars," he said over the music. Shelby slid him fifteen dollars and winked. "Keep the change." She snagged both shot glasses and handed me one. "To old times and old friends."

Tears stung my eyes. The old times weren't what I wanted. I wanted Joe. I wanted to hear his voice one more time, assuring me that I'd be okay. That somehow, someway, we'd make it through this. But he probably hated me after everything I put him through. I clicked my glass to Shelby's and shot the contents. It was delicious, a citrusy sweet burst in my mouth that heated my throat as it slid into my belly. I set my glass on the bar. "I might need another one of these."

"Yes!" Shelby pumped her fist. "Tamara's back. Back again. Tamara's back, Tamara's back, Tamara's back." She sang, throwing her hands in the air and swaying in a circle.

I laughed. It was strange that of all the people on the planet, Shelby Turner would be the one cheering me up tonight. Maybe that's how life worked. The people who hurt you the worst were also the ones who held the power to heal you.

"Hey, Zack," Shelby said. "We need another couple of shots."

CHAPTER 23

December 31, 8:20 p.m.

DAKOTA

That afternoon, I did laundry, washing every article of clothing I had with me. I told myself I was preparing for the move tomorrow, but honestly, I wanted my clothes clean so I could have choices. I must have changed my outfit at least six times. In the end, I wore a black T-shirt, a hoodie I stole from Tamara and my best jeans, though they were a bit snug on me from the extra food I'd eaten since getting sober. The dressing fiasco caused us to run behind schedule. By the time we found the Redding Civic Auditorium and parked, we were thirty-five minutes late.

"This place looks more like a giant factory where they make car parts than a concert hall," Tim said with a chuckle as we walked up the sidewalk.

"Right? Or a prison." Outside, it did have a dreary institutional feel to it.

He gave me a sideways grin. "You *are* on a date with a cop."

There was that word again. *Date.* It sounded so official and scary. Yet a part of me savored the word, letting it spark the raw nerve in my stomach that Tim's closeness always brought.

Tim opened the glass door for me and handed the guy behind the desk our tickets. We followed the music down the hall to the ground floor seating and found our spot, only seven rows from the front. How much had he spent on these tickets? We squeezed past a few people and took our seats. Tim's hand brushed against mine, causing the feeling in my belly to intensify. Taking in a deep breath, I focused on the stage.

The opening act was pretty good. Their name was Reverb, and they had this nice folky sound that accented Segar perfectly. The main singer and lead guitarist stood out from the rest of the band. His voice had a deep soulful resonance to it that made me want to listen to him the whole night. He was also quite attractive with Adonis-like features and chin-length dark hair that fell over his face when he sang.

"Thank you so much, Redding, California. You have been an amazing crowd. This final song is a bit special to me. I wrote it for a girl a long time ago." He paused for a moment, a faraway look gathering in his eyes. "I guess she'll forever have a piece of my heart." He strummed the guitar softly and sang into the microphone.

"I was born in an American town, where the mountains touch the face of God,
and she was born on the wrong side of the tracks.
A city girl with a life full of pain,
I picked her up in the pouring rain,
thumbing her way to nowhere from the past."

The lyrics and the melody dug deep into my soul, making me long for something different, something more in my life.

"She said, I've been through hell,
but you can take what's left.
I'd gladly take what's left of that girl."

Tim's gaze on me heated my skin.

"What's left is a fallen angel,

what's left is a fallen angel,
what's left is the chance of a new life,
in the arms of this cowboy.
What's left is a will to carry on,
when you thought your life was over.
What's left is a fallen angel for me.
Just for me."

Tim's hand slid around mine, and I met his stare. My skin tingled, and my stomach fluttered. Two parts of me fought with one another. I wanted to pull my hand from his and run out of the building. I would never be somebody's angel, not even a fallen one. Unless that meant a demon ... which I was confident this song wasn't referring to that.

The other part of me wanted to wrap my hand around Tim's and hold on forever. I wanted to believe the words he said were true. That if the past would have been different, if I hadn't been abused by my brother and my dad, I could have had a normal life where there wasn't pain layered upon pain.

For a moment, I stayed frozen, staring into Tim's eyes in the dim room, listening to the song, feeling the emotions it stirred in me—emotions I didn't even know I was capable of. Then I curled my fingers around his.

"She wrapped me in her arms like a lover and slowly closed my eyes
so I could see.
The beauty of her world and all its wonder,
she showed to me, she gave to me."

Tim's face slowly inched toward me. I licked my lips, the anticipation warming my insides. His mouth softly met mine, and heat pulsed through my abdomen. I pushed myself into him, my lips growing urgent against his. He pulled me closer to him. I felt the kiss in my chest, in my knees, and all the way to my toes. Around us, the crowd cheered as the song ended. Tim broke away, keeping his arms around me. "I almost forgot where we were." He said through a jagged breath.

I settled into a spot under the crook of his arm and tried to imagine that I was a normal girl from a normal family. For that moment, I wasn't Dakota Jensen, a damaged junkie. I was an innocent girl on a date with her childhood sweetheart. I inhaled through my nose, taking in his scent, wishing we could stay here forever, basking in whatever chemicals his closeness was releasing in my brain. This was a different kind of high. One I'd never felt before, yet way better than any other. And like any other high, I knew it couldn't last. The low would come, and I'd pay for it for days if not weeks. But for now, the addict in me would take everything Tim would give me.

CHAPTER 24

December 31, 9:40 p.m.

JOE

I stood in my kitchen, staring at my powered off phone, throat aching, a thousand awful images assaulting my mind. Tamara in Charlie's embrace, him comforting her in ways that only *I* should. Acid churned in my guts, and my free hand folded into a fist. I fought back the urge to punch the wall.

Get ahold of yourself, man. You don't know anything for sure.

But why would Charlie have answered Tamara's phone? Bile climbed my throat as another round of disturbing thoughts crashed over me. When Tamara and I split last year, she had slept with Kyle. My heart fractured at the thought. If she was in Washington finding comfort in another man ... we were truly over. I didn't think I was ready for that.

I opened and closed my hand several times, trying to distract myself from the agony in my chest. Maybe I should head to the Brickhouse, get completely drunk and mouth off to someone so I could release this pent-up anger. I inhaled three breaths to suppress the rage. I shouldn't be alone right now. These dark thoughts were bound to build into something worse.

I powered on my phone. It immediately pinged with three notifications of voicemails from Tamara. A terrible mixture of anger and longing overwhelmed my whole being. Why did loving her hurt so damn much? I ignored her and sent a group text to the guys from Wholehearted Man, asking them for prayer. Then I dialed Caleb's number.

"Joe, my man. How ya doing?" In the background, rhythmic beats of hip-hop music played.

I cleared my throat. "I'm not good. I called Tamara earlier and a guy answered her phone."

It sounded like he choked on his drink. "That's terrible."

"Right? What am I even supposed to do with that?" My hand clenched again. Maybe I should head to Washington and track this Charlie guy down.

"What are you going to do?"

"I don't know. I need to leave this house before I start punching inanimate objects."

He was quiet for a beat. "You could go to a meeting."

I was sick of meetings at this point. "No, that would only make it worse."

"Joe, I'm gonna be honest with you. I'd invite you here, but I've been drinking. I don't want to be the reason you fall again."

I considered this for a minute. Which was tempting fate more —staying here wrestling with my demons alone or heading to a party with Caleb? "It'll be fine," I said, though inwardly I wondered if it were true. "I won't drink. I shouldn't be alone right now." There were too many vivid nasty pictures to contend with.

"You sure?"

"Positive."

"Okay, I'm dropping a pin right now."

A second later, my phone vibrated. "Thanks, I'll see you in a few."

As I drove across town, I kept thinking of Tamara with Charlie. Most guys I knew wouldn't help a woman the way Charlie had helped Tamara unless he had feelings for her. Now she was alone and vulnerable, and he was conveniently there to step in and save the day. Just like Kyle had.

Clenching my jaw, I stomped on the accelerator. I needed to

get out of the sick places in my head. Fast. Tamara was a different person now. She loved me. Even if we were broken up, she wouldn't go sleep with another man.

Then why had she been showering at his house?

My throat ached for a drink. *God, please help me.* I couldn't let this woman affect me like this anymore. I couldn't keep letting her be an excuse for me drinking. It wasn't what I wanted.

I slowed and took a left on Industrial. Perhaps it was time to really let her go. Perhaps she wasn't the person I thought she was. Perhaps she didn't love me the way I thought she did. A bitter empty feeling gathered in my guts as I made another turn. Tamara was ruining me. I had to shut her out forever.

A few minutes later, I parked in front of the address Caleb had sent. The neighborhood was upper-middle class, but the large houses were similar with a prefab feel to them. Cars lined the driveway and littered the streets. I shot Caleb a text to let him know I'd arrived and waited. He replied almost immediately.

I'll meet you at the front door.

I turned off my phone and threw it under my seat. Knowing myself, if I had it with me, I would be checking it the entire time. I climbed out of my Jeep and walked to the house.

Caleb opened the door, a half-baked grin on his face, hands in the air. "My brother." The smell of liquor emanated from him as he wrapped me in a bear hug. "So glad you could join us," he said, a slight slur in his voice. Caleb didn't drink that often, which made him a lightweight. He pulled away from me. "There's somebody I want you to meet."

I followed him into the house, weaving through clusters of people. The place was nice with modern art lining the walls of the hallway. Plush white carpet covered the floors of the large living room, which had a matching beige couch and loveseats. On the far side of the room was a table loaded with a large assortment of alcoholic drinks. By the appearance of the people partying, they were taking full advantage of it. My mind raced at the thought of another night of drowning my sorrows and forgetting this drama with Tamara for good. I shook my head.

No. I couldn't do that to myself.

Caleb led me to a pretty redhead standing by the sofa, holding a bottle of water. "Joe, this is Hailey." Even in his buzzed state, the way he said her name had a certain reverence to it.

"Nice to meet you. I've heard a lot about you." She was around five seven, slender, with pale blue eyes and a smattering of freckles across her nose and cheeks. I guessed she was a few years older than Caleb, which surprised me since he tended to date younger women.

"Likewise," I said, even though Caleb hadn't mentioned her. The only thing I knew was what his family had said at Christmas.

Caleb leaned in and whispered in her ear. She smiled, her eyes sparkling with amusement. My heart twisted at the intimacy, and I once again ached for Tamara. A serious role reversal was happening right now. It was me who normally doted over a woman while Caleb was the third wheel.

"Hey, babe, could you do me a favor and go grab Joe a coke from the kitchen?"

Babe? They were on that level?

"Sure."

"I'm good," I said.

Caleb shot me a look. "No, you definitely need a drink."

"Okay ..." I chuckled.

"I got it." She kissed Caleb on the side of his mouth and turned toward the kitchen.

"Make sure it's non-alcoholic!" Caleb called after her.

Great. Now she and the whole room knew I was an addict.

Caleb threw an arm around me. "Isn't she amazing?"

"Uhh, yeah, for the whole thirty seconds I was around her, she seemed great."

Caleb thrust a finger in my chest with a sickening grin on his face. "Do you know what you need?"

"No, but I'm sure you're gonna tell me."

"You need to meet someone new. Check out the hotties here tonight." He waved around the room.

"You're nuts, bro."

"Come on," he slurred, leaning into me, a cheesy smile lighting his expression. "I can be your wingman."

Lifting my hands in the air, I shook my head. "I don't even know where Tamara and I stand at the moment."

"You said it yourself. Another guy answered her phone."

"I know but finding someone new when I'm so wrapped in her seems like flirting with disaster."

"I don't mean a relationship. I'm saying a fling. A one-nighter. You know what they say," he said with a singsong voice, grin growing wider.

"If you tell me the best way to get over someone is to get underneath someone else, I will coldcock you." I deadpanned.

Caleb guffawed and pushed off of me. "Always so serious."

Hailey returned with a can of coke and handed it to me.

"Thank you," I said, not only for the coke, but for rescuing me from Caleb's shenanigans.

"Hey, babe, are any of your friends here single? I think we need to help my man here with the ladies."

She giggled and scanned the crowd. "Let me think."

Great. They were ganging up against me.

"I believe Sadie's single."

I shook my head. Ridiculous.

"Who's Sadie?" Caleb asked.

"Three o'clock." She nodded in the direction of a blond wearing a slinky dress that hugged her toned body.

Caleb's eyes bulged and he grabbed my shoulder. "She's perfect. Let's go."

"I'm good, bro. I told you, I'm not interested in anything like that."

"Are you blind? You know what?" He turned to Hailey. "You hold him here. I'm going to go get her." Then he ambled boldly across the room—a man on a mission.

"Awesome," I said under my breath with a strong hint of sarcasm.

"You don't think she's pretty?" Hailey asked, curiosity tingeing her features.

Sure, she was pretty. In fact, most men on the planet would probably find her attractive. "It's complicated. I'm actually engaged. We're going through a rough patch, but I'm hoping it will still turn around."

"Caleb never mentioned you were engaged," she said.

I averted my eyes. "I think he would rather have me be with someone else."

She tilted her head to the side, a sympathetic look lining her features. "Do you mind me asking why?"

I chewed the side of my cheek, not wanting to go there. "Tamara and I have been through some hard times. I slipped a few times in my sobriety since we've been together, and I think he blames her."

"Sounds like you love her."

"I do." I was pretty sure, even if we were officially breaking up, I always would.

"I hope love prevails then. No matter what Caleb thinks," she said, her eyes twinkling.

"Me too." I thought of Charlie answering Tamara's phone again and nausea twisted my guts. The thing was, I couldn't see us making it through this, no matter how much I wanted reconciliation. I eyed the table full of alcohol again as Caleb staggered toward us with the attractive blond by his side. My fight or flight receptors flared, telling me to get out of there. This was a mistake. Staying here was dangerous, but a part of me didn't care. I was tired of always having to be the strong one.

CHAPTER 25

December 31, 11:15 p.m.

DAKOTA

The concert had been amazing. Bob Segar played his best stuff and ended the night with "Turn the Page," which seemed like a fitting song to ring in the New Year.

Tim held my hand on the way to the car and opened the door for me. It felt so strange to have a guy treat me with respect after all the pain men had caused me, but for the moment, I allowed myself to go with it, letting myself feel what I wanted to. It was a welcome reprieve from the withdrawals and constant self-condemning voices. Every time doubt would rise, I'd ignore it and lean into Tim.

This was our last night together. Might as well live in the moment. Be in the now, deal with the consequences later. When we got to Sage's house, Tim and I joked around while he made hot chocolate. He poured the hot cocoa into a thermos and collected a few thick blankets from his room.

"Come on. Follow me. I want to show you something."

I lifted an eyebrow and gave a goofy grin. "I don't know. My mama told me to never follow boys into dark places."

He adjusted the blankets and thermos to hold them with one hand and grabbed me with the other, pulling me forward. "It's okay, ma'am. I'm a cop. You're safe with me."

"Does that mean you're going to frisk me?" My cheeks warmed. What in the hell was I doing?

"Only if you ask me to," Tim said in a whisper and tiptoed past Sage's room. He turned the doorknob on the front door quietly, careful not to make a sound.

Outside, the sky was clear, not a single cloud in the expanse. The dark backdrop made the stars twinkle like diamonds in the sky. We walked to the middle of the field. Tim let go of my hand and spread both blankets out, one on top of the other. He lifted one of the blankets, sat on the bottom one and motioned for me to do the same. My stomach fluttered, and I shivered, partially from the cold, the other part from nerves. I settled into the spot next to him.

Tim leaned back, lying on the blanket, and tugged on me to do the same. "It's easier to see the stars this way."

I hesitated for a moment, but then leaned into him and focused on the massive sky. We lay there for a long moment in silence, watching as the stars blinked at us. Tim caressed my shoulder, and I shivered again.

"You cold?" He drew me in closer and tucked the blankets around my opposite side.

"A little. It's worth it though."

He rested the top of his head against mine. "Yeah, I've loved watching the stars since I was a kid. Especially on clear nights like this."

"It's stunning," I said, heat expanding in my core.

"You see that line of three stars right there." He pointed at a collection of stars. "That's Orion's belt, and over there is one of his hunting dogs."

I nuzzled into the crook of his arm. "How do you know?"

"My grandmother was a stargazer, but she was also into astrology." He shook his head, a smile in his voice. "She believed our stories were written in the stars."

I snorted. "Sounds like some woo-woo romantic bull crap to me."

He laughed. "She was definitely a bit different, but she taught me about the stars and constellations. Some of my favorite moments as a child were staring at the stars with my grandma."

"And here I thought your favorite childhood memories were with me." I poked him in the side, smiling. "But nope, I was bested by your kooky, old grandmother."

"Hey." He tickled me, and I giggled. "I'll have you know, that kooky, old woman was a genius. See over there." He pointed at another cluster of stars. "That's the Twins, better known as Gemini."

Just then, a shooting star zipped across the sky. I gasped. It had been years since I'd seen a shooting star. For a long moment, I stared at the sky in awe as something came alive in my chest that I thought had died eons ago. My icy heart was somehow beating. Feeling. Another shooting star and then another.

Tim leaned in close and whispered, "Make a wish."

I turned toward him and searched his face, pulse thrumming in my ears. I needed a million wishes to set things right. First, I'd wish that I could go back in time and stay close to Tim rather than getting mixed up in the life I had. I paused, lingering on everything that one different choice would have changed. I would have never brought drugs home, which meant Tamara wouldn't have had to take my beating, and she wouldn't have left home. I would have never gotten involved with Ryan, and Gabriel would be alive. A tear trickled down my cheek. I guessed I only needed one wish to make those million things right.

"What's wrong?" His thumb wiped at the tear.

I shook my head. "Just thinking about wishes."

He put his finger over my mouth. "Don't tell me. Otherwise, it won't come true."

"I haven't wished anything yet. I'm only thinking about them."

"I have a wish." He leaned his face toward me and brought his lips to mine. Closing my eyes, I kissed him and drank in his soft passion as the sadness and regret faded. At that moment, as I felt the tenderness and heat of his touch, I wished, with what was left of my heart, that we could stay like this forever.

CHAPTER 26

January 1, 1:45 a.m.

TAMARA

The room swayed as I leaned my head against the bar, waiting for Charlie to finish closing. The place had cleared after last call, and Shelby had left a half-hour ago with the drummer from the band. I wasn't sure how many Blue Kamikazes we'd drank. I lost track after my fourth. Or was it the fifth? Who knew or even cared? Joe sure didn't. I must have called at least ten times, but he was ignoring me again like I didn't even matter to him.

His silence made me feel invisible, transparent because if Joe didn't care anymore, I had nothing left. It wasn't like Danny, though Danny had hurt enough. But when he and I split, though I was wounded and it hurt like hell, I knew I'd eventually heal. I'd move on and build a life with someone else. With Joe, it was like ... damn ... the best parts of myself had been torn from me. If he was gone, truly gone, I didn't know how to keep breathing.

"You ready?" Charlie's voice said from behind me.

"I think so." I stepped from the bar and stumbled.

"Whoa, girl. Easy now." Charlie placed a steadying arm around me and helped me to his car.

I pressed my head against the window on the way home and focused on breathing. In and out. In and out. That's all I had to do to stay alive. Why did I feel like I was dying then? Why did it hurt to breathe? Wasn't drinking supposed to numb the pain? In this case, it amplified the sorrow.

"You okay over there?" Charlie asked as he turned into his driveway.

I shook my head and wished I could cry, but the tears were stuck in my lungs, suffocating me.

There was a long silence before Charlie exited and rounded the vehicle. He opened my door, and I fell onto the driveway. Charlie helped me to my feet and steadied me as we stepped into his house, leading me to his couch. "I'll get you some water." He went into his kitchen and returned moments later with the full glass that he handed to me.

The room spun a bit as I took a drink. "He hates me, doesn't he?" I slurred and put the glass aside, darkness seeping over my soul.

"He doesn't hate you, Tamara. He's probably hurting and confused." He sat on the couch next to me.

"Do you think, he thinks ...?" I gestured between us.

"Probably." His eyebrows pinched together in a sympathetic look.

Didn't Joe know how much he meant to me? I would never hurt him like that. Thoughts of Kyle assailed my mind. I *had* hurt him like that before, but that was different. *I* was different back then.

"I'm so sorry, Tamara." Charlie slid a comforting arm around me. "I feel horrible."

"It's not your fault." My words slurred as I leaned into him. "You've been a good friend to me."

"He's a lucky guy, Tamara."

I raised my head and the room spun. "Are you crazy? I'm such a mess."

"A beautiful mess." He tucked a lock of hair behind my ear, lips curving into a fond smile.

I laughed a scornful laugh and rested my head on his shoulder.

"You don't even know me, Charlie." My words sounded like a mumble, and I could feel the alcohol drowning my brain, tugging me under.

"I know enough."

I couldn't make sense of Charlie's words. He seemed to have a high opinion of me, but I didn't understand it. Couldn't he see that I was a selfish person, continually hurting the people I cared for in some way? Joe had loved me deeply and unwaveringly, and I had screwed it up. That was what made this so painful. I had no one to blame but me.

"My own father kicked me out of his life, and Joe won't even talk to me. I think that says enough about who I am."

"The stuff with your dad is complicated, but I believe this thing with Joe will be all right."

His words swirled around me, seeming to echo in my mind. "Why do you think Joe's lucky?"

He stayed silent for a long time, and I wondered if he even heard me. Or maybe I didn't say the words out loud.

"I think one of your best qualities is how deeply you love people." He leaned away from me, his eyes scanning my face. "When you love someone, it's like you don't see anyone else. They're your whole world. That's how you were with Danny. And now with Joe. If he doesn't see that, he doesn't deserve you."

A flicker of defensiveness rose in me. "Joe's wonderful. He's the best thing that has ever happened to me."

"You've said that, but where is he? You're going through some really hard things. He should be here. If you were my girl, I would never make you face your family alone."

That wasn't fair. A person could only take so much. "Maybe he needs me to be there for him for a change."

"Maybe," he said in a whisper. "I just hate to see you like this."

"Me too." Tears trickled down my face, bringing the slightest sense of relief. "Thank you for being here, Charlie."

He pulled me closer to him. "Absolutely, girl. I got you. Always will."

The room spun, and nausea tore through me. I bolted off the couch and into the bathroom, where I hurled the night's contents into the toilet.

CHAPTER 27

January 1, 2:35 a.m.

JOE

Over the last hour, the party had thinned a bit, but fifteen people remained. Five, including Caleb and Sadie, were dancing in the center, completely wasted. A handful of couples were sprawled on the various couches making out while the rest were off in the kitchen or outside drinking.

I remained in the same spot most of the night talking with Hailey and Sadie. Sadie had hung all over me and was a decent conversationalist until she hit her drink and frustration limit that I hadn't made a move and joined Caleb on the dance floor.

Hailey, however, stayed with me, mostly sober, nursing a glass of wine. For the last hour, she sat attentively listening as I shared with her the story of the previous month's events. The more I shared with her, the less of an urge I had to drink. She was amazing. I could see why Caleb fell for her.

We both focused on Caleb as he jumped on the coffee table with his shirt off, swinging it over his head, hips pumping with the music like a stripper.

I covered my mouth with my hand, stifling a laugh. "Should we go get him?"

A fondness twinkled in her eye. "Nah, he's slightly nuts but harmless."

I chuckled and took a drink of my third coke. With the caffeine and sugar combo, I probably wouldn't be able to sleep tonight. "That's a good way to describe him. So, I take it you're okay with his shenanigans."

"Absolutely. His liveliness is what endears me to him the most. The last guy I dated was too much like me, and we were so bored."

I nodded, thinking of Tamara. "Opposites do attract, don't they? I guess I am more worried about the mess."

"Eh, it's okay, I already hired a team of house cleaners scheduled for—" she glanced at her watch and shot me a goofy grin "—seven hours from now."

"This is your house? I had no idea. It's nice."

"Thanks. I inherited it from my parents when they passed."

My heart hit a speed bump, and for a split second, I considered asking how they died. Had it been an accident like my mom? I shook off the urge. It was too deep and personal for our first time talking. Then again, I had told her the details of the most gruesome season in my life since losing my mom, but still. "Sorry to hear that. My mom died when I was seventeen, and I never knew my dad."

Knowing flitted over her face.

"What?" I threw her a confused glance.

She narrowed her eyes and took a sip of her wine. "On a scale of one to ten, how honest do you want me to be with you, considering it's the first time you've met me?"

I considered her question for a few moments, unsure. Did I really want to go here? Why not? "I can appreciate a straight shooter."

She hesitated for another few beats before she spoke. "Okay but know I'm saying this because of my experience. When my parents died, there was this huge thing that had been stolen from me. It made me feel powerless. For a long time, and sometimes even now, I have this overwhelming need to control. It makes my world feel safe. When you were sharing your story, I got an inkling you were the same way."

For a moment, I sat stunned, awed by her insight, wondering if she was right. Had I been trying to control my circumstances because I felt powerless? Perhaps. The thought made me want to grab one of the bottles of vodka off the table and empty it down my throat.

I met Hailey's compassionate gaze. "It's okay, you know. You're going to get through this."

I took in a deep breath, letting her words comfort me. "Thanks. You're kind of great at listening and reading people."

She shrugged. "It's my job. I'm studying to be a clinical psychiatrist, and I'm getting paid for it now. So based on our talk tonight, you owe me a few hundred dollars."

I laughed. She was a jokester too. Perfect for Caleb. Just then, both Sadie and Caleb returned. Caleb extended his hand to Hailey for her to join him on the dance floor as Sadie sprawled herself across my lap. Hailey mouthed a 'sorry' as Caleb dragged her to dance.

"Good luck," I said with a wink.

"Enough talking," Sadie leaned in. "When are you going to kiss me?" She moved in close enough to feel her breath against my face. Her nearness caused a surge of adrenaline to pulse through me. She was definitely attractive, but ... Tamara crossed the screen of my mind. She owned every bit of me, and I wasn't sure that would ever change. But then, she might be with Charlie—

My thoughts were interrupted as Sadie's lips met mine and her hands slid around my neck. At first, they were comforting, like my problems could melt away with the feeling of her mouth against mine. Tamara's face flashed before me again. I stiffened. I couldn't do this. I didn't want this. After all the suffering she had put me through, I only wanted Tamara. Pushing Sadie aside, I stood and weaved my way through the drunk people and out the door to my car.

CHAPTER 28

January 1, 9:35 a.m.

DAKOTA

After kissing under the stars for hours, Tim led me into the house and into his bed where he held me for the rest of the night. It was a foreign feeling to be held by a man, especially a man who claimed he loved me.

Once he fell asleep, I sat and watched his torso rise and fall, wondering what he could possibly see in me. Why, after all these years of watching me go down the wrong path, did he even care? Eventually, I nestled into him as the questions swam around in my brain. Somewhere around three, I drifted off to the sound of his breathing. Being in that place of comfort should have felt safe. Instead, I dreamt of the worst moment of my childhood.

I was five years old and hiding under the bed with Tamara. Gabriel's cries filled the air along with my father's voice screaming at him. "You're worthless!" *Whack!* The sound of my dad's hand on skin. "You're so dumb!" *Crash!* His body being thrown against the wall. "You can't do anything right!"

Tears streamed down my face, and Tamara's comforting arm circled my tiny frame. Why wouldn't he stop beating him? What did he do to deserve this?

"You will never amount to a damn thing!" Another crash followed by a *whack*. What felt like forever, I lay frozen, a crying concrete statue, as my brother was beaten at the hands of that monster. I wanted to scream. "Stop! Stop! You have to stop!" But I'd been afraid he'd beat me too.

Instead, I hid under the bed, praying that someone would intervene. Nobody did. An hour or so later when the house went quiet, I tiptoed into Gabriel's bedroom and climbed into bed with him. I wrapped my arms around his abdomen and rested my head on his chest. In that moment, I was a little girl, comforting her favorite brother, wishing she could take his pain from him. Then he slipped his hands under my clothes and touched me in ways no brother should.

I woke with a start, tears pouring onto Tim's chest. I couldn't keep living in this fantasy land. My scars ran too deep. I'd never be free of them. Tim deserved far better than a damaged junkie. I rolled away from him and sat. His hand came around my wrist. "Don't leave. We only have a few more hours together."

I stood, my insides shaking. "I can't do this, Tim."

Confusion lined his brow as he sat up in bed. "You can't do what?"

"Whatever this is." I motioned between us.

"Did I do something?" he asked softly. "Last night was wonderful. Please, come back to bed." He reached for me. "We can talk this through."

I shook my head and stepped away. "There's nothing to discuss. Last night was a mistake."

"No. That's not true. I love you, Dakota."

"Stop saying that. You don't love me. You don't even know me. You're in love with the person I was when I was a child. You're in love with a freaking ghost."

Tim jumped out of bed and took ahold of my arms. "You're telling me you didn't feel anything between us last night?"

I yanked my limbs from his grasp. "You don't know a thing about me. You don't know the terrible things I've done. I'm a liar, a cheat, and a thief."

"You may have done some of those things, but that's not who you are."

"Oh yeah? I watched my own brother die at the hands of a psychopath and didn't turn in his murderer!"

Tim stepped back, mouth gaping.

"That's right. Gabriel's dead. Ryan killed him and threw him on a fire pit. I've carried his ashes around with me for the last five years. I had them in your house along with my other dark secrets."

"Dakota, I'm so sorry. I'm sorry you had to carry that alone." He lifted his hand toward my face.

I withdrew from his touch, refusing the comfort. "You sound exactly like Tamara, and I don't understand. Doesn't justice matter to you? Don't you care what the law says? I was an accessory to murder."

"You were a child."

"You don't get it! I'm no good. After my sister forgave me for doing all that, I stole her car so she wouldn't make me tell the rest of my family. That car in the driveway is a stolen vehicle." I placed my hands in front of me, wrists together. "Here I am, Officer. I turn myself in. Cuff me, throw me in jail and destroy the key because that is what I deserve!"

He seized my wrists and drew me to him, eyes shaded with an emotion that almost ripped my heart wide open. "I need you to hear me. I don't give a damn about you breaking the law. At this moment, I'm not a cop. I am a man who loves a woman who has been through hell. Do you understand me? Let me love you, Dakota."

"I can't." My lower lip trembled. I didn't know how. I wasn't even sure what love was, and at this point, I was too damaged to learn. I ripped out of his grasp and bolted from the room.

CHAPTER 29

January 1, 10:10 a.m.

TAMARA

I woke, head spinning, queasiness mingled with fear clawing at my stomach. Thoughts of the night before crashed over me, making my brain hurt. Joe refusing to talk to me, shots with Shelby, Charlie taking me home. I couldn't believe I allowed Shelby to talk me into drinking with her. I thought I had changed, but I kept making the same mistakes. Nausea tore at my stomach, and I ran to the bathroom, barely making it to the toilet before hurling. *God, please forgive me.*

Sounds of pots and pans clanging from the kitchen pierced through my skull, and the smell of coffee and bacon returned me to the toilet. Crushing pressure settled over my chest, squeezing the air from my lungs. What if Joe never spoke to me again? What if my dad kept me out forever? All this would have been for nothing. I gasped for air but couldn't breathe under the weight of this sorrow. The room spun as I picked myself up and fled through the back door.

I ran toward the beach, my inner storm building with each step. Dark clouds loomed in the distance, ready to release their tears. I sucked in a hard inhale and dug my heels into the sand. "God, where are you? I need you!" I stomped onward, anger rising in my veins. "I followed you here. You told me to come, but my life has only gotten worse." A large gust of wind blew around me, but I trudged forward toward the ocean. "I don't understand, God! Why am I here? Why would you take Joe from me!" My heart fractured, splintering apart in a thousand little pieces.

I stepped to the edge of the water, watching it swell into large waves. "You promised me beauty for ashes, but I've only seen more pain. You promised me my family would be restored, but we're just as broken as ever. You promised me my dad would walk me down the aisle to Joe, but Joe won't even talk to me, and my dad hates me!" I fell to my knees as I yelled at the ocean.

The water rose to the shore, lapping at my knees, sending shivers through my body. "Why would you do this to me?" I cried, slamming my fists into the sand. "Why would you give me hope only to snatch it away? Why would you make me believe in heaven and then lead me into hell?" The looming clouds yielded their rain. "I can't do this anymore, God. I've lost enough. I've been through enough!" Tears spilled over, mingling with the rain.

Lightning streaked across the sky, followed by booming thunder. The ocean swelled, rising and falling with the wind. "God, help!" I screamed into the wind. "God, you promised me a better life. You promised me—" My words cut off, the life draining out of my fight. I didn't know what to do. I felt completely lost. "This battle is too big for me, Lord. I can't do this anymore."

For the next ten minutes, I wailed and cried, releasing the anguish as the storm raged around me. I thought maybe I'd sense God in this wild, electric storm, but the only thing I felt was my doubt and my own inner tempest. "God," I whispered. "Please speak to me. I feel so lost."

A sunburst broke through from behind the dark clouds and created the most brilliant, blinding light in the sky. I sheltered my eyes, yet the light was too bright. It caused my stomach to churn again. I turned to the side and vomited onto the sand. Hunching over, I held my abdomen while rocking back and forth. The wind slowly died down as a strange calm settled over the water.

I am with you.

A whisper so faint resounded deep within me. Chill bumps rose on my skin as more tears formed and fell.

"God, are you really still with me?" Through the blurry blinks, I returned my gaze to the sky. The bright light softened, revealing the most brilliant rainbow, hovering over the water. Could this rainbow be here for me?

My thoughts brought me to Sunday school when I was a child. One of the few times my parents had brought me to church, the teacher had spoke on Noah and how God had given him a rainbow as a sign of his promise to him.

Warmth filled my stomach as I stared at the rainbow, a sense of awe consuming me. In the middle of fumbling through the darkness of my past and present mistakes, God followed me once again to remind me of his promises. He truly was a kind father, just like David had told me.

Sometimes when God gives a promise, it's because we're about to face something hard. David's words played through my mind. He had no idea at the time how right he'd been. But he also said how important it was to pray into them. Why hadn't I listened? Why was it so hard to believe what God had promised me?

I focused on the rainbow again, stood and dusted the sand off my pants. After that meeting with David, I had gone home and declared to the darkness that I was done running from it. That I resolved to hold onto the hope my family would be restored. Why had I stopped fighting so easily? Why had I returned to my old ways? I was better than this, stronger than this. Tenacity merged with my guilt, and I rushed to Charlie's house with renewed strength in my steps.

Charlie sat on his couch, holding a plate of food when I came through the door. "Good morning." He gave me a curious glance. "Where have you been?"

I stood on the welcome mat, dripping, realizing for the first time how cold I was. "At the ocean, praying."

"Nice. You okay?"

"I'm good. I think. I need to go do something." Shivering, I pointed to the guest bedroom.

His eyebrows twitched with confusion. "All right, I made plenty of breakfast if you get hungry later."

Internally, I recoiled at the thought of food. "Thank you, Charlie. For everything," I said and forced myself to walk at a normal pace toward my room.

I shut the door behind me and changed into dry clothes before digging through my bag for my journal. Opening it, I flipped it to the page where I had my list of promises.

Beauty for Ashes

"God, you promised me that you would give me beauty for ashes," I said with conviction. "You showed me that flowers would spring forth from the ashes of my past. I hold you to your word and trust that the ashes of my life will be replaced with beauty. Gabriel's death will not be in vain. My family will be restored." As I said the words, a fire ignited in my belly as if the Holy Spirit himself was speaking through me. I looked at the next promise on the list.

Dad will walk me down the aisle to Joe.

"God, you gave me a vision of my dad giving me away on my wedding day. I believe that my relationship with my dad and Joe will be restored. I ask forgiveness for running away from home, and for what I did to Joe by leaving. I have faith this promise will be fulfilled in my life."

The years of my life will be restored.

I tapped on my Bible app, found Joel 2:25 and read it aloud. "'I will restore to you the years that the swarming locust has eaten.' God, you told me through this verse that you will restore the years that were stolen from me. All the years spent running in fear, all the years missing my family's lives, all the years lost, I believe that you will restore them all."

Faith rose from within me, and another memory came. A few days before giving Hope to Levi and Sarah, God had given me a promise that Joe and I would have children of our own. I lifted my pen and wrote that promise as well.

Joe and I will have a baby.

"God, when I gave Hope to Levi and Sarah, you told me you would give me children with the man I love." I strode across the room with my journal in my hand. "I trust that you will not only restore our relationship but also bring us a baby conceived in love."

For the next hour, I wrote every promise God had given me in the book and spoke them out loud. Halfway through, it felt like God was in the room with me, on my side, declaring with me. There was still no call from Joe, my dad, or Dakota. Nothing outwardly changed, but inside—I felt different.

"Thank you, God, for being with me. Thank you for bringing me this far. Thank you for forgiving me and giving me the strength to move forward. Thank you for giving me faith again."

Lines ran through my head, and instantly, I knew that there were words that would finish the poem I'd been adding to.

I flipped the page and wrote the words, emotions flooding over me.

I need you, but I run
You are bright, I can't face you, so I hide
but you follow
I return to the garbage and throw up
I flee through the darkness but fall
And you follow

169

As I wrote, the comfort of his love covered me like a cozy blanket. Tears fell onto the page. "I am so sorry, God, for the many ways I've failed you."

You are forgiven.

The words reverberated in my spirit and more of the poem came.

> *You are here, I feel your glory*
> *I give up and turn, you extend your hand.*
> *I have eyes, I see your face*
> *I can hold your hand to finally leave this place*
> *I can live with you forever*
> *And you follow*

I closed my journal with tears in my eyes. I was done doing things my way. In my heart, I chose to fully surrender to God. As I did, a weight felt like it lifted from me. My life was no longer my own. I was truly his.

I may not have had what it took, but he did. He was able to make me the best daughter, fiancé, and future wife. He held my dreams and promises in his hands. I'd given him the ashes of my life, and in the right time, he would exchange them for beauty. I was sure of that.

CHAPTER 30

January 1, 11:50 a.m.

JOE

I stared through the window as I sat at my kitchen table, sipping my coffee and contemplating what this New Year would mean for me. This was supposed to be a day of new beginnings. The calendar flipped over, and the divine reset happened, but for me, there were so many things out of place and pending, I didn't know how to keep up.

The paperwork for the insurance claim had been much more detailed than I ever imagined. It could take months to sort through. Which meant it would take months before a check would be issued. In a different world, I might have been able to manage, but the fact that I had mortgaged my house threw a monkey wrench in the whole thing. Within a few months, if I didn't have that money, I could lose my house and my car.

Hell, I could lose everything. My chest tightened, and I took another sip of coffee. Outside, the evergreen trees swayed, dancing in the wind as if they liked the turbulent weather they seemed to thrive in. Why couldn't I be strong like that? Things would have gone differently with Tamara. *Tamara.* My mood sunk deeper. It was time to face her, to face whatever was to become of us.

I stood and crossed the kitchen to where my phone was

charging. I powered it on, and the message notifications from last night popped on the screen. I gnawed on the inside of my cheek, fighting the miserable ache her name brought. I pressed play, and her worried, desperate voice came out of the speakers, begging me to call her. Sadness and relief swept through me. The sound of her voice and her words made me see two things: one, nothing had happened with her and Charlie, and two, my ignoring her had hurt her deeply.

Praying a silent prayer, I hit the green icon.

She answered in the middle of the first ring as if she'd been watching her phone. "I'm so glad you called."

Closing my eyes, I let her voice comfort that place that only she could touch.

"Joe?" She questioned, alarm ringing in her voice.

"I'm here." A thousand words lodged in my throat, making it impossible to talk. I miss you ... I love you ... I'm sorry ...

"I don't even know where to begin," she said through a deep sigh. "I know it's only been a week, but a ton has happened. Things became hard in Aberdeen, so I'm staying with Charlie for a little while."

She was staying with Charlie? I did *not* like this. I believed Tamara's motivations were pure, but that didn't stop *him* from trying to make a move on her. I suppressed the jealousy and spoke. "Why didn't you come home?"

She quieted for a few beats. "I didn't know you wanted me to."

That was fair, I guess. It wasn't like I'd been warm to her since she left.

"And if I'm being honest, I'm not sure I'm done here," she said. "Charlie offered me a job and a place in his guest room. He's been a good friend."

A bitter taste formed on my tongue. *I* had been a good friend to her once, but then we became so much more.

"I can't tell you how sorry I am." Her voice came out hoarse like it was hard to say the words. "I've had a ton of time to think, and I understand how much I hurt you. You've been there for me so many times, and I haven't been there for you." She paused, and I could imagine the tears that poured over her beautiful face.

A few tears seeped from my eyes as well.

"I wish I could make things right with us. There are many things I would change. I'm so, so sorry."

Her words were like a salve on my aching heart. Why did she have to be so far away? If she were in front of me, I'd hold her close and assure her that we'd make it through this, but her distance reminded me of the insanity that we'd been through and caused doubts to flicker. I honestly didn't know how we'd make it through this, but this conversation seemed to be a step in the right direction.

It was my turn to talk. To tell her I wasn't the man she thought I was— that I had failed. "I appreciate what you're saying, but I'm really broken right now."

More silence. Anxiety formed a knot in my guts.

"What do you mean, Joe?"

Swallowing hard, I opened and closed my fists, trying to form the words, but they didn't come. I couldn't tell her about my mistakes. I couldn't be this vulnerable with her. Not now. "It's been really hard since you left me."

"I'm sorry, Joe."

I sighed. "Me too."

"How did we get here?" A lifetime of sorrow hung on her words.

An enormous knot gathered in my throat. What a weighted question. I had no idea how to respond.

"Where do we go from here?"

I wanted to tell her that I was coming to get her. That I'd be there tonight, and I'd take her home. But as much as I missed her, as much as I wanted her close, the relationship we had before needed to end, and that truth just about killed me. "I don't know …"

A sob came through the phone. "I love you, Joe. That will never change."

"I love you too, T." With all of my fractured heart. "But I'm not sure if that's enough."

CHAPTER 31

January 1, 12:40 p.m.

DAKOTA

For the rest of the morning, I locked myself in my bedroom, unable to face Tim. I mulled over last night, from us kissing to waking in his arms. I couldn't believe I let myself get carried away with him like that. I couldn't believe I told him about Gabriel. I couldn't believe I told him I stole Tamara's car.

At this moment, I'm not a cop. I'm a man who's in love with a woman who's been through hell!

Inwardly, I flinched at the words. I ached for a cigarette, but that would mean leaving this room and facing Tim.

Tell me you didn't feel that last night. His words wouldn't fade —a lot like the memory of the way he'd held me. Truthfully, I *had* felt something. Something I never thought possible. But there was this darkness so deep within me, tangled with the abuse and the shame, buried underneath layers of lies. Tim truly deserved way better than I could ever offer.

A knock at the door. I froze and held my breath, hoping he would leave.

Another knock. "Dakota, please open the door. I'm leaving. I want to say goodbye."

I chewed my lower lip and stared at the door, staying still.

Please, Dakota.

So many times, I'd pushed him away, but this tore at my insides, splitting me apart. I slowly crept to the door and twisted the lock.

When it swung open, Tim stood there, his features clouded with a brooding, intense look. "Can we talk?"

I made a sweeping gesture with my hand. "Come in." A part of me wanted to reach for him, to let my defenses crumble, to let him embrace me once more.

He walked across the room and turned toward me, an ancient sadness behind his eyes. "I don't understand life sometimes." He glanced at the floor, hesitating before making eye contact. "Dakota, I don't understand why I had such a good life as a child, great parents with decent jobs. They were loving and kind and supported me in anything. But you." He grew silent for a second, his gaze deepening with sorrow. "It's like you drew the short straw in every area of life. Your parents neglected you, your brother molested you, and now you tell me that he died in front of you. I can't even imagine what that was like."

It was absolute hell.

"The worst thing that ever happened to me was seeing my best friend go down a terrible road and being completely powerless to stop it." He took a step closer to me. "I know you're not ready for me to love you, but someday, I hope you can. But more than that, I hope you find the peace and healing you need."

I didn't think that was possible.

He drew me into an embrace. "Always know I'm here for you in whatever way you need me to be."

I rested against him, holding him, wanting to hang on with every ounce of my strength. "Thank you, Tim. You're the best friend I've ever had."

"Allies." He took a step back and smiled sadly.

"Forever."

"One other thing. I did some digging. Tamara never reported her car stolen. Why do you think that is?"

I shrugged, exhaling. "I don't know."

He brushed a lock of hair from my face and his hand landed on my shoulder. "I think it points to something huge. Your sister loves you. I think she's trying to send you a message."

I met his gaze once more.

"Dakota, take the car to Tamara. Make things right with her. Let her in."

I thought of the kindness Tamara had shown me when she'd found me. She was so full of love and forgiveness, but she wasn't the only one involved. There was Romeo too. He wouldn't be as forgiving as Tamara. After what happened at the diner, he hated me. I could never go back there. "I'll consider it," I lied.

He pulled me into another embrace. "You take care of yourself, Dakota," he said and withdrew himself before walking out of the room.

A cold vacant feeling filled me, and chills ran through my body. Keeping him out was the right thing to do. I fetched my duffel bag from the closet and started packing. Tim had gone. Now it was my turn. It took ten minutes to pack my belongings. I picked up the big blue Narcotics Anonymous book off the dresser and held it tight, feeling the weight of it in my hands.

For a few moments, I allowed the grief of what this book represented to overwhelm me. A few nights ago, I had read the first couple chapters. I was pretty sure I had the first step done. I could wholeheartedly admit I was powerless over my addiction. My life had been unmanageable for longer than I could remember. I wasn't quite sure how that would help me in the long run, but it was doable. I shoved the book into my duffel bag, zipped it and left my room. I hurried down the hall. With her nephew gone, Sage would want me to leave.

Through the front window, I could see her grooming one of her horses. Should I go say goodbye? I at least needed to thank her for her hospitality. I put my bag in the trunk and headed toward her. "Hey, Sage, I'm taking off. I wanted to thank you for letting me stay here."

"You're welcome." She ran the brush along the horse's mane. "You heading to stay at the shelter with Naomi?"

I shrugged. "I don't know. I think I'm better off on my own. Less casualties that way."

Sage set the brush in a bucket and peered through the fence. "Now that's a great idea. Why don't I point you to the nearest drug dealer and we'll call it good?"

Glowering at her, I threw a hand in the air. "What do you want from me?"

She shook her head, placing a hand on her hip. Next to her, the horse winnowed. "Did you even look at that book I gave you?"

"Sure did." I shifted my weight from foot to foot. "I even did the first step."

"Oh, that must have really cost you something."

"I don't need this." I turned on my heel and stomped to my car.

"I know, right? You don't need anybody!" she called after me.

I climbed into the car, jammed the key in the ignition and turned it. The engine didn't engage, and the whirring noise had returned. I tried again. Same result. I cursed under my breath and tried again. Nothing. *I thought Tim had fixed it.* I pounded on the steering wheel as a string of expletives flew from my mouth. I couldn't be stuck here. A tapping noise came from the window. Turning, I glared at Sage.

Lifting an eyebrow, she flashed a wry smile and jerked her head toward the house. "Come have some coffee with me." My abdomen clenched, and my muscles tightened. A bottle of vodka sounded better. Sage opened the door for me. "Come on. I know a mechanic who owes me a favor."

I ran my hand over the steering wheel, hesitating for a second.

"I know you're terrified of owing people, but, Dakota, everybody needs a little help sometimes."

"Awwww." I pressed my hand against my chest and gave my

best sarcastic tone. "That's a beautiful saying. Did you get it from the book you gave me?"

Sage laughed hard and slapped her leg. "I swear. You're straight after my own heart."

Not the reaction I'd expected. "Whatever."

"You want help or to sit in the dead car?" She opened the door wider.

I shook my head and climbed out. "Fine, why not? It's not like I have anything better to do."

She chuckled again. "You amuse me, Dakota."

"At least I'm good for something." I followed her up the stairs to the deck and through the door.

"You're good for more than a good laugh. You're worth a lot more than you know."

She didn't have a clue.

Once in the kitchen, she filled the reservoir of the coffee pot with water and added grounds before pressing the start button. "So, you made it through the first step, huh? Did you read any further?"

"Not really." The aroma of fresh coffee filled the air. "After that, it lost me."

She took a couple of mugs from the cupboards. "How so?"

I found this line of questioning irritating. "You say you know a good mechanic?"

She shot me a look. "Why don't you answer my question first, then I'll answer yours."

"Fine." I sighed. Clearly, I was at her mercy. "I'm not a big fan of the whole higher power stuff."

"Why?"

"That's another question. And I don't see how that's any of your business."

"It's a simple question. I'm not here to judge, but maybe in some way, I could help you."

Why did she have to pry so hard? "Do you really want to know?"

She nodded, keeping her hard gaze on mine.

"Because if there is a God, or a higher power or whatever you want to call it, he's never done a damn thing for me."

"I could understand how you feel that way."

"You do?"

"Absolutely. I completely get it. You've been through hell, and you need somebody to blame." She poured two cups of coffee and handed me one.

"Yeah, my sister is a hard-core Christian. Like she seriously believes that God is good and that he actually loves us, but if that were true, why was I born into my effed-up family where my dad abused us and—" The words caught in my throat. I couldn't tell her about Gabriel. That was off-limits.

Sage stirred some cream into her coffee. "I'm not sure. It's the age-old question. Why do bad things happen to good people and all that jazz? Maybe nobody knows for certain." She took a drink of her coffee, features contemplative.

I sipped the yummy hot liquid. I wasn't a good person per se, but I had been a child.

She set her mug on the table. "The thing is, when it comes down to it, it doesn't matter."

Her words struck the middle of my chest like a dull hatchet, and anger flared inside of me. "Of course, it matters. It has to matter. How can you believe this higher power can restore us to sanity if he's not trustworthy? If he's the force that allows children to be murdered and raped? Or, in my case, abused?"

She quieted for a beat. "I guess I see it differently than most people. My higher power is like a light universal energy. But there's also an opposite energy—one that brings nothing but destruction."

I raised an eyebrow. "That sounds like some Luke Skywalker, Darth Vader bull crap. May the force be with you and all that."

She laughed, her eyebrows raising. "That's the thing with the program. We turn ourselves over to a power that is greater than ourselves as we understand him. This is how I understand him. Your higher power can be the Flying Spaghetti Monster if you want it to be. As long as you have a power greater than yourself that you are surrendering to."

My mouth dropped open. The Flying Spaghetti Monster? She had to be joking. "That seems hokey to me. If I'm going to surrender my life to a higher power, I want it to be real. Not some mumbo-jumbo-woohoo-force-B.S."

She raised her hands in the air. "I get it. I had the same struggle, but I'm going to tell you right now, that second step isn't one you can avoid if you want to get better."

I took another sip of my coffee. "I'll think about it. Now, how about that mechanic?"

She grabbed her cell and scrolled through her contacts. "I'll give Ray a call and see what he can do."

I listened and drank my coffee as she talked to Ray, savoring what was sure to be my last cup of this amazing stuff. A few minutes later, Sage hung up the phone and turned toward me. "Ray will be here in a few days."

"A few days? Great. Where does that leave me?"

"The same place you've been for the last week. In my guest bedroom."

"Listen, I appreciate you letting me stay here, but Tim's gone. You're not obligated to me in any way."

"I wasn't obligated to you when Tim was here either." A slow grin curved her lips. "Maybe I like you, or maybe your higher power is watching out for you better than you know, girl."

I drank the last of my coffee. My higher power? I wanted to tell her to stick her higher power crap where the sun didn't shine, but I held my tongue. She was being generous. Keeping my attitude to myself for the rest of my stay here was, without a doubt, the best move. I rose to my feet, walked to the coffee pot and poured myself another cup.

"But as you said, I'm not obligated to you in any way, so if you are going to stay here, eating my food, and drinking my coffee, you are going to work hard for it."

I smirked and set the coffee pot into its spot. Some hard work to get my mind off things sounded strangely good. If nothing else, this was going to be an interesting few days.

CHAPTER 32

January 2, 9:00 a.m.

TAMARA

Last night, I dreamt of Joe. He was locked in a transparent box separated from me and the rest of the world. He sat on a wooden chair, hunched over, head buried in his hands. I beat on the box in an attempt to free him, but there was nothing I could do. He was stuck there, trapped in his sorrow, cut off from the people who loved him. I pounded on the glass and shouted his name, but he seemed deaf to my cries.

I shook myself awake and prayed for Joe. Rolling over in bed, my thoughts lingered on the dream and the conversation with Joe yesterday. For a moment, it had felt like a step in the right direction, until I heard the doubt and fear in his voice. *I love you too, T. I'm just not sure if that's enough.* That one line sent me reeling for the rest of the day. Since we'd first become a couple, Joe had been my rock, yet this thing between me, my family and losing the restaurant had devastated him. He didn't have the strength to love me like he used to.

Maybe I could have enough love for both of us. Was there a way to woo him back to me? Would he even let me close enough to try? I wasn't sure. I prayed again for Joe, putting my trust in God to fulfill his promises to me.

The smells of Charlie's cooking, wafting from the kitchen

made my stomach turn. What was wrong with me? I stumbled out of bed, room spinning. I threw on a hoodie and walked across the house to the kitchen.

"Morning." Charlie stood in front of the stove, wearing pajama bottoms and a T-shirt, his hair tousled from sleep. "I'm making an omelet."

Another wave of nausea rolled over me, turning my intestines into a knot.

"You want—" He peered at me, his eyebrows furrowing. "You don't look so good."

"I don't feel so good." I sat on the stool and inhaled deeply, praying the dizzy sick feeling would pass.

"Can I get you a cup of coffee? A glass of water?"

I shook my head slightly. "Give me a minute." The frenzy in my belly intensified. I hopped off the stool, unsteady on my feet as I ran to the bathroom and heaved into the toilet. Vertigo swayed the room for a few moments, and the feeling of deja vu pressed hard against me. Last time I vomited like this was when I was pregnant with Hope. I heaved again.

No ... No. Freaking. Way.

My pulse thundered in my ears. When was my last period? I breathed in deep to calm my racing heart and did a mental check of the last couple of months. I hadn't been regular since after having Hope. And when I thought about it, I had been nauseous a lot lately. I ran my hand over my belly, overwhelmed with the thought of Joe's baby possibly growing inside of me. What would I even tell him? How would he react? One thing I was sure of, if I was pregnant with Joe's baby, I would never let it go. This child would be mine to keep. I pulled myself off the floor and went into the kitchen.

Charlie sat at the table, eating his omelet. "You okay?"

"I think I need a ride to the store."

"Sure, what's up?"

I ran my hand through my tangled bed hair and sighed. "I need a pregnancy test."

Charlie choked on a bite, eyes bugging. "Wow, okay, yeah, give me a second." He shoved the last bit of omelet in his mouth and stood. "Let me go slip on some jeans."

"Thank you."

Within minutes, I was in Charlie's car, riding toward Ocean Shore's IGA, the local market—the only place in town that would have what I needed. As we parked, I glanced around to see if there was anyone I knew. Not that it mattered. I entered the store and hurried to the pharmaceutical aisle while Charlie stayed in the car. I purchased three types of tests, each claiming they were extremely accurate after only one day of a missed period and bolted to the car.

A half-hour later, I'd taken two of the pregnancy tests and both of the results were glaringly clear. I was definitely pregnant. How was this even possible? I had to be the most fertile woman on the planet to get pregnant on the first time, twice. Of course, I hadn't been taking birth control since giving birth to Hope, but still.

Shame settled over me. I had drunk a lot the other night while drowning my sorrows and I was pregnant? I placed my hand on my tummy. *I'm sorry, baby.* Joe would kill me if he knew I drank while carrying his child. I stared at the two positive tests. There was nothing I could do to change it now. I needed to move forward and do better.

"Tamara?" Charlie rested a gentle hand on my shoulder. "How are you doing with this?"

I turned to him, panic rising. "How am I going to tell Joe?"

"I thought you guys were talking again?" He tilted his head to the side, voice soft.

"We are, but I don't know. The way he sounded yesterday, it seemed like he wasn't ready to move forward with us. There's a lot of damage that's been done." I knew Joe. If I told him now, he'd be here in a heartbeat. I didn't want him to feel obligated to be with me because it was the right thing to do.

"You have to tell him. He deserves to know."

"I know. I just need to figure out how."

Charlie took the phone from the coffee table and handed it to me. "You just do it. The sooner the better."

Swallowing hard, I took the cell from him and stood. He was right. I needed to do this. On the way to my room, I scrolled to Joe's name and hit send.

"Hello."

"Hey, how are you?" I asked, relieved that he answered and that yesterday hadn't been a fluke.

"I'm okay. I'm getting ready to head into an appointment with the insurance adjusters."

I bit my bottom lip. "Oh, I'm sorry. If this isn't a good time I can call later."

"I have a few minutes. It's good to hear your voice."

My heart swelled at his tone. I wished he was here with me for this moment. This was the kind of news that should be given in person. "Ahh, I needed to talk to you."

"What's up?" His voice had a tinge of concern in it.

I paced the bedroom floor, trying yet failing to form the words. "What are you doing tomorrow?" What was I doing? This was stupid.

"Hmmm. Let me check my schedule. No job. No prospects. My big appointments are scheduled for today. Yep, pretty much nothing."

"I'm sure you didn't forget, but tomorrow's my birthday."

"I could never forget," he said sweetly.

I smiled, my heart melting. "I wanted to invite you to Ocean Shores to celebrate with me."

He was quiet for a long while as if he was considering. "I don't know, T. I'm pretty broke right now. I could barely afford gas money, let alone anything else."

If he didn't have the money, that meant—

"I haven't wanted to touch our wedding fund."

A pang of guilt flitted through me. Did that mean he still had hope for us? Why had I used that money for my trip? I'd been adding the money back little by little, but it was building slowly. I gulped hard and responded. "Seeing you would be enough of a gift."

Words climbed my throat. I wanted to tell him now. This was such big news to keep from him, but it would be better to do it in person.

After another long silence, he responded. "I'll see what I can do."

CHAPTER 33

January 2, 6:00 p.m.

JOE

I sat at the table, reviewing the statement the insurance adjuster had given me, head aching. The meeting earlier today had been a real drag. Though I'd given her the paperwork and inventory list she'd asked for, she said there couldn't be any movement until the police confirmed through their investigation that I hadn't been involved in starting the fire. It made me sick. How could they think that I was somehow in league with Ryan to torch my own diner? They said the fact that I had recently purchased the place made it more suspicious.

Ridiculous.

Standing, I walked across the room and opened my fridge, searching for something to eat though I wasn't that hungry. I caught a glimpse of the magnet picture of Tamara and me from one of those silly booths in the mall. Loneliness bombarded my soul, along with an immense sense of longing. I touched the picture, and my throat went dry. Should I go to her? I didn't know how to face her after her failures and mine. It would mean looking her in the eyes and telling her that I'd failed once again. It would mean admitting that I wasn't the man she thought I was.

Shaking off the thought, I took the milk out of the fridge and poured myself a bowl of Raisin Bran. Dinner of champions. I chuckled and thought of Tamara. This was more her kind of dinner. I swear the girl would have Cinnamon Toast Crunch for every meal if it weren't for me. The ache in my chest increased as I shoveled the cereal into my mouth. Why did I have to miss her this much? Why couldn't I let her go? I took another bite and worked at suppressing the lonely feeling. Even if I wanted to drive to Ocean Shores, I didn't have a dime to my name. There was the wedding fund, but ... I shook my head. Using it would feel too much like I was throwing in the towel on us. And as angry as I'd been since she'd left, I wasn't ready for that.

No matter how much I fought it, my heart would forever be Tamara's. I was nothing without her. I set the spoon in the bowl and pinched the bridge of my nose. There was no fighting it. I needed to be there tomorrow. If I had to, I'd use credit. I had a $20,000 Visa Platinum card. I'd only used it a few times and paid it off each month. If nothing else, I could live off that until the insurance money came through. My mom had warned me of the dangers of credit cards ... *Screw it.*

I poured the rest of the cereal down the drain and picked up my laptop. A few minutes later, I had a room booked at the Collins Inn and Seaside Suites in Ocean Shores. It would cost me $150 a night, but in the end, I hoped it would be worth it.

I ran upstairs to find my duffel bag. It sat in my closet, partially packed from when I had stayed at Caleb's house. I threw in a few more jeans, shirts, clean underwear, and a hoodie before zipping the bag. I felt lighter than I had all week as I tossed my bag in my jeep.

I typed Ocean Shores into my GPS and headed to the nearest gas station. In less than three hours, I'd be in the same town as Tamara. The thought both scared and excited me. I wanted to be with her, but I knew things would have to drastically change if we were to work. I hoped beyond hope that Tamara would be ready for that.

CHAPTER 34

January 3, 8:30 a.m.

TAMARA

The sun poured through the window and woke me from my dreamless night. I peeked outside and smiled at the perfect weather. If Joe did make it here today, I'd take him to my favorite part of the beach. Then when we were there, I could tell him about the baby. I ran my hand over my abdomen, imagining his reaction to the news. Last year, he'd been so sweet when I'd carried another man's child, but this baby would be ours. We would be a family. That's if he still wanted to marry me. I didn't even know if he was going to make it today anyway. He had never called me last night.

I reached for my phone, and a familiar jolt of queasiness settled over my stomach. "Good morning to you too, baby." I patted my belly.

Would it be bad to call Joe again? Should I give him his space? No. Forget that. We've had plenty of space. If he wasn't coming here today, I'd tell him over the phone. I tapped on Joe's name and noticed a message from him.

Sorry for the late text. There was a huge accident North of Vancouver, but I am here at the Collins Inn and Seaside Suites.

Anyway, since it's past midnight, Happy Birthday! I'll see you in the morning.

I threw off the blanket, excitement surging through my veins. Joe was here in the same small town I was in. Circling the room, I tried to figure out the first thing to do, my mind in a daze. A part of me wanted to run over there in my pajamas, morning breath and all, but I couldn't do that. I wanted to be beautiful for him. I dumped the contents of my bag onto my bed and dug through it. It wasn't like I had brought anything fancy with me.

I found fresh underwear, jeans, and a navy-blue sweater. For now, clean would have to suffice. At least I'd smell good. Opening the bedroom door, I scanned the house for Charlie. The scent of fresh coffee came from the kitchen, so he had to be awake. I stepped out of the room, and he came through the front door, holding a stack of mail and the newspaper. "Good morning. Happy Birthday!"

"Thank you, Charlie." I beamed, smiling from ear to ear. "It's a happy birthday indeed."

"Oh yeah? Do tell."

I raised my phone in the air, holding it up like a trophy. "Joe's here! He came. Charlie, I am so sorry to ask this of you since you have already done so much for me, but would you please help me do something special for him?"

"Wait a second." He walked across the room and placed the mail on the table. "Isn't *he* supposed to be doing something special for you?"

"You don't understand. Joe is the king of big gestures. For once in our relationship, I'd like to give back. I want to show him how much he means to me."

"What exactly do you have in mind?"

I discussed a few ideas with Charlie, but unfortunately, none of them seemed to reach Joe's level of thoughtfulness. I had nearly given up when Charlie suggested an idea far better than any of mine. It meant he would be doing a lot more work than I felt comfortable with. I tried to tell him no, but he insisted. I had to admit, his idea was perfect, and after everything I'd put Joe through, he deserved the whole world if I could give it to him. The nice thing was that Charlie had already taken the day off to celebrate with me. Too bad he'd be doing more working than celebrating.

After a quick shower, I dressed and put on make-up. I considered blow drying my hair, but I couldn't stay away from Joe for a minute longer. Crossing the room, I hugged Charlie and thanked him again before donning my jacket.

"Don't mention it." He waved me on. "Have fun, birthday girl!"

I wagged my eyebrows. "Oh, I will."

On the way to the B&B, I bought two coffees at Beach Treasures and speed-walked the rest of the way. The Collins Inn was adorable, and the attached restaurant smelled amazing. I'd have to bring Joe here for breakfast after taking him this coffee. I went upstairs to room seven and hesitated before knocking on the door, nerves pricking in my core. It had only been a little over a week since I'd seen him, but it felt like a lifetime ago. Should I have called first?

Don't be ridiculous. He drove the three and a half hours to see me. Surely, he wanted me here.

I tapped on the door three times and waited, chewing my bottom lip. A stirring in the room and footsteps before the door opened, revealing the most beautiful sight I'd seen in over a week. Our gazes locked, and my heart pounded. There were so many things I wanted to say, but the words were buried under a thick knot in my throat. It took a moment to compose myself, and I lifted the coffee toward Joe. "I brought you coffee. A mocha with whip cream."

"You trying to get me fat?" He accepted the cup with a slight smile, but the sadness in his aura made him feel distant.

"Thank you for coming today. I've missed you." I stepped forward and put my free arm around him.

He stood there for a moment, completely motionless as if he was unsure of what to do. Ever so gently, he brought his arm around me and pulled me closer to him. I pressed my head against his chest like I'd done a thousand times before, but this time it felt different. He felt different, like he was here within my grasp, but completely out of my reach. Sorrow bombarded my soul. How could I fix us?

"I missed you too." His voice sounded weak like the words hurt to say. "Happy Birthday."

"Thank you." I drew away and took a sip of my coffee. The dream I had the other night with Joe being trapped behind an invisible wall ran through my mind. In that night vision, I hadn't had the strength to reach him. Inwardly, I prayed that God would give me the key to breakthrough to him now. "So, I have a surprise for you."

Joe's eyebrows furrowed. "Aren't I supposed to be spoiling you today?"

I reached for his hand and wound my fingers through his. "You being here is gift enough."

Again, that reluctant smile that didn't reach his eyes. Had he come here to end things with us once and for all? My heart shook at the thought.

He regarded our hands locked together, me holding on for dear life. "I don't think so. It doesn't work like that. Not on your birthday."

I stepped in closer to him. "Ever since the beginning of our relationship, you've been the giver. This year for my birthday, I want to reciprocate. It's my turn to give, Joe."

He shrugged with a weak smile. "Since I'm completely broke, I'll go with it. What's the surprise?"

"Oh, that's coming way later."

"You realize that you're terrible at this. If the surprise is later, why tell me now?"

"Great question." With my hand on my hip, I threw him a

coy smile. "You'll have to teach me because you're right. I have no clue what I'm doing."

"I'm pretty sure it's hopeless, just like your cooking." He smirked.

"Hey!" I smacked him playfully. "Be nice."

The silly banter reminded me of who we were before the insanity and loss. I loved to see Joe smile again. Even if it was brief.

He sipped his coffee. "So, what's on the agenda for today until the big surprise?"

"Well." I put my finger on my chin with a pouty grin. "I thought we could start with breakfast downstairs and then we could go for a walk on the beach."

Joe took a half bow. "Sounds like a great plan, birthday girl."

My heart threw an irregular beat. Now if only I could break down his invisible barrier before I revealed that I was pregnant. I didn't want him reconciling with me because of a sense of false responsibility. I wanted to win his affection and trust again. I wanted him to see the depth of my love for him. My dream of Joe trapped in the glass box came to mind again, and I prayed for some way to break through it.

CHAPTER 35

January 3, 9:15 a.m.

JOE

Tamara's hand in mine felt a bit comforting as she tugged me forward, but it also stung a little. There were a billion things that needed to be worked through between us, yet here we were, slipping into our old Joe and Tamara act. I couldn't help it though. Being with her made me feel more like myself, but this gnawing ache below the surface kept begging to be resolved. Today wasn't necessarily the day for that, though. I would forget my own questions for now and focus on her birthday.

I followed her downstairs to an empty table, taking in her beauty and joy. Something was different about her, and I couldn't quite put my finger on it—a lightness in her countenance that had not been there since before the adoption.

"This town seems great. Tell me, how did you end up here again?" I pulled out a chair for her and she sat.

She fiddled with the silverware placement, averting her gaze. "Things didn't end well with my dad. Which is really sad, because it went great with the rest of my family. My mom was happy and relieved to see me, and my brother Nathan invited me to Christmas breakfast with his family. He has two adorable children. I wished I would have found them first. I think you would have liked them more than Dakota. They're actually normal people."

Dakota's name caused the whole nightmare that had happened in Vancouver to tumble over my mind in a split second. My chest ached, but I did my best to ignore it. I couldn't dwell on that now. Today belonged to Tamara. Not me. I took a sip of my coffee and tried to smile.

A lady came and took our order, but I'd lost my appetite.

"My dad though, he's still angry at me for leaving the way I did. He blames me for our broken relationship and denies the abuse ever happened. I never even got a chance to tell them that Gabriel died before he made me leave." She paused to take a breath, sadness hovering over her features.

I almost wished I hadn't mentioned it. I liked to see her happy. It reminded me of why I loved her and why I had come. This stuff with her family only added weight to the distance between us.

"My dad turned Nathan against me before I left Aberdeen. I haven't even heard from him or Mom since leaving. I was in the middle of dinner with Charlie when Nathan called and went ballistic on me for the way I treated dad."

Guilt and jealousy took jabs at my stomach at the same time. *I should have been the one who'd been there for her.* But Charlie had been there at the opportune time, ready and willing to swoop in. "I'm sorry, Tamara."

She reached for my hand across the table. "It's okay. I know that it's going to be all right in the end. I'm just thankful that you're here."

Not the words I expected from her. "How can you say that?"

She tilted her head to the side, softness in her eyes. "God promised me it would. I trust him."

My guts twisted around her words, feeling uneasy. "What do you mean?"

"I've dug into my relationship with God through this." She hesitated, her expression thoughtful. "He's felt close lately. The other day when I was praying on the beach, he gave me a rainbow."

I forced a smile, unsure what to say. I was glad she had leaned on her faith through this trial, but I couldn't quite relate. Since the diner burnt down and Tamara left, I could barely speak to God and he sure didn't feel close. "That's great." I forced out.

Her brow creased slightly. "Is it? You don't have to say it if you don't feel it."

I went quiet for a moment, uncertain.

The waitress came with our food. Tamara had ordered a fruit bowl and cottage cheese, and I got eggs, sausage, and country potatoes.

"I want you to be honest with me, Joe," she said, picking at her food with her fork.

I shrugged. "It's a lot to take in. I'm not sure if I can handle this right now. Let's keep things light."

"If that's what you need. I'm just glad you're here. I've missed you terribly." She popped a strawberry in her mouth and grinned.

I grabbed my fork and dug into the potatoes, ignoring the pit in my guts. Was being here the right thing for us? It wasn't like I could start where we left off like nothing had happened. At some point, we would have to have a talk, and if I was being honest, I was afraid our differences might be too great. Was being here giving her false hope?

After breakfast, we walked along the beach, and Tamara reached for my hand. It felt foreign, but I couldn't deny there was a part of me that was soothed by her presence. The feeling of her hand in mine made me believe even for a split second that hope remained for us, but I didn't know how to get there.

As we walked, she asked me questions about my time over Christmas. Images of drinking alone in my bedroom jabbed at me. I wanted to unload this weight, to tell her how much hurt she had caused me and that I drank heavily multiple times, but I didn't know how to let her in again. For now, I brushed off the hard subjects, made small talk, and went through the motions. I had to be strong and happy for her today. We could work through the hard stuff later.

After a few hours of walking, strained talking, and then forced smiles in an ice cream shop, she took me by the place where she'd been staying—a nice bungalow near the beach. She gave me a hug and asked me to return in an hour for the big surprise. I let her go and walked to the B&B.

Would the big surprise be that she was ready to choose me over her family? That she would finally abandon this ridiculous journey of trying to make her family fit into a perfect little box? Because if it was anything less than a one hundred percent change, I didn't know if I would have enough fight in me to keep going forward with us.

CHAPTER 36

January 3, 11:47 a.m.

DAKOTA

I shoveled another horse biscuit into the dung pile and wiped my brow. It was only sixty-three degrees today but shoveling this crap had me sweating. The last few days, I'd been shadowing Sage's routine in order to make myself useful. I peeked at Tamara's car and cringed. Today was her birthday, and that made my guilt meter twist up ten notches. At least I was getting help.

Well, sort of.

I was sober. As far as working the program, yeah, that wasn't happening. Over half the steps spoke of making peace with a higher power. When I dwelt on that, my guts would turn, and my muscles would ache for the next high. So, for now, I had to white knuckle it because me and God was *not* happening.

"Penny for your thoughts." Sage came around the corner, carrying a saddle in front of her.

"I was thinking of my sister. It's her birthday today."

She hung the saddle on the rack. "Have you called her?"

Averting my gaze, I glanced at a bucket of horse crap. "No."

"Bad blood, huh?"

I set the shovel aside and blew a stray hair from my face. "It's complicated."

"It always is. You'll get there, though." She dusted off her hands and stepped toward me. "You gotta work those steps. It will take time, but things will come together."

I took a smoke from my pack. "I'm not sure if the program is really for me."

"Still the higher power thing?"

I lit a cigarette, pulling in a deep drag. "I think I'm doing okay on my own."

She barked a laugh. "That's only because you haven't been tested yet. You need to dig deeper, Dakota. What has you running so hard from surrender? It's so much easier once you do."

Grimacing, I puffed on my smoke. "We've already had this conversation. How can I trust a God that allows a child to be abused by the people who are supposed to love her the most?"

"Maybe you should ask the higher power. He or she is not afraid of your questions."

I glared at her. "There is no god. And if there is, he or she is an angry being in the sky that doesn't give a damn what happens in my life."

She raised an eyebrow. "You sure?"

"Fine." I threw my half-finished cigarette to the ground and stormed toward the woods.

Within a few minutes, pine trees and brush surrounded me. I looked around at the trees but moved forward, needing my space from Sage and her relentless questions.

But what if she was right? What if I couldn't do this by myself? What if as soon as I left Sage's house, I returned to my old ways?

"Okay, higher power," I said sarcastically. "Where are you? More importantly, where *were* you?" I plucked at a fern and broke a piece off. The only sound was the breeze rustling the trees and a scurrying animal. I kept walking, breathing in the fresh air and sending angry comments into the empty sky.

Every accusation I threw out while meditating on my horrible past made me even angrier. If there was a higher power, how could he let all the terrible things happen to me? "Where were you, higher power, when my dad was beating Gabriel?" I picked up my pace to a run, and my pulse raced. "Where were you when the rest of my siblings were cowering under Dad's verbal assaults? Where were you when my brother was molesting me? Where were you?" I yelled the last line, letting the sky feel every bit of my anguish.

I stopped running and fell to my knees. Tears mixed with my heavy breathing. "Where were you?" I cried for a long time, the deafening silence filling the area.

I was alone.

I'd always been alone, and I'd always be completely alone. I wiped my face and sat back. Through the trees, I spotted a small creek. I stood to my feet and walked toward the water and sat down. I slipped my hands into the bubbling stream. Flashes of Tim and me swimming in the river near his house when we were kids came before me. I lay back and watched the sky as the tops of the trees blew in the wind.

A flock of birds flew by, soaring in the sky. I thought of Tim and how when we were kids, he'd meet me in the woods near the park where we'd laugh and play for hours, completely losing track of time. I focused on the sound of the water as I remembered those fun-filled days when nothing else mattered.

My thoughts shifted to Tamara taking the beating from Dad for me. The hits were so vivid. Every smack from my dad radiated through my mind. She loved me enough to willingly take the pain for me. Tears made my eyes sting. Tamara had sacrificed herself for me, and in some ways so did Gabriel. He followed me to the power lines that night because he somehow thought I'd been worth fighting for.

That's where I was.

On the edge of my vision, a deer came next to the brook around twenty feet down stream. My pulse quickened, and a strange understanding crept over me. Even after years of being shunned by me, Tim had hung around as the best friend anyone could have. And then Tamara too. She somehow was able to love me unconditionally without ever being taught how. Tears streamed down my face. Could a higher power be in the middle of this?

It did seem like the times I had been afraid as a child, Tim had been there for me, lending me his strength, protecting me from allowing the darkness to fully take hold of my soul. "Higher Power, I'm not sure who you are, but if you sent Tim and Tamara to protect me, thank you." I wrestled with the thought, trying to allow it to dig deeper in me. Could a higher power be loving me through other people? Helping me when I didn't deserve it?

I threw a rock into the stream, and the deer scurried off. I had to admit, compared to many other stories I'd heard from friends, my life could have been worse. The fact that I was even here, sitting in this beautiful forest getting sober when many of my friends were dead or lost in drugs was far more than I deserved.

I wasn't sure I would ever be ready to surrender, but a part of me couldn't deny that there was some good in the universe, and I had to change. Tim had been right the other morning. I needed to return Tamara's stolen car. I needed to finally confront my past. Maybe if I took the steps to right my wrongs, pay my penance, I could be free. Maybe I, Dakota Jensen, too could be a part of the good in the universe. Maybe.

CHAPTER 37

January 3, 4:15 p.m.

TAMARA

I wiped the steam from the mirror and took in my reflection. Shelby would be here any minute with an array of clothes for me to wear tonight. Hopefully, she'd bring an outfit that wasn't too ... Shelby. Nervousness rattled my insides as I thought of my evening with Joe. I prayed tonight would go better than this morning. Though being with Joe had been wonderful. He'd been a gentleman and laughed on cue at my jokes, but I could feel his pain beneath the surface, and there didn't seem to be a way to cut through.

The doorbell rang, and Charlie answered it. I wrapped a towel around me and scurried to the bedroom. Shelby followed behind me, a pile of clothes slung over her arm and a couple of pairs of shoes in the other hand. She was dressed modest, in dark skinny jeans and a white shirt, make-up understated, opposite of how she normally wore it. Perfect for the role she was playing this evening.

"Thank you for helping me tonight."

She set the clothes on the bed and turned to me. "Absolutely, chica." She picked up a shimmering purple dress off the bed. Or was it a shirt? It didn't have much material to it. "Now, I personally think you should go with this one."

Laughing, I shook my head. "I would never wear that. Not tonight. Or ever."

"Fine." She threw the dress aside and grabbed the next one. "I thought you were trying to win this Joe guy back. That dress would definitely do it."

I rolled my eyes. "It's not me, Shelby, and you know it."

She threw a cheesy grin. "Suit yourself. What about this one?" It was white and flowy with a floral print.

"It's better."

"More like boring. I stole it from my mom's closet."

"It's more me than that one. What else you got?"

She lifted the last one—a classic form-fitting black dress. It was a little shorter than I usually went for, but I'd make it work. "That's the one."

She squealed and clapped her hands together. "You're going to be so hot! Can I do your make-up?"

"Not happening."

Her bottom lip protruded into a goofy pout. "You're no fun sometimes."

"Yeah, well, you're too much fun sometimes, so there's that. Now give me a few minutes to get dressed. I'll meet you in the living room in fifteen minutes."

"You mean I have to hang with Charlie?" She paused dramatically, lifting her hand in the air, palm forward. "By myself? Eww."

"It will only be a few minutes. Go see if he needs help."

She sauntered to the door with an attitude. "Girl, you owe me one."

"Yeah, right."

After she left, I dropped the towel and put on my underwear before slipping the dress over my head. It was a tad loose around the chest but other than that, it fit like a glove.

A half-hour later, I emerged from the bedroom, wearing the black dress and red stilettos, hair and make-up done to perfection.

Charlie's house had been redecorated for the evening. He and

Shelby had pushed the couch back to make room for the dining table and strung white twinkle lights across the ceiling for ambiance. The table was nicely set for two with champagne glasses and a tapered candle in the middle of it. The smells coming from the kitchen were amazing. Grilled meat, garlic, and another aroma I couldn't pinpoint.

Charlie walked out of the kitchen, Shelby trailing him. "Dang, girl! Looking good! Hey, if things don't work out with you and Joe tonight, I'm so getting your number." He winked with a chuckle.

My face warmed. Shelby smacked Charlie, something I would have done if I were closer to him.

"You are looking hot in my dress," Shelby said.

"This place is amazing, guys. Seriously, thank you both for doing this." There was only one thing I forgot. I returned to the room and retrieved the pregnancy test that I'd wrapped in a small box yesterday. I slipped it in my purse to give to Joe at the right moment.

The doorbell rang, and Charlie and Shelby both bolted into the kitchen. Overhead, light music began to play. I smiled on the way to the door. Charlie had certainly thought of everything down to the last detail. I opened the door, and Joe stood in front of me wearing dark jeans and a light blue oxford, sleeves rolled to mid-arm. He held a single long stem red rose.

My heart melted. He was seriously the most perfect man ever created. He handed me the rose. "I wish I could give you more."

I brought the flower to my nose and inhaled deeply. "It's perfect. Thank you. Come in."

He peered around the room, his gaze landing on the table. "What's this?"

"Surprise," I said, in a sing-song voice, smiling.

His eyes met mine, and it seemed like he was really seeing me for the first time today. For a moment, he looked at me the way he used to, appraising me from head to toe. "You're breathtaking."

Heat swirled in my stomach, working its way to my face. I

wanted to reach for him and pull him close, to kiss him like I used to. I swear I could see the same desire in his eyes.

He peeked around me at the table. "You did this?"

I grinned sheepishly. "I had some help from a few friends. Come and sit. Dinner is almost ready."

Mock horror lit Joe's face. "You didn't cook, did you?"

"Oh, come on. You know me better than that."

He chuckled. We both sat. As if on cue, Shelby walked into the room with a bottle of sparkling cider. "Hello. My name is Shelby, and I'll be your server tonight."

Joe's eyes practically bulged out of their sockets. I probably should have warned him that we were friends again, but that subject never came up today.

Shelby poured us both a glass of cider. "Your salads will be ready in a few minutes. What sort of dressing do you prefer?"

Joe leaned back in his seat, amusement lighting his face. "Let's see. Does this establishment have blue cheese?"

"As a matter of fact, I believe we do," she said with a flirtatious smirk.

"I'll take ranch." I shot her a glare.

"You got it." She left as abruptly as she had come.

Joe leaned in and spoke quietly. "Was that who I think it was?"

"Yep. We made up on New Year's. Whose dress do you think this is?"

His eyebrows lifted. "Well, this night is full of surprises."

He had no idea. The biggest surprise was yet to come.

CHAPTER 38

January 3, 6:00 p.m.

JOE

My heart and mind were locked in a battle. Sitting across from Tamara, with her smiling warmly at me, and wearing that dress, caused the good memories to surface. Yet this last month our love had been tried in the furnace, leaving me worn and battle-scarred. Again, I ignored the heartache and focused on Tamara's face glowing in the candlelight. I wasn't sure if she'd ever looked so beautiful.

After the salads, Shelby brought us two plates with ribeye steaks and loaded baked potatoes. It was delicious. Charlie was probably the master chef behind the curtain. Tamara certainly couldn't make a steak like this. At the end of the meal, Charlie and Shelby delivered a small chocolate cake with a candle in the middle of it and we sang happy birthday to Tamara.

She laughed and blew out the candles. Shelby set the cake between us with two clean forks. I stood to shake Charlie's hand. "Nice to meet you. You did an excellent job with the food."

He extended his hand. "Thanks. It's great to meet you too." Charlie turned to Tamara and smiled. "But we're going to leave to give you two some time alone."

Tamara stood and gave them both a hug. "Thank you. You

both are awesome. Are you sure you don't want some of the cake?"

"I'm more in the mood for a Cosmo." Shelby winked as she opened the door. "You both have a great night."

As soon as the door closed, Tamara returned to her seat. "This part wasn't planned by me."

I sat as well. "You have some great friends."

"Yes, they are certainly amazing." She grabbed a fork and took a bite of the cake. "Mmmm. So good. You gotta have some."

I patted my belly. "I don't know. I'm pretty full."

"Come on, babe. Help me eat it."

My heart fumbled over the word 'babe.' That was the first time she had used a term of endearment like that since I had been here. I brushed off the feeling and reached for the fork.

She took another bite and set the fork next to the plate. "There's something I need to tell you."

I stopped eating mid-chew, pulse quickening.

She stretched her hand across the table, reaching for mine. I hesitated, beholding the ring she still wore, and then folded my hand around hers. They were cold. They were always so cold.

She hesitated before she spoke, searching my face. "I want you to know how truly sorry I am. I know how much I hurt you when I left like I did."

I swallowed hard. Images of me drinking alone in my apartment a few days before Christmas feeling completely abandoned swept over me. Then the thought of Sadie kissing me at Hailey's party made me sick.

"It didn't hurt me, Tamara. It crushed me," I said, voice hoarse.

She came to me and knelt. "I'm so sorry. I've had a lot of time to think, and I can clearly see the things I did wrong. I am sorry for being impulsive and not listening to what you needed. I forced you to make decisions you weren't ready to make, and I wasn't supportive of your dreams. I am truly sorry, Joe. I want you to know things are going to be different. Going forward, I promise to let you into every decision."

It was difficult to believe the words. I wanted to. I really did. But things had gotten so out of control, and she hadn't taken my feelings into consideration at all. I wanted this change, but was the promise of it enough?

"I know you feel like I chose my family over you. And maybe in some ways I did. It was really messed up and confusing. I hope it's not too late to say I choose you now. Because, Joseph Michael Phillips, you have been the absolute best part of my life. I love you with my whole being and I always will."

I willed myself to believe her words. "I love you too, T."

"I have one more surprise for you." She stood, went to her purse and retrieved a small rectangular gift. She moved her chair around the table close to me and handed me the gift before sitting.

What would fit in a box this size? Had she gotten me jewelry? "What is this? I'm the one who's supposed to be giving you things today."

She pressed the gift against my chest. "Open it."

I tore off the wrapping and opened the box. A slender stick with two pink lines? My head snapped up to meet her gaze.

"You're pregnant?"

She nodded, tears welling in her eyes. "You're going to be a dad, Joe."

A father? I was going to be a dad? Tamara was pregnant with *my* baby. A truckload of emotions landed in my gut.

"How long have you known?"

She shook her head. "Only since yesterday morning. I would have told you before, but I wanted to tell you in person. I wanted to make it special."

The air was sucked out of the room. I didn't know how to feel or what to say. This last year, when she'd been pregnant with Hope, I'd wished a thousand times that the baby she carried was mine.

"The crazy thing is, the other day, God reminded me that he promised me before I gave up Hope, he'd give me more children in the future, with you. I had no clue when he reminded me that, that I was already pregnant. And you're here, and it feels like we're getting on track. It feels like the beginning of promises being fulfilled. That means that the other stuff God said could happen too."

My head spun along with a twinge of panic. There was still a ton for us to work through. Even with the pregnancy, I didn't know where we stood. I hadn't had a chance to tell her about my failures. Would she see me the same way once I did?

"What other stuff exactly?"

"I don't know. Mostly family restoration, and I did see a vision of my dad walking me down the aisle."

The thought repulsed me. After everything he did to her, she wanted him to be a part of our wedding? "You can't be serious. I can't keep doing this, Tamara. You say you choose me, but then you want him at our wedding?"

"I'm not sure that I do. I only know what I saw. And I do want healing for him. I want restoration for my whole family."

"At what cost though?"

"I'm sorry, Joe. I'm not trying to upset you. I'm sharing my heart with you. I'm not planning to do anything, okay. I just want things to be right with *us*. As far as I'm concerned, you're number one. You are my family, Joe." She took hold of my hand and placed it on her stomach. "I don't want to do anything else to jeopardize that." The fear in her countenance just about undid me.

I swallowed the lump forming in my throat. "Listen, Tamara, I'm sorry. I didn't mean to freak out, but I can't keep doing this anymore. I'm not as strong as you think I am. In fact, I'm weaker than you could possibly imagine."

Tears stung my eyes again. Tamara looked at me like ... I don't know, like I was some sort of superhero. Like I could handle anything that she threw at me, but if I were a superhero, she'd be my kryptonite. I swallowed again and caressed her abdomen. It was time to tell her the truth.

"If you had told me you were carrying my child a month ago, I would have been the happiest man alive. I would have believed that every one of my dreams were coming true. But I'm not sure if I have what it takes to be a good dad or a good provider."

She ran her hand over my shoulder. "You're going to be a great dad, Joe."

For a brief moment, her touch comforted me. I braced myself with a long inhale and locked my gaze with hers. "You don't understand. When you left, I fell down. Hard. I went on a bender a couple times. Then at one of my lowest points I went to a party and let one of Caleb's friends kiss me. It meant nothing, and I hate myself for being so weak." I stayed quiet for a long moment, staring at her beautiful face.

Her intense green eyes were sad, but they were steadfast. "That doesn't define you. You are not your mistakes. You're the one who taught me that."

I hung my head. "I can't be strong anymore."

"You don't have to be strong. Let me be strong for you for a change." She stood but kept hold of my hand.

I rose along with her. She turned toward me and drew me to her, holding me like that for a long time in silence. The barrier I had placed between us started to melt. I caressed her shoulders and arms with tenderness like I used to. After a few minutes, she pulled away. "I want you to know that you don't have to be strong for me all the time. I'm sorry that I ever made you feel like you had to."

I stroked the side of her cheek. "I want to be strong for you."

"I know, but it doesn't change my feelings for you. I love you as much when you feel weak as when you feel strong." She placed my hand over my heart.

Why was it so hard to let go of my mistakes?

"Can I pray for you?"

I nodded. Her connection with God seemed stronger than mine had lately.

"Dear Father, I ask for your help in this moment. I pray that you would overwhelm Joe with your love. Lord, please show him it's okay to be weak. Show him that you love him in his weakness even more than I do."

As Tamara prayed, thoughts of the dream I had a little over a month ago circled my mind. Her splashing in the waves with our children. My little boy running to me arms wide open, begging me to pick him up. The feeling of peace I'd received from the dream flooded over me. Having a family and giving them my love was my greatest desire.

Tamara quieted, and the atmosphere in the room grew with the intense love I felt. "I keep hearing a phrase in my head," she said in reverence after a long moment.

"What is it?"

"He sets the lonely in families."

Her words shot to the center of my being, causing the dream to become more vivid. Tears fell down my face.

"What's God saying to you, Joe?"

I kept my eyes closed and spoke. "I'm seeing a picture of the dream I had after we slept together. The one of us on the beach with two children."

"He sets the lonely in families," she said again with the same reverential awe. "I think that's his promise to you, Joe."

"Yeah, maybe." I opened my eyes and peered at her face. It had this subtle glow to it that hadn't been there before. Was it the pregnancy?

She wiped the tears from my face again. "We're going to get through this, Joe. We're going to be stronger than before."

"I want to believe that, but even with all this, I still feel broken." I paused for a moment to find the right words to communicate my feelings without hurting her. "In some ways, it doesn't make sense. Our two promises almost seem contrary to each other."

"How so?"

"I mean the stuff with your family. I know how important it is to you, but, Tamara, our whole world busted apart at the seams because of Dakota. And I'm not sure where I stand. I don't want to force you to choose. But maybe that's because I'm afraid you'll choose them again."

She took hold of both of my hands. "I choose you, Joe. You're the one I can't live without." She placed my hands on her belly again. "It's always going to be you. You are my family. I see that now."

CHAPTER 39

January 4, 7:15 a.m.

JOE

I woke with a heavy heart, not sure what to do. I wanted to do the right thing for Tamara and the baby. I wanted to be a good father. I wanted to be the man she thought I was. More than any of that, I wanted to believe God could work all this out the way it was supposed to be. I threw on a hoodie, jeans, and tennis shoes and headed outside for a run.

As I ran on the beach, thoughts bombarded me, swirling around in a tangled mess, impossible to make sense of. Why would God make me a father now when I was so broken? What if I couldn't do this? What if the pressure became too much and I started drinking again? I never had a father growing up. How was I to be a good one?

And what about Tamara? Could I actually make her choose after everything she'd been through? As much as I wanted her to drop her family and come home with me, that didn't seem fair. Why did this have to be so complicated? I loved Tamara with my whole heart. She was carrying my child. We were engaged. This should be as simple as breathing, but there was so much more wrapped into it, and for some reason, I couldn't let the past month go.

The wind stirred around me as I ran toward the ocean. The weather was cold like it had been, but sunny with blue skies. Within a few minutes, I was at the beach, watching the swell of the ocean as the waves came and pull back. It was no wonder Tamara loved this place. The vastness of the ocean had a way of putting life into perspective. I wasn't sure what the answers were, but watching the raw power of the waves spoke to me of the greatness of God. It was he who gave boundaries to the water. It was he who had spoken this into existence. Surely, he could figure out my life.

Do you trust me?

The question stung as much as it brought comfort. My whole life I'd been taught that God was trustworthy, first by Mom, and then by other people I loved, like Levi and David. But lately, with the events surrounding me, it had become difficult to believe.

I want to, Lord ... I do. It's just been so hard. So painful.

A gust of wind blew across my face, bringing with it the briny smell of saltwater.

Son, give me the pain.

I dropped to my knees in the sand.

I don't know how.

I closed my eyes. In my mind, I saw a picture of a giant set of hands reaching to me from the sky—hands that were big enough to carry the whole world. I began putting the things that had hurt over the last month into them. First, the insanity of what had happened in Quilcene, Trudy nearly dying, then sleeping with Tamara. I paused for a long time on the diner, realizing that in purchasing the place, I, in my own way, had been trying to take control of the situation. Our lives had been spinning, but instead of surrendering and trusting God with our future, I'd taken matters into my own hands. Exactly like Hailey had said at her party.

"God, please forgive me. I'm sorry for trying to control our lives and not trusting you." I remembered then that Tamara had warned me. She told me she didn't think it was a good idea to buy the diner. In fact, she'd been quite adamant about it. Yet I'd plowed forward despite her reservations. I had done the same thing to her that she had done to me. *I'm sorry, God.*

My son, give me the shame.

A horrible feeling burnt my guts until I yielded the mistakes to him. Then I gave him the other stuff. The diner burning, almost losing Tamara, and the next morning when she had abandoned me.

"I forgive her for that, Lord, and I forgive Dakota too. I release both of them to you."

Tears fell down my cheeks as I saw a truckload of pain placed into the giant hands. I no longer felt shackled by it like I had. Images of that night came when I found myself at the liquor store and then letting Sadie kiss me. Another round of shame berated my soul.

Forgive yourself, my son, for I have forgiven you.

I hung my head. I didn't know how. Why could I forgive everyone else, but not myself?

"God, help me!" I cried as the pressure grew.

Let it go.

"Yes, Father." I choked on the words. "I forgive myself for drinking. I forgive myself for hurting Tamara. I let go of my shame. I give it to you. I put my trust in you. Have your way in my life. I surrender." Another layer of heaviness broke off my heart. For the first time in at least a month, I felt like myself again. I raised my hands in the air and shouted for freedom's sake. I didn't know what the future held. I was unsure of the right move, but at that moment, the only thing that mattered was the connection I had found with God again.

I opened my eyes and looked around at the empty beach. As I did, a strange sensation overwhelmed my entire body. This was the beach from my dreams. The beach where our lives were supposed to be.

Suddenly and sharply, my whole world came into focus, and a feeling of deja vu wrapped around me. I had been here before, though I hadn't. Could it be that Tamara had been on the right path from the beginning? Could it be that this was where we were destined to live?

CHAPTER 40

January 4, 9:10 a.m.

TAMARA

I folded another pair of jeans and placed them into my duffel bag. After last night, one thing was certain. Joe needed to know that I was fully in with him. I needed him to know that I absolutely one hundred percent chose him. I wasn't sure what would happen with my family, but at least I could say that I tried to be a part of their lives again. For now, I had to surrender that fight and resume my life with Joe.

Father, I give my family to you. I trust you with the fulfillment of your promises. Thoughts of my dad, beaming, full of pride as he walked me down the aisle toward Joe, played through my head. That seemed impossible at this point, and me leaving with Joe made it even harder.

I folded a sweater and stuffed it into the bag. That was okay. They had my number. They knew I had tried. At least my mom knew I was safe and that I loved her.

I took hold of my brother's ashes and stared at them for a long time. Why hadn't I at least told them about Gabriel? No matter if they wanted me in their lives or not, they deserved to know. Maybe I could meet with Mom on the way through Aberdeen and tell her. I set the ashes aside. Unsure.

A knocking at the door brought me out of my thoughts. I

rushed across the room and opened the door. Joe stood in the doorway, appearing fresh, with a lightness in his countenance that hadn't been there yesterday. He stepped in, pulled me into him, and lifted me, spinning me around.

Joy surged through my entire being. Something had changed between last night and today. Something big. "Good morning to you too," I said through a laugh as he set me on the floor.

"There is so much I have to tell you." He cupped his hands around my face, searching my gaze, eyes deepening with emotion. "But first I need to do one thing." His lips came to mine so softly with a tenderness I felt in the core of my being. I melted into him, sliding my hands around his neck, pulling him closer. It had been way too long since he'd touched me like this, but none of the chemistry had faded between us. If anything, it had only intensified, like gasoline on fire. He withdrew his lips from mine after a few minutes and rested his forehead on mine the way he had the first time he kissed me.

"I love you," he whispered.

"I love you more."

He tenderly caressed my arms, sending shivers through my body. "Not possible."

We stood like that for a while, feeling the comfort of each other's embrace.

"I could stay like this the whole day," Joe said.

"Me too." I smiled at him.

He brought his hand to my cheek again, tracing the length of my face. "I'm sorry for my part in this."

I shook my head. "This was my fault, Joe."

"That's not true. I'm as guilty as you were. I didn't really ever support you in finding your family." He drew away from our embrace. "And I completely ignored your feelings when it came to buying the diner."

I placed my hand on his chest, heart sorrowful. "No, Joe, don't do that. I knew it was your dream, and I should have supported you."

The corners of his lips lowered as his eyebrows pinch together. "You don't understand, Tamara. You were right. I was afraid and tried to control the situation. Things had gotten crazy, and instead of trusting God, I took matters into my own hands. And when the diner burnt down, I blamed Dakota and you for ruining my dreams. I hardened myself toward you because of my own need to be in control. I'm so sorry, Tamara. Please forgive me."

"I do. I love you more than you could possibly know." I weaved my hand through his and tugged him to my room. "You see this." I pointed at my packed bag. "I'm going home with you if you'll have me. I choose you, Joe."

"No, Tamara. You can't do that."

Confusion and sadness worked through me. "You don't want me to come with you?"

He placed his hands on both sides of me. "I'm not saying that. Of course, I want you with me every second of every day. It's just, I no longer want you to choose. I believe you need to do what you came here to do."

"But it hurt you so much. We almost lost each other because of it."

"A big part of that is because I wasn't trusting God with you. I was holding on so tight because I feared losing you. But, Tamara, I think you've been on the right track from the beginning. I had this moment on the beach with God." A distant look filled his eyes as if he saw something in the horizon that I couldn't. "Tamara, he showed me that this was the beach from my dream. I know it sounds crazy, but when I saw it, everything came into focus. This is where we're supposed to be. This is where we're meant to end up."

What was he saying? I couldn't quite wrap my mind around it. Ocean Shores had been my favorite town on the planet before it became a place of sorrow, but that didn't matter anymore. I'd forgiven Shelby and Danny too, for that matter.

"The other day, you said you had a list of promises. Could you show me that list?" Joe asked.

"Absolutely." I walked across the room and snatched the journal Joe had given to me a little over a month ago. I flipped it open to the first page before handing it to him.

He scanned the list, eyes misting over. "I never want to stand in the way of the things God has put inside you, Tamara. From this moment on, I want to champion you and stand with you believing these promises will be fulfilled."

His words were so earnest and sincere, they found me breathless, and it took a few moments to find words to say. "That's wonderful, Joe. Thank you."

"Your promises are my promises, and my promises are yours. Do you have a pen?"

I found a pen in my purse and handed it to him.

Underneath my list of promises he wrote.

Own our own business
Have two beautiful children
Have a healthy marriage full of love and vibrancy.

After Joe made his additions, he held me, letting the love we shared weave the broken pieces of our relationship together once more. For that moment, we were perfect again. We were whole. My heart was so full, I felt like it might explode. I didn't know how God would fulfill some of these, but we were now both on the same path to discover that together.

CHAPTER 41

January 5, 9:50 a.m.

DAKOTA

I stole my sister's car after she opened her home to me and forgave me for what I did to Gabriel.

As I stared at the last line I'd written, my insides twisted and turned into knots. I chewed my inner lip, trying to push down the sick feeling.

The past few days, I had read almost the whole book of Narcotics Anonymous. The more I read, the surer I was that I needed to face Tamara, to let her know how sorry I truly was. I hadn't fully worked through Steps Two and Three, but I'd been trying. For someone like me, learning to surrender to a higher power could take my whole life. So, I decided to skip to Step Four. Making a searching and fearless moral inventory of ourselves. This step had been torture as I confessed my wrongdoings on to a yellow slip of notepad paper. Well, more like both sides of three pieces, but who was counting? For some reason, that last line hurt me the most.

For years, I had hated Tamara for leaving me like she did. I'd judged her as a coward for running away, but in reality, her leaving had been my fault. She'd done the best she could under the circumstances. Pressure grew in me as I thought of the years of each other's lives we'd missed because of my mistakes. And now I had gone and done it again. I had driven a wedge between us by stealing her ring. But she had forgiven me for taking her ring, right? She even forgave me for Gabriel. Surely, the car would mean less than either of those two things.

"Dakota," Sage called through my door and knocked three times.

I glanced at the line one last time and stood. "Come in."

She entered. "Looks like Ray's done with the car."

I glanced at the piece of paper, feeling that strange peace I'd felt in the woods. Was it a sign?

So dumb.

I shook my head. I didn't recognize these new thoughts. I'd been so used to the foggy haze the drugs had brought from the bitterness of life. Without them, I could see myself thinking differently, feeling differently. Whether it was a sign or not, taking Tamara's car to her was the right thing to do.

"What have you been doing?" Sage glanced over my shoulder.

"Step Four."

"That's a rough one." She shook her head and blew out a low whistle. "Staring your crap in the face is never easy."

"Yeah, I feel like it's time for me to go and face my sister."

"That sounds like a great step in the right direction. I'm proud of you, Dakota."

Her words felt strange. I didn't think I'd ever heard them before. I gave her a half-smile. "Thanks. I appreciate the help you've given me."

She reached her arms toward me, offering a hug. I hesitated and then stepped into her embrace. "You're welcome." She held on for a few seconds and broke away. "When were you thinking?"

"I'm mostly packed. I think it's time."

"You want a bite to eat before you leave? We have that leftover Chicken Marsala."

Tempting. That was one thing I'd surely miss—Sage's

cooking. "I know myself. I need to get going before I talk myself out of it."

Sage agreed, and twenty minutes later, I was packed and driving toward Redding. Overwhelming gratitude hit me as I left Sage's driveway. She had gone above and beyond for me over the last ten days, even after Tim left. Yearning worked through me at the thought of his name. We hadn't spoken since he left except for a few short texts. It was easier that way. I turned on the radio and adjusted the dial to a classic rock station.

For the next ten miles I stayed on 299 East, then I wove through Redding before hitting I-5 North. I stomped the accelerator once I hit the freeway and tried not to dwell on what lay ahead.

How would Tamara react when I got there? What had happened after I left that morning? What if me stealing her car was the last straw, especially after the fire? I had seen the way Romeo had looked at me after what had happened that night. He'd tolerated my presence for Tamara's sake, but really, he hated my guts.

I accelerated and merged to pass. I had to stop thinking like this. I had to control my thoughts, or they would control me. "God grant me the serenity," I said and cringed. Praying didn't feel right to me. With my own strength I would end these thoughts. I could do this on my own.

Who was I kidding? The only thing I'd ever been able to do was to get high.

For hours, I struggled around the same thoughts: Tamara, sobriety, God, and the devastation and sorrow in between. When I'd been on the farm with Sage, life felt easier, sobriety felt easier. But like she said, I hadn't been tested yet. Was this my first test? Because if it was, I was failing miserably.

A hundred miles into Oregon, I glanced up and saw a big billboard advertising a casino a few miles ahead on Exit 99. A huge part of me wanted to say screw it—to pull off there and spend the remainder of my money getting so wasted I wouldn't have to think of the mess my life had become for at least five hours.

No.

I wouldn't do it. I would stay strong. I would stay sober. Thoughts of a double shot of Stoley's going down my throat caused my fingers to clench around the steering wheel. It would be only one drink. Ha. Yeah, right. It was never one drink. It was always the whole bottle. Just like it was never one line.

When Exit 99 came, the part that had guided me most of my life took over, and I swung off, no longer in control. I pulled into the casino and parked, pulse racing. What was I doing? It had only been twelve days since I quit, but trashing even one sober day felt costly.

What does it matter? You'll never truly be free.

The thoughts were right. I was incapable of change. I inhaled deeply and shut off the car. I went through the motions of getting out and locking it behind me.

This isn't right. What about Tim? And Tamara ...

I took a few steps forward, the battle in my mind raging.

Screw them. Screw the whole world for that matter. None of it matters.

As I stepped into the building, I thought of the last time I'd been at the casino. That's when things had begun to change. That night, Tim had saved me from Ryan's cronies and then later from Lisa.

Lights from the slot machine beckoned me, and I shook off the memory. Tim and I were over before we even began.

I love you, Dakota.

His voice hit my thoughts as I stepped forward to the quarter machine and stared.

"Can I get you a drink, hun?"

I turned toward the voice. A dark-haired cocktail waitress with kind green eyes stood in front of me. She reminded me a bit of Tamara.

We can be the change in our family.

My heart hammered against my rib cage. I couldn't keep doing this. The only way out of the darkness was to meet it head on. Turning, I ran from the casino to Tamara's car. I climbed into the car and stuck the key into the ignition. I turned the key. A loud grinding sound filled the air. *No.*

I turned it again. The same noise. *No! No! No!* This stupid, no good, piece of crap car! I hit the steering wheel, cursing. "God!" I punched the seat. "Please help! I need help!" I turned my focus to the casino. In my mind's eye, I saw the gang of demons sitting on top of the building taunting me, beckoning me to come play. I turned my head to ignore them. "I don't want to do this anymore, God. I want to change. But I need help!"

CHAPTER 42

January 5, 2:30 p.m.

TAMARA

Joe and I snuggled on the couch in his room at the bed-and-breakfast. One of his arms rested around my shoulder, and his opposite hand gently caressed my stomach as if he was loving on the precious life growing inside. "How is it the longer that I'm with you, the more I feel like myself?" Joe whispered, his voice tender.

"'Cause I'm your other half." I said, joy overwhelming me. I'd been ecstatic when he'd decided to stay another night. After the trials of the last month and the separation, having this time of quiet with him felt healing to my soul. The longer he held me, the deeper I could feel God embrace us both and the more whole I felt.

"Yeah," he said after a few thoughtful beats, moving his hand sweetly over my belly. "What do you think we have in here?"

"Hopefully, a healthy baby with all its fingers and toes." I placed my hand over his.

"I think it's a girl," he said.

I thought of Hope and my niece, Ivy. I liked the idea of having a girl. Not that I could ever replace Hope, but it would be great to have the chance to raise a daughter of my own. "I hope you're right."

He kissed my cheek and his lips lingered near my face. "I need to talk to you about something. What would you think about me putting my house on the market?"

I lifted my head, my brain hiccupping. I loved Joe's house. For so long, I'd imagined living there with him. I couldn't see it any other way.

"Do you think that's a good idea with everything that's going on in Vancouver?"

He tilted his head from side to side, seeming to weigh my words. "With the diner gone, I have no job to keep me there, and most of the insurance stuff can be dealt with remotely. I know there is a lot to consider. I was awake half the night thinking on it."

I nodded and tried to hide my panic as my mind worked through his words. "It feels like a big step."

His smile was a bit rueful. "It is, but for me, it feels like a step of faith. Besides, it makes the most financial sense. From what I understand, it's a seller's market right now. When I borrowed the money for the diner, the house appraised for two hundred seventy-nine thousand. My loan was for eighty-five percent of that."

"And that means what exactly?" Math certainly wasn't my strong suit, and my pregnancy brain and the stress of this new idea made it worse.

"It means that if I sold it for what it's worth, I'd turn a thirty-grand profit. That would be enough to see us through for a while until we figure out housing and jobs here."

I let that sink in for a minute. "Sounds like you've really thought it through."

"I have. And on top of that, I want to be here with you while you sort through things with your family."

I rested my head against him and considered his words. Having that kind of influx of cash would be helpful, and I could let go of the idea of living in his house if it meant him being here with me now.

"If that's what you want to do, I support you."

"So, you feel okay about it?"

"For the most part."

"Okay," he said, slowly nodding his head. "Tomorrow when I head home, I'll get ahold of a realtor."

Anxiety swirled in my core. Deep down, I knew things would be fine, but there were a ton of moving parts. It was hard not to be a bit nervous, especially with a little one on the way.

"It will be all right. I'm sure Charlie will keep me working if need be." In fact, I was on the schedule for tomorrow night.

Joe stiffened. "I don't want you bearing that load. And I sure as heck don't want Charlie to be taking care of you."

I met Joe's gaze. Was he jealous of Charlie?

"Babe," I said softly, seeing for the first time how hard it had been for him that I kept turning to Charlie for help. "I can quit Midways and find another place to stay until our wedding."

Having to pay for another place would seriously dip into our wedding fund, but I was pretty sure I'd do anything he asked me at the moment. I cringed inwardly at the thought. I hadn't told him I'd used the wedding fund yet.

"No, it's not like that." He brought his hand to my face, tenderly tracing my jaw. "I trust you, and I want you to work if you want to, but I want to be the one who takes care of you, of our family."

Joe brought his lips to mine, sweetly lingering there for a few minutes.

"I do like working for now, but I love that you want to take care of me. You will have plenty of opportunities for that when our baby comes."

"Looking forward to it." He kissed me again.

I leaned away from him. He was the sweetest ever. Sometimes I couldn't believe how lucky I was to have him in my life.

"In full honesty, I do need to tell you something. I've borrowed from the wedding fund a few times since being here. I have been working on repaying it, but this trip got more expensive than I hoped. I'm sorry." It hurt how many times I've been having to apologize lately.

He drew farther from me, a question in his features. "How much?"

"I'm not sure. A few hundred." Maybe more.

Joe opened the bank app on his phone. "Wow, okay."

I peered over his shoulder, and my stomach tightened. The balance was lower than I thought it would be.

He quietly stared at the screen for a few minutes. "Okay, thank you for telling me."

"Are you upset?"

"A little, but it will be all right. Even if we have to go a little lower budget for our wedding."

He was right. We still had a little more than two thousand in the account, and at least another month to add to it. "I am surprised you are taking this so well."

He swiped away the bank app and turned to me. "There is too much stuff going on at the moment to sweat the small stuff."

Across the room, on Joe's nightstand, my phone rang. I considered ignoring it, but it could be important. I slowly withdrew from him, stood and walked across the room. I picked up the phone, focusing on the screen. A Washington phone number. I accepted the call and brought it to my ear.

"Hello."

"Tamara?"

Dakota. My heart jolted at her voice, and I turned to Joe. I was ready to hear from her, but was he? "Yes." Silently, I prayed this would be good news.

"I bet you didn't expect to hear from me." Same old sarcasm.

My grip tightened around my phone. "I didn't. Are you okay?"

"I know you probably hate me for taking your car. It was a terrible thing to do. I was just so screwed up in the head. I mean the fire and you wanting me to face Mom and Dad with the truth.

I wasn't ready." Her words poured out fast like a fire hose on full blast.

"It's okay, Dakota. Calm down."

Across the room, Joe shot up in his seat at full alert. I put the phone on speaker. If he heard what Dakota said, we'd be able to have a more informed conversation regarding it. From now on, each decision I made concerning my family would be thoroughly discussed with him.

"Don't tell me to calm down. Not right now. I need to say this."

Joe's eyes narrowed, and my heart dropped. He hadn't heard the rest of her apology.

"I know it's not long, but I've been sober for twelve days. I stayed the holidays with Tim and his aunt."

"You've been in Quilcene this whole time?"

A beat of silence. "No, I've been in Whiskeytown, California."

I gaped at the phone, disbelieving. California? She drove my car to California? Joe crossed the room and placed his warm hand on the small of my back.

"I've been reading this Narcotics Anonymous book and trying to work the steps."

"Trying to?" That didn't sound promising.

She exhaled an exasperated breath. "Yeah. They want me to surrender to a higher power and make a list of my wrongs."

Joe's features held a sad thoughtful expression.

"It sucks, but, Tamara, it's made me realize how awful I've been. I wanted to make things right and bring your car to you, but per usual, the universe is screwing with me."

"I'm sorry, Dakota, but I'm not following."

She let out another deep sigh, or she could have been smoking. I couldn't tell. "I'm trying to tell you that I was bringing your car to you, but it broke down. I swear, Tamara, this thing is a complete dog turd. This is the third time it's broken down on me."

I had no idea what to say. My first reaction was to offer to rescue her, but how would Joe feel with that choice? "Could you hold on a sec?"

"Err, sure."

I tapped the mute button to talk to Joe. "What do you think? I know she's put us through a lot, but should we go get her?"

A silent war raged behind his deep hazel eyes. "I don't know. She sounds sincere, but you never know. And we may need to tow your car back to Vancouver. Ask her where she is."

I nodded and clicked on the volume. "Where are you?"

"I'm not sure. I'm in the parking lot of a casino in Oregon. I took Exit 99."

Joe and I exchanged a glance, and an electric current went through me. Was he thinking the same thing I was? It had to be more than a coincidence that she pulled off on that exit. "Hold on again."

An irritated sigh came through the line. "Fine. Whatever."

I muted the phone again. "Can we go get her? I have a good feeling about this. I'm sure Charlie knows someone with a car trailer."

"Absolutely. This suddenly feels like a God thing."

"Be careful. You're sounding a lot like David." I winked at him with a smile.

"That's not such a bad thing, is it?"

"Not at all."

I shot Charlie a text and unmuted the call. "Joe and I are going to come get you, but it's going to take a while. We're in Ocean Shores."

"Ocean Shores? What are you doing there?"

I made eye contact with Joe again, searching for guidance. How much should I divulge if she was struggling with her sobriety? Joe shook his head slightly, which I interpreted as to keep it brief.

"Just visiting friends," I said and hoped she couldn't hear the lie in my voice.

Joe furrowed his brow with a funny smirk. I shot him a look that said, *Yes, babe, I know I'm a terrible liar.*

"You have friends in Ocean Shores? That's close to Mom and Dad."

I bit my lower lip. "Yeah, they're close."

"So, you've seen them?"

My mouth felt dry. "Yes. But let's discuss that in person."

"Okay ..."

Joe typed on his phone and turned it toward me. His GPS showed a six-hour drive.

"Tell me one thing." Dakota's voice sounded weak. "Do they know?"

The question tore through my heart with a jagged blade, and I focused on the floor. "No. But, Dakota, you sit tight. Joe and I will be there in six hours."

"Six hours? Damn, sis, that could be rough."

"It's the best I can do. I'll see you soon."

I ended the call and saw that Charlie had texted me back. "Good news. Charlie said his uncle would let us borrow his trailer. Are you sure you are okay with this?"

He shrugged, raising his hands in the air. "Dakota and I have had our differences, but this feels right. Plus, it would be good to have your car again."

Grinning, I grabbed my purse and keys off the nightstand. "It's come full circle with this 99 thing, hasn't it?"

"Yeah, it has." Joe smiled while opening the door. I whispered a quick prayer of thankfulness as I followed Joe outside to his Jeep.

As we drove toward Dakota, I kept wondering why she had decided to stop at that exit? Was she stopping there to drink? Or something worse?

CHAPTER 43

January 5, 9:40 p.m.

DAKOTA

I rested my head on the steering wheel, head pounding, skin crawling, a sick nauseous feeling taunting and begging me to go into the casino and drown the pain with vodka. The last few hours had been hell, but I had fought through. I had smoked almost a pack and a half of cigarettes and punched the steering wheel and dashboard until my hands were sore. Perhaps when I had a place of my own, I'd invest in a punching bag. That way, when the battle got too intense, I could release it on the bag.

A jeep with an attached trailer parked beside me and cut the engine. I jolted up. The door opened, and Tamara exited the vehicle. Thank God. I wasn't sure how much longer I could have resisted. I climbed out and she practically pummeled me.

"I'm so glad you called, Dakota." She pulled back, grinning brightly. "Twelve days, huh? I'm so proud of you."

I regarded her, not knowing how to respond. I'd expected a good solid tongue lashing, not a warm hug and beaming pride. There was no questioning it, Tamara was certifiable. Her love for me and those around her made her insane.

Romeo stepped around the vehicle. I braced myself. Was this going to be the whole good cop, bad cop routine? Tamara, for whatever crazy reason, loved me. Romeo didn't.

"Hey, Dakota." His features appeared friendly as he pointed at the car. "Why don't you pop the hood, and we'll see what's wrong with this clunker."

"Hey! Lay off the car, babe. She's treated me well over the years," Tamara said.

I chuckled sarcastically. "Yeah, right. This thing is a piece of junk."

Tamara shot me a playful glare. "It's because she doesn't belong to you. She was like, oh no, you ain't taking me from my girl, Tamara."

Joe nodded with a lighthearted grin. "It's like she was trying to buck you off the saddle, Dakota."

"You guys are nuts." I reached into the car and unlatched the hood.

"What exactly did it do when you tried to start it?" Joe asked

"Nothing. It was like the other times this happened. The mechanic just changed the starter this morning."

Romeo stepped around me, got into the car and turned the key. A clicking sound, but no ignition. He climbed out and lifted the hood, disappearing behind it. Then Tamara did too.

Why wasn't she angry with me? Why wasn't she screaming at me and calling me a horrible person? I sure as hell deserved it. And what about Romeo and the diner situation? Surely, he blamed me for the fire, even if Ryan had been the one who started it. I had been the one who he had a vendetta against. These people were a whole different breed. I lit a smoke and waited, taking in this one familiar vice, the one thing I'd surely never quit. A minute later, the hood slammed shut. I jumped, a tad on edge.

Tamara walked to the driver's side door. "Joe says he thinks it's the alternator. We'll be towing it home to Vancouver."

Romeo brought the Jeep around the front of the car and backed up. Then he got out, walked to the back and we pushed the car onto the trailer.

I took another drag of my cigarette and threw it to the

ground, wishing I had time to finish. It was going to be a long ride.

"You ready?" Tamara asked.

"As I'll ever be."

We climbed in the Jeep and headed north to Portland. Tamara fiddled with the radio and landed on a classic rock station, playing *Sweet Home Alabama*. I relaxed into the seat with a grateful sigh. At least she didn't switch it to the Christian station.

For a while, I zoned out the window, watching as Romeo sped by the other cars. Then the questions began to assail me. What had happened when she met with Mom and Dad? I looked at Tamara in the front seat, quietly holding hands with Romeo. I bit my lip and considered how to broach the subject. Should I talk about our family business in front of him? How much did he know? What details had she shared with him? It didn't matter, I guess. She'd probably tell him whatever I said later anyway.

"Thank you, guys, for coming to rescue me. I really appreciate it."

"I'm glad you called," Tamara said, turning her head.

I looked at the floor, avoiding eye contact. "At least you have your car now."

"You don't get it, do you? I care a hundred times more about you than that stupid car. A vehicle can be replaced. A sister can't. I want you in my life, Dakota."

I bit my lip and focused on a car passing us, resisting the tears that wanted to come. She, like Tim, so easily ripped past my barriers into who I really was—a weak little girl who stopped at nothing to keep people out.

"I'm sorry for taking your car. I'm sorry to you too, Joe, for the diner situation."

He caught my reflection in the mirror. "I forgive you, Dakota." His voice was soft. Kind.

"I don't understand how you both can be so nice."

"I know what it's like to need forgiveness," Joe said, sincerity showing in his features. "I know what it's like to have to face people after hurting them. It's not easy. It took a lot of courage to bring Tamara her car."

I averted my gaze once more. He was absolutely right. Calling Tamara after the damage I'd caused had been one of the hardest things I'd ever done, but there was one thing that would be even harder. Facing the rest of my family with the truth.

"So, Tamara, what happened with Mom and Dad? Why didn't you tell them?"

Tamara and Joe exchanged a glance, and he nodded his head slightly.

Fear struck my guts and slithered around my spine, giving me a nasty round of chills. What weren't they telling me?

"It's been harder than I thought," she said, voice low. "Things didn't go well with Dad from the beginning."

Surprise, surprise.

"Mom was great. I even spent Christmas with Nathan."

"You guys have been there since Christmas?"

Tamara grew quiet and gave Joe another glance before bringing her hand to her chest. "I have."

She went by herself? I couldn't imagine Romeo being comfortable with that. He hadn't wanted her out of his sight after the fire.

"It was wonderful being with the family." Tamara continued her story without explaining. "Even if Dad was being rude and giving backhanded compliments."

"Oh, boy." That definitely sounded like Dad.

"Anyway, I couldn't bring myself to tell them."

"Understandable." I hadn't been able to bring myself to do it ever.

"Do you know what's weird though?" she asked.

"Like everything with our family," I said.

Joe snickered. Tamara didn't appear to find the humor in it.

"Nathan pretty much has this perfect life with his wife, Amanda."

I nodded. I'd only met her one time, but she seemed like a decent person.

"When I spoke of Dad's abuse, he became defensive and told me I was wrong. He insisted Dad never abused us."

"Wow. Can you say denial?" I said, my fingers itching for a cigarette.

"Right? I mean, were we even raised in the same house?"

"That's more common than you would think," Joe interjected, placing a hand on Tamara's. "People construct their own ideas of reality when the actual reality is too hard to bear."

I wish I could have done that. I'd always medicated mine with drugs.

"They generally reject anything that challenges their constructed reality," Joe said.

"That makes sense, I guess," Tamara said. "Dad is in complete denial that he ever abused any of us. He gave me the boot for alluding that there was something I needed to forgive him for."

Frustration stirred in me. I'd been there the night he'd beaten Tamara to a bloody pulp. Those images would never be erased from my consciousness. As much as I tried to numb them with drugs and partying, they were permanently stuck there. "I'm sorry, sis. I know what he did to you."

"I don't know what to do. I had planned on telling him and Mom about Gabriel that night, but instead, he kicked me out and turned Nathan against me. I haven't heard from Mom, so I'm guessing he laid down some sort of edict concerning me."

"I think we need to confront him together," I said before I changed my mind and ran in the opposite direction.

Tamara's head jerked toward me. "What are you saying?"

I swallowed hard, pushing down the fear, then looked her square in the eye. "It's time to face him together."

Panic struck Romeo's face. "What would that accomplish exactly, except making him angry?"

"Yeah, Dakota. I don't want to confront him. I only want to

talk to him. To make him see that he needs to get help so he can be in our lives again."

Why did Tamara have to be so damn forgiving? Didn't she want to see him pay for what he did to her and the rest of the family, because I sure as hell did?

Anger smoldered in my guts, but I shoved it down. "We talk to him then," I said, to smooth things over with Romeo. I didn't know what good it would do, but I was done holding my secrets in. For the moment, I had the courage to face my dad, but I wasn't sure how long that would last.

CHAPTER 44

January 6, 12:12 a.m.

TAMARA

When we got to Joe's house, Dakota settled into the living room for the night. Joe and I went upstairs to his bedroom to have some time to ourselves. The drive home had been a bit tense after Dakota mentioned confronting our dad together. Joe had grown quiet, and I knew that he didn't like the idea. I didn't know how to feel about it, but Dakota seemed determined.

Joe heaved a deep sigh as he sat on the bed.

I stood in the doorway, taking in his weary appearance. "Tell me what you're thinking."

He ran his hands through his hair and sighed again. "I don't like the idea of you going to your dad's by yourself with Dakota. She's sober, but she's still volatile. From what you've told me about your interactions with your dad, it could be a recipe for disaster."

I walked across the room and sat next to him. "I understand where you're coming from. But what's the worst that can happen?"

"Babe, you've told me how abusive your dad is. What if he hit you? Or worse?"

I considered his words, wondering if that were a possibility. I didn't think it was. Sure, my dad had verbally abused my mom our whole life, but he'd never hit her. The only times when he'd been physical with us kids were when we were in trouble. Then the full force of his rage would emerge.

"I don't think that would happen. He's only ever hit us when he was disciplining us when we were kids."

"Tamara ..." He tilted his head to the side, tender concern lining his face. "You told me yourself that he beat you when you were sixteen. I wouldn't consider that being a kid. And didn't he abuse your mom?"

"You're right, but I had lived under his roof. He had seen me as a kid. And with my mom, he'd bully her using fear and intimidation tactics, but he never hit her." Inwardly, I cringed at the minimization in my own words. It seemed that the old adage was true. The abused had a tendency of protecting their abuser.

"I don't know, babe. That sounds like a stretch. I don't want you putting yourself into dangerous situations for the sake of your dysfunctional family. I know you love them, but this feels dangerous." Fear darkened his hazel eyes.

"I hear what you're saying, and I know that I've only ever painted my dad in this ugly way to you." I placed my hand over his. "But underneath that, there is a human being who's in deep bondage. What if I can reach him?"

Worry lines appeared in his forehead. "It's insane to me that after what he did to you and the rest of your siblings, that you'd still want to help him."

He was right on so many levels, but for reasons I didn't comprehend, I couldn't let him go. Yes, he'd hurt me and my family, but he was my dad and a human being who carried his own sorrow. That didn't excuse what he had done. Not by a long shot. But if he could take responsibility for his actions and seek the help he needed, maybe he could be the dad I wanted him to be. "I know. I don't fully understand it, but nobody is beyond redemption, right?"

He pinched the bridge of his nose. "That's true, but you can't just invite him into your life again."

"I'm not. Not without getting the help he needs."

He stayed silent for a few seconds. "Can't you wait for another day so I can go with you? I'd feel better if I were there."

"I honestly think it would be better if it were the two of us for now." I scooted in closer to him and leaned against his shoulder. "But I want to respect your feelings, so if you don't think we should, we will wait."

He slid his hand on my back, and made circles with it, taking his time before he spoke. "No, I trust you. If you feel this is right, I support you. Please promise me though that you will be extremely careful. If you feel the slightest bit of danger or aggression, I want you to leave immediately."

"I will, Joe, I promise."

CHAPTER 45

January 6, 1:00 p.m.

JOE

The Uber parked in front of my house, and I climbed out. Tamara and Dakota were sleeping when I left in the morning to take the car to the shop. Last night, they spoke of leaving today and talking to their dad together. I still hated the idea of them going to their parents' house without me, but I was learning to let go of control. I was learning to trust that Tamara could take care of herself. I was learning to trust that God would keep her safe, even when I couldn't.

As I walked into the house, sounds of Tamara's laughter bellowed from the kitchen—one of my favorite sounds on the planet. Smells of pancakes and coffee wafted in the air, and my mind hit a speed bump. Was Tamara cooking in my kitchen? I hung my jacket on the coat hook and hurried down the hall. Tamara and Dakota stood near the stove, talking and laughing between themselves. Flour had spilled on the front of Tamara's shirt with a little in her hair and on her cheeks. Smiling, I stepped toward the stove. "What in the world is happening right now?"

"I'm cooking," Tamara said in a sing-song voice, raising the spatula, a grin spreading across her face.

I shot Dakota a look of mock horror. "And you didn't stop her?"

She lifted her mug in the air with a goofy smirk. "You should know by now, there's no stopping this girl."

"I'm pretty sure you can't screw up pancakes. You just add water to the mix and pour it in the pan. Besides, these are Mickey Mouse shaped. I have to practice for you-know-who." Tamara patted her belly and winked.

Dakota's eyes bugged out. "You're pregnant?"

"You're going to be an aunt, sis."

Her mouth dropped open. "Didn't see that one coming."

"That's all you have to say?" Tamara narrowed her eyes and curled her upper lip.

"What do you want me to say?" Dakota asked.

Tamara put her finger on her chin and peered at the ceiling. "Um ... 'Congratulations?' Or, 'wow, sis, I'm super happy for you. You're going to be a great mom.'"

"Sorry, yes to all those things. You will be a great mom." Dakota glanced at the tiled floor. "I kinda have some less happy things on my mind right now."

The atmosphere in the room shifted, feeling a bit heavy.

Tamara's face grew serious. "Are you having second thoughts about going?"

One could only hope.

Dakota shook her head. "No. I'm just not looking forward to it."

"Me either." Tamara placed her hand on Dakota's arm. "But we'll have each other to lean on. We'll get through it together."

I wished I'd be going with them today in case things didn't go well. Maybe I should reschedule my meeting with the adjuster and skip the Wholehearted Man group tonight. "Are you guys sure you don't want to wait one more day so I could come with you?"

"No," Dakota said. "I need to do this now."

Before she lost her nerve. That was fair, I guess. Not that I liked it, but I understood.

Behind Tamara, smoke rose from the frying pan. I hurried across the room and removed it from the heat.

244

"Oh, man," Tamara said, turning toward the pan. "That's not fair. You guys were distracting me."

I smiled at her. She was too adorable. "Really, babe. If you think we're distracting, wait until you have a couple of kids running around."

Dakota snorted a laugh. "You best keep practicing, sis."

"Whatever." She crossed her arms in front of her and glared at us. "Y'all are rude."

"Everyone has their talents. Cooking just isn't yours. That's why God gave you me." I dumped the pancake into the garbage, put fresh oil in the pan and added more batter.

The next fifteen minutes where full of laughter as Dakota and I took turns ribbing Tamara and her slapping it back at us. It felt good—like the way family should be, free and light without pain clouding things up. After the drama and insanity, it amazed me that this right here was even possible. If only things with her dad could go this well.

I placed the stack of pancakes in the center of the table and each of us grabbed a plate and fork.

"You want to discuss the plan?" Tamara asked.

"The plan? Why does there need to be a plan?" Dakota put air quotes around the word *plan*, using a mocking voice. "I'm more of a shoot from my hip kinda girl."

"And that's worked so well for you?" I deadpanned.

She pointed her fork at me. "You may have a point."

I dug the three hundred dollars from my pocket that I'd withdrawn from the wedding fund and slid it across the table. It hurt having to do it, but this would be the best way to make their plan work. "Tamara told me you owed your dad money. I think the best thing you can do to soften him is to pay him back."

Dakota eyed the money and shook her head. "I don't want to take anything else from you."

Tamara scooped up the cash, took hold of Dakota's hand and put the money in it. "Take it, Dakota. Believe me, it's the best way. You can return the money when you get a job."

"Fine." She shoved it in her pocket. "I'm not sure it will make much of a difference."

My core surged with anxiety, and I breathed in slowly. "Both of you need to listen carefully. I know this is going to be hard, but I want you to promise me that you'll go into this meeting as humble as possible. Go slow and go low." I made eye contact with Dakota. "I think you should let Tamara do most of the talking."

Dakota pushed her stack of pancakes away. "We'll be fine, Joe. You don't have to be crazy about it."

Tamara placed her hand gently on Dakota's. "I think he's right. If we're going to get anywhere with Dad, we have to be respectful. Don't let him set you off, or he'll throw us out again and we'll be at the same place we started."

"Or he'll do worse," I interjected, unable to reign myself in.

Dakota shot me a dirty look. "What do you mean worse?"

"Come on." I tilted my head to the side. "You know what I mean. He could get violent."

A scowl painted her face. "That's unlikely. He's more verbally abusive with his adult children."

"I understand, but I want you both to promise me that if he gets the least bit aggressive you both will leave."

"I've already promised you, Joe," Tamara said, her gaze on her barely touched breakfast. Why wasn't she eating? Was she struggling with morning sickness? Or worrying over today?

"I know." I reached for her hand. "I'm just concerned for you two."

"You don't need to worry," Dakota said. "We made it our whole childhoods living under his roof. I think we can handle a twenty-minute conversation."

"She's right, Joe." She squeezed my hand, giving me a reassuring smile. "I'm scheduled to be working for Charlie at seven, and since we'll have to go slower hauling Charlie's trailer back to him, we should leave as soon as possible."

I tried to return the smile, but the angst made my face feel heavy. "That's something else we haven't discussed. Is Dakota going to stay at Charlie's with you?"

Dakota rolled her eyes and lifted her hands in the air. "Oh my gosh. Do we have to figure out every detail?"

Tamara gave me an apologetic glance before answering. "I haven't asked him yet. He's already helped me a lot over the last few weeks."

"Stay at the inn tonight," I said, shrugging off Dakota's rudeness. "I never checked out." I'd been in too big of a hurry rescuing Dakota to think of such things.

"Babe." Tamara caressed my hand, concern lining her features. "That's a lot of money to be spending."

It was a lot of money, but this settlement would come through eventually. "It'll be okay."

After the meal, I walked them to the Jeep. Dakota climbed in the passenger seat. I checked the trailer to secure it and then met Tamara on the driver's side. She turned to me, and I pulled her close, whispering a prayer for protection and comfort as they set off to face her dad.

CHAPTER 46

January 6, 4:15 p.m.

TAMARA

I scanned the driveway as I parked in front of our parents' house, foreboding swirling in my guts. Mom's car was gone, but Dad's semi was parked in its normal spot. Why couldn't she have been here today? I grabbed the box of pastries I'd purchased from a local bakery and opened the Jeep door, internally saying a prayer for the thousandth time today. God had told me that he'd always be with me, but a part of me wasn't sure this was the right move. I mean, what would be different bringing Dakota here?

I left my backpack that held Gabriel's ashes and stepped up to the walkway. No use bringing those now. If Mom wasn't here, telling him seemed like a terrible idea. Once at the door, I knocked on it three times. Through the curtain on the door window, I could see my father approaching. My pulse quickened, adrenaline pulsing electricity through my veins. I turned toward Dakota. Fear-filled eyes stared back at me.

For a millisecond, I was transported to our childhood where I'd do anything to keep her safe. I had to fight the urge to take hold of her hand and run.

"Are you sure about this?"

Dakota grabbed my hand and nodded.

The door opened behind us. "Tamara?" Dad spoke with apprehension.

I turned to him, blood pounding in my ears. He peered around me, gaze landing on Dakota. "What are you thinking, bringing her here? I told you she's not welcome on my property. And neither are you, for that matter."

I shoved the box of pastries in his direction. "I'm sorry, Dad, but we need to talk."

He sneered at the box. "What's this?"

"A peace offering. They're from a local place here in town."

"You think you can buy me off with some donuts?" He scowled at us.

Dakota came forward and held out the money Joe had given her. "No. But I will start this conversation with an apology. I stole money from you to buy drugs. That was a terrible thing to do, and I am very sorry."

He took the money and the pastries, face bewildered.

"Dad, please let us in," I said.

He eyed us both again and silently waved us in. We followed him into the living room. He set the pastries on the coffee table and sat in his recliner.

Dakota and I sat on the couch. I took in a deep breath to gather myself before I spoke. "Dad, we came here today because we want healing for our family. Dakota has gotten clean and I'm getting married. We both believe it's time to put the past behind us and begin to rebuild our family."

Dad eyed the donuts, but a softening in his countenance made me believe he was listening. I shot up a quick prayer. He reached for an apple fritter, brought it to his mouth and took a large bite.

I looked over at Dakota and then at Dad, racking my brain on how to continue. "Dad, we want you in our lives again."

Dad nodded, the lines of his face softening. "I want that too. I love my kids. I always have."

My heart swelled at his first admission of love since I'd been home. "I am glad to hear that." I composed myself with a long inhale. "The thing is, in order for that to happen, there needs to be some big changes."

Dad frowned, his eyebrows pinching together. "What do you mean?"

"Dakota and I want you to get help for your anger issues."

He glowered at me. "What are you saying?"

I responded in a slow, calm voice. "I want you in my life again, but I think it's fair to ask you to own up to what you did to us."

His face turned red and a vein throbbed in his neck. "You can't stop with this, can you? You say you want to be a family again, but then you come here spewing your lies!"

Fear, with its sharp talons, climbed my throat. Swallowing hard, I glanced at Dakota. Her leg pulsed, and she bit her lower lip as if she was restraining herself from speaking.

I jumped in before she had a chance to make things worse. "Dad, the truth is, your anger issues and abuse have devastated this family."

He stood, face red, hulking frame towering over us.

I glanced at the door. I had promised Joe I would leave if my dad became aggressive, but I sat frozen, unable to move if I wanted too.

"Abuse? You don't know a damn thing about abuse. You want to see abuse?" He turned and lifted his shirt. "My father beat me every day of my life! I have scars on my back to prove it. That's abuse. None of my kids have scars, not a damn one."

"We have emotional scars." My voice elevated as a tear slipped down my face. Why couldn't he understand? Why couldn't he admit to the pain he caused?

"Emotional scars? Gimme a break! I gave you kids everything. I sacrificed my life to put food on the table, and this is how you repay me. You have no—"

"Stop it!" Dakota yelled as she bolted from her chair. "Just stop it! One of my earliest memories was hiding under the bed while you beat the crap out of Gabriel. You say none of us had scars. Well, he did!"

"Dakota." I stood and placed my hand on her wrist, adrenaline causing my heart rate to spike.

"No!" She ripped her arm from my grasp. "He needs to know. You broke us, Dad! Your abuse and anger ruined our home! Be a man and own it!"

Dad took a few steps away and relief settled my pulse. "I don't have to take this from you. I don't know what I did to have such rotten daughters."

"You're the reason we're like this!" Dakota thrust her finger in his direction. "You're the reason Gabriel's dead!"

Dad's jaw slackened. "What did you say?"

The atmosphere in the room changed from hot to freezing cold.

Dakota's face had turned an ashen shade and she spoke slowly to enunciate each word. "I said, you're the reason Gabriel's dead."

"Gabriel's not dead," he said, more to himself than us. "He left town, like Tamara."

I shook my head. "No, Dad, he's dead."

"You're lying."

"We're not lying!" Dakota screamed. "Why would we lie about this?"

"You're a couple of no good liars! Get the hell out of my house!"

Dakota's face crumpled into a mask of grief as tears poured down her cheeks. I'd never seen her so vulnerable. "Dad, I promise you, I would never lie about something like this."

"Get out!" He crossed the room and ripped open the door.

"Dad, please believe us. We—"

"Out!" he yelled. "Get the hell out of my house and never come back."

"Come on, Dakota." I gripped Dakota's hand and dragged her from the house.

On the way to Joe's jeep, the craziest calm settled over me.

Despite how terrible that had gone, it was done. We had told him. I no longer had to carry the burden of this secret. Beside me, Dakota trembled. I put the car into gear and drove forward, unsure of what the next twenty-four hours would bring. Once the shock of the news wore off, would he realize we weren't lying? Would he tell my mother and the rest of the family? I could imagine Mom's devastation upon hearing the news. Would she call me to confirm the story?

An earth-shattering scream erupted from Dakota, and she punched Joe's dashboard. "Why! Why? Why were we born into such a damned screwed up family? Why couldn't they love us the way we needed it?"

It had been a mistake to bring her there. Why hadn't I been strong enough to tell them myself?

She pounded the dashboard again as another round of gut-wrenching sobs filled the air. "It is Dad's fault Gabriel's dead. It's Dad's fault he molested me."

I took a turn toward Ocean Shores, gripping the steering wheel tighter. My heart felt as if it were being mangled in a meat grinder. How could I comfort her after that? "I shouldn't have brought you there."

She quieted for a few minutes as her body shook through another round of tears. "Sometimes, I think if I close my eyes long enough, I could make a wish and I'd have a different reality, some other stories to tell, but then I open them and realize nothing will ever change. I can't erase my past like a damn whiteboard."

I had no idea what to say to that. I had suffered in this life, but my pain was like a shadow compared to hers. "I shouldn't have brought you there," I repeated stupidly.

"Could you please stop doing that? You have been amazing through this. I know how much he hurt you, Tamara, and yet you faced him with strength, keeping calm in the face of his delusional lies." She paused, her lower lip trembling. "You're a freaking superhero as far as I'm concerned and the best sister a girl could have."

What did she say? Many times, I'd felt like I'd failed her and now she was saying I was a hero? It didn't quite make sense, but I took it in and let it touch those hurting places inside of me. "I love you, Dakota."

"I know you do. You've proved it a thousand times."

Blinking, I fought tears, but a few escaped. I hoped beyond reason that this, as difficult as it was, would be another step toward seeing my family healed.

A long road, full of potholes and detours lay ahead for Dakota. It would take time and hard work for her to recover. She would forever carry the scars of our past, but through faith, I could see her set free. I could see her discovering the many wonderful things that were in her and building a new life with someone like Joe, someone who'd love her through it.

Ten minutes later, we parked the Jeep in front of the inn. It was difficult with the trailer still attached, but I managed. I didn't have time to take it to Charlie now, plus I had no idea how to detach the thing. Maybe Charlie could help me after work. We unloaded our things and walked through the lobby. I lugged my duffel bags upstairs and opened the room with Joe's keycard. Dakota followed behind me, eyes red, countenance sadder than I'd ever seen on her. I'd been so used to her rough exterior and sarcasm, this new side of her had me concerned. Maybe it would be good though. Maybe it meant that she was finally dealing instead of coping with her pain.

"I'm going to go call Joe. You can have the bed if you want." I wished I didn't have to work tonight so I could stay with her.

She gave the slightest smile, though her countenance seemed heavy. "We can share the bed, sis. This thing is huge. It'll be like when we were kids."

I smiled at the thought before grabbing my phone and heading outside to have a few moments of privacy. I clicked on Joe's name and hit the button.

He answered quickly. "Hey, you."

I let the tenderness of those two endearing words wrap around me, wishing he were here to snuggle up to.

"How did it go with your dad?"

I shook my head, though I knew he couldn't see me. "Not good. It got pretty elevated before we left. I wanted to leave like you told me to, but I was frozen."

"But you're okay?"

I gazed at the ocean and inhaled, letting the beauty settle me. "I am, but I don't think I should have brought Dakota there. She's really broken right now, and I don't know what to do for her."

"I don't think we could've stopped her. She seemed determined."

My eyes prickled as I thought of her screaming in the car, blaming my dad for her ruined life. "I know. It was difficult though. I've never seen her like this."

"I'm sorry, babe. Why don't you tell me what happened?"

I sucked in a breath as longing for Joe squeezed my chest. I couldn't wait for the day that we'd never have to separate again. For the next few minutes, I shared with Joe the relatively short interaction with my father, ending with him kicking us out of his life forever because he thought we were lying about Gabriel.

"He thought you were lying?"

"Yeah ..." I said, guts wrenching. What kind of monsters did my dad believe he raised to lie about such a thing?

"I'm sorry. I wish I were there."

"Me too. I miss you." I held the cell tighter, reaching to feel his love through the phone.

"How are you doing with this? I know you were hoping for reconciliation." The tenderness in his voice soothed the ache in me.

"I'm okay. A bit sad and somewhat disturbed, but ..." I paused for a moment and searched my heart. How could I describe what was happening within me? I was concerned for Dakota, but something deeper than that had given way. I believed

God would take care of this, even if us going there today had been a mistake.

"I don't know. I still have this crazy faith that everything is going to be all right." A memory flitted through my mind. Almost a year ago, while dealing with suicidal depression, I'd heard that song Rock-a-Bye by Shawn Mullins. I had sung from the top of my lungs that everything was going to be all right. Later that morning, Levi had written the lyrics on his ticket he had left for me.

"Wow," Joe said with reverential awe.

Warmth ran through my core. "What?"

"You're kind of amazing me right now."

"How so?" I watched the sun dip behind a cloud.

"The girl I knew a few months ago would have been devastated by this. You would have been in tears for days. But right now, you sound strong. You may be a bit sad, but not broken."

I pondered his words for a long moment. What exactly had changed? Somewhere along the way, I had begun to trust, and faith had sprouted from that place, giving me light for these dark moments.

"I'm proud of you, Tamara."

I took in his kind words, heart-swelling. Honestly, he'd come a long way too. Before, he wouldn't have let me go face my dad without him. "I think we've both grown a lot."

"Yeah, we have, haven't we?" I could hear the smile in his voice. "Hey, sorry to change the subject, but I do have news. I talked to a realtor today. Because the house was recently appraised for the loan, it should be easy to get onto the market. He said he could have it listed by the weekend."

"That's great." I looked at the ocean again, watching the waves crash against the shore. I couldn't believe that this was going to be my home.

"You should put in your thirty-day notice at your apartment."

"Okay. Yeah. But we don't even know where we're going to

live here." I placed my hand on my belly, thinking of the precious life growing inside. There was a lot to figure out before this child was born, but at least Joe and I were in a good place.

"I know. Things are unsettled right now. I'll ask the guys to pray for us tonight."

"What guys?"

"I started going to this men's group at Hope Chapel."

Hope Chapel... sadness crashed over me. I would miss that place. And David too. I hadn't even talked to him since leaving town. I should call him and let him know what was going on with me.

"Levi invited me into his small group." Joe continued, "I'm getting ready to walk in."

"Okay. Have a good time. I love you."

"Love you."

I ended the call and headed into the inn to get ready for work.

CHAPTER 47

January 6, 7:00 p.m.

JOE

I sat in church distracted as Joshua spoke. My thoughts drifted to Tamara and how much she'd grown recently. The previous month and a half had made me doubt she was ready for marriage. But seeing the transformation in her over the last week and talking to her today after the confrontation with her dad shifted my image of her. She wasn't this wilting flower anymore. She was a strong, resilient woman, full of faith and tenacity. She was ready to not only be a wife but the mother of my child. The storm that I thought had broken us had actually prepared us.

Suddenly, I knew what needed to be done. We couldn't wait for another three months to be married. She was already pregnant with my child. It was time to put things in the right order in front of God and man. Joshua finished his talk and excused us to our small groups. Levi and I walked across the room to meet Logan and Rod.

"Hey, guys," I said, grinning.

"What's going on with you, Phillips? You're glowing." Rod said, putting his hand out for a shake.

I shook hands with him and glanced at Levi, slightly nervous to make my big announcement. "Let's say things have changed dramatically since our last meeting."

Rod patted me on the back. "That's great, man. I've been praying."

"I'm excited to hear. I love a good testimony." Levi beamed.

Another wave of anxiety. What would Levi think of me once he knew I'd slept with Tamara. I hadn't wanted anyone to know, especially Levi.

We fetched a few chairs and made a small circle. The guys quietly waited for me to talk.

"I don't know how to say this exactly, but turns out I'm going to be a dad."

Levi's expression was hard to read. Was he disappointed in me?

"I know it probably looks bad, but it only happened once."

"Nobody's judging you here, brother," Rod said, offering a sympathetic smile. "Sometimes our biggest mistakes become our biggest blessings. When I was in college, I got caught using drugs, which made me lose my basketball scholarship. But that very thing caused me to turn my life around. Through that failure, I found my relationship with God."

"Yeah, man," Logan said. "The truth is, my wife and I were pregnant when we got married, but we rushed to the altar to hide it."

Levi nodded in agreement.

"I'm considering pushing up the date as well, but it's not because I want to hide anything. It's because I don't want to wait another second to make her my wife. I would have married her months ago if she were ready."

"And you believe she's ready now?" Levi asked.

I nodded slowly. If only he could see the growth in her, he'd agree. "I don't know how it happened, but there has been this beautiful transformation in her. You'd be proud, Levi."

He smiled. "I believe it. I love Tamara like a daughter. And I have to say, if she were my daughter, I couldn't think of a better man for her, Joe."

"Thank you. That means a lot," I said, but his words struck

me in an unexpected way. Suddenly, I wanted, no, needed Tamara's dad to see her the way Levi did, the way *I* did. I wanted him to know what a great person she had become despite his abuse and the heartache he caused her. And more than that, I wanted to have his blessing before I went forward with marrying his daughter.

I shook the thoughts off and readjusted my attention to the group which had switched to Rod. Over the last week, work had been steady, and they had found a new bookkeeper. She seemed to know what she was doing, and so far, things had run smoothly.

I tried to keep my focus on his words, but the more I did, the more my mind kept traveling to Tamara's dad. Could I change his mind about his daughter? Tamara couldn't make him see reason, but maybe I could. How would I even get his address? Tamara surely would caution me not to go there, but the more I considered it, the more I knew I wanted to talk to her dad, man to man.

When the meeting ended, we prayed for one another, then Levi walked me to my Jeep and gave me a big hug. "I'm glad you felt comfortable talking tonight. I know you love Tamara deeply."

"I do," I agreed.

"I think you're right to move up the wedding date," he said. "You two belong together. There's no reason to prolong the process."

I laughed and opened my car door. "Amen to that."

"You let me know if you need anything."

I climbed in my car and rolled down the window. "I will. Thanks for everything." I turned the key, and the engine roared to life.

He threw a wave, and I returned it as I drove from the parking lot. As soon as I left Levi's sight, I called my room in Ocean Shores. Tamara would be at work, but it wasn't her that I needed to talk to.

After the fourth ring, Dakota answered, voice groggy from sleep. "Hello."

"Dakota, it's Joe."

"Tamara's at work," she said through a yawn.

"I know. I wanted to talk to you."

"About what?"

"I need your parents' address."

She was silent for a full thirty seconds.

"Dakota?"

"Why?"

"I need to talk to your dad."

She barked a laugh. "You're insane."

She was probably right, but I couldn't shake the idea. "Can I please have the address?"

She rattled it off and ended the call.

I said it aloud, again and again, committing it to memory. Whether it made sense or not, I would be going to his house tomorrow.

CHAPTER 48

January 7, 12:15 p.m.

JOE

Last night, I stayed awake for hours, searching for houses in Ocean Shores. I found a few two bedrooms I thought I could afford, not that I could truly afford anything right now. On the drive to Aberdeen, I called to check on the properties and made an appointment for later in the afternoon. I had one more thing to do before heading to Ocean Shores and ask Tamara to move up the date—talk to Tamara's dad. My palms were sweaty as I pulled up to the street address Dakota gave me.

I exited my car and stepped to the sidewalk. A semi was parked in front of the house on the street. An older model Honda Accord and a Toyota Sienna minivan sat in the driveway. He obviously wasn't alone. I wasn't sure if that was a good thing or not. I had imagined facing him by myself. Perhaps it would be better this way. Perhaps with people around, he'd be less likely to become aggressive. I stepped to the door and knocked three times. A few seconds later, a middle-aged woman with graying hair opened the door a crack. Her face had the same oval shape as Tamara's, but it was aged with slightly sunken eyes and deep worry lines on her forehead.

"May I help you?" she asked, her voice kind.

"Yes. My name is Joe Phillips. I'm Tamara's fiancé."

Eyes widening, she swung the door open. "Oh goodness. Is everything all right?"

I smiled a reassuring thing, to help put her at ease. "Oh yes. I hoped to speak with your husband. Is he home?"

She glanced behind her tentatively but moved aside, gesturing me forward. "Come on in. I'm Theresa."

"Nice to meet you." I smiled and took a step forward. The house was a tad cold and smelled like old hardwood floors and Lysol. Anxiety rattled through my guts. Should I be here right now?

"Paul," she called. "There's somebody here to talk to you."

I followed her into a small living room where two men sat drinking PBR tallboys. For a split second, that ancient thirst dried the back of my tongue, but I swallowed hard, squashing it immediately. I'd *never* allow myself to entertain those thoughts again. I had too much to lose.

"Nathan, Paul, this is Joe, Tamara's fiancé."

Nathan rose to his feet and stuck out his hand, a jovial expression on his face. "So, you do exist. I was beginning to think she made you up."

I laughed and took hold of his hand. "Oh, I'm real."

Paul stood slowly, caution lining his brow. "To what do we owe the honors?"

Anger immediately sparked in my core. This was the man who had caused Tamara so much pain. Images of taking him outside and beating the living crap out of him engulfed me. It took great restraint to bury the thoughts and extend my hand toward him. "Hello, sir. I wanted to stop by and introduce myself and perhaps have a word with you."

He regarded my hand for a few seconds before he took hold of it and gave it a firm shake.

I matched the tightness of his grip, holding my ground. "Could we speak privately?"

He glanced at Nathan and then at Theresa. "Whatever you want to say can be said in front of family."

I kept my focus on him, trying to get a better read. Was he scared to be alone with me? Could he see the anger in my eyes the way I saw the coldness in his? "Okay, but for the record, Tamara doesn't know I'm here, but she did tell me about coming here with Dakota yesterday—"

"They were both here yesterday and you didn't tell me?" Tamara's mom asked, voice sharp.

Paul scowled at her. "There was nothing to tell. Only more of their BS lies. I didn't want to upset you."

"I would have liked to have seen them. I haven't seen Dakota in years."

"Theresa," Paul said. "Let the man talk."

Inwardly, I prayed that God would cool the embers burning in my chest. I peeked at Nathan, who quietly chugged his beer. More temptation invaded my thoughts. This conversation would be easier if I had a drink or two in me. I almost laughed at the thought. What a lie. If I had drank before coming here, I may have already lost my cool.

"Mind if I sit here?"

"Please." Nathan scooted over on the couch, and I sat next to him.

I turned to Paul, searching for the words that would crack his hard exterior. It had been clear in my mind last night, but now that I was here, it felt like a jumbled mess in my head. *God, help me.*

"Sir, I first want to say that I don't have the first clue as to what a family is supposed to be like. I never knew my father, I have no siblings, and my mother died when I was a teenager."

"That's terrible." Theresa covered her mouth, features a mask of sorrow. "I'm sorry."

"Thank you."

"Theresa, why don't you get the man a drink? Would you like a beer?" Paul asked and focused his gaze on me.

Theresa moved toward the kitchen.

My mouth felt dry. "No, please, water would be fine." I

turned to Paul and made eye contact. "But if I did have a family, I would fight to keep it together."

Paul tensed in his seat, hands clenching into fists. "What are you trying to say?"

Nathan gazed at the floor as he fiddled with the edge of the beer can. What was his opinion of this conversation?

Theresa returned, handed me a glass of water and sat in the recliner next to her husband. I took a large swallow and set it on the coffee table, bracing myself as I said the next words. If he was already getting angry about the other stuff, this next part might send him over the top. "What I'm saying is from what I understand, when Tamara came here yesterday to ask for you to get help, you turned her away."

Paul waved both of his hands in a quick jerky motion. "What a load of crap. Obviously, Tamara's lies have poisoned you against me."

Another blast of anger rose like a blowtorch, searing my insides. *God, help me not lose it.* "With all due respect, sir, Tamara's not a liar."

Paul's jaw hardened and a vein pulsed in his neck. "What exactly are you implying?"

A sick part of me wanted to push him the rest of the way in this second, but that would help nothing. I needed to seriously tone this conversation down for the moment, to get on his good side. Otherwise, he'd never hear what needed to be said. "I'm saying that I want you to know your daughter is amazing. She's the most loving and forgiving person I know. Sir, I already asked her to marry me before she found you, but I'm here now because I would like your blessing."

"An old-fashioned man, huh? I like that." His expression softened and he stood. "Sure, son, you seem respectable, and Tamara mentioned you're a businessman. You can marry my daughter with my blessing." He walked over and extended his hand to me.

I stood and took his hand with a firm shake. "Thank you.

That means a lot to me." Although it bothered me how easily he said yes. They didn't even know me.

Nathan slapped his hands together. "All right, sounds like a reason to celebrate. You still got that bottle of Ardbeg, Pop?"

My face went hot, feeling a new pressure grow inside of me at the mention of the expensive bottle of scotch. I didn't want to have to explain my addiction to my in-laws on our first meeting.

Theresa smiled and gave an encouraging nod.

"I think you're right, son." Paul walked over to the liquor cabinet and pulled out a green bottle.

My pulse thudded in my ears. This was *not* the direction I had seen this going. I had been more afraid of things getting physical, not being tempted by aged scotch.

Paul filled three glasses with the liquor and handed one to me before giving one to Nathan. "Welcome to the family."

I raised a hand in the air in protest, my face on fire with embarrassment. "Oh, none for me, please."

"Come on, son." He patted me on the shoulder with a toothy grin. "I know you already asked her, but we're celebrating."

"Yeah, come on, Joe. Take it as a family initiation." Nathan raised his glass toward mine.

Family initiation? I eyed the drink, swallowing the shame and fear. A part of me wanted to drink it so I wouldn't have to tell them. My throat tightened, and I swallowed again. "I can't. I'm a recovering alcoholic."

Paul's head tilted, then he took my drink and poured it into his glass. "It's fine. We all have our kryptonite."

"Thank you for understanding," I said, relief washing over me.

"I guess that means more for us," Nathan said with a laugh and shot half his glass. "To Joe and Tamara getting married." Nathan raised his glass to Paul. "One sister down, one more to go."

"Now that would be a miracle," Paul said as they both smirked and clinked glasses.

Indignation rose in me at their exchange. "Sir, can I ask you something?"

"Sure, son, you're family now." Paul set his glass on the counter.

"Why are you letting me marry your daughter? You don't even know me."

"I'm not following you. Do you want to marry her or not?" He took the bottle and poured more into his and Nathan's glass.

"Yes, of course I do, but I don't feel you know the value of the woman you are giving away." There I said it. At least the truth was out instead of being stuck in my gut, causing it to turn with fury.

"Excuse me?" His eyebrows furrowed, and his jaw hardened.

"This all feels transactional, like because I owned a business, I am good enough for your daughter." I wanted to say that I found it despicable, but I kept that part to myself.

He looked at Nathan and then to me, his features hard. "Son, if you have something to say, you better get to—"

"I'm saying, when my daughter is grown, you better believe that I would be sitting in a chair like that one cleaning a shotgun when some punk kid comes around wanting to marry her." I took a moment to compose my thoughts. "He's going to have to earn it. I will demand he tells me what he sees in my daughter and gauge if he is worthy of marrying my treasure."

"What do you want from me?" He raised his free hand in the air. "That girl broke my heart. She brought drugs into my house and then just abandoned us. She chose to leave us for six years. *Six years.* I had no idea if she was strung out somewhere, living on the streets, or dead for that matter. In my mind, Tamara wasn't going to amount to anything. Please forgive me if I'm a bit eager to see her marry a decent guy with a head for business. I don't know what she told you about me, but I want what's best for my kids."

As angry as I was, for the briefest moment I tried to see it from his point of view. He'd been hurt deeply by Tamara, but the truth was, she hadn't brought drugs into his house. Dakota had.

Tamara had only been trying to protect Dakota, but by doing that, she'd poisoned her dad's perspective of her.

"I understand how that could be difficult. Could I please tell you how I see your daughter? Can I tell you why I want to marry her?"

Paul took another sip of his scotch, his eyes shadowed with years of sadness. "I'm listening."

"When I met Tamara, she was pretty closed off, but even then, I found myself drawn to her. She was smart, funny, beautiful, and so strong. As she began to let me in, I started to see her brokenness and struggle, but she was such a fighter through it. Quite honestly, she amazed me, sir. She was handed an extremely tough hand last year when she found herself pregnant as a result of date rape, and instead of becoming bitter, she gave birth to that baby and gave it to a couple who were desperate to have children."

I paused for a moment, reigning in my emotions. The gift of life Tamara had given to Levi and Sarah always wrecked me when I thought about it. I had witnessed how much it cost her, and a part of me would be forever in awe of her for it. "We recently discovered that Tamara is pregnant again, and we want you to be in our child's life."

Theresa's mouth dropped open. "Tamara's going to have a baby? Oh, that's wonderful."

"Yes." I smiled at her, hoping I didn't ruin anything by telling them before Tamara did. "We're both excited for it." I turned my attention to Paul, who sipped his scotch, his expression thoughtful. Was I getting through to him? "But, sir, in order for us to feel safe having you in our house and around our kids, we want you to acknowledge what you did to her and to get help for your anger issues."

Rage flared in Paul's eyes, "This is unbelievable. I will not admit to any such thing. I am *not* the one to be blamed here."

"Then, as a man, I am here to tell you that you're in the wrong. You're willing to shut your daughter out, and give up ever holding your grandchildren, for what? I can't believe you are too proud to take responsibility for your actions."

Paul dropped his glass, lunged forward at me and clutched the collar of my shirt. "What gives you the right?"

"Hey! Dad, stop!" Nathan yelled, pushing him back, face growing red. "You need to leave!" He shoved my chest.

I raised my hands in surrender. "I'm leaving, but there's one more thing you are wrong about. Tamara would never lie about Gabriel dying."

Behind me, there was a sharp inhale of breath.

"What did you say?" Nathan said as horror crossed his face.

This was the first they had heard of it?

"Get out, you liar!" Paul yelled, coming at me again. "Get out of my house before I throw you out."

I looked at Nathan, and then at Paul. "It's not a lie. Call Tamara. She'll tell you." I bolted through the door, berating myself for coming here in the first place. I was a fool to think I could change anything.

CHAPTER 49

January 7, 1:00 pm.

TAMARA

After sleeping in and taking an easy morning at Joe's hotel room, Dakota and I headed to the convenience store for some breakfast, though it was past noon. Dakota chose a Pop-Tart and a coffee while I got a box of saltine crackers. It wasn't the healthiest breakfast, but it was the only thing I could keep down for the first meal of the day. We left the store and walked toward Charlie's house, quietly munching on our food.

Last night, work had been busy, but after the bar closed, Charlie helped me bring the trailer back to his uncle's house. While we were together, I told him Dakota's story and about her being homeless for the moment. He listened intently for the most part until the end. Then raising a playful brow, he'd asked me if she were cute. I had smacked him playfully and told him yes, but that she was off-limits for both of their sakes.

Five minutes later, we were at Charlie's house. I gave a quick rap on the door and pushed it open. He sat on the couch wearing jeans and a gray T-shirt, freshly showered and shaved.

"Dakota, this is Charlie."

"Hey, Dakota." He threw a wave. "Nice to meet you."

"Likewise." A slight sarcastic ring came through her tone, which gave me relief after her episode last night.

Sarcasm was her superpower, a barrier she used to hide behind.

"Welcome to Ocean Shores. You gonna be here a while?"

"Anything is possible at this point. I'm taking one day at a time." She shrugged.

"Great rule to live by," he said.

"Yeah. I read it in the Big Book."

"The Bible?" Charlie grinned, but I couldn't tell if he was joking.

Dakota narrowed her eyes with a smirk. "No, like the Big Book, not the good book. It's from NA."

Charlie laughed. "I'm messing with you. My uncle is in recovery. He's eight years in. They have a couple of meetings that meet here in town."

"Good to know." More sarcasm.

I smiled. Goodness, I loved this girl.

My phone rang, and I dug it out of my pocket. Joe's picture lit the screen.

"Hey," he said when I answered. "Are you at Charlie's?"

"Yes."

"Okay, I'm pulling into town. I'll be there soon. We need to talk."

My stomach flipped and turned, doing acrobatics Olympians would be proud of. "What's going on?"

"I'll explain when I get there."

The call ended, and I stared at the phone, my mind racing. Why was it when people said they needed to talk, my mind tended to jump to the worst conclusion? He may have good news, right? But why were my intestines bunching in knots? I focused on Dakota and tried to reengage with the conversation. Charlie was telling Dakota of the things to do in Ocean Shores, which wasn't much if you were flying sober. Dakota threw in a few comments here and there, but Charlie did most of the talking.

"Hey, Charlie, Joe is going to be here soon," I said, jumping into the conversation. "Can you entertain Dakota for a bit while we talk?"

A playful grin brightened his face. "It would be my pleasure."

"Watch yourself. Last time I heard, Dakota had a cop for a boyfriend."

She glared at me like I'd crossed a boundary. "I don't have a boyfriend."

I heard Joe arrive and cut the engine. "Whatever you say. You should see your face whenever you mention him. You definitely have the hots for, what's his name? Tom? Jim? No. Tim," I said, teasing her.

She shot me a withering look. I giggled and blew her a kiss. My phone rang as I walked outside. Nathan? My pulse quickened. What did he want? Had Dad told him the news of Gabriel's death? Or was he calling to yell at me like he had last time? I shoved my phone in my pocket and turned my attention to Joe as he stepped out of his Jeep. A somber expression hung on his handsome face.

"What's wrong?" I asked, worry flickering.

"I did something. Tamara, I'm so sorry." He walked toward me, the lines of his features etched with regret.

What could he have possibly done?

He took hold of my hands, an apology in his touch. "During the meeting last night, I got it in my head that I needed to talk to your dad."

"What?" I said, unable to disguise the irritation in my tone. Why would he go there without talking to me?

"I know, it was stupid. I don't know what I was thinking." He shook his head. "I mainly wanted to tell him how amazing you are and that you weren't crazy for wanting him to get help."

Joe went to defend my honor to my dad? That was one of the sweetest things he'd ever done for me.

"You can imagine it didn't go well. My words got twisted, and I was a lot more aggressive than I meant to be. In the end, he threw me out of the house."

Of course, he had. No one was allowed in his house if they dared defy him. "What else happened? Tell me everything."

"Let me see. Your mom answered the door. She was sweet."

"You met my mom?" The thought made my heart happy.

"Yes, and your brother Nathan. He was nice too. Until your dad lunged at me. Then he jumped on your dad's side and yelled at me to leave. I hope I didn't make things worse."

"Babe, no. There's no way you could have after what Dakota and I did yesterday." At least, I hoped not. I didn't want him feeling bad for this. He had good intentions when going there, and that was what mattered.

"There's one more thing I need to tell you," he said as my phone buzzed.

Was that Nathan again?

"As I left, I told your dad you would never lie about Gabriel's death. Both your mom and Nathan acted like it was the first time they heard of it."

Dad never told them?

"I'm sorry, Tamara. I shouldn't have gone there without telling you."

"It's all right." I looked at my phone. It *was* Nathan again. My pulse rate doubled. "You may have knocked something loose." Whether it was good or bad remained to be seen. I turned my phone to show him the screen. "This is the second time in the last few minutes that he's called."

"Oh yes, answer it."

I answered the phone and put it on speaker. Whatever he was going to say, it would be in front of Joe. "Hello."

"Is it true?" His voice sounded strained as he spoke. "Please tell me it isn't true."

I made eye contact with Joe. He nodded, encouraging me to talk.

"It's true." My heart fractured as I said the words.

"How do you know? What happened?" He sounded desperate as if he was trying to grab onto anything but the truth.

I recalled the story Dakota had told me in my living room, moisture gathering in my eyes. "Dakota said he and Ryan got into a fight at the power lines."

"Ryan Cooke?"

"Yes. He hit his head on the bumper of a truck really hard. Dakota thought he'd been knocked out, but a few minutes later she realized he wasn't breathing. She tried to give him CPR, but she didn't know what she was doing.

Ryan threw his body on a bonfire and threatened the people who were there that if they said anything, he'd kill them." A cold wind blew around me, and I shivered.

He was quiet for a minute. "That doesn't make sense. Everyone was afraid of him?"

He obviously hadn't seen Ryan in action. "Yes."

"When did it happen?"

Blinking back tears, I gripped the phone tighter. "Almost five years ago."

"This can't be true. Why didn't Dakota ever report it?"

"She almost went to the police, but Ryan told Dakota that he'd kill the rest of her family if she told. A few days later, he set fire to the trailer park and tried to pin it on Dakota."

"No. That can't be right. Mom filed a missing person report on him a week after he went missing. Wouldn't the cops have found some sort of evidence?"

"I don't know. Without a crime reported or a body, they had very little to investigate. You know how understaffed Jefferson County Police Department is."

"This can't be real." His voice was empty, distant— completely void of emotion.

I focused on Joe again. His face held a depth of compassion that gave me the courage to talk through the sadness overwhelming me. "I didn't want to believe it either, but Dakota brought me his ashes when she came to me in Vancouver."

"You have his ashes?"

I worried my lower lip. "Yes. I've had them since before Christmas."

"Send me your address. I'm coming there, and I'm bringing Mom." He ended the call, and I sent him my location. Nathan was bringing my mom? I wasn't sure how I'd handle her grief. The weight of it might rip me wide open.

I leaned into Joe and prayed as his arms came around me that God would give me strength for this moment. What about Dakota? This moment would be ten times harder for her than me. I had to be strong for her.

Pulling away, I headed toward the house, Joe trailing behind me. Dakota sat on the couch on the opposite side of Charlie playing with her phone.

"Can I talk to you for a minute?"

She stood and followed me into my room, leaving Charlie and Joe in the living room. I heard them making small talk as I shut the door behind me.

"You're not going to believe this, but Joe went to Mom and Dad's house to confront him about our conversation yesterday."

Dakota plopped on the bed. "I know, sis. How do you think he got the address?"

My jaw dropped open. "You knew and didn't say anything?"

"Didn't seem like my place." She gave a nonchalant wave. "That's between you and Romeo."

A part of me wanted to smack her. But honestly, this wasn't what mattered now. "It's fine. I came in to tell you Mom and Nathan are on their way here."

Her head snapped to attention. "What? They are coming here? Like right now? Why?"

"Yes. I talked to them on the phone. They know about Gabriel."

A scared, vulnerable expression crept over Dakota's face.

I crossed the room and sat next to her. "It's going to be okay. We'll get through this together. They might want answers, or they might just want to cry. Either way, we need to be prepared."

"I don't know if I'm ready to face Mom." Her voice cracked. "She doesn't deserve this. I've already put her through enough."

"Yes, but she's strong, and I know she wants you in her life." I thought of the moment I had with Mom in my motel room. She had been so sad that three of her children had abandoned her. She'd never have Gabriel back, but it wasn't too late for us to heal.

A stray tear fell down Dakota's face. "I know, but this is hard."

I took hold of her hand, giving it a firm squeeze. "I understand, but I believe this moment right here is what Gabriel wanted for us. I believe when he came after you to save you, he wanted us to come closer together rather than let our struggles pull us apart. You carried the sorrow of his death alone for too many years, but because you let me into that pain with you, we are stronger. Let's invite the rest of our family in."

She wiped her face and peered at me with a sadness that crushed me. "Okay, but I need you to promise me something."

"Sure, sis. Anything."

She glanced at our hands locked together. "I don't want them to know what Gabriel did to me. That's between me and you."

I nodded, my throat suddenly thick and dry. I didn't know how to feel about keeping this secret, but if that was the way Dakota wanted it, I would respect her wishes.

A text came through my phone.

Almost there.

That was quick. "They'll be here any minute." I unfolded my hand from Dakota's and stood. Dakota wrapped her arms around her waist and sat there with that same vulnerable expression as before. Was she ready for this?

"You coming?" I asked.

She gave a slight nod. "I need a minute."

"Okay, sure." I took the ashes from my bag before heading

into the living room. Joe sat on the couch, watching the sports channel.

"Where's Charlie?"

Joe grabbed the remote and muted the volume. "He had to run to Midways. There was an issue with the new cook."

I set the ashes on the coffee table and settled in next to Joe.

He slid his hand over my back. "You doing okay?"

"As good as I can be." I leaned my head against his shoulder and inhaled. "I'm concerned for Dakota." Heck, I was concerned for my whole family.

Joe drew me in closer, holding me tight, wordlessly communicating his support. I was so grateful that he was here for this moment.

Dakota emerged from the room, ambling slowly, her face a few shades paler than usual. She sat next to me. Inwardly, I prayed that God would cover this moment.

There was a knock at the door. I rose, walked across the living room and opened the door. Nathan stood in front of me, his eyes swollen. Amanda stood beside him, countenance drawn. Mom stood behind them, her limbs encasing her stomach, eyes as red as Nathan's.

"Come in," I said and stepped out of the way to let them in. "Joe, this is Amanda, Nathan's wife."

Joe stood to meet her and shook her hand. "Nice to meet you."

Dakota stayed curled on the couch, her gaze averted to the floor. Mom crossed the room, knelt in front of her and pulled her into an embrace. Dakota's body was stiff, but her lips trembled. Then she broke, unable to contain her emotion.

"I'm so sorry, Mom. I'm so sorry." She pressed her head into her neck.

Mom joined Dakota on the couch, drawing her in closer. "It's okay, baby, it's okay. It's not your fault."

I wiped my tears with my sleeve and glanced at Nathan, who for once was speechless, looking like a scared little boy. There was nothing humorous at the moment for him to hide behind. He stood stoic, face frozen like glass.

I picked the jar of ashes off the table and handed them to Mom.

"Oh, my baby," she cried softly, clutching the jar, her face contorting with sorrow. "My sweet, sweet boy."

"I don't understand why Dad didn't tell us," Nathan said in a whisper, his lower lip trembling. "Why isn't he here?" His eyes welled with tears.

The questions hung between us for a few moments, then Nathan's expression shifted as if he were seeing the truth about Dad for the first time.

"I'm so sorry, Tamara. I was awful to you."

I crossed the room and hugged Nathan for a long time. "It's okay. I forgive you."

In the light of this loss, none of that mattered. I was just glad that he was here and we were letting each other into our lives and into our grief.

Nathan pulled away from me and sat next to Mom. Amanda squeezed in next to them and rested her head on Nathan's shoulder.

My heart felt fragile underneath the heaviness of the grief in the room.

Joe came, stood close to me, and drew me into his embrace, and I broke. Being surrounded by loved ones allowed a new door in my soul to open and more tears to flow. I buried my head into him, allowing myself to get lost in my own grief. It hit me once more that for the rest of my days on this planet, I would never see Gabriel again. I'd never hear his silly belly laugh when he did something stupid. I'd never see that compassionate look in his eyes when he knew I was having a hard day.

In my mind's eye, I saw a picture of Gabriel standing next to Jesus, gloriously full of joy, unshackled by the brokenness of this world. I would never see him again here on earth, but there could be a day when all of us would laugh together again in heaven. I cried into Joe's chest, releasing my grief.

I'm not sure how long we stayed like that. It felt like an eternal moment. One that couldn't be counted in seconds or minutes. Instead, it was measured in sorrow and grief. Pulling my head from Joe's chest, I peered around the room. For the most part, the tears had dried, and everyone seemed relaxed. Amanda and Nathan were holding each other, and Dakota sat on the couch, curled up next to Mom.

Time slowed again as I could feel the tangible comfort of the Holy Spirit descend on us. As terrible as this was, it felt like a collective wound was healed in us today. I cracked a pained smile. Maybe, just maybe, this was the beginning of the reconciliation our family desperately needed.

CHAPTER 50

January 8, 6:15 p.m.

DAKOTA

After Nathan, Amanda, and Mom left, I went outside for a smoke. I stared at the sky, taking in the large expanse, trying to sort through the thoughts in my head.

For years, I had run from this moment of telling my family the truth, believing that they'd hate me. What a lie that had been. I had never felt more loved and embraced as I did when Nathan and Mom pulled me into the center of their grief. I had felt no rejection, only the simple assurance that I still belonged to them, no matter what pain I had caused them.

But what I couldn't understand, now that the moment was over, was why I felt so empty. I had the craziest desire to go get high, even after all that love had been lavished on me. What was wrong with me? Had the secrets and lies I'd kept been an excuse? Had I completely sabotaged my life on purpose? Possibly. I lit the smoke and sucked in a large drag. If that was the truth, was there any hope for me?

Behind me, the door opened and closed. I took another puff, ignoring the sound.

Romeo came and stood beside me. "How ya doing?"

I turned to him, somewhat confused. I'd been positive he

endured my presence for Tamara's sake. "Oh, you know, livin' the dream."

He squinted and scratched the side of his head. "So, basically you're ready for the next hit or line or whatever your drug of choice was?"

I raised an eyebrow. "Perceptive."

"From one addict to the next. I get it." He leaned against the side of the deck, a knowing look on his face.

Tamara hadn't mentioned he was an addict. I swear, these people were everywhere. "Does that mean you're gonna give me some compelling ounce of wisdom to help me through my hour of need?" I asked with as much snarkiness as I could muster.

He leaned against the deck rail, his gaze fixed on the ocean. "No, but I was going to see if you wanted to hit a meeting with me."

"A meeting?" I asked, taken aback.

"Sometimes they're the worst," he said with an apologetic smile. "But other times, they can really help."

I stared at him for a long moment. Had I stepped into an episode of the Twilight Zone?

"I checked the schedule earlier. There's one getting ready to start." He peeked at his phone. "In around ten minutes. You in?"

I inhaled another drag and watched the smoke drift from my mouth. "Why not?"

"Cool. I'll go tell Tamara."

"Is she coming?"

"Nope. Just me and you," he said and walked into the house.

I smoked the rest of my cigarette while waiting for Joe to return. He was probably in there being all lovey-dovey with my sister. Sickening. I didn't know how much more I could take of them.

A few minutes later, Romeo emerged from the house and headed to his car, gesturing me to follow. I took a few steps forward, unsure. I'd never been to a meeting before, and I wasn't sure what to expect. I climbed into the car and buckled myself in, bracing for what the night would hold.

It only took a few minutes to reach the community center in this small town. The room was cold and a bit cluttered with fifteen chairs or so set in a circle. Great. Were we going to hold hands and sing Kumbaya?

A few people milled around, and a bigger bunch gathered around a coffee urn, waiting for their turn to fill their Styrofoam cups. Romeo nudged me and jerked his head toward the crowd of people. "It's a staple at meetings. A legal substance to which most of us are still addicted."

I smirked and stepped in that direction. "I'll drink to that."

As we grabbed our cups, he made small talk with the locals, asking about the area and the job market. I ignored him as I sipped the warm sludge and thought of Tim. Had Sage called him after I left to let him know my plans?

The meeting was called to order, and I took a seat on the nearest chair. Romeo settled into the spot next to me. The people seemed average to me—a mix of ordinary faces that would easily blend into a crowd. An older lady with thin lips and a crooked nose stood and asked us to join her in the serenity prayer.

I remained silent but saw that Romeo seemed to be mouthing the words with a certain reverence. I suppressed the massive eye roll that had become more of a reflex than anything. The guy was too freaking sincere. It irritated me.

I folded my hands in my lap and then unfolded them to distract myself from my judgmental thoughts. Truth was, he was a great guy, my sister adored him, and he'd been nice to me even after the catastrophe that I caused in his life.

I spaced out during the announcements, thinking of Tim again. I should probably shoot him a text to let him know I was okay. Joe handed me a collection bucket, and I had to resist the urge to take a few dollars from it as I passed it along. I was *so* going to hell.

The woman spoke again. "Tonight, we will be focusing on

Step Ten and our need to continuously take personal inventory and when we do wrong to promptly admit it."

There were a few moments of silence before a man in his early forties spoke. "Hi, I'm Randall, and I'm an addict."

"Welcome, Randall," the rest of the group chanted.

He looked around the room, took in a long, deep breath and launched into his story. "A little over a year ago, right around Christmas, I loaned my brother-in-law some money. It wasn't much." Shrugging, he lifted his hands in the air. "Only a few hundred dollars. But instead of returning the money at his next payday as we agreed, he avoided me for months. Even over the holidays. At first, I tried to let it go. But after a while, it got to me. Eventually, I started to resent him. The more bitter I became, the more the desire for the drugs grew. Finally, I realized before God that I was committing the sin of unforgiveness. I wrestled with it for weeks. I didn't understand. I'd done the right thing by helping my family, but in the end, the bitterness cost me a whole lot more than the money. It cost me my peace, and it could have ruined six years of sobriety."

He paused for a moment, shifting from foot to foot. "At that point, I found my brother-in-law and told him to consider the debt completely forgiven. The relationship isn't the same, but it's not because of me."

Cracking my knuckles, I bit my lip, hating that I could relate with the brother-in-law in that story more than anything else. With the years of sorrow that I had caused my family, it had been easier to stay away to avoid the ways I'd disappointed them.

Several other people spoke, each having their own stories of overcoming their issues by constantly taking a moral inventory. One lady went way off topic, droning on about helping her neighbor move her furniture and cleaning her carpets. After that, I peeped at the clock. Only fifteen more minutes until the meeting was over.

"My name is Joe, and I'm an alcoholic."

He was going to speak? Oh man, this could be embarrassing. Maybe I should leave now.

"Today I have fourteen days sober."

What? No way. That was one day less than me. I would have guessed he had years under his belt.

"Before that, I had eight months and before that, I had three years." A small laugh and then a pause. "I know everyone here has their own sad story. The malady within them that causes them to drink or do drugs. For me, my story started when I watched my mom die when I was seventeen years old." Joe paused, seeming to linger on the memory.

The room was so silent, I could hear my own pulse.

"That moment in the ICU when I watched her life slip away was the day when my whole world went tilt. I knew then that nothing was certain, and everything could change in a split second."

My throat tightened, and I fidgeted in my seat, trying hard to push down the emotions gnawing to the surface.

"For the next few years, my life went spinning off its axis. I hurt so many people. I burnt every single bridge. I got a girl pregnant and talked her into getting an abortion. There were many times I wished for death."

I couldn't make sense of the words I was hearing. Joe seemed like Mr. Perfect. I would never have guessed he had been capable of self-destructing like I had.

"A few years into it, I met this woman. She was way out of my league, but somehow, she was into me. I latched onto her, thinking she could save me, but in the end, I devastated her too. That was when I started to get the help I needed. It's been a long journey, and a lot of work. And I will say this step we're discussing tonight is one of the most important steps. One of the biggest things I've seen lately while taking personal inventory is my need to control." He focused on his hands, seeming to gather his thoughts. "When life starts spinning, instead of trusting God, I have a tendency to take matters into my own hands. Recently, it almost cost me my relationship with my fiancé, and it did temporarily cost me my sobriety."

What had happened after I left? Fourteen days ago was Christmas. Right after the fire, he had drunk, yet he and Tamara seemed happy together. They were nauseatingly perfect. Or so I thought.

Joe ended his speech, and the facilitator thanked him for sharing. A few minutes later, the meeting ended, but I couldn't help but see Joe differently. He, like Sage, had gone through loads of heartbreak, and yet here he was, doing his best to be a good man and loving my sister with all he could. Maybe someday, after hard work and facing my issues, I could be a good person. And maybe, I could love someone too. I thought of Tim again, and that ache returned. Forget sending him a text. I needed to call him.

The car ride was quiet as we drove to Charlie's, for which I was grateful. Between what had happened earlier with Mom and Nathan and this meeting with Joe, there was a ton to process. And I definitely didn't want to talk about it. In fact, isolating myself somewhere and not speaking to anyone for the next three days sounded like a great idea. We pulled into Charlie's driveway. Joe killed the engine, and we exited the vehicle.

The smell of hamburgers and fried food hit my nose as we entered the house. Charlie and Tamara were standing near the kitchen.

"Perfect timing," Tamara said, then she hurried across the room to give Joe a hug.

I shot Charlie an irritated eye roll and then looked at Tamara. "Get a room."

Charlie sniggered and lifted a bag. "I brought home burgers for dinner."

"Thanks, man," Joe said, untangling himself from Tamara. "I'm starved."

I was hungry too, but after the day's emotional turbulence, I wasn't sure if I had the energy to eat.

"No problem. I rented a movie on the way home too. You guys are welcome to stick around and watch it with me."

Tamara and Joe exchanged a look. "What movie?"

Charlie lifted a movie case. "The Glass Castle. It has Woody Harrelson in it."

"Nice. I'm in. He's a good actor," Joe said.

Tamara agreed and came closer to me. "How you doing, sis?"

"I'm beat."

"Yeah, it's been a hard day. You could go rest in my bed if you're not into the movie thing."

"I think I'll take you up on that." I yawned and gave her a hug before stepping toward her room.

"Hey," Charlie called after me. "You sure you don't want one of these before you lie down. I made them myself at the pub. My heart attack burgers are way better hot."

I hesitated, my tummy snarling at me. Would it be rude to take it into the room with me? I rolled my eyes at my own thought. Since when did I care? "Thanks, Charlie." I crossed the room and took a wrapped burger from the bag.

"Don't forget the fries." Charlie pointed at the other bag on the counter.

I threw him a wry smile, took a bag of fries and headed to Tamara's room to have a moment to myself.

CHAPTER 51

January 8, 9:27 p.m.

TAMARA

Charlie's burger was fantastic. It was a double stack of perfectly seasoned beef, sautéed onions, bacon, Swiss cheese, and an over medium egg on top. Somehow, I'd finished the whole thing and it settled well. After dinner, we gathered in the living room. I snuggled with Joe on the couch while Charlie started the movie and sat in the recliner.

Since Charlie had picked the movie, I expected it to be an action flick. One of those kinds with over-the-top shoot 'em up scenes and a bunch of unrealistic special effects. It wasn't that in the least bit. From the moment the movie started, I was drawn in by the main character, a woman, Jeanette Wall, who had done well for herself as a journalist.

In that first scene, on her drive home after having dinner at an upscale restaurant, she notices a woman picking through garbage in a Dumpster, then realizes it's her mom. From there we watched her poverty-stricken childhood, where she, along with her siblings, were neglected by their whimsical artist mother and highly intelligent alcoholic father.

As the movie played on, I found myself relating with several main story lines. Of her siblings, Jeanette seemed to have this special connection with her dad like I had. Though he was an alcoholic and his mistakes caused their family to have a ton of instability in their lives, she genuinely loved him and believed in him. After years of alcohol abuse and neglect, she finally understood he'd never change, and when she had the chance, she left home. That part was difficult for me as I watched her do as I had and leave her little sister behind.

The end of the movie hurt the worse though, when after all the pain the dad had caused her, there was a moment where I saw how much he loved her. Even through his dysfunction, he was able to see her and admit that he had hurt her. Would I ever get that resolution from my dad? At the moment, that seemed like an impossible desire, one that hurt me more the longer I held onto it. Tears streamed down my face as the credits started and pictures flashed on the screen.

"You okay?" Joe whispered in my ear.

I nodded and wiped the tears away.

Charlie stood and turned on the light. "That wasn't what I expected. I only picked it because of the actor."

"I liked it," Joe said.

I breathed in, overwhelmed, wishing I had a place to go to be alone with my thoughts. I needed space to process my emotions. I stood. "I'm going to go for a walk."

Joe eyed me warily and glanced at Charlie. "Baby, it's freezing outside."

"I know. I need a few minutes though." I walked to the door and took my coat off the hook.

It was cold outside, but the night air was calm. I started toward the beach as the sadness overwhelmed me again. The movie had opened this raw deep place—this longing for my dad that, except for a miracle from God, would never be fulfilled. I'd seen that vision of my dad proudly walking me down the aisle, but what if it had been only wishful thinking? What if I'd seen that in my mind because there was this part of me that would always want our relationship restored, no matter how much he'd hurt me?

I kicked at a hill of sand. Why couldn't he acknowledge what he did and get help so he could be in my life? Was I not worth it to him? Why couldn't he at least meet me halfway? I trudged forward, my feet heavy. I wished I could let him go, but a part of me not only wanted him in my life, but needed him.

I gazed at the star-filled sky and wondered if I would ever truly be free of what my dad had done to me. If he never changed, if he never saw how much he hurt me, would this hole inside me ever be filled? Would I be a broken little girl longing for healing for the rest of my life?

If my dad changing was the source of my healing, then I was screwed. Each time I'd tried to make any step toward him, it had only made it worse. He wasn't even speaking to me now. I walked along the beach for a long time, sorting through the gnarled mess of emotion that the movie had stirred in me. Turning, I started toward Charlie's. I wasn't going to be able to make sense of this stuff tonight. It could take years to work through questions this deep.

In the dark, footsteps came toward me, and my pulse quickened. I reached into my coat pocket for my phone, but it wasn't there.

"Tamara?" Joe's voice came through the night air, and relief washed through me.

"Oh, my goodness." I clutched my chest. "You scared the crap out of me."

"You scared me first. You said only a few minutes. I tried calling you, but your phone was on the coffee table."

"Sorry. I got caught in my head."

Joe took hold of my freezing hands. "I could imagine, with the events of the day and then that movie."

We started walking toward Charlie's house again. "Yeah, it was a lot."

We strolled in silence for a few minutes before I shared my thoughts. "I think I might be delusional regarding wanting my dad in our wedding."

He stopped and turned toward me, taking hold of my other hand. "How so?"

"That movie made me think. It made me see I have such a desperate need for my dad to acknowledge what he did to me and want to be in my life that my wires may have been crossed."

I could see now that most of my interactions with my dad had been driven by this need, and that had only made things worse between us.

Joe quietly rubbed my arms. I wished he would say something. Something to cool this scorching ache in my chest.

"I think I may have royally messed things up." I confessed.

"Tamara," Joe said my name with the same reverence that he had on the phone yesterday. "I'm so sorry that he failed you as a man and as a dad. I want to validate your feelings. You don't deserve what he did to you, and it's not your responsibility to fix things with him."

Then why did I feel so responsible? I stepped in closer to him, needing his comfort and warmth.

"Last night when I talked to Levi, I was overcome by this need for your dad to see you. I mean, truly see you. I wanted for him to know that despite his abuse and rejection, you have become one of the strongest women I know."

How could he say that after everything we'd been through together?

"I know that this is hard, but no matter what happens, whether he can acknowledge what he did to you or not, whether he's in our wedding or not, I want you to see how far you've come. The girl I met a couple years ago was closed off and would have avoided anything painful. Now you're facing your pain courageously, not quitting even when it feels like every door has slammed in your face."

I shivered, and Joe drew me in closer. "I know it doesn't carry the same weight as it would coming from your dad, but, Tamara, I see who you've become, and I'm so proud of you. I believe you're going to be the best wife and mom ever."

His words wrapped around me, cooling the embers, refreshing my soul. He was right. It wasn't the same as hearing the words from my dad, but in some way, they meant more coming from Joe. He knew me better than anyone on the planet, and I could tell he meant what he said.

Truth was, my dad didn't know me. He had chosen to let his rage and unforgiveness blind him from who I had become. That was on him. But I wouldn't make that same mistake. Deep down, in this place of hurt, I had to choose to forgive him. I had to learn to surrender this need for him to acknowledge the pain he had caused me, because I had to heal. I had to believe I could find peace, no matter if my dad ever changed or not.

I leaned my head against Joe's torso. "Thank you, Joe. You have no idea what that means to me."

He held me in silence for a few more minutes. "There's something I wanted to talk to you about."

I glanced at his face, though it was nearly impossible to see under the dim light of the moon.

He took hold of my hands again and ran his finger over my engagement ring. "I know that you've been hesitant in the past when it comes to us rushing to the altar, but Tamara, I believe it's time. I want to go forward with this. Could we please move the date up? I don't want to spend another moment without you as my wife." He rested his hand gently on my belly. "I would love for the three of us to live under one roof."

My heart swelled at his words. In the past when we discussed moving up the wedding, I'd resisted because I believed I wasn't ready. But what if it was really because of this pain I kept wanting my dad to heal? My insides burned, but this time in a good way. As scary as it felt, it was time to release that place to God. To trust that even if I never got what I needed from my dad, God would fill it.

"When were you thinking?"

"Would the twenty-first work?"

In my mind's eye, I watched the last bit of the dream of my

dad being at my wedding slip away. It was time to go forward with my future, whether he was in it or not.

"Can we have a real wedding?" Maybe I could get Nathan to walk me down the aisle.

"Absolutely, babe."

My mind spun around the details that would need to be put together in two weeks, and anxiety filled me. Could things come together that quickly and would the money we had left cover everything? Leaning into Joe, I mentally released each detail to God, and the buzz in my lungs calmed a bit.

I could do this. *We* could do this. "Yes. I believe I'm ready," I whispered.

His strong arms crushed me against him. "You just made me the happiest man alive."

Excitement stirred within me despite the day's sadness. In two weeks, I would be married to this wonderful man. That thought in itself brought enough joy to carry me through.

CHAPTER 52

January 8, 11:01 p.m.

TAMARA

After saying good night to Joe, I went into the house to tell Charlie the news. I found him sitting on the couch with the sports channel on, watching as a sportscaster reflected on a football game earlier in the day. I took a seat next to him 'on the couch. "Thanks again for dinner and the movie."

He muted the television and turned toward me, empathy in his gaze. "I'm sorry about the movie choice. I had no idea how close to home it would be for you."

I shook my head. "It's fine. It helped me work through some things I didn't know I needed to."

He tilted his head with a tentative smile. "This is probably why I remain single. I'm constantly making jackass moves with good intentions."

"Gotta work on that timing," I teased with a laugh, but inwardly I racked my brain for someone great I could introduce him to. "I have some news."

"Oh yeah?"

"Joe and I moved the date up on our wedding to the twenty-first of this month."

Charlie's eyebrow lifted. "That's really quick."

I bit my lip, my eyes jetting to the side. "I know, but it feels right."

"Can't argue with that. Let me know if there's anything I can help with."

"Thanks, Charlie."

He'd already helped me with so much, I was pretty sure I owed him my right kidney. My thoughts went to Dakota in my bedroom. I hadn't had a chance to ask him about Dakota staying with us for a few days until we found a place for her.

"There is one thing."

"What's that?" He leaned back and put his feet on the coffee table.

"In case you were unaware, Dakota is crashed in my room right now." I cringed inwardly, annoyed that I was having to ask him for another favor.

"I'm well aware of that."

I rubbed my hands on the front of my jeans. "Would you mind if she stayed with us for a few days while we get her sorted out?"

"I don't know," he said with a playful smile. "Two cute girls staying under my roof and neither of them are my girlfriend. Sounds like a sick joke to me."

I smacked his arm.

He chuckled. "Of course, she can stay."

"Thanks, Charlie. I seriously owe you." For this and every other kind thing he'd done for me. "I'm going to head to bed. I have a long couple of weeks ahead of me."

I said goodnight, went to my room and slowly opened the door, careful not to wake Dakota. I undressed and got into an oversized T-shirt and yoga pants, contemplating purchasing sexy pajamas for when I was married to Joe. I wouldn't want to sleep next to him dressed like this. Crawling into bed, I gently pulled the covers over me.

"Tamara," Dakota whispered in the dark.

Shoot. Oh well. At least I tried.

"I have a question for you." Her voice was soft.

"Yeah?"

"What happened in Vancouver after I left with your car."

I didn't want to speak of this, especially not with Dakota. She didn't need to know how much tension she had caused between me and Joe. "Joe wanted me to go to the cops, and I refused, which caused a huge fight."

She rolled toward me. "You should've turned me in."

"Why? So you could be stuck in the system with a felony? What good would that do? I would rather sacrifice my car than do that to you."

She stayed silent for a long time. "At the meeting this afternoon, Joe told his story. He said he fell off the wagon."

"Yeah ..." It was hard to imagine, my perfect man, broken to the point that he'd turned to the bottle. "But he didn't stay in that place, and he's here now."

She was quiet again, and I hoped she didn't have any more questions for me. Today had been full of enough grief. I'd rather think about happy things. "Joe and I decided to move our wedding date up."

"That's great, sis."

"I hope you'll be my maid of honor."

"Wow." Her body tensed. "That's a big step. Are you sure you would trust me with such a task?"

"Absolutely. I wouldn't want anyone else."

"You're not going to make me wear one of those froufrou dresses, are you?"

I laughed too loud. "I ask you to be my maid of honor and this is what you're worried about?"

"I don't even like dresses, let alone froufrou ones."

"Fine, no froufrou," I said, but honestly, I wouldn't want anything like that. I wanted my wedding to be understated, simple, and elegant.

"All right, count me in."

The conversation shifted after that. She spoke of her time

with Tim and Sage and how great they both had been. I wasn't sure what it was, whether it was the time with Nathan and Mom or going with Joe to that NA meeting, but something seemed different in her. Softer. I wanted to ask her, but I was scared to rock the boat by calling attention to it. Somewhere around one in the morning, we drifted off to sleep.

CHAPTER 53

January 9, 10:30 a.m.

TAMARA

As soon as I woke, I darted to the bathroom. Though tiny, the baby already rested on my bladder. I washed my hands and splashed water on my face, then walked to the bedroom. I picked up my phone to text Joe and noticed the time. It was already ten thirty. I couldn't afford to sleep in. Counting today, I had twelve days left to plan my wedding.

I clicked on Joe's name and saw that he had texted me ten minutes ago saying he'd be here soon and that he had something important to show me. I threw on some clothes and went into the living room, leaving Dakota fast asleep on the bed.

Charlie stood in the kitchen, cooking, creating smells that made my stomach turn.

"Good morning." I walked past him and retrieved the box of saltines from the cupboard.

"Nice breakfast," he teased.

"It's the only thing I can keep down this early." I stuffed a cracker into my mouth and sat at the kitchen table.

He slid an omelet onto a plate, grabbed his coffee, and joined me. "Whatcha doing today?"

I swallowed my bite. "I'll probably go dress shopping and

search for a place to have the wedding. Preferably, one with a reception hall."

He lifted a fork and dug into his food. "I wanted to talk to you about that."

I squinted at him, confused. "About what?"

"What would you think about using Midways for your reception? You cover the cost of food, and I'll take care of the rest."

"Are you sure? That seems like a lot."

"I insist. It will be my wedding present to you."

I gave him a doubtful look. "You don't have to do this. You have already done so much, and I planned on having a simple reception."

"Perfect. This will be simple, and now you can cross it off your to-do list."

I stood and threw my arms around him. "Thank you! You're the best!"

"Just make sure you introduce me to one of your hot single friends that night."

"Oh, so you have hidden motives?" I laughed and stepped away. I didn't have many single friends. Maybe Claire ... hopefully, she could make it on such short notice. "I'll see what I can do, but seriously, Charlie, you're a great guy. I'm sure love is right around the corner for you."

The doorbell rang. I walked across the house to answer it. "That's probably Joe."

I swung the door open wide. "Twelve more days." Joe stood there beaming, wearing jeans and a throw over. "Come on. I want to show you what I've been doing this morning."

"I'll see you later, Charlie," I called over my shoulder and followed Joe to his Jeep.

We got in and he reversed out of the driveway.

"Where are we going?"

"That's for me to know and you to wonder about."

"Not this again." I examined the vehicle with a goofy smile. "Where's the blindfold?"

He made a clicking noise with his mouth. "Darlin, you need to see this time."

I laughed. "Always changing the game, aren't you?"

He waggled his eyebrows. "It keeps things interesting that way."

Within minutes, we were driving on Ocean Shores Blvd. Joe parked in front of a nice home with a wraparound front porch facing the beach.

He turned off the car and waved toward the building. "What do you think?"

"It's lovely."

He opened his car door. "Come on." He jumped from the Jeep and walked toward the house. I followed him.

"This place would be a perfect starter home for us. It's on the higher side of our budget, but it's a two-bedroom with an amazing spacious kitchen and open floor plan."

I smiled at his joy and followed him into the house. It was nicer inside than out. It appeared as though it had been recently remodeled with beautiful wood floors.

"How far on the higher side?" A house this nice on the beach could not be cheap.

He tugged me into the kitchen filled with new appliances. "It's twelve hundred a month."

I looked around the room. That wasn't a bad price considering the space and location. "How much to move in?"

"First month and deposit would be one thousand eight hundred."

I drew out a whistle, thinking on how low our cash flow was at the moment. "That's a lot to come up with."

"I've been racking my brain trying to make it work. What would you think about using the wedding fund?"

Was he serious? That would fully drain our account. How could I plan a wedding without any money?

"I don't understand. Are you wanting to get married at the courthouse?"

I wasn't sure why the words hurt so badly to say. Possibly because it would mean the dream of my dad giving me away would be officially dead.

"Baby, no." Joe came closer and cupped my face with his hand, his gaze searching mine. "You deserve a real wedding."

His love wrapped around me in that familiar way, strengthening me.

"I have a credit card with a twenty-thousand-dollar limit. We'll need to be frugal, but we can use it for the wedding."

Another scratch in the proverbial record. I hated the thought of using credit for our wedding. "I don't know, babe. I don't want to start our marriage in a ton of debt."

"I know. I don't want to either, but we'll be getting money from selling my house, and the settlement here soon will be able to pay it right off."

I could feel the worry lines deepening in my forehead. "But we don't know when either of those things will happen. We can't count on that for finances."

He gazed at me, eyes pleading. "I hear you. I'm planning to get a job as soon as we're moved. I just need to get these things in order."

I glanced around again at the immaculate kitchen. "This place is amazing, and I would love to live this close to the ocean."

"Me too." He nodded and took hold of both of my hands, knotting his fingers with mine. "Is it all right if I use the money and fill out the application?"

I inhaled deeply, inwardly releasing my anxiety to God once more. "Okay, yes. I think we should do it."

A grin crept over his face, "Are you sure? I'm excited about this, but I know this is a huge decision. I want you to be completely on board."

I smiled and kissed him. "Yes, I am."

"Awesome!" He pumped his fist in the air in victory before

giving me another quick peck on the cheek. "I'm going to make a phone call to the landlords. I hope to get us moved while you plan the wedding."

I looked around the house for a few more minutes, feeling this crazy surreal sensation tingle through me. This would be the home Joe and I would come to the night we were married. Those were the steps he'd carry me over. I ran my hand over my belly. This was the house we'd bring our baby home to. This is where we would start our forever. I let myself soar there for a few minutes while I wandered from room to room, then reality struck. Before I could start forever, I needed to plan the details of my wedding. It was time to gather the troops. I reached for my phone and texted Nathan.

What's Amanda's number?

A few seconds later, a text came through, sharing her contact. I clicked on it and hit send, stepping outside. Across the yard, Joe wore lines in the grass, seeming to be having a serious conversation.

"Hello," Amanda answered.

"Hi, this is Tamara." I kept my eyes on Joe, concern pinging my stomach.

"Hey, how are you doing?"

"I'm okay. How's Nathan?" Should I have called him first to check in with him?

"He's doing all right. Last night was rough. After he got home, he called Josiah with the news."

Sad. I could imagine how that conversation went.

"He was awake half the night after that."

I glanced at Joe again. Worry lines creased his forehead and his cheeks were blotched red. What was going on with him? He'd been elated a few minutes ago, but now he seemed to be carrying a huge weight.

"What can I do for you, Tamara?" she asked, breaking the silence.

I took in a deep breath to brush off the worried feeling. "I'm calling to see if the offer still stands with you helping with my wedding."

"Absolutely."

"Awesome, because Joe and I decided to move the date to the twenty-first of this month."

"What?" Her voice pitch elevated an octave. "That's like two weeks from now."

"I know. That's why I need your expertise."

"Wow, okay, yes. I'm in."

"Great. First thing on the agenda is finding a wedding dress. Would you be available to go shopping with me this afternoon?"

"Sure. I'll have my mom watch the kids."

Ivy's tiny angel face came before my vision, squeezing my soul with longing. That little girl had sneaked into my heart so easily. "What do you think about Ivy being the flower girl?"

"Oh, my goodness. She would love that," Amanda said.

My heart melted at the thought of her walking down the aisle in a princess gown sprinkling flowers on the floor. "Sweet. I'll be there at one."

I hit the end icon and scrolled to Shelby's name. Never in a million years would I have thought I would have included her in my special day. In some ways though, I was thankful for her. If she hadn't hurt me the way she did, I would have never met Joe.

Before I could hit send, my phone rang, startling me. Mom's number flashed on the screen. I answered it.

"I just got off the phone with Josiah." Her voice had this raspy quality to it that made me want to cry. "We're trying to find a way to get the family together to have a memorial for Gabriel." Her voice grew quiet on the last two words as if she was having trouble speaking. "The soonest he'll be able to make it will be the seventeenth. Will you be around?"

The seventeenth. That was four days before my wedding. It would be close, but at least it would mean Josiah would be here for my big day.

"Yeah, Mom. I didn't have a chance to tell you yesterday, but Joe and I are moving to Ocean Shores."

"Oh, that's wonderful, honey."

Joe ended his phone call and came to stand next to me, his features weighed down.

"Yeah, with the baby coming, I wanted to be close." I twisted my engagement ring on my finger. "Also, Mom. Joe and I decided to move the date to the twenty-first of this month."

Complete silence.

"Mom?"

"Sorry. This is a lot to take in. How are you going to plan a wedding in two weeks?"

"I have no idea. I hoped you could help me. What are you doing this afternoon?"

"Nothing. I took a personal day off of work."

"I know you probably needed the day to yourself after last night, but Dakota, Amanda and I are going wedding dress shopping, and I'd love for you to join us. I could use all the help I could get."

"I think spending the day with my girls is exactly what I need."

"Great, I'll fetch you on the way to Amanda's around twelve forty-five. I love you." Oh man, if Shelby tagged along, the car would be crowded.

"Love you too, sweetie."

I ended the call and turned to Joe. He wore that stressed expression that happened sometimes when things weren't going well. "You all right?"

"That was the insurance company on the phone."

"What happened?"

"They're low balling us. Big time." He raised his hands in the air and blew out a breath. "The number they offered us would barely cover the clean-up and rebuild, let alone paying the employees and our loss of income."

"Can't we fight them on it?"

"Yes, and I will be getting in touch with my attorney, but that means it will take a lot longer to get the money from them."

"Joseph Michael Phillips," I said tenderly. "We're going to be okay."

He crossed his arms in front of him, eyebrows pinched together. "I should have never bought that diner. This is such a nightmare."

"Hey." I slid my hands around him. "It's going to work out. It's only a matter of time."

"Look at you." His features softened as his hands came around my back. "How did you get such great faith?"

"This right here." I kissed his cheek. "It's my first promise fulfilled. God restored our relationship. Number two is that Dakota is here and she's sober."

"And this is promise number three," Joe said as he placed his hand on my belly.

"Exactly." I smiled. "We have to keep moving forward in faith."

Joe inhaled deeply. "You're right. That's the only thing to do."

"You better believe it. Now, I have a wedding to plan, and you have two lives worth of stuff to move."

Joe pulled away, nodding in agreement. "Once I sign the paperwork on the house, I'm going to go to Vancouver and start packing."

I inhaled through my nose, suppressing the overwhelming anxiety trying to engulf me. "Sounds like a plan I'm heading dress shopping today, and I'll be on the hunt for a wedding venue after that."

Joe tilted his head to the side, eyes soft. "I would offer to help, but I'm going to have my hands full with the move."

"That's okay. There is one thing though. Could you please call David and ask him to marry us?"

"Sure thing, babe."

I snuggled into him once more and breathed in his scent, letting his embrace calm my anxious heart. The next two weeks may be insanely busy, but it would be worth it the moment we said our vows.

CHAPTER 54

January 10, 12:01 p.m.

JOE

I blasted the radio as I drove toward Vancouver to drown the thoughts ... well, more like to ignore my doubts. There were three things I was sure of: I was going to be a father, I was going to marry Tamara, and I was supposed to move to Ocean Shores. But at this moment, things with our finances were unsteady, and the one thing I thought would turn the tides just got shot down. If I were to get the money I had coming, I needed to get a lawyer involved, which meant it could be months or even years until I'd see a dime. I didn't have years though. I needed the money to come through so I could rebuild and sell the place. I heaved a deep sigh.

God, show me what to do.

We have to keep moving forward in faith. Tamara's words played through my head. She was right. I had to let go of the things I couldn't change and work on the things I knew I could. To put one foot in front of the next and trust. If I had to, I could get multiple jobs in Ocean Shores. I would do what it took to take care of my family.

First step—put the wedding stuff in order. I found Caleb's number and called him.

"Joseph, my man. What's going on?" Caleb's voice came through the speaker.

I smiled. We hadn't spoken since New Year's, and there was a lot of catching up to do. Hopefully, he'd be happy for me in spite of his issues with Tamara. "Hey, bro, just calling to see what you were doing on the twenty-first?"

"You know I don't plan that far in advance."

"I'm going to need you to because I'm getting married, and I want you to be my best man."

"What?" He choked on the word. "Your love life is seriously giving me whiplash."

A part of me wanted to fill him in on how things had changed, but I knew he wouldn't understand. There might always be a weird tension between him and Tamara, but that was okay. She was the woman I loved. I didn't need to defend that to him.

"We made up on her birthday and, are you sitting?"

"No, I'm in the driveway."

I changed lanes to pass a slow driver. "Turns out, you're going to be an uncle."

"What?" His voice pitch rose three octaves. "Wow, congratulations, man. That's awesome."

"You think?"

"Yeah, and I'll be in that wedding. I know I've had my doubts about Tamara, but I can see how much you love her. You know what they say? You can't deny love. Can't buy it either."

I laughed. "Thanks, Caleb. Should I mark you down for a plus one?"

"Yes, sir. I'll take the steak. Hailey will have the chicken."

"You'll be lucky if you get a hamburger at this point." Heck, we didn't even know where we were going to have the ceremony.

"Nothing wrong with a hamburger, but I gotta go for now. Love ya."

"Ummm, me too."

"Oh my gosh. Sorry, man. Force of habit with the woman, you know."

Whoa! Caleb and Hailey were saying the L-word? That was major. "It's cool. Talk to you soon."

Chuckling, I ended the call. That was one thing to check off my list. Next and maybe more important was David. I hit his name and the phone rang over the speakers. Four rings later, it went to voicemail. I left him a message for him to call me. Then I went through the rest of the list of phone calls, letting people know Tamara and I were getting married on the twenty-first at a location that would be announced soon. Trudy was ecstatic, Claire was overjoyed, and both wanted to know if there was any way they could help.

After going through the list, I decided to try calling my realtor, Andrew Beck. He answered quickly with too much cheer in his voice.

"Hey, Joe. What can I do for you this fine afternoon?"

"I know it's only been a few days, but I wanted to check on the house."

"It's going good. There's been some interest. I showed it twice yesterday, and I'm planning an open house this week."

"Sounds great. I'm going to be moving my stuff over the next few days. Will it be okay that it's unfurnished?"

"I think it will be fine. Like I said before, it's a sellers' market, and we have your place marked at the right price."

A niggling sensation worked through my brain. "Hey, can I have you look into something for me? I own that lot on the corner of 99th and Highway 99. I'd planned to rebuild, but I was wondering how much I could get for the lot as is."

Noises of fingers moving across a keyboard. "Residential is my specialty, but I can check with my team and let you know."

"Sounds good. Thanks, Andrew."

"You bet."

I clicked the red button and cranked the radio. For now, that was all I could do. The rest was in God's hands. I remembered the set of large hands God had shown me on the beach. I smiled and pictured placing this new set of problems in them.

I didn't know how things would work out, but I was finally learning to trust. He was a good Father. He had good things planned for my life. In this moment, believing this, no not only believing, but knowing this deep down, was enough.

CHAPTER 55

January 10, 12:42 p.m.

TAMARA

It was nice to have my car again, but it was a bit crowded with Shelby, Dakota, Amanda, and Mom. Good thing the three girls in back were tiny, otherwise, they wouldn't have fit.

Amanda directed us to the Rose Bridal Boutique in downtown Aberdeen, which she said had beautiful dresses for a decent price. I hoped by 'decent price' she meant around five hundred because that was the most I felt comfortable charging.

We climbed out of the car and made our way into the boutique. A pretty woman with short hair wearing a leopard print blouse stood by a rack of bridesmaid's dresses, organizing them according to color.

"Good afternoon, ladies." She peeked over her gold-rimmed glasses. "How may I help you today?"

Shelby pushed me forward. "This girl is getting hitched and needs a dress."

"Wonderful. My name is Rose, Rose Roden." She stepped from behind the rack and stuck her hand toward us. "I'm the owner of this establishment."

I shook her hand. "I'm Tamara."

She gave me a quick once over. "Are these lovely ladies with you the wedding party?"

"It's going to be a small wedding. My sister, Dakota, is the maid of honor. These two are helping with the details but aren't in it." I pointed to Amanda and Shelby then looped my arm around Mom. "And this is my mom."

Rose placed her hand on her chin, with that same assessing look. "I see. When is the date?"

"The twenty-first," I said.

"Of what month, dear?"

"January."

"Great. A year from now. I love it when brides plan ahead."

I glanced around at the ladies, butterflies swimming in my tummy. "No, I meant eleven days from now."

"Oh. Wow. Okay. That certainly changes things." She hurried across the room and opened a filing cabinet behind the counter. She pulled out a form and handed it to me. "There are so many things involved when planning a wedding. Eleven days is pushing it. What size dress do you wear? Let's hope we already have a dress here that you love because we can't rush anything that quick."

Anxiety fluttered in my belly. She was right. Could we pull it off? "I'm a size four," I said, my voice weak.

Mom placed her hand on mine with a gentle smile. "It will be okay. It will come together the way it's meant to."

I breathed in deeply and nodded.

Rose's gaze turned sympathetic. "She's right. Let's work on getting you a dress today." She glanced toward Dakota. "And you too, young lady."

Dakota gave her a curt smile and turned away to hide an eye roll.

"What is your price range?" Rose asked me.

"I budgeted five hundred dollars."

She bit her bottom lip and peered around the store. "Okay, let's see what we have in stock. Is there anything specific you're looking for?"

"I'm not sure. I was thinking simple and elegant."

She smiled. "Well, with your figure, I think most of these

dresses would look amazing on you." She walked to a rack and grabbed a slip and bustier. "Follow me." We trailed her to the fitting rooms, and she handed me the undergarments. "You get these on, and I'll start bringing you dresses. What are the colors of your wedding?"

"Ivory and burgundy," I said, slightly unsure.

"Great. I'll get some dresses for the maid of honor as well."

Behind us, Shelby dug through the gowns on the nearest rack. She lifted a shimmering black dress that would barely reach her mid-thigh. "I think I found what I'm wearing to your wedding," she said with mischief in her expression.

"How is it that you find the skimpiest thing in the store without even trying?" I asked with a laugh.

"It's a gift." She snickered.

A few minutes later, Rose returned with several gowns for me to try on. The first two were not good, and the others agreed. The third was better but didn't feel quite right. The fourth and fifth were even worse. Too much fluff and frills. The one on the mannequin in the window would be perfect, but I was afraid it might be too expensive. It was an A-line princess style with an off-the-shoulder sweep. The top had beautiful, embroidered lace, and the bottom was a gorgeous flowing chiffon.

Amanda noticed me eyeing it. "How about you try that one on?"

"I don't know. It looks expensive."

Amanda ignored my caution and waved to Rose, who was off searching for more dresses with my limitations. "Can she try on that one?" She pointed at the mannequin.

Rose's countenance brightened. "Oh, yes. It's a bit above your price range, but we could open a line of credit if you need."

"I don't know …"

"Try it on, sweetie." Mom interjected.

Shelby nodded. "You have to at least see how if fits you. Yolo, girl."

"Did you seriously just *yolo* my wedding dress?"

She pursed her lips. "Sure did."

I laughed. "Fine. I'll try it on."

Dakota exited the changing room, wearing a burgundy, asymmetric, hem high waist, sleeveless chiffon dress.

"Dakota, you look amazing," Amanda said.

She grimaced. "You're lucky I love you, sis."

I smiled, "I think it's perfect."

Mom nodded.

"You look hot," Shelby piped in.

"Oh, that does look nice. It would go great with this dress." Rose walked toward us, holding the gown I had requested. "Here you go."

My insides fluttered. The dress would go perfect with Dakota's, but how much would it cost? I tried to ignore the pestering thoughts as I stepped into the fitting room. I slipped the dress over my head, zipped it as far as it would go and looked in the mirror. Goosebumps covered my skin. I loved it. It was absolutely perfect. It was elegant, beautiful, and it fit like it was made especially for me. I didn't think it would even need alterations.

I stepped out of the fitting room. Mom gasped and covered her mouth, tears welling in her eyes. "You're beautiful, honey."

"That is definitely your dress, chica," Shelby said.

"As much as I hate this kind of stuff, I have to say I agree," Dakota said, her arms crossed in front of her. She had already changed into her jeans.

Amanda squealed, clapping her hands together. "You must say yes to that dress."

I peeked at the price tag. It said $899.99. Wow. This dress was amazing, but I didn't want to start my marriage with that kind of debt and there were other expenses to consider. "I'm sorry, I can't afford it."

"That is completely understandable. We will find a gown in your range." Rose started toward the rack.

"That won't be necessary." Mom dug in her purse. "I will be paying for both your and Dakota's dresses."

My jaw dropped open in shock. "What? Mom, you can't do that. That's over twelve hundred dollars between the two."

"I can do the math, honey." She took her wallet from her purse with a smile. "Your dad and I are doing pretty well for ourselves these days, and I have some money saved for special occasions."

"Oh, Mom." I pulled her into a hug. "Thank you."

She held me tightly for a long moment before stepping away and wiping at her glistening eyes. "It's the responsibility of the bride's parents to pay for the wedding, so I want to take care of the rest of the details too."

"What, Mom, no!"

She lifted a hand in protest. "Please, Tamara, I've missed so much of your life. Please let me do this."

"But what about Dad? He won't be on board with this decision."

"He doesn't need to know everything I do." She winked and turned from me to the register. "After this is cake shopping," she called over her shoulder.

I stood dumbfounded, unsure of how to feel. For the last six years, I'd been used to having to take care of myself. It felt good to have a parent again. I couldn't wait to tell Joe. I excused myself and stepped outside, hitting the call button as I walked.

"Hey, beautiful," he answered. "How's it going?"

"Great, but I'm a bit overwhelmed."

"What's happening?" he asked sweetly.

"My mom just offered to pay for the whole wedding." I couldn't believe it as I said it.

"Babe, that's amazing! Especially now!"

A gust of wind blew on my face, bringing with it the smell of the surrounding restaurant food. "I know it is. I've just never felt this kind of support from my family."

"It sounds like another miracle."

I smiled. "It does, actually. Now we need one more."

"What's that, babe?"

"We need to find a venue for the wedding with this short of notice."

Joe was silent for a few beats. "Have you considered the bed-and-breakfast I've been staying at? They have that beautiful big room that opens toward the ocean. And it is off season, so it could be available."

Marrying Joe in front of the ocean would be like a dream come true. "I guess it's worth a shot."

"Why don't you call them and let me know."

"Okay. Have you talked to David yet?"

"Yes. He said he'd be honored to marry us."

"Yay! One more thing to check off. I love you."

"Love you too."

The ladies poured out the front door of the shop.

"Cake time," Amanda said, waving her hands in the air.

"Okay, yes." I lifted one finger. "I need to make one more phone call."

"I'll drive then," Dakota said.

I shrugged and followed them to the car. I climbed in the back so Mom wouldn't have to and googled the bed-and-breakfast phone number.

Amanda gave Dakota directions as she drove.

I pressed the call button and waited for an answer.

"Collins Inn & Seaside Suites. This is Samantha speaking. How may I help you?"

"Hi, Samantha. My fiancé is staying in your inn, and we are wanting to rent your banquet room that faces the ocean on the twenty-first if it's available."

"Let me check, but I'm pretty sure it's booked that weekend for a wedding."

My heart sunk. That place would have been perfect.

The sound of fingers moving across a keyboard came through the phone. "Hmm. Oh wow. There's been a recent cancellation."

"Awesome. How much is it?"

Dakota drove into the parking lot of the local bakery and parked. Samantha told me the price, which was actually quite a bit lower than I'd expected. The only issue was we were not allowed to bring any outside food or drinks, which seemed reasonable.

"We'll take it. Can you reserve it under my fiancé's name?" If Mom wanted to pay for it, she could settle up with us later.

"Sure, but we'll need to confirm it with him," Samantha said. "What is his name?"

"Joe. His name is Joe Phillips." I tried to suppress my excitement, but I sensed it overtaking my face.

"Great, you're set. Please let your wedding party and guests know they get a discount by using your name. We have plenty of rooms available that week."

"I will, thank you." I ended the call, beaming. I couldn't believe things were coming together so fast.

CHAPTER 56

January 17, 2:50 p.m.

TAMARA

I walked onto the pier and inhaled the crisp afternoon air. Joe came and stood beside me, and I leaned into him. In a few minutes, the rest of my family would be here for the commemoration of Gabriel's life. Then we'd spread his ashes into the water and say a final goodbye. Tears welled as I thought of everything that had brought us to this moment. Two years ago, today, I blazed into Vancouver thinking my car was on fire and met the most amazing man. One year ago, today, Hope was conceived. And today, I'd be eulogizing my brother as my family mourned over him. What was it with this day bringing both sorrow and joy?

Joe's grasp tightened around me. "How are you doing?"

"A bit sad. I wish I knew what to expect." Would my dad even show today? Or had he stayed in denial?

"I understand, but I want you to know that no matter what happens today, you're going to be okay. Over the last month, I've seen you learn to draw your strength from God alone. You've been through hell and back, and you're still standing. I'm so proud of you T."

A tear spilled over, and I wiped it from my cheek before snuggling into Joe, a fresh resolve rising in me. I ran my hand over my stomach, thankful he was here to remind me of the truth. Whatever the day held, God would strengthen us through it. And in four short days, we would meet at the altar and say our vows, sealing us together for the rest of our lives.

Up the beach, Nathan parked his minivan, then a black Traverse parked right next to it. Was that Josiah's car? Mom said he would be arriving this morning. I withdrew from Joe and started toward them. Nathan and Amanda got out and helped Colton and Ivy from their car seats. Josiah climbed out of the other vehicle along with a pretty blond. She circled the car and brought an infant from the backseat. Dakota came walking over. I smiled. All of my siblings were here, right in front of me.

Josiah noticed me and came running in my direction. "Look at you," he said, and wrapped me in a bear hug. I embraced him back, tears threatening to come again. I hadn't realized how much I missed him. I hadn't realized how much I missed each of them.

Josiah pulled away. "Come and meet your niece. She's the cutest darn thing you'll ever see."

I followed him to the blond woman holding the baby. I couldn't remember her name from when mom had told me before. "Tamara, this is Lindsey." He leaned over and spoke the next words tenderly. "And this is our little Mia."

She was beautiful, with chubby cheeks and strawberry shaped lips.

"She's adorable."

She smiled and cooed at me while kicking her legs.

A tan, older model Honda Accord drove in beside us. Dad sat in the driver's seat with shades on, his face hard. Had Mom coerced him to come? Had they fought over it? The hard set of his jaw made him appear more angry than sad.

Glancing around, I took my whole family in. Colton had taken a liking to his soon to be Uncle Joe. He stood close to him, pointing at the shells on the beach.

A somber look fell over Josiah's face as Dad climbed out of the car, followed by Mom holding the jar of ashes. Her eyes were puffy, her face drawn in lines of sorrow. I walked to Mom and embraced her, and she cried into my hair. I glanced at Dad, who remained quiet. Josiah offered his hand to shake, but Dad kept his focus forward, walking silently to the rest of the family.

When Mom let me go, I tried to take the ashes from her, but she shook her head and grasped the jar in a tight embrace along with more tears. I nodded. Josiah put his arm around her as we slowly moved toward the rest of the family.

Mom placed the ashes in the middle of us, and we gathered in a circle around it. For a long moment, we stood in silence, each of us retreating into our thoughts.

Josiah broke the silence. "I think we all would agree that Gabriel was the best brother we had. He was kind, helpful, and kept a great attitude no matter what. He was deeply loved and died way too early."

Nathan chuckled sadly. "I remember around six years ago, the three of us brothers decided to take an impromptu camping trip. Josiah brought his RV and let Gabriel sleep in there since he didn't have a tent. The next morning, Josiah and I woke early and sprinkled breadcrumbs on the roof. Soon, a bunch of birds flew over, pecking at the metal roof. He ran out of the RV buck naked, holding a pillow around him, screaming. We played so many pranks on him that camping trip, and some were a little mean, but he was a good sport and never retaliated. That was our last camping trip together."

Dakota cried softly. "I'm sorry, Gabriel. I'm so, so sorry."

I wrapped my hand around hers. I was the only one in this circle who knew the true depths of her pain. Even after what he had done to her, she had carried the guilt of his death.

"I'm sorry to each of you. For many years I've run from this moment, numbing myself from what I'd done." She quieted, suppressing a sob. "I was high the night he died. He came to the power lines that night to try and save me. The only thing he wanted was for me to get clean, and I pushed him away." She sniffed through her tears. "If I had left with him that night, he would be alive right now. He died because of me."

"This isn't your fault." I put my arm around Dakota.

Mom came and stood next to her, pulling her into an embrace. "You gotta let that go, baby. You have to forgive yourself." Her voice was hoarse as she spoke, coming out in stilted breaths. "We *all* have to forgive ourselves."

Nodding, I wished so deeply that she'd finally release the guilt of this horrific tragedy that wasn't her fault. I glanced at Dad, who stood motionless, a concrete statue. Why couldn't he let go of his pride and anger and care even a tiny bit that his kids were hurting?

God, please break through to him! My silent scream rose to the heavens as the wind blew around me, bringing a chill. I shivered, but on the inside, the gentleness of a subtle whisper, nudged me to speak.

Tell them about the ashes.

For the briefest moment, I wasn't on the beach with my family, but in the spot where our childhood home had burned to the ground. Jesus stood in front of me, the fire of love gleaming in his eyes. The warmth that I'd felt in my living room that day wrapped around me, giving me the confidence to speak.

"A few weeks before I knew that Gabriel had passed, he came to me in a dream." I gazed around the circle, taking in each one of their grief-stricken faces. "He told me that night that I needed to find our family. The thing is, I'd already been trying to find you guys. I had an intense need within me to be with you all again. A need I couldn't deny anymore."

I withdrew from Dakota and Mom, who were locked together in an embrace. "I found Dakota first, and this is when I learned about Gabriel." I paused and took time to meet each of their sorrow-filled gazes. "The moment Dakota told me what had happened, I was so devastated, I didn't think I could keep breathing. My whole body and soul were consumed with suffocating grief, but then the craziest and most beautiful thing happened. I had a vision."

I hesitated. Would they be ready to hear the next part? Would they think I was insane?

"Jesus came into my living room and asked me for Gabriel's ashes. I didn't want to give them to him. They were the only thing I had left of him, and I couldn't let them go."

I made eye contact with Dakota. Her face held a sad vulnerability. I glanced around the circle once more. Everyone but Dad seemed to be receiving me well.

"He asked me three times for the ashes before I surrendered them to him. As I did, each of you came into the picture, standing in the place where our trailer had burnt down. Jesus took the jar, opened it and sprinkled the ashes around us. From that place, flowers sprung up, blooming into a beautiful garden. After that the vision ended—" I paused, feeling strength enter me.

"Gabriel had been on the power lines that night because he wanted Dakota to be free to live a long and happy life. I believe he wants that for each of us. Dakota, what did you say his last words were concerning our family?"

Dakota wiped her cheek but kept her gaze on the sand. "He said our family had lost enough."

Mom let out a soul-piercing cry, and Dad flinched.

"I agree with Gabriel. Our family has lost enough, and I believe it was because many of us, including myself, were selfish." I glanced at Dad. His face was still cold. "I'm so sorry that I ran away and abandoned all of you. I told myself that I was doing the right thing, but the truth was, I was acting weak and afraid." I wiped at my tears. "But I believe that today marks a new day. Gabriel's desire was that our family would be brought together and healed. It's time that we let the past go and let the healing begin. So today, for Gabriel's sake, let's do everything in our power to be a family again."

A loud noise came from my dad, and he dropped to his knees, his face contorted with anguish.

"Dad! Are you all right?" Josiah ran toward him.

Dad clutched his chest. I ran to him and the others came closer.

"Get back! Give him space!" Nathan yelled. Was he having a heart attack?

"Gabriel can't be gone!" Dad cried from a deep guttural place. "He can't be." Tears streamed down from behind his sunglasses. "I'm sorry. I'm so, so sorry." He hunched over on his knees, wailing again and again. "I don't want to lose any more of my kids. Oh, God, forgive me."

I fell to my knees in front of him. Could it be that this was the first time it sunk in to him that Gabriel was actually gone? Did God use my words to infiltrate his hard shell? I leaned over to embrace my dad, and for the first time, his arms came around me. The rest of the family joined us on their knees.

"I am sorry, Tamara." His glasses fell to the ground. "You were right," he said through a deep sob. "Please forgive me. I can't lose any more of my kids."

My heart was overwhelmed with sympathy and sadness at the same time.

He drew back and looked at me. His lids were almost swollen shut from the tears he must have been crying the entire day. He peered around at us, lingering on each of our faces. "I'm sorry for allowing my anger to hurt you all. I swore I'd never be like my father. I tried to keep the anger at bay, but it was a part of me." His face slumped with shame.

Suddenly, I was drawn into a scene of my dad as a little boy playing with his toys full of joy as his father came in. The hulking man stepped on one of his action figures, and his face turned beet red as he pulled out his belt. The beating I saw in my mind's eye was way worse than anything that our dad had done to us. Sorrow and compassion filled me. That was where the cycle of abuse began, but today, it would end through our forgiveness. "I forgive you, Dad."

"Dad, I forgive you too." Dakota's voice shook as she spoke.

A dam burst inside of Josiah. "I forgive you, Dad."

"I forgive you," Nathan whispered. "I love you, Dad."

I glanced at Joe. His eyes were glossy with tears as he watched this sacred moment happening with my family. The words of forgiveness continued to flow, and Nathan helped Dad to his feet. We took turns hugging each other, letting the tears melt away years of grief. I wasn't sure what this would mean for my family, but thankfulness overwhelmed me as I realized this was a huge step toward one more promise being fulfilled.

CHAPTER 57

January 17, 4:26 p.m.

DAKOTA

For a long time after we spread Gabriel's ashes, I walked along the beach by myself while the rest of my family headed to Midways for lunch. They had asked me to join them, but I needed some time alone. The huge weight that I'd carried for years had been released from my shoulders—something I never thought would be possible.

I breathed in deep and stared at the ocean. What now? Who was I now that I didn't have to carry this secret anymore? There were parts of me that still were marred and twisted, but something happened today that was so miraculous and breathtaking, I was sure it had changed me forever.

My dad had actually apologized. He'd finally seen, after these many years, the damage he did to us, and he was willing to change —to even go through the steps to get the help he needed. If my dad could make such a huge step. If he could change, anyone could. That meant *I* could. I didn't have to let the molestation and abuse define me anymore. I didn't have to let my past mistakes define who I was. Today was a brand-new day. A day where I could put my past to rest.

I reached for my phone, found Tim's name and hit send.

"Dakota?" he answered, a question in his tone.

My heart expanded to the sound of his voice. His effect on me continued to scare the hell out of me, but I could feel a new courage rise within me. Fear had stolen too much of my life. It was time to look that thief in the face and take back what was mine. "Do you believe in miracles?" I asked.

Tim was quiet for a few seconds. "I'm not sure."

"I think I just witnessed one." I thought of the noise my dad made when he fell to the ground. I honestly thought he had been dying. Perhaps a part of him had.

"Oh yeah? You gonna tell me about it?"

How does someone explain a moment like that? It felt like the shattered pieces of my family had rejoined together, creating this beautiful mosaic. It would never look the way it had before. Gabriel was gone—a missing part of the whole—but as we came together to heal, those shattered parts could make texture and character.

Wow. I think I may have drunk the Kool-Aid. I felt like I was seeing life with a different set of lenses. My mind had shifted, and I was becoming a whole different person. "Someday, I hope to be able to explain it to you, but for now, there's this one part that pertains to you." I swallowed the fear that was trying to rise.

I could hear Tim breathing through the phone, but he stayed silent, waiting for me to finish.

"I think ..." Why did this have to be so hard? "If you still want to." Emotions flooded over me as I thought of our shared history and our night together in Whiskeytown. "I've been so scared to love people, Tim. I've been so scared to be loved. But after today, I think I'm ready to let you love me."

More silence. A big part of me wanted to say, "Kidding!" Or any other sarcastic thing I could say in the moment to ease the sting. But instead, I waited for too many agonizing seconds.

"That does sound miraculous."

I kicked at a mound of sand. That's all he was going to give me after that? I guess that was fair. I had pretty much thrown him out of my life after our night together.

"What are you doing four days from now?" I asked.

"I don't know. Polishing my gun collection." He chuckled. "Why do you ask?"

In the distance, a bird descended into the water and caught a fish with its beak.

"Well, Tamara's getting married, and I was wondering if you'd like to come with me."

"Are you asking me on a date?" He enunciated the word date.

"I guess I am."

"Where is this said date going to be located?"

"Ocean Shores. The twenty-first at 5:30 p.m. Sharp."

"I'll be there. Just so you know, Dakota, I've loved you since we were kids. It's never faded. And I'm sure I'll love you until we're old and gray, whether you're ready for it or not."

For the first time, his words penetrated past the barren walls of my heart, hitting me in places I thought had died forever. Before I could think better of it, the words tumbled from my mouth. "I love you too, Tim." I saw then that I always had.

CHAPTER 58

January 18, 9:30 a.m.

TAMARA

The next morning, I waited at the bed-and-breakfast restaurant for Joe and my parents. I arrived early so I could get a better feel for the room that Joe and I would be married in. For the most part, it was ready. The only thing we would need to do the day of the wedding was to bring in a simple arbor and a few flower arrangements. The part I loved the most was the huge window that opened toward the ocean. There wasn't a more perfect place to marry Joe.

Josiah and Lindsey had already taken advantage of the wedding block discount and moved into one of the suites, and several other guests would be arriving tonight. I smiled at the thought of gathering Claire, Trudy, Roger, Levi, Sarah, and David together in the same place.

I scanned the menu and checked my watch. Joe would have normally been here by now, but he'd been going nonstop with the big move. He'd been staying in the new house over the last week, but he'd made it absolutely off limits to me. He said I couldn't see the finished product until our wedding night, which I thought was adorable, but it made me super curious.

"Hey, beautiful." Joe's voice came from beside me. "Sorry I'm late."

"It's okay."

"I'd hoped to talk to you alone before your parents arrived."

We had been surrounded by family the whole day yesterday. After Mom and Dad left in the late afternoon, Nathan, Josiah, Dakota, Joe, and I headed to Midways and spent the rest of the evening catching up on each other's lives. Amanda and Lindsey had taken the children to Nathan's house while we hung out. It was a great time full of laughter and tears, but I never had a chance to debrief with Joe.

"That was incredible yesterday," Joe said as he took a seat across from me.

"I've been in complete awe the whole morning."

Across the room, I noticed Mom and Dad walk into the restaurant. I stood and waved them over. Mom saw me and gave me a bright smile, then Dad noticed me too. His lips curved slightly upward as they strode toward us.

"Good morning," I gave Mom a hug while Dad shook Joe's hand.

"This is a nice place," Dad said and wrapped me into an awkward but warm embrace. I squeezed him tightly, feeling my heart melt.

We let go of each other and sat at the table. The waitress came and poured our coffees and took our food orders.

"Theresa tells me you guys are moving to Ocean Shores," Dad said, sipping on his coffee.

"Yes, we are. We wanted to be close to family," I answered, fidgeting with my napkin.

"I think that's wonderful," Mom said.

"Tamara said you own a restaurant in Vancouver. What are you going to do with it if you move here?" Dad asked.

Joe shot me a look, and inwardly, I cringed. I never had a chance to tell my family about the fire.

"There was an incident right before I came that I haven't told you," I said, feeling my cheeks turn bright red. Hopefully, this wouldn't hurt the progress we had made.

"What kind of incident, honey?" Mom asked, alarm in her voice.

"There was a fire," Joe said.

"A fire?" Deep lines folded across Dad's forehead as his eyebrows rose.

"It was a total loss." I squeezed Joe's hand again.

"That's awful. What terrible timing," Dad said.

Joe frowned and focused on the steam rising from his coffee. "Yeah, the insurance company is trying to lowball me, but I have a few other things I'm working on."

"Oh yeah?" Dad took another sip of his coffee. "Tell me about it."

"I own a home in Vancouver that I've put on the market. It's a sellers' market, and I have a bit of equity in it, but I'm also seeing what I can get for that piece of land without rebuilding."

"I see." Dad brought his hand to his chin, a thoughtful expression lining his brow. "Well, if you need any help while you're getting on your feet, please let me know."

"Thank you, sir." Joe glanced at me and smiled. "I appreciate the offer, but I believe we are going to be okay."

Dad shook his finger at him with a playful gleam in his eye. "It's time to drop the sir bit. We're family. And while I can appreciate a man who prefers to stand on his own, please know the offer is on the table if you need it."

"That's generous, Dad, thank you," I said.

"Sure thing, kiddo." He stirred more cream into his coffee.

Joe's phone rang and he checked it. "Do you mind if I answer this?"

"Go ahead." Dad gave Joe a wave. "Hopefully, it's good news."

Joe stood and walked out of the restaurant, answering the phone as he left.

"I like him, honey." Mom leaned in and squeezed my hand.

"He's a good one," Dad said with a wink.

"I'm glad you approve." It meant a lot that they both liked him.

Dad's expression grew serious, and he averted his gaze. "I need to tell you something."

I was silent, unease wiggling through my chest.

"This morning I made an appointment with a therapist." He paused for a few beats before making eye contact. "I want you to know that I meant what I said on the beach yesterday. I'm so sorry for everything. I've been blind over the years, but I'm sincerely going to get help. I know it's going to take a while to earn your trust, but I want to make things right."

Waves of joy overwhelmed me. I'd pretty much resigned myself to this never happening, but here it was. My dad was making a genuine effort to be in my life. "Thank you, Dad. That means more than you know." I reached my hand toward him. "I wanted to ask you something."

"What's that?"

"Will you please walk me down the aisle on my wedding day and give me away?"

His eyes misted over again, but this time, a large smile overtook his face. "I would be honored to, cupcake."

I smiled at the endearment he used to call me as a child. Of course, I knew that there would be years of rebuilding our relationship, but something deep and healing happened yesterday that had changed us.

The waitress came with our food. I had ordered a fruit plate with cottage cheese, but now that it was here, my tummy acted like it might reject it.

Mom ordered the veggie omelet and Dad got the lumberman's breakfast. A triple egg and cheese scramble with onions, ham and cheese, hash browns and a triple stack of pancakes.

"Honey, you really need to watch your cholesterol." She scolded Dad.

He batted her words off as if they were a pesky fly. "I'm as healthy as a horse."

"That's not what your numbers say."

"Could you please let me enjoy my food in peace?" He spread butter over his pancakes and poured a ton of maple syrup on top. "You don't see me nitpicking your food choices."

"That's because I'm careful about what I eat." She cut into her veggie omelet and took a bite.

I smiled at their banter. Would this be Joe and me someday? I couldn't imagine that, but in their exchange, it was apparent the deep love Mom had for Dad.

Joe approached the table with a huge grin on his face. He took a seat next to me and peeked at his plate of food. "You won't believe what just happened."

I glanced across at the table at my parents, thinking of the miracles that had taken place lately. Nothing would surprise me at this point.

"This morning a cash offer came through on the house for over ten thousand dollars more than the listing price."

"No way!" I dropped my fork.

"Yes way. And there is more."

"More?" Dad asked, tilting his head.

Joe looked at each of us around the table, his gaze landing on me. "The realtor listed the diner lot yesterday morning and today there is a bidding war going on between two major fast food chains. If both sales go through, we could put a sizeable down payment on a restaurant here within a few months."

"Wow," was the only thing I could say. I was completely stunned.

Dad smiled and dug into his stack of pancakes. "Looks like you won't be needing any help from me after all."

My heart felt like it could burst. God had faithfully brought us through these darkest of trials, and now both of our dreams were on the verge of coming true.

CHAPTER 59

January 21, 5:26 p.m.

JOE

Nerves ran through me as I walked down the aisle to take my place at the altar. Through the glass wall facing the ocean, the sun was about to dip behind the water, and the sky was lit in beautiful purple and orange hues. Breathtaking. I took my place and turned toward the small crowd, taking in the familiar faces.

Tamara's family sat in the front row. Behind them were Trudy, Roger, Claire, Samuel, and Hailey. Charlie stood by the door helping people when they arrived. I had to hand it to him, overall, he had shown himself to be a good guy and a great friend to Tamara. Once I started hanging out with him, I couldn't find an insincere thing in him.

Levi and Sarah came through the door with Hope. This would be the first time Tamara had seen her since the adoption, but we had both decided we wanted them to be here today. Levi had played such a big role in both of our lives, it had felt right. They took a seat behind Trudy and Roger as music began to play from the speakers overhead. That was the cue for everyone to get into place. David strode the aisle toward me, smiling fondly. "You ready for this?"

I patted my front pocket where my vows were neatly hidden. "As I'll ever be."

"Great, because it's time." He took his place behind the glass pulpit. Shelby walked in with a guy I didn't recognize and sat across from Tamara's family. Tim followed behind them and sat next to Nathan.

A minute later, the music changed. Ivy came into view, holding a basket, wearing an ivory flowy dress with burgundy flowers embroidered into the skirt. She walked up the aisle beaming, scattering pink and red petals as she went. Dakota and Caleb appeared in the doorway and slowly walked down the aisle.

Caleb was dressed in a black tux with a burgundy vest that matched Dakota's dress. Dakota looked completely different from the first time I'd met her. The hardness in her countenance had softened, and a new light shone in her eyes. When they reached the front, Caleb stood next to me and flashed me a huge smile. I mirrored his grin, resisting the urge to give him a high five. Dakota took her place across from me.

The first few notes to *Bless the Broken Road* by Rascal Flats played, and Tamara appeared in the doorway next to her dad. All the breath was stolen from my lungs. She was absolutely stunning. Her gown was simple yet elegant, hugging her trim waist and flowing to the floor. Her hair was half-up and long curls ran past her shoulders. She held a single long stem rose. The kind I had brought her on our first date. She smiled at me, and my heart felt like melting wax inside my chest. This beautiful angel was going to become my wife today.

"All rise," David said.

The crowd stood and turned to face Tamara. She took her first step toward me, and I was completely undone. Today would be the start of our happily ever after.

CHAPTER 60

January 21, 5:35 p.m.

TAMARA

This moment felt surreal—almost unbelievable—but it was real. This was my real-life dream coming true. I was walking down the aisle toward the love of my life. We were about to commit the rest of this life to each other. And my dad was actually holding my arm, supporting me as he brought me to Joe. The last four days had softened the years of hurt. My dad and I were taking steps toward complete healing and because of it, he was able to be a part of this most special day.

Heart swelling, I focused on Joe as I walked toward him. The adoration in his gaze was enough to bring me to my knees. I steadied myself on Dad's arm and glanced at him. His face beamed with pride and love, exactly like the vision I had seen in my head on the way home from Quilcene.

A baby cooing brought me out of my thoughts, and I turned toward the noise. The most adorable infant bounced on Levi's lap, smiling and cooing at me. Hope. My throat tightened with mixed emotion. Sadness and joy, but more than that, love. Hope was here with her parents, and it felt right, as if the whole picture was finally complete. Everyone that I truly loved was gathered in this one room to witness my vows to Joe. Outside, the sun crested over the ocean, causing the water to glisten in the most brilliant way. I didn't think I could have asked for a more perfect moment.

Dad and I reached the end of the aisle and paused.

"Who gives this woman in holy matrimony?" David asked.

"Her mother and I do," my dad said as he placed my hand in Joe's before leaving my side and taking his place next to Mom.

I handed my rose to Dakota and turned to Joe, looking deeply into his eyes. They were misted over and so full of love. Tears welled in my eyes too.

"Dear friends and family, we are gathered here today to witness the merging together of two lives. Biblically, marriage is a sacred covenant where two lives are brought together and, in every way, become one. I've had the privilege of getting to know both Joe and Tamara over the last year, and I've seen wonderful growth in each of them. I witnessed their love for God and their love for each other. I believe that God has brought them together, and it is a great honor for me to be here today." David prayed a blessing over the service and took a few minutes speaking of the sacredness of marriage before he asked us if we had our vows ready.

Joe nodded and took a piece of paper from his vest pocket. He unfolded it and read, "I, Joseph Michael Phillips, take you, Tamara Christine Jensen, to be my wife." He searched my glistening gaze. "You have taught me more about love than any other person on the planet. You've shown me that it's not only about feelings, though my feelings run deeper for you than I ever thought possible. I've seen, through your actions, what true love is. First with Hope and then with the rest of your family. Your love has given me hope, joy, and has made me a better man. From this day forward, I vow to cherish you and to always be there for you. I promise to be your navigator, sympathizer, sidekick, best friend, and husband. Finally, I promise you myself. Without you, I am nothing—with you, I am more than myself. I can't promise to love you perfectly, but I vow to love you with everything I am and everything I have."

His voice was full of conviction as if he was speaking from the deepest parts of himself. "I will champion your dreams and fight alongside you as I build my dreams around you. I will protect you from harm, stand with you in troubles, and look to you when I need protection. I promise to be the man that I see now in your eyes—today, tomorrow, and for always. I love you with all my heart. I am completely yours."

David handed me a handkerchief, and I blotted the tears from my cheeks. I brought my gaze to Joe. He was the most perfect man ever created. I didn't have a paper to read from, but I didn't need one. I knew exactly what I wanted to say.

"Joseph Michael Phillips, I take you to be my husband." I swallowed the lump building in my throat as images from our love story played before my vision. "I've told you before, and I'll say it again. You have been the absolute best part of my life. When we met, I believed that true love wasn't possible for someone like me. I was so broken that I had erected a wall around my heart two feet thick and a mile wide. But somehow, you still saw me. You pushed past my walls and in doing so, you made me believe in love again. I know this hasn't been an easy road for you, but your love for me has completely changed my life. I want to thank you for loving me so purely, so unselfishly."

"Today, I give you all that I am and all that I have. I give you my heart, my faith, my life. I choose you today. And I will choose you again tomorrow. I will go on choosing you the day after, and every day for the rest of our lives. From this day forward, I join my life with yours. Wherever you go, I will go. Whatever you face, I will face. I promise to love you without reservation, comfort you in times of distress, encourage you to achieve your goals, laugh with you and cry with you, grow with you in mind and spirit, always be open and honest with you, and cherish you for as long as we both shall live."

Joe smiled at me through the tears that streamed down his face. I handed him my hanky and a sprinkle of laughter sounded behind us.

"Now it's time for the exchanging of rings," David said.

Caleb handed Joe my ring.

"Joe, place the ring on Tamara's finger and repeat after me," David said.

Joe brought the ring to my finger and repeated David's words to me with sincerity and truth. "With this ring, I seal my promise to be your faithful and loving husband as God is my witness. I give you this ring as a sign of my love, and with everything I have, I honor you and take you for my wife."

When he was finished, I took Joe's ring from Dakota. I brought the ring to Joe's hand and repeated after David as I slid the ring on his finger. "With this ring, I seal my promise to be your faithful and loving wife as God is my witness. I give you this ring as a sign of my love, and with everything that I have, I honor you and take you for my husband."

"By the power vested in me by God and the state of Washington, I now pronounce you man and wife. You may kiss the bride," David said with a broad smile on his face.

Joe leaned in, lips meeting mine. This kiss was like no other kiss I'd ever experienced. Deep and pure, loving and passionate. The kiss that sealed our union. The kiss that changed me forever. I was no longer who I was yesterday. I was now Tamara Christine Phillips. I was Joe's wife, and that somehow changed my whole world.

Joe drew back with a smile and whispered, "Hello, Mrs. Phillips."

I grinned at him, heart swelling and melting at the same time.

"Ladies and gentlemen, I present to you, Mr. and Mrs. Joe and Tamara Phillips."

A round of applause erupted. Joe took my hand and we turned toward our friends and family and walked down the aisle together to start our future.

CHAPTER 61

January 21, 7:35 p.m.

TAMARA

When I arrived at Midways, I was amazed at how Charlie had transformed the place. The pool tables were covered with white tablecloths, and the dart boards had been taken down and replaced with large canvas pictures of me and Joe. The ceiling was bordered with white twinkle lights, and each table was set with a small vase, each holding one long stem rose. In the middle of the room were two tables. One was smaller and held a three-tiered cake, decorated with white and red frosting. The other table was loaded with two large pans of lasagna, salad and garlic bread. Our guests poured in and rounds of congratulatory hugs ensued.

The next hour was filled with eating, cutting the cake, and a couple of awkward toasts from Caleb and Dakota. Joe and I danced our first dance and then Dakota joined Dad and me for the father daughter dance. From there, music blared from the jukebox, and Shelby led the charge to move the crowd into a dance party in the center. Dakota took Tim by the hand and joined the bunch. Nathan and Josiah dragged their wives onto the dance floor. Even my dad was sitting at a table next to Mom tapping his foot with a smile on his face.

I laughed at the scene and sat back next to Joe, overcome with gratitude, still in awe that everyone had made it on such short notice.

Joe placed his hand softly on the small of my back and leaned in. "This feels like a dream," he whispered in my ear. "I can't believe you're finally my wife."

"You better believe it." I slipped my hands around his neck with a playful smile. "You're stuck with me now."

"I wish we could skip the rest of the reception and take some time to ourselves." He kissed me sweetly, but there was an intensity behind his lips.

I moaned and rested my head against his. "We'll leave soon, but first there is something I need to do." I stood and grabbed both my journals from my purse and headed toward the stage, strength and peace encircling me. I'd been unsure about doing this today, but in this moment, surrounded by the people I loved, many who had changed my life, it felt right. I walked across the stage and picked up the microphone. "Hi, everyone. Joe and I are going to be leaving soon, but before we do, I wanted to say thank you to each of you for coming. I want to thank my parents for helping us with the wedding and Charlie for everything over the last few weeks, including throwing us this fantastic reception." I paused and peered around the room, my gaze landing on Levi who held Hope, Sarah standing next to him.

My heart filled with joy again. "I want to thank Levi Taylor. It was your prayers and light that brought me to God, and for that, I am eternally grateful. I want to thank David for being the world's greatest pastor. Your guidance and love have caused me to grow so much over the last year."

I turned my attention to Joe and smiled. "Joe, I want to thank you for standing with me and holding me together when I thought I might fall apart. I owe you my whole life." I pointed toward the sky. "And I'd like to thank God for following me through the darkness and not relenting until he rescued me with his love."

I opened my first journal and found the poem I had finished a few weeks ago. "I'd like to read you a poem about the redemptive journey God has taken me through. When I wrote this, I never thought I'd share it, but now with my loved ones gathered in the same place, I would like to be vulnerable and let you into my journey." I composed myself and read the words on the page.

I am walking,
but I know not where I go.
I look around this forsaken place
without a care in the world,
wandering the lonely streets without a purpose.

I paused as I remembered where I'd been when I wrote those lines. It was a year after I left Ocean Shores. I'd been so broken and depressed, my existence had felt pointless. Scanning the room, I spotted Shelby at a table near the place she and I had been when Danny sang to me from this stage. She winked and blew me a kiss. I'd been devastated by what they had done to me, but that was far from the end of my story.

A man stands in front of me, and all around me at the same time.
I look at him, but only darkness surrounds my vision.
I know this man, I know this place,
I have been here before, but I do not want to stay.
So, I run.

I turn away, but he calls out.
I try to run, but my head is filled with tormenting cries.

Deception consumes me, his lies, my bread.
I have no face to show the world. The glow of my life burns out, So, I
hide.

I skimmed the crowd. There were several people in the room who hadn't allowed me to hide. My gaze landed on Trudy first. I was so thankful that she had seen past my brokenness and not only hired me, but promoted me. Then I spotted Claire. She was a good friend who seemed to see me better than I was. I found Charlie and made eye contact. He had been the catalyst that sent me in the right direction, and over the last few weeks, he'd become family. He nodded at me with a smile, and I returned to the page.

The weeks become like days in this place without love.
Searching the dark streets striving for touch.
I run and I run, but I stand still.
My motion leaves me in this place I call home.
So, I cry.

My thoughts fell to Kyle. I had left with him that night because of my deep loneliness. I'd been desperate for love and I'd opened myself in all the wrong ways, wanting so badly for someone to fill those hurting places, but in the end, it caused me more hurt.

There must be more to this lonely life.
The garbage I eat will not satisfy.
I scream for more,
but my call is unheard.

It felt as though every eye in the bar was staring at me, pulling the next words from me, but I hesitated, thinking of the garbage I used to fill myself on. I whispered the next line, inviting the room to feel how small I felt during that time.

My love is lost, and my end is near,
So, I fall.

I'd written those last lines in one of my lowest points, believing I was no good for anyone. Too damaged for anyone to love. I'd run from Joe after sleeping with Kyle. Thinking that I'd destroyed my whole life, I sunk into despair. I had ripped my apartment apart that night in anger, desperate to find anything to give me hope.

That's when I'd seen and read the journal Levi had left for me. Waves of emotion flooded over me as I remembered the moment of me running to the church and how God had saved me, restored my relationship with Joe, and provided me two amazing people to take my baby.

I looked over at Levi, Sarah, and Hope again. Hope was such a beautiful child. It had devastated me to give her away, but now I could see how amazing and healthy she was and surrounded by parents who loved her. It filled me in a special way to watch the interaction with them today. I switched to my second journal and spoke the next line loudly as a declaration of God's goodness.

Suddenly, light cuts the darkness like a sword its foe!

I scanned the crowd again. Trudy held her heart, beaming at me. My focus landed on Dakota, who held Tim's hand. She'd been the reason I'd written that line. It was after that session in David's office where Jesus had come into my darkness. Dakota stealing my ring and abandoning me in Quilcene had ripped my wounds open, but in the midst of it, I saw that I was an overcomer. That day I knew I was a fighter and that I could stand in true faith for my family. I locked gazes with David, who smiled at me like a proud father. I took a deep breath and exhaled the next few lines.

Warmth enters me, and the cold retreats.
You are here.
I feel you.
I need you.

I regarded the next line, closed my eyes and whispered it.

341

But still, I run.

Those four words had defined my life for so long ... But somehow throughout every mistake I'd made, God had chased after me. In doing so, he had redeemed my life.

You are too bright,
I cannot face you, so I hide, but you follow.
I return to the garbage and throw up.
I flee through the darkness and fall.
But you follow.
You are still here,
I feel you.
I need you.
I give up and turn.
I have eyes,
I can see your face.
I take your hand and stand.
Finally! I can leave this place.

And you follow.

I closed my journal. There was a brief silence, then the room erupted into applause. Up on this stage, being vulnerable with my journey, gave me fresh eyes to see. I saw then the purpose of my life, the purpose in the struggle.

Much like a woman going through the travail of childbirth to see the beautiful baby as the result. Because of what I had gone through, Dakota was on the path of sobriety, my family was doing better, and Joe and I were healthy enough to start our life together.

Joe came beside me, wrapped me in his strong arms and spoke into the mic. "Thank you all for being here tonight and being a part of our special day. We love you, and I look forward to getting to know those of you I just met over the rest of my lifetime. But for now, we have to say good night."

I laughed as he swept me into his arms and carried me off stage through the crowd. I ducked and waved as the throng threw rice at us. When I passed by Charlie, I mouthed the words 'thank you,' not envying him to have to clean this mess. He waved me on with a wink. Joe set me down, and together we raced to his Jeep.

The ride home brimmed with excitement as I curled myself around Joe's arm in the front seat. The moon and stars overhead lit the darkened sky and the beauty of it made me think of our story. Through the darkest night, Joe had been the light, illuminating my heart so I could truly see what love was. My heart exploded with bliss as we hit the driveway of our new home.

"We did it." I smiled at Joe.

"That we did," he said, leaning over for a kiss. His lips felt like magic as they connected with mine. We no longer had to subdue our passion. There were no more boundaries that separated us from each other, and that truth ran through me like electricity. I threw myself passionately into the kiss, sliding my hands around his neck, pulling him closer, eager for more.

"Easy, now," he said with a chuckle, drawing back.

"Hey, we no longer need to put on the brakes. We're married now." I pouted.

He bit his lower lip through a smile. "I think I'd like to make it to the house first."

My cheeks flushed hot at my own reaction to him. "You may have a point."

He gave me a quick peck on the lips and hurried from his seat, rounded the Jeep, and opened my door. "Mrs. Phillips."

He held out a hand and helped me from the car. As soon as I was on my feet, he lifted me into his arms and carried me across the driveway and up the steps over the threshold where he hesitated. Behind us, sounds of the ocean crashed against the shore. He smiled at me and kissed me tenderly. "You ready for this?"

I nodded, my gaze steadied on him.

"All right then." He opened the door and brought me into our new home. Joy overwhelmed me once more. I hadn't seen it since he moved our furniture from our old places. My gray loveseat fit perfectly next to his blue couch. My old wooden trunk matched with his end tables. I loved it. I rested my head against his. I wouldn't kid myself to think our lives would be smooth sailing from here, but in that moment, I was finally home.

Epilogue

JOE

Two years later

I left my office and headed to the front to check in on the workers before I left for the evening. The tables in the restaurant were set elegantly for dinner with white tablecloths, lit candles, and water glasses.

I'd purchased the bed-and-breakfast we were married in eight months after Tamara and I moved here. It took a lot of work and remodeling to make it perfect before we reopened it under the new name of *Emily's Rose Garden Inn and Cafe*, after my mom. The restaurant was exactly what I dreamed it would be, an upscale eatery using many of my mom's special recipes. The suites were an added bonus.

My phone rattled as I walked into the staging area. I pulled it from my pocket and answered it.

"Hey, Joe." Tim's voice came through the line. "Are thing's set for tonight?"

I smiled at the nerves in his voice and peaked into the banquet room where Tamara and I had said our vows. There was a single table in the middle of the room, lined with a burgundy tablecloth, elegantly set for two. "Yup. Everything's golden."

"Great. You don't think it's going to be too much for her? You know how she gets."

I chuckled. He had a point, but Dakota had come a long way over the last few years. In the beginning of their relationship, she'd gotten spooked about the commitment, which triggered a huge fight and a small relapse. After a week and a half on Tamara's and my couch, Dakota came to her senses and worked things out with Tim. They had been going strong ever since. "I'm sure she'll love it." Tamara and I had helped him with this idea. What better place for him to propose than the very spot where they reunited for good?

"But do you think she'll say yes?"

I shut the door and started back to the front of the restaurant. "She'd be crazy not to."

Tim was silent for a beat. "We both know she has a tendency toward crazy."

I laughed again. "Dude, you need to take a deep breath. It's going to be fine."

"You're right. You're right. I'm just freaking out a little. I'll see you later tonight."

I ended the call as I found Maria, the general manager. "How are the books this evening?"

"Great, Mister Phillips. Ninety percent of the rooms are reserved, and we have a full house for most of the night."

"Awesome." I told her at least ten times to call me Joe, but for some reason, she insisted on being formal. I wasn't sure I liked it. It made me feel old, but I did appreciate the respect. I glanced around the restaurant, once more running through the mental checklist of what was needed, but it seemed like things were covered.

"You can leave for the day, Mister Philips. We have it taken care of."

The greatest and worst part of having a fantastic team was that sometimes it felt like they didn't need me. Even though Maria took care of most things, I enjoyed playing a part. I peeked at the time. "I have a few minutes. I'm going to check on the kitchen."

She shook her head with a smile. "You better not keep your ladies waiting."

"I won't." I laughed, walking toward the back. Tamara had been wonderful, encouraging me to follow my dream and run the place. Our only agreement was that I daily made time in the late afternoons for my girls. Most days, even on cold days like today, we'd walk the ocean route to our home, taking in the beauty and combing the beach for sand dollars and other treasures.

Pushing open the double doors, smells of fresh garlic, oregano, and seared meat overwhelmed my senses. The prep cook stood near the large sinks, shucking oysters for the special tonight and the line cooks were busy preparing meals for the current patrons. The kitchen was twice as big as the Highway Ninety-Nine Diner, which made it easier to move around in. "Smells great in here, guys."

Brandon, the line cook standing closest to me, pointed a spatula at me. "It's because we learned from the best."

I waved him off with a smile, knowing he was blowing steam at me. I loved my team. I'd spent a few months training them when we bought the place, but most of them came with years of experience. There was not much they didn't know. He grinned and turned his attention to the food.

"Dadda!" I heard the sweetest little voice in the world call to me. I turned around. Lillie walked through the kitchen by herself like she owned the place. I knelt with my arms stretched wide, beckoning her to run to me. Her dark curly hair bounced with each step. I smiled broadly, lifted her and carried her through the door.

Lillie Rose Phillips was the spitting image of her mother. She had the same oval shaped face, beautiful symmetrical features, and sparkling green eyes, but sometimes when I looked at her, I could see bits of my mom in different parts of her mannerisms.

Tamara stood by the open kitchen door, one hand on her

swollen belly. She wore blue jeans, a flowy black blouse, and matching boots. I kissed her cheek and ran my hand over her baby bump. Baby number two, who I strongly believed would be a boy, would be joining us in a little over four months.

"Dadda go bu bu." She leaned her body toward the door, using her weight to tug me outside.

Tamara ran her hand over Lillie's hair and smiled, but there was a sadness in her eyes that I hadn't seen for a while. "We were at the library learning about dogs, and trains, and bears, but she's been wanting to go to the beach with Daddy the whole day."

"Let's not keep her waiting any longer then." I took Tamara's hand in mine and walked to the front of the inn and outside.

Once on the beach, I set Lillie on the sand. She ran forward twenty feet, spinning and twirling, a lot like her mom had done on our first date. I chased after her as she ran away giggling. After a few minutes, she slowed and began her normal routine of combing the beach for treasures. Tamara and I followed her closely, oohing and awing over the shells she found.

"Dadda, dis purdy." Lillie lifted a tiny heart-shaped quartz.

I leaned toward her with a smile. "Sure is, sweetheart, but not near as pretty as you."

She grinned and ran off again. This was hands down my favorite part of the day. After fifteen minutes of following Lillie's rabbit trails, we reached our plot of sand.

Lillie found her favorite tools and started digging. Tamara let go of my hand and wandered toward the water, gazing into the distance, seeming to relish the scenery.

I watched her for a moment, growing concerned for the distance I could sense in her.

"Dadda, Dadda." Lillie beckoned my attention.

I knelt beside Lillie and helped her scoop sand in the bucket with my hands. "What are you building, sweetheart?"

She said a few incoherent words as she patted at the sand with a plastic shovel. My heart expanded as I watched her joyfully play. Then I glanced at Tamara and concern pricked at my senses.

Again, something about her seemed off. Perhaps the combination of pregnancy hormones and running after Lillie had finally caught up with her. I stood and dusted off my jeans as I made my way toward Tamara.

Once I reached her, I gently took her hand and tugged her toward the dock. "Come on."

I rested against the railing along the dock and pulled her into me. "What's going on with you?"

Swallowing hard, she fidgeted with the button on her coat, and then stole a glance at Lillie. "I got a call from Mom today. She's concerned about Dad's health." She quieted again and closed her eyes for a beat before reopening them. "This morning they found out that he's in the beginning stage of cirrhosis of the liver. I did some research while at the library. If he stops drinking now, it would mean a better prognosis, but if he doesn't ... it could be bad."

I took in a sharp exhale and pulled her closer.

Addiction ran deep in Tamara's family and though Paul had come a long way with his abuse and anger issues, he hadn't stopped his heavy drinking. Nathan hadn't either. It was a subject Tamara and I prayed about often.

"I'm so sorry, Tamara." The words felt cheap, but they were all I had at the moment.

A stray tear rolled the length of her cheek. "Even though it's been two years, it feels like we've barely found each other again. I'm not ready to lose him."

I gave Lillie a quick glance. She was thoroughly immersed in the sandcastle she'd been working on. Then I pulled Tamara around to face me, searching her gaze.

"Listen to me. God has brought us through so, so much, and we've seen him come through time and again. We know he's trustworthy. He will bring your dad through this and give him the strength to stop drinking."

"I hope you're right." That ancient sadness shown behind her eyes.

Faith surged through me, emboldening me to say the next line. "I promise you I am."

"I love your faith, Mr. Phillips," Tamara said as she relaxed into me.

"I love yours," I whispered in her ear.

More than once over the last few years, her trust in God had carried me through my trials. She never downplayed the hardships but was there to magnify how big our God was, and now I'd return the favor.

We gathered Lillie on the way to our home and as we climbed the walkway, I whispered a prayer of thanksgiving for our family and for healing for Tamara's dad. Tamara and I stood at the window and continued to watch the sunset while Lillie banged on one of those colorful xylophones.

As the sun set and the colors faded, I thought about the last few years and the lessons I'd learned. Truth be told, I didn't know how things would work out with Tamara's dad. But I'd learned that God was trustworthy and even when bad things happened, he was able to bring life from death. He was able to take horrible circumstances and bring healing to the deepest wounds. I wasn't exactly sure how he did it, but it always amazed me to see the beauty emerge from the ashes.

Dear Reader,

Thank you so much for coming on this journey with us. Jesse and I hope you enjoyed reading this series as much as we enjoyed writing it. For me personally, it has been quite an adventure. Each book has been eerily prophetic as we set out to write them. From the beginning, God would often use the very writing we'd just written to personally minister to me weeks or months later. This book has been no different.

As you read in the previous Letter to Reader in *Ninety-Nine Ashes*, you saw it was one of the hardest books I wrote in my career, but in many ways *Ninety-Nine Promises* was harder. Not so much because of the content, but because of my expectations. Like the theme of *Promises*, I thought surely the pain of the "Ashes" season of my life was behind me. I thought God would move me past that season and start fulfilling the things he had promised me. But as Tamara found, grasping ahold of the promises of God continued to be a struggle.

I believed God had promised that he would restore some broken areas of my family that I'd been praying about for years. That he would bring healing to my emotions and restore my ministry school experience from the year before, so in faith, I returned for a second year. Surprisingly, a few months into my studies, my husband lost his job, my family was still hurting, and I started having severe panic attacks as my mental health waned. I cried out to God, wondering why when He promised transformation, I still only saw hardship. As I prayed through this moment, I heard God whisper in my spirit, "It's time to write your victory song." Immediately, I knew what he meant. Even though these promises had not yet been fulfilled, God was saying it was time to *write Ninety-Nine Promises* as a declaration for a future hope.

A few years ago, Jesse shared a sermon with me that his pastor had preached about the siege of Leningrad during World War II. In 1941, the Germans fully encircled the city, cutting off all supply lines. In the 900 days the siege lasted, the city's civilians refused to surrender even as they endured rapidly increasing hardships. However, in the midst of the death and hopelessness of the siege, a man by the name of Dmitri Shostakovich chose to compose his seventh symphony. During a time when his people were fighting for the very right to exist as a nation, he had the resounding purpose to prove to the world that they hadn't given up. When finished, loudspeakers were strategically set up throughout the city and even aimed over the walls at the enemy as a direct act of defiance, sending the clear message that they would never surrender. Prior to the performance, they pounded the enemy with a round of shells to silence them and make way for the music. On August 9th, 1942, one year before they would see victory, Leningrad performed their victory song.

Ninety-Nine Promises is my victory song. While we were writing it, I too felt like I was under siege. I was in a ton of debt, I was struggling emotionally, and there were certain things in my family that looked like they would never change no matter what I did. But I chose in the face of that to write a book that proclaimed that God was big enough to fulfill His promises in the face of great opposition. I believe that this book was meant to inspire hope in the hearts of the readers that no matter what battle they are facing, no matter what it looks like, God is able to bring the breakthrough and he is always faithful to his promises.

Now as I write this letter, I've seen the beginning of God's promises fulfilled in my life, but again we are now facing a different kind of enemy in the form of a global pandemic. Even though many are giving in to fear, I believe it's time to submit to God's perspective. In every shade of death, he sees a banner of life. In every hopeless situation, he knows a strategy to overcome. He knows the end of our story, and he is singing over us, *Victory!*

I believe in this season and in the years to come, God is releasing creativity in each of us to inspire hope. So let us dare to write our victory song while we are still in the ashes. Let us stand, live, and declare that even while we are under siege, God is still good. Let us dare to hold onto the promises of tomorrow and inspire hope to the world by releasing our victory song today.

Blessings in Christ,
Elisheba Haxby and Jesse Vincent
ElishebaHaxby@gmail.com
AuthorJesseVincent@gmail.com

> *God promises us that if we give Him the ashes of our lives,*
> *He will exchange then for His beauty,*
> *no matter how big our ash heap seems to be!*
> *~ Heidi Baker, CEO of Iris Ministries*

Next In Series

Thank you for reading Ninety-Nine Promises!
If you enjoyed it, continue the series with:

Book 4: Ninety-Nine Chances

First chapter of Ninety-Nine Chances below:

JANUARY 20, 7:39 P.M. – DAKOTA

As I walked out of the weekly Narcotics Anonymous meeting, my muscles tightened, and chills shot down my spine. Everything inside of me screamed that I was being watched. I scanned the parking lot, but nothing was out of the ordinary. Just a handful of people walking toward their cars.

Fumbling through my purse for my keys, I tried to push aside the unsettling sensation.

What was wrong with me lately? Why couldn't I just enjoy this newfound happiness I had worked so hard for?

For years, my life had been consumed by addiction and struggle. But now, I was finally starting to feel like my feet were firmly planted on solid ground. My relationship with Tim was stronger than ever, and it had been over a year since my last relapse. Yet, there was still a lingering fear that this happiness could all come crashing down at any moment—that somehow, despite everything, I'd manage to screw it all up again. The sickening feeling gnawed at my gut and refused to let go, no matter how much I tried to push it aside.

With my keys clutched tightly in my hand, I rushed to my car. My hand shook as I clumsily unlocked my 1993 Honda Civic. Calm down, Dakota. You're being ridiculous. Ryan's dead. No one was coming for me. It had been over two years ...

I sank into my seat and turned the car on before scanning the parking lot for the final time. A deep blue Mustang with tinted windows sat off to the left on the far side of the lot. Had I seen that car before? It didn't matter. My nerves were getting the best of me.

These were the moments I had learned to be extra careful. When my mind started playing tricks on me. It meant the addict was close to the surface, begging to get out. Cranking up the radio, took a deep breath, and counted backward from ten. The serenity prayer flitted through my head. It was still hard for me to say out loud. I'd come a long way with the higher power thing, but there were still places of resistance.

I gave the Mustang one last look, then backed out of the parking spot and peeled out of the parking lot, desperate to put the meeting and my unease behind me. My tires squealed as I made the turn onto the main road, and my heart pounded in rhythm with the beat of the music flooding from the speakers. Unwell by Matchbox Twenty played on the radio. Rob Thomas' voice, laden with melancholy and regret, echoed my own unease.

A quick glance in the rearview mirror sent my heart racing. A few cars back, the Mustang followed, gliding smoothly around the corner with an ease that sent a chill down my spine.

What the freak? Were they following me? My fingers gripped the steering wheel tightly as I made a sharp turn onto a backroad leading to my house. In the mirror, I could see the car continuing on the previous road.

Wow. I was seriously losing it. Nobody was following me. No one was watching me. I was just a complete paranoid mess. I changed the radio station and ignored my racing heart. One of these days, the demons that tried to torment me would fully be gone. Until then, I needed to fake it. To pretend that everything was okay.

I pulled into the driveway at the home Tim had purchased earlier this year and breathed in a sigh of relief. He had sold his home on Quilcene and purchased this one in Port Hadlock wanting to give us a fresh start in a new town. Not to mention it was closer to his job at the Jefferson County Police Department. Some days though, twenty minutes away from my hometown didn't feel like far enough. Memories lurked around every corner, and I still ran into people I used to party with on a regular basis.

I opened the car door and stepped out before making my way into the house. When I walked in, Barenaked Ladies One Week was playing, and the smell of popcorn wafted in the air. Tim stood in the kitchen, back to me, shaking a cast iron pan over the stove.

A smile formed on my lips at the sight of him—Tim, in his faded jeans and police academy sweatshirt, cooking dinner. He was so ordinary, so domestic, so unlike the life I knew before.

As quietly as possible, I tiptoed toward him, suppressing the giggle that wanted to rise. I jabbed his sides with a sudden "Boo!"

He screamed like a girl and spun around. "Uh! You are so paying for that!"

Smiling broadly, I backed away. He lunged for me, grabbing my sides and tickling me.

I squirmed and fought against him as laughter erupted from my mouth. "Stop! You're gonna burn the popcorn!"

"Oh well." He laughed, tickling harder. "There's plenty where that came from!"

I fought back for a while but soon we were both laughing so

hard it was hard to catch our breath. Tim's eyes locked on mine, his gaze warm and loving. His laughter faded into a soft smile as he moved closer, his hands still resting on my sides.

This was the man I'd known since childhood, the one who never ceased to amaze me with his kindness and dedication. His expression held a gentleness and heat that melted away all of my worries.

He kissed me softly yet passionately as he drew me in. My hands found their way around his shoulders as his encircled my waist. And just like that, between his playfulness and then his love, the fear that had weighed heavy on me five minutes ago had vanished, replaced with this safe feeling of being loved. Only Tim could reach these places inside of me.

Smells of burnt popcorn filled the air. "Oh crap." Tim pulled away from me and rushed to the stove.

"Told you!"

Rolling his eyes, he pulled the burning popcorn off the heat. "And I told you we could make more." He leaned toward me and kissed me again, sweet and slow, before pulling away, searching my face. "And I'd say it was worth it."

My heart sped up under his gaze. There was so much emotion behind his expression that, after all this time, I still wasn't sure how to handle it. I averted my gaze to break the intensity. "You better make that popcorn, or we'll never get to our movie."

He hesitated and then turned back to the popcorn mess.

"I'm going to change into something more comfortable for the movie." I walked to our bedroom, dug through my dresser, pulled out some sweats then headed to the bathroom.

As the door clicked shut behind me, I caught a glimpse of myself in the mirror. My eyes were wide and surprised, my face flushed with laughter and warmth. I reached up to touch my lips, still tingling from his kiss. The girl in the mirror didn't look haunted anymore, not like she used to. There was still an echo of the old fear, a shadow in the depths of my eyes, but being with Tim seemed to chase away those ghosts.

I sighed, my chest rising and falling steadily in the mirror. Was I worthy of this? This love, this warmth, this peace? After all that I had done in my addiction, the lying, the stealing—Gabriel's death... I wasn't sure. I swallowed back the doubt that rose with these questions, the doubt that had always been a part of me, intertwining itself with every thought and action.

Turning on the water, I tried to push away the thoughts that pestered me.

I rinsed my face, the cool water seeping into my skin, washing away the residual traces of the day. I pulled on my sweats, and the comfort they brought was palpable.

On the way back to the living room, I snagged one of Tim's oversized hoodies and slipped it on over my head. I breathed in through my nose, inhaling his musky, earthy scent. It smelled like home.

I stepped into the living room, and Tim was standing there, holding a large bowl of popcorn.

"You ready for this." He smiled broadly, threw a piece of popcorn in the air, and caught it with his mouth before grabbing the remote. We had been talking about doing this for weeks, but both of us had been busy.

"As I'll ever be," I smirked at him and then settled into the couch. Because you're about to finally be proven wrong."

"Whatever." He rolled his eyes as he flicked on the television.

Ever since we were kids, we've had the same disagreement about which Star Wars episode was the best. Episode three is my favorite, yet he swore episode five was the best movie of all time.

Tim sank into the couch next to me, placing the popcorn on his leg so we could both reach it. "There's no way for you to prove me wrong with this. It's strictly opinion. You have yours, and I have mine. We're just going to have to agree to disagree."

"Yeah, right." I scoffed. Twelve years of this ridiculous argument and now he wanted me to agree to disagree? No freaking way.

"Most people on the planet, myself included, disagree with you on this."

"And you made my point for me. Most people are idiots." I reached into the popcorn and grabbed a handful.

"Touché," he said with a chuckle, then lifted the remote and pressed play.

When I first met Tim, I was probably one of six people on the planet who hadn't seen Star Wars. He would throw out references all the time because he thought it was cool or something. When I told him I had never even watched one episode, he was dumbfounded. How was it even possible to grow up in America and not have seen Star Wars?

The following weekend, he begged me to come over for a movie marathon. It was a rainy Saturday, and my parents were fighting anyway, so I accepted.

He gathered a bunch of pillows and blankets in his house and set us up a comfy spot in front of the television. We binged all six episodes from start to finish, starting from episode one. And this is what started our playful feud.

To this day, Tim regreted showing me them in what I would say was the correct order.

Tim's arm slipped around my shoulders, pulling me closer to him. As the story began, a sense of contentment and belonging settled around me.

The opening crawl filled the screen, and sounds of John Williams' iconic music swelled as I leaned into Tim. For the moment, I let go of our silly banter and got lost in a galaxy far, far away.

Sometimes I wished I could be with Tim like this all the time and never have to leave the house. Being with him had always been the place I felt safe.

The popcorn bowl slowly emptied as the movie progressed. For a while, I was completely immersed in the world of Jedi and Sith, lightsabers and epic duels. But somewhere in the middle of the movie, a line spoken by Yoda turned anxiety in my guts once more. "Fear is the path to the dark side. Fear leads to anger. Anger leads to hate. Hate leads to suffering."

A sudden chill swept over me, making my skin prickle. It was something I had heard a thousand times, yet this time it hit differently. It was like Yoda was speaking directly to me, his words echoing my own fears.

A shiver ran down my spine. I could practically feel Ryan's cold, menacing gaze on me, his hands choking the life out of me. Stop it, Dakota. Ryan was dead. Yet his memory was as alive as ever, a ghost that refused to be laid to rest.

Fear is the path to the dark side.

So many years of my life had been stolen by fear. My fear had truly led to my dark side. And to so much suffering.

Thoughts of earlier that day intruded into the moment, and trpidation settled into my chest. That deep blue Mustang... it had seriously seemed like it was following me. Should I tell Tim about it? No. I shook off the thought and tried to refocus on the movie. I was just being paranoid.

Was this fear trying to lead me into the darkness once more? Damn it! I couldn't let that happen. I had too much to lose now.

"You okay, Dakota?" Tim's voice broke through my spiraling thoughts, and I turned to look at him. His gentle gaze was filled with concern, his warm brown eyes flickering in the soft light from the TV.

I shook my head. "Yeah, I'm good." I lied, not wanting to go there. This was something I needed to process by myself for a while.

"Have you finally realized how wrong you've actually been?" He said with a grin, leaning in for a kiss.

"You wish." I teased with a smirk, but inwardly there was a gnawing ache in my guts.

His lips met mine, and the pain eased a bit. Tamara told me once that love was the antidote for fear. Sometimes when I was with Tim like this, I actually believed her. Sliding my arms around his neck, I invited his kiss to become deeper. For a moment, I allowed myself to forget about Ryan, about the Mustang, about everything. There was only me and Tim. His arms were my haven, his warmth a welcome respite from the demons that often haunted me.

His hand cradled my face, and he whispered, "I love you," again and again in between kisses. Tim had been my guiding light since we were kids. His love had never given up on me, even when I pushed him away so many times.

"Remember what tomorrow is," he said softly, kissing me near my ear. I smiled, though I wondered if this was the reason for the fear, the reason my mind was playing tricks on me. Tomorrow was our two-year anniversary when we officially got together. The day he met me in Ocean Shores for Tamara's wedding. It was kinda weird that our anniversary was the same as my sister's wedding day, but it felt right in a way. Tamara's love, just like Tim's never faltered, and so it was fitting that the two occasions were etched in time together.

Two years though... It was a big deal for me. I'd never done anything for two years straight except for meth. Were these darker sides of who I was, working to sabotage this? I couldn't let my darkness win. I could not let this happen.

Over the last few years, Tim had become everything to me. He was my new addiction. I needed him like I used to need that next hit of meth. Damn. I hated myself for thinking of Tim like that. He was so much more than an addiction.

"Coda," he whispered, his brow furrowing as he cupped my cheek, his thumb brushing against my lower lip. "What's wrong?"

"Absolutely nothing," I said, pulling his face to mine once more. He didn't need to know about my internal struggle. All I wanted him to know at that moment was that he was enough to quiet my demons. I crushed my lips against his and let his love consume me until I forgot every awful thing my dark side had done.

Acknowledgments

This book journey has been amazing, and we have so many people to thank. Since this is the last book in the series, we would like to specifically acknowledge those who have walked with us from the beginning of our writing journey, through the highs and lows, through the ashes and fulfilled promises.

Of course, we would like to start with our families. Thank you to our parents for believing in us and supporting us literally from birth, for our siblings, and the rest of our family— Thank you!

Next, we want to thank our close friends who have rejoiced when we rejoiced and mourned when we mourned. Thank you, Maddie, Melanie, Megan, Derek, Luke, Chris, Jen, Marra, and Zane. Your love, your cheerleading, and support keeps us going!

We also want to thank our partners, primarily our amazing editors: Marnie, Kit, Kristin and Michaela. Thank you, Gary, for providing your amazing songs to add. And thank you to our beta readers Cathi C, Jessie, Marra, and Grace. Also thank you to Maddie, Marylyn, Rose, Rod, Diane, Susan and Melanie for supporting us financially.

And finally, we want to thank our mentors. Christina, who helped us improve our books, and to Jim Rubart, who encourages us to keep reaching higher and provided valuable insights to grow us as writers. Everyone involved in this journey played a pivotal role, and we appreciate all your help. Thank you!

About The Authors

Elisheba and Jesse met in Youth With A Mission in 2001. Elisheba was impressed by Jesse's creative mind and his dedication to story crafting. Jesse was impressed by Elisheba's deep walk with Jesus and her commitment to emotional authenticity. They became friends and years later decided to start writing together through a set of supernatural circumstances.

Jesse carried the idea for their first book, Ninety-Nine, since 1999. At the time he knew it was a download from God, but struggled to write from an emotionally raw woman's point of view. Throughout the years when bringing this frustration to God, God simply responded with "this is not your story." Then in 2010 Elisheba heard from God to start writing and that her stories would lead people into an encounter with the love of God. She brought this word to Jesse and it clicked for both of them to work together on this project. The idea was conceived and nine months later the first book was birthed.

The journey of writing and publishing was quite challenging, filled with many hurdles and mistakes. But every step of the way God met them, helped them, and healed them. Over the many years of writing together, learning the craft, and pursuing inner healing, they decided to start a business to help other authors do the same. They wanted to combine their belief that God wants to create through His people with the need to help creatives be healed enough to partner with God and produce this creativity. To do this, they founded Above The Sun, LLC.

For more writing by Elisheba Haxby, Jesse Vincent, and Above The Sun, please visit:

ElishebaHaxby.com
AboveTheSun.org

What's Your Story?

Above The Sun is a community of hope-filled creators who believe the world can be transformed through authentic stories. Our mission is to develop authors who are committed to becoming whole in order to successfully bring their message to their unique areas of influence. If you have a book in you and you are willing to do the work to release it, we would love to connect.

Visit us at AboveTheSun.org